During the darkest, quietest hours between midnight and dawn, four patrol flyers departed Araminta Station, armed with such weaponry as the armory was able to provide. At high speed they darted around the curve of the world: across Deucas, over the Western Ocean, then slanted down so as to approach Ecce at low altitude. Up the Vertes River they flew, barely skimming the surface of the water, the better to evade whatever detectors might be operating on the summit of Mount Shattorak.

Where Glawen had landed the Skyrie, the raiding party veered away from the river to fly low over the swamp and up the slope of the volcano, and so arrived at the summit.

Twenty minutes later the operation was over. The communications shed had been destroyed, along with a gun emplacement. The hanger sheltered seven flyers, including the two most recently captured from Araminta Station. The base personnel offered no resistence.

But the leaders, having had warning of the raid, had departed hours before. . . .

Tor books by Jack Vance

JACK VANCE

ECCE AND OLD EARTH

A TOM DOHERTY ASSOCIATES BOOK
NEW YORK

This is a work of fiction. All the characters and events portrayed in this book are fictitious, and any resemblance to real people or events is purely coincidental.

ECCE AND OLD EARTH

Copyright © 1991 by Jack Vance

Cover art by Vincent di Fate

A Tor Book
Published by Tom Doherty Associates, Inc.
175 Fifth Avenue
New York, N.Y. 10010

Tor ® is a registered trademark of Tom Doherty Associates, Inc.

ISBN: 0-812-55701-8
Library of Congress Catalog Card Number: 91-18799

First edition: September 1991
First mass market printing: September 1992

Printed in the United States of America

0 9 8 7 6 5 4 3 2 1

Dedicated to

My indispensable son
John

JOHN ADKINS

ECCE AND OLD EARTH

PRECURSORY

I. THE PURPLE ROSE SYSTEM
(Excerpted from: THE WORLDS OF MAN, 48th edition.)

Halfway along the Perseid Arm near the edge of the Gaean Reach, a capricious swirl of galactic gravitation has caught up ten thousand stars and sent them streaming off at a veer, with a curl and a flourish at the tip. This strand of stars is Mircea's Wisp.

To the side of the curl, at seeming risk of wandering away into the void, is the Purple Rose System, comprising three stars: Lorca, Sing, and Syrene. Lorca, a white dwarf and Sing, a red giant, orbit close around each other: a portly pink-faced old gentleman waltzing with a dainty little maiden dressed in white. Syrene, a yellow-white star of ordinary size and luminosity, circles the gallivanting pair at a discreet distance.

Syrene controls three planets, including Cadwal, an Earth-like world seven thousand miles in diameter, with close to Earth-normal gravity.

(A list and analysis of physical indices is here omitted.)

II. THE NATURALIST SOCIETY

Cadwal was first explored by the locator R. J. Neirmann, a member of the Naturalist Society of Earth. His report prompted the Society to dispatch an official expedition to Cadwal, which, upon its return to Earth, recommended that Cadwal be protected as a conservancy, or natural preserve, secure forever from human settlement and commercial exploitation.

To this end, the Society registered the world in its own name, and after securing the Certificate of Registration found itself in sole and perpetual tenancy of Cadwal Planet, with no further formalities other than periodic renewals of the certificate: a task devolving upon the secretary of the Society.

The Society issued an immediate decree of conservancy: the Great Charter, to which were attached the Regulations of Conservancy: the basic political instrument of Cadwal. Charter, By-laws and Certificates were stored in the Society's archival vaults, and an administrative staff dispatched to Cadwal.

III. THE WORLD CADWAL

The landscapes of Cadwal were endlessly various, often spectacular and almost always—to human perceptions—pleasant, or inspiring, or awesome, or idyllically beautiful. Tourists who made the rounds of the wilderness lodges always left Cadwal with regret and many returned again and again.

The flora and fauna were approximately as diverse as those of Old Earth, which is to say that they challenged generations of research biologists and taxonomists with the profusion of their species. Many of the larger beasts were savage; others exhibited aspects of intelligence and even what seemed to be an aesthetic capability. Certain varieties of andrils used a spoken language which, try as they might, linguists were unable to interpret.

The three continents of Cadwal were Ecce, Deucas and Throy. They were separated by expanses of empty ocean, unbroken by islands or smaller masses of land, with a few trifling exceptions.

Ecce, long and narrow, lay along the equator: a flat tract of swamp and jungle, netted by sluggish rivers. Ecce palpitated with heat, stench, color and ravenous vitality. Ferocious creatures everywhere preyed upon one another, and made the land unsuitable for human settlement; the Naturalists had attempted not even a wilderness lodge on Ecce. Three objects alone broke the flat landscape: one dormant and a pair of active volcanoes.

The early explorers gave Ecce little serious attention; no more did the later scholars, and Ecce, after the first flurry of biological and topographical surveys, remained for the most part a land abandoned and unknown.

Deucas, five times as large as Ecce, occupied most of the north temperate zone on the opposite side of the planet, with Cape Journal, the continent's southernmost extremity, at the end of a long narrow peninsula which thrust a thousand miles below the equator. The fauna of Deucas, neither as grotesque nor as monstrous as that of Ecce, was yet, in many cases, savage and formidable, and included several semi-intelligent species. The flora tended to resemble that of Old Earth, to such effect that the early agronomists were able to introduce useful terrestrial species at Araminta Station: bamboo, coconut palms, wine-grapes and fruit trees without fear of an ecological disaster.*

Throy, to the south of Deucas and about equal in area to Ecce, extended from the polar ice well into the south temperate zone. The terrain of Throy was the most dramatic of Cadwal. Crags leaned over chasms; dark forests roared in the wind.

Three small islands, all ancient sea-volcanoes, were located off the east coast of Deucas. These were Lutwen Atoll, Thurben Island and Ocean Island. Elsewhere the oceans spread open and empty around the globe.

---

* The biological techniques for introducing new species into alien surroundings without danger to the host environment had long been perfected.

IV. ARAMINTA STATION

An enclave of a hundred square miles had been established on the east coast of Deucas, halfway between Cape
Journal to the south and Marmion Head to the north. Here
was Araminta Station, the agency which monitored the
Conservancy and enforced the terms of the Charter. Six
bureaus performed the necessary work:

Bureau A: Records and statistics.
　　　　 B: Patrols and surveys: police and
　　　　　　 security services.
　　　　 C: Taxonomy, cartography, natural sciences.
　　　　 D: Domestic services.
　　　　 E: Fiscal affairs: exports and imports.
　　　　 F: Visitors' accommodations.

The original six superintendents were Deamus Wook,
Shirry Clattuc, Saul Diffin, Claude Offaw, Marvell Veder,
and Condit Laverty. Each was allowed a staff not to exceed
forty persons which they all recruited from family and guild
kinships, and which brought to the early administration a
cohesion which otherwise might have been lacking.

After many centuries, much had changed but much
remained the same. The Charter prevailed as law of the
land, though certain factions were intent upon modifying
its terms. Others—notably the Yips of Lutwen Atoll—paid
no heed whatever to the Charter. At Araminta Station, the
original rude encampment had become a settlement dominated by six palatial edifices, where lived the descendants
of the Wooks, Offaws, Clattucs, Diffins, Veders and Lavertys.

As time passed, each House developed a distinctive
personality, which its residents shared, so that the wise
Wooks differed from the flippant Diffins, as did the cautious
Offaws from the reckless Clattucs.

The station early acquired a hotel to house its visitors;
also an airport, a hospital, schools and a theater: the
'Orpheum.' When subsidies from Society headquarters on

Old Earth dwindled and presently stopped altogether, the need for foreign exchange became urgent. Vineyards planted at the back of the enclave began to produce fine wines for export, and tourists were encouraged to visit any or all of the wilderness lodges, which were established at special sites and managed so as to avoid interaction with the environment.

Over the centuries, certain problems became acute. How could so many enterprises be staffed by a complement of only two hundred and forty persons? Elasticity was necessarily the answer. First, collaterals* were allowed to accept middle-status positions at the station.

By a loose reading of the Charter, children, retired persons, domestic servants and 'temporary labor not in permanent residence' were exempted from the forty-person limit. The term 'temporary labor' was extended to include farm labor, hotel staff, airport mechanics—indeed, workers of every description, and the Conservator looked the other way so long as the work-force was allowed no permanent residence.

A source of plentiful, cheap and docile labor had always been needed at Araminta Station. What could be more convenient than the folk who inhabited Lutwen Atoll, three hundred miles to the northeast? These were the Yips, descendants of runaway servants, fugitives, illegal immigrants, petty criminals and others, who at first furtively, then brazenly, had taken up residence on Lutwen Atoll.

The Yips fulfilled a need, and so were allowed at

---

*Collateral: Only forty Wooks, Offaws, Clattucs, Diffins, Lavertys and Veders could be reckoned 'Cadwal Agents.' The excess became 'collaterals' (co-Wooks, co-Lavertys, co-Clattucs, etcetera), and upon their twenty-first birthday were required to leave the house of their birth and seek their fortune elsewhere. The occasion was fraught always with heartbreak: sometimes fury and, not infrequently, suicide. The situation was criticized as 'brutal' and 'heartless,' especially among the LPFers of Stroma, but no remedy or better method could be devised within the intent of the Charter, which defined Araminta Station as an administrative agency and a business-place, not a residential settlement.

Araminta Station on six-month work permits. So much the Conservationists grudgingly allowed, but refused to yield an iota more.

V. THE CONSERVATOR AND THE NATURALIST OF STROMA

At Riverview House, a mile south of the agency, lived the Conservator, the Executive Superintendent of Araminta Station. By the terms of the Charter, he was an active member of the Naturalist Society, a native of Stroma, the small Naturalist settlement on Throy. With the waning of the Society to little more than a memory, the directive necessarily had been interpreted loosely and—at least for this purpose, where no realistic alternative offered itself— all Naturalists resident at Stroma were considered equivalent to members of the Society.

A faction dedicated to 'advanced' ideology, calling itself the 'Life, Peace and Freedom Party,' began to champion the cause of the Yips whose condition they declared to be intolerable and a blot on the collective conscience. The situation could be relieved only by allowing the Yips to settle on the Deucas mainland. Another faction, the 'Chartists,' acknowledged the problem, but proposed a solution not in violation of the Charter: namely, transferring the entire Yip population off-world. Unrealistic! declared the LPFers, and ever more categorically criticized the Charter. They declared the Conservancy an archaic idea, non-humanist and out of step with 'advanced' thinking. The Charter, so they asserted, was in desperate need of revi-sion, if only that the plight of the Yips might be ameliorated.

The Chartists, in refutal, insisted that both Charter and Conservancy were immutable. They voiced a sardonic suspicion that much of LPF fervor was hypocritical and self-serving; that the LPFers wanted to allow Yip settle-ment of the Marmion Foreshore in order to set a precedent which would permit a few deserving Naturalists—no doubt defined as the most vigorous and ardent LPF activists—to establish estates for themselves out in the beautiful Deucas countryside, where they would employ Yips for servants and farmhands and live like lords. The charge provoked the LPFers to such violent spasms of outrage that cynical Chartists asserted that the vehemence of their protests only underscored their covert ambitions.

At Araminta Station, 'advanced' ideology was not taken seriously. The Yip problem was recognized as real and immediate, but the LPF solution had to be rejected, since any official concessions would formalize the Yip presence on Cadwal, when all efforts should be exerted in the opposite direction, i.e.: transfer of the entire Yip population to a world where their presence would be useful and desirable.

This conviction was reinforced when Eustace Chilke, the Station airport manager, discovered that the Yips had long been systematically stealing from the airport warehouse. Their booty was primarily spare parts for the Station flyers, which in due course could be assembled into whole flyers at Yipton. They also took tools, weapons, ammunition and energy packs, apparently with the connivance of one Namour co-Clattuc, Agency Commissioner of Temporary Labor, and in this connection Namour and Chilke came to blows. The two fought an epic battle. Namour, a Clattuc, fought with typical Clattuc flair and courage; Chilke fought a methodical backroom style: essentially a technique of backing the opponent up against a wall and pummeling him until he fell to the floor, exactly as Namour eventually found himself doing.

Chilke was born near the town Idola, on the Big Prairie of Old Earth. Early in his life little Eustace was influenced by his grandfather Floyd Swaner, a collector of stuffed animals, old oddments, purple bric-a-brac, rare books, and anything else which caught his fancy. When Eustace Chilke was a child, his grandfather presented him with a wonderful ATLAS OF THE UNIVERSE, depicting all the inhabited worlds of the Gaean Reach, including Cadwal. The ATLAS stimulated young Eustace to such an extent that he became a wanderer: half vagabond, half jack-of-all-trades.

The route which brought him to Araminta Station was

devious but certainly not accidental. Chilke one day
described the circumstances to Glawen:

"I was working as a tour-bus operator out of Seven
Cities, on John Preston's World." Chilke told how he
became aware of "a big pie-faced lady with lots of bosom,
wearing a tall black hat," who joined Chilke's morning tour
four days in succession. At last she engaged him in conversation, commenting favorably upon his conduct.

Chilke responded modestly: "It's nothing special, just
my stock in trade."

The lady introduced herself as Madame Zigonie, a
widow from Rosalia, a world to the back of the Pegasus
Rectangle. After a few minutes of conversation she suggested that Chilke join her for lunch: an invitation which
Chilke saw no reason to refuse.

Madame Zigonie selected a fine restaurant where they
were served an excellent lunch. During the meal she
encouraged Chilke to talk of his early years on the Big
Prairie and the general facts of his family background.
Presently, as if on sudden impulse, Madame Zigonie mentioned her clairvoyant powers which she ignored only at
grave risk—to herself, her fortunes, and all others involved
in the revelations. "Perhaps you have wondered at my
interest in you. The fact is that I must hire an overseer for
my ranch and my inner voice insisted that you were the
right and proper person for the position."

"That is very interesting," said Chilke cautiously. "The
salary is high and you plan to pay a substantial advance?"

"You will be paid in the standard fashion, after you
render the duties I will require of you."

"Hm," said Chilke. The remark was ambiguous and
Madame Zigonie, large, somewhat over-dressed, with small
narrow eyes glinting from a broad-cheeked face the color of
putty, lacked all appeal.

In the end Madame Zigonie's inducements overcame
his reluctance and Chilke became superintendent of the
Shadow Valley Ranch on Rosalia.

Chilke's duties required that he direct the activities of
a large work-force, composed entirely of indentured Yips,
brought to Rosalia by a labor contractor named Namour.

Chilke's puzzlement with circumstances became extreme when Madame Zigonie declared her intention of marrying him. Chilke refused the honor, and Madame Zigonie discharged him in a rage, though she neglected to pay his salary.

In the town Lipwillow on the Big Muddy River Chilke was approached by Namour and offered a job as airport manager at Araminta Station. Namour here far exceeded his authority, but Chilke managed to secure the post on his own merits. Madame Zigonie's off-again on-again romantic interest and Namour's sympathetic assistance was a mystery to which he found no ready solution. Other even more urgent mysteries hung in the air. How many illicit flyers had the Yips constructed from the stolen parts? How many had they acquired by other means? If such existed, where were they located?

The superintendent of Bureau B was Bodwyn Wook: a small man, bald, yellow of skin; thin, active and sharp-eyed as a ferret. Bodwyn Wook was notable both for his caustic tongue and his indifference to the dictates of stylish convention. The discovery of the Yip thefts prompted him to a swift response. Yipton was raided; two flyers and a machine shop were destroyed.

Another sinister discovery followed hard upon the first. Yips of the Araminta work-force were found to be armed with a variety of weapons, as if in preparation for a grand massacre of Agency personnel.

The work-permits were instantly canceled; the Yips were sent back to Yipton. When questioned, Namour merely shrugged his shoulders and denied complicity in the affair. No one could prove differently and, indeed, it seemed incredible that the personable and popular Namour would involve himself in crimes so horrendous, and suspicion, while always latent, lost its edge as time went by. Namour proceeded with his regular routines, indifferent to lingering doubts.

Namour was a person impossible to categorize. He was strong, innately graceful and of good physique; his features were classically regular. He wore his clothes with flair and seemed to know everything worth knowing. At all times

Namour conducted himself with an engaging deliberate
ease and understatement, suggesting passion under careful control: an attribute which many ladies found appealing, and indeed Namour's name had been linked with many
others, including both Spanchetta and Smonny, whom he
apparently served on a continuing basis as a joint paramour, to the satisfaction of both.

Namour was not universally admired, especially at
Bureau B. His critics considered him a stone-hearted
opportunist, lacking all compunction and capable of any
crime. This view, in the end, proved correct, but before
Namour's crimes could be brought home to him, he quietly
slipped away from Araminta Station, to the intense regret
of Bodwyn Wook.

VI. THE YIPS AND YIPTON

The typical Yip was by no means deformed or unpre-
possessing: to the contrary, at first glance, the ordinary Yip
seemed extraordinarily handsome, with large luminous
hazel eyes, hair and skin of the same golden color, well-
shaped features and excellent physique. The Yip girls were
notorious up and down Mircea's Wisp for their comeliness,
docility and mild disposition, and also for their absolute
chastity unless they were paid an appropriate fee.

For reasons not wholly understood, Yips and ordinary
Gaeans were mutually infertile. Some biologists suggested
that the Yips were a mutation and represented a new
human species; others suspected that the Yip diet, which
included molluscs from the slime under Yipton, gave rise
to the situation. They pointed out that Yips indentured to
work on other worlds, after a passage of time, regained a
normal procreative ability.

Yipton had long been a tourist attraction in its own
right. Ferries from Araminta Station conveyed tourists to
Yipton, where they were housed in the Arkady Inn: a
ramshackle structure five stories high built entirely of
bamboo poles and palm fronds. On the terrace Yip girls

served gin slings, Sundowners, coconut toddy: all formu-
lated, brewed or distilled at Yipton from materials whose
nature no one cared to learn. Tours were conducted around
the noisome yet strangely charming canals of Yipton, and
to other places of interest, such as the Caglioro, the
Woman's Baths, the Handicraft Shops. Services of an intimate nature were provided both men and women at
'Pussycat Palace,' five minutes' walk from the Arkady Inn
along creaking bamboo corridors. At Pussycat Palace the
attendants were mild and obliging, though the services
lacked spontaneity and were performed with a careful, if
somewhat absentminded, methodicity. Nothing was free. At
Yipton, if one requested an after-lunch toothpick, he found
the reckoning on his bill.

Along with profits derived from tourism, the current
Oomphaw* of the Yips, one Titus Pompo, earned money
through the off-world indenture of labor gangs. The
Oomphaw Titus Pompo was assisted in this particular
enterprise, and others more disreputable, by Namour co-
Clattuc.

VII. STROMA

In the first few years of the Conservancy, when Society
members visited Cadwal, they presented themselves, as a
matter of course, to Riverview House, in the expectation of
hospitality. At times the Conservator was forced to entertain as many as two dozen guests at the same time, and
some of these extended their stays indefinitely, that they
might pursue their researches or simply enjoy the novel
environment of Cadwal.

One of the Conservators at last rebelled, and insisted
that visiting Naturalists live in tents along the beach, and
cook their meals over campfires.

At the Society's annual conclave, a number of plans

---

*The title, originally a term of derision, had been originated by a
tourist from Clarendon, Algenib IV. The Oomphaw's elite police were
the Oomps.

were put forward to deal with the problem. Most of the programs met the opposition of strict Conservationists, who complained that the Charter was being gnawed to shreds by first one trick, then another. Others replied: "Well and good, but when we visit Cadwal to conduct our legitimate researches, must we live in squalor? After all, we are members of the Society!"

In the end the conclave adopted a crafty plan put forward by one of the most extreme Conservationists. The plan authorized a small new settlement at a specific location, where it could not impinge in any way upon the environment. The location turned out to be the side of a cliff overlooking Stroma Fjord on Throy: an almost comically unsuitable site for habitation, and an obvious ploy to discourage proponents of the plan from taking action.

The challenge, however, was accepted. Stroma came into being: a town of tall narrow houses, crabbed and quaint, black or dark umber, with doors and window-trim painted white, blue and red. Seen from across the fjord, the houses of Stroma seemed to cling to the side of the cliff like barnacles.

Many members of the Society, after a temporary stay at Stroma, found the quality of life appealing, and on the pretext of performing lengthy research, became the nucleus of a permanent population which at times numbered as many as twelve hundred persons.

On Earth the Naturalist Society fell prey to weak leadership, the peculation of a larcenous secretary and a general lack of purpose. At a final conclave, the records and documents were consigned to the Library of Archives, and the presiding officer struck the gong of adjournment for the last time.

On Cadwal the Naturalists of Stroma took no official notice of the event, though now the sole income of Stroma was the yield from private off-world investment. The Charter remained as always the basic law of Cadwal and Araminta Station continued its work as usual.

* * *

VIII. PERSONS OF NOTE, RESIDENT AT ARAMINTA STATION, STROMA AND ELSEWHERE

At Clattuc House Spanchetta and Simonetta Clattuc were sisters, more alike than otherwise, though Spanchetta was the more earthy and Simonetta — 'Smonny,' as she was known — the more imaginative and restless. Both grew to be large, big-breasted young women with profuse heaps of curling hair, small glinting heavy-lidded eyes. Both were passionate, haughty, domineering and vain; both were uninhibited and possessed of boundless energies. During their youth, both Spanny and Smonny became obsessively fixated upon the person of Scharde Clattuc and each shamelessly sought to seduce him or marry him or by any other means to possess him for their own. Unfortunately for their hopes Scharde found Spanny and Smonny equally distasteful, if not repugnant, and sidestepped the advances of each as courteously as possible, and on several occasions with a desperate absence of courtesy.

Scharde was sent off-world to an IPCC* training mission at Sarsenopolis on Alphecca Nine. Here he met Marya Aténè, a dark-haired young woman of grace, charm, dignity and intelligence with whom he became enamored, and she with him. The two were married at Sarsenopolis and in due course returned to Araminta Station.

Spanchetta and Smonny were deeply outraged and grim. Scharde's conduct represented personal rejection and also — at a deeper level — defiance and a lack of submissiveness. They were able to rationalize their rage when Smonny failed to matriculate from the Lyceum and, on becoming a collateral, was forced to move out from Clattuc House, coincidentally at about the same time Marya arrived, so that the blame could easily be transferred to Marya and Scharde.

Heavy with bitterness, Smonny departed Araminta Sta-

---

*IPCC: the Interworld Police Coordination Company, often described as the single most important institution of the Gaean Reach. Bureau B at Araminta Station was an IPCC affiliate, and qualified Bureau B personnel became, in both theory and practice, IPCC agents.

tion. For a time she ranged far and wide across the Reach, engaging in a variety of activities. Eventually she married Titus Zigonie, who owned Shadow Valley Ranch, comprising twenty-two thousand square miles on the world Rosalia, as well as a Clayhacker space yacht.

For the labor necessary to work his ranch, Titus Zigonie at Smonny's suggestion began to employ gangs of indentured Yips, brought to Rosalia by none other than Namour, who shared the proceeds of the business with Calyactus, Oomphaw of Yipton.

At Namour's urging Calyactus paid a visit to the Shadow Valley Ranch on Rosalia, where he was murdered by either Smonny or Namour, or perhaps both working in tandem. Titus Zigonie, an inoffensive little man became 'Titus Pompo, the Oomphaw,' though Smonny wielded all authority.

Never had she relaxed her hatred of Araminta Station in general and Scharde Clattuc in particular, and her dearest wish was to perform some destructive atrocity upon them both.

Meanwhile, Namour, with utmost sang-froid, once again took up his duties as paramour to both Spanchetta and Smonny.

Marya meanwhile had borne Scharde a son, Glawen. When Glawen was two years old, Marya drowned in a boating accident under peculiar circumstances. A pair of Yips, Selious and Catterline, were witnesses to the drowning. Both declared themselves unable to swim and therefore helpless to aid Marya, and in any event it was none of their affair. So went most of the joy from Scharde's life. He questioned Selious and Catterline at length, but both became stolid and uncommunicative, and at last Scharde, in disgust, sent them back to Yipton.

Glawen passed through childhood, adolescence, and at the age of twenty-one reached his majority. Like his father Scharde he cast his lot with Bureau B. Glawen took after his father in other ways too. Both were spare of physique, narrow of hip, square of shoulder, sinewy and quick rather than massive of muscle. Glawen's features, like those of Scharde, were hard and blunt in a rather gaunt flat-cheeked face; his hair was dark, thick and cut short; his skin, though tanned, was not nearly so weather-beaten and brown as that of Scharde. Both men were economical of motion; both at first glance seemed somewhat sardonic and skeptical, but the dispositions of both were far less grim and austere than their first impression suggested. Indeed, when Glawen thought of Scharde, he thought of someone who was kindly, tolerant, absolutely honorable and totally brave. When Scharde considered Glawen, he found it hard to contain his pride and affection.

From Stroma the current Conservator, Egon Tamm, had come to Riverview House with his spouse Cora, their son Milo and daughter Wayness. A dozen young men of the Station, including Glawen, immediately fell in love with Wayness, who was slim, dark-haired, with dark gray eyes in a face alive with poetic intelligence.

A suitor of longer standing was Julian Bohost, also from Stroma: an earnest, highly articulate member of the LPF. Wayness' mother Cora approved of Julian, his fine voice and exquisite manners. It was an article of faith among her friends that Julian was a young man with an important political future. On this basis, she had encouraged Julian to consider himself betrothed to Wayness, though Wayness had carefully explained that her own thinking went in a different direction. Julian smilingly refused to listen, and continued to make plans for their joint future.

Julian's aunt was Dame Clytie Vergence, a Warden of Stroma and an LPF bellwether. Dame Clytie was a large woman, assertive and single-minded, and determined that the manifest rightness of LPF philosophy should win the day, despite all opposition and especially despite any references to the edicts of 'that crabbed old trifle of pettifoggery,' here referring to the Charter. "It has long outlived its usefulness! I intend to blow away this obfuscation and bring new thinking to bear!"

To date, the LPF had been unable to implement any of their reforms, since the Charter was still the law of the land against which the LPF could not legally transgress.

At an LPF conference, a subtle ploy was evolved. Near Mad Mountain Lodge, migrating banjee hordes regularly engaged in terrible battles, which the LPFers decided to stop, whether they destroyed the ecological equilibrium or not. Here was a cause, thought the LPF theoreticians, which every right-minded person must support, even though the principles of Conservancy were compromised.

Acting as Dame Clytie's official representative, Julian Bohost set off to visit Mad Mountain, that he might inspect the environment before making specific recommendations. He invited Milo and Wayness along for company; Wayness arranged that Glawen should fly the aircraft, much to Julian's disgust, since he had learned to dislike Glawen.

The excursion ended in disaster. Wayness finally made her disinterest clear to Julian. The next day Milo was killed in an accident arranged by three Yips, possibly after incitement by Julian, though the circumstances remained unclear.

Back at Araminta Station Wayness informed Glawen of her imminent departure for Old Earth, where she will reside for a time with her uncle Pirie Tamm, one of the few surviving members of the Naturalist Society. Milo would have accompanied her, but now Milo is dead, and she must share with Glawen a secret of enormous importance, in the event that she were to die on Earth.

During a previous visit to Earth, by chance she discovered that the original Charter, together with the Certificate of Registration — in effect the deed of ownership to Cadwal — had become lost. She now intended to search for the lost documents, before someone else found them — and there were indications that other persons unknown were engaged in just such a search.

With Milo dead, Wayness must now go off alone. Glawen would happily have accompanied her but for Bureau B constraints and lack of funds. He assured Wayness that he would join her as soon as possible; for the moment he could only urge caution upon her.

* * *

At Araminta Station Floreste co-Laverty, a person of flamboyant style and great aesthetic creativity, had long managed the Mummers, a troupe recruited from among the young folk of Araminta Station. Floreste trained the Mummers well and infused them with his own enthusiasm, so that they toured the worlds of Mircea's Wisp and beyond, with great success.

Floreste's great dream was the construction of a magnificent new Orpheum, to replace the creaking old auditorium now used for performances. All moneys earned by the Mummers went into a construction fund, for which he also solicited contributions.

A series of horrid crimes was discovered at Thurben Island, in the eastern ocean south and east of Lutwen Atoll. The crimes had their origins off-world and Glawen was sent to investigate. He returned with proof that Floreste, acting in concert with Namour and Smonny, was responsible. Namour quietly took his leave of Araminta Station before the crimes could be brought home to him; Smonny was at least temporarily inaccessible at Yipton but Floreste was sentenced to death.

During Glawen's absence off-world, his father Scharde had flown out on a routine patrol, but had never returned. No distress calls had been heard; no wreckage had been found. Glawen could not believe that Scharde was dead, and Floreste hinted that his suspicions were correct. He undertook to tell Glawen all he knew if Glawen, in return, would guarantee that Floreste's money should go to the use for which Floreste intended: the construction of a new Orpheum; to this contract, Glawen agreed, and Floreste drew up a will, bequeathing all he owned to Glawen.

Floreste's funds were on deposit at the Bank of Mircea, in the city Soumjiana on the nearby world Soum. Smonny, for the sake of convenience and fluidity, kept her own funds in the same account. The arrangement was temporary, but Smonny delayed too long; the entire account came into Glawen's possession upon Floreste's death.

Floreste's final act was the composition of a letter, in which he told all he knew in regard to Scharde.

Glawen has only just opened the letter, to learn that Scharde Clattuc, to the best of Floreste's knowledge, is yet alive. Where? Glawen will not know until he reads the letter in its entirety.

CHAPTER I

I.

The sun had set. Glawen Clattuc, wet and shivering, turned away from the ocean and ran up Wansey Way through the twilight. Arriving at Clattuc House, he pushed through the front portal and into the reception hall. Here, to his annoyance, he discovered Spanchetta Clattuc, at the foot of the grand staircase.

Spanchetta stopped short to take critical note of his condition. Tonight she had draped her own majestic torso in a dramatic gown of striped scarlet and black taffeta, with a black vest and silver slippers. A rope of black pearls wound round and round her great turban of dark curls; black pearls depended from her ears. Spanchetta paused only an instant to look Glawen up and down, then with averted eyes and curled lip she swept off toward the refectory.

Glawen proceeded to the chambers he shared with his father Scharde Clattuc. He immediately stepped from his dank garments, bathed under a hot shower and started to dress in dry clothes but was interrupted by the chime of the telephone. Glawen called out: "Speak!"

The face of Bodwyn Wook appeared on the screen. In a sour voice he said: "The sun has long since set. Surely you have read Floreste's letter. I expected your call."

Glawen gave a hollow laugh. "I have seen only two sentences of the letter. Apparently my father is alive."

"That is good news. Why were you delayed?"

"There was trouble on the beach, which ended up in the surf. I survived. Kirdy drowned."

Bodwyn Wook clapped his hands to his forehead. "Tell me no more! The news is disturbing! He was a Wook."

"In any event, I was just about to call you."

Bodwyn Wook heaved a sigh. "We will report an accidental drowning and forget the whole sickening affair. Is that understood?"

"Yes, sir."

"I am not altogether easy with your conduct. You should have expected such an attack."

"So I did, sir, which is why I went to the beach. Kirdy hated the ocean and I thought that he would stand clear. In the end, he died the death he dreaded most."

"Hmf," said Bodwyn Wook. "You have a callous nature. Suppose he shot you from ambush, and destroyed Floreste's letter: what then?"

"That would not be Kirdy's way. He wanted me to look into his face while he killed me."

"And if Kirdy altered his custom, for this particular occasion?"

Glawen considered, then gave a small shrug. "Your reprimand, in that case, would be well deserved."

"Hmf," said Bodwyn Wook with a grimace. "I am severe, certainly, but I have never gone so far as to reprimand a corpse." He leaned back in his chair. "We need take the matter no further. Bring the letter to my office and we will read it together."

"Very well, sir."

Glawen started to leave the chambers, but stopped short with his hand on the doorknob. He reflected a moment, then turned back and went to the side-room which served as utility room and office. Here he made a copy of Floreste's letter. The copy he folded and placed in a drawer; the original he tucked into his pocket, then departed.

Ten minutes later Glawen arrived at the Bureau B offices on the second floor of the New Agency, and was immediately admitted into Bodwyn Wook's private chambers. As usual, Bodwyn Wook sat in his massive leather-

upholstered chair. He held out his hand. "If you please."
Glawen gave him the letter. Bodwyn Wook waved his hand
toward a chair. "Sit."

Glawen obeyed the instruction. Bodwyn Wook
extracted the letter from its envelope, and began to read
aloud, using a nasal drone not at all in accord with the
extravagances and felicities of Floreste's language.

The letter was discursive and sometimes rambled off
into an explication of Floreste's philosophy. He expressed
pro forma contrition for his deeds, but the words lacked
conviction, and Floreste seemed to intend the letter as a
justification for his activities. "There is no question, and I
state this positively," wrote Floreste. "I am one of a very few
persons who may properly profess the designation
'Overman'; there are few indeed like me! In my case, ordinary strictures of common morality should not apply, lest
they interfere with my supreme creativity. Alas! I still am
like a fish in a tank, swimming with other fish, and I must
obey their procedures or they will nip my fins!"

Floreste agreed that his dedication to 'Art' had persuaded him to irregularities. "I have taken shortcuts on the
long and tedious route to my goals; I have been trapped,
and now my fins must be nipped.

"Had I to do it all over again," mused Floreste, "I surely
would have been more careful! Of course it is often possible
to gain the accolades of Society even while one is arrogantly
flouting and demeaning the most sacred dogmas which are
its very soul! In this respect, Society is like a great cringing
animal; the more you abuse it, the more affection it lavishes
upon you. Ah well, too late now to worry about these
niceties of conduct."

Floreste went on to ponder his crimes. "My offenses are
difficult to weigh on an exact scale, or balance against the
benefits derived from the so-called 'crimes.' The fulfillment
of my great goal may well justify the sacrifice of a few futile
wisps of humanity, which otherwise would have served no
purpose."

Bodwyn Wook paused to turn a page. Glawen observed:
"The 'futile wisps' of course would not agree with Floreste."

"Naturally not," said Bodwyn Wook. "His general thesis

is certainly arguable; still, we cannot allow every vagabond dog-barber who calls himself an 'artist' to commit vile crimes while pursuing his Muse."

Floreste turned his attention to Simonetta; she had told him much about herself and the events of her lifetime. After storming from Araminta Station in a fury, she had wandered the Gaean Reach far and wide, living by her wits, marrying and remarrying, consorting and reconsorting, and in general living a self-willed adventurous life. While a member of the Monomantic Cult she met Zadine Babbs, or 'Zaa,' as she called herself, and a brute of a woman named Sibil de Vella. The three banded together, became 'Ordenes' and assumed control of the cult.

Smonny soon tired of routines and restrictions, and abandoned the seminary. A month later she met Titus Zigonie, a small plump man of submissive character. Titus Zigonie owned Shadow Valley Ranch on the world Rosalia, as well as a spacious Clayhacker Space yacht: attributes which Smonny found irresistible, and Titus Zigonie found himself married to Smonny almost before he realized what was happening.

A few years later Smonny visited Old Earth, where she chanced to encounter one Kelvin Kilduc, current Secretary of the Naturalist Society. During their conversation Secretary Kilduc mentioned the former secretary Frons Nisfit and his peculations. Kilduc suspected that Nisfit had gone so far as to sell the original Charter to a collector of ancient documents. "Not that it makes any difference," Kilduc hastened to add. "The Conservancy now exists by its own momentum and will do so forever, Charter or no Charter, or so I am assured."

"Of course," said Smonny. "Naturally! I wonder with whom the wicked Nisfit dealt?"

"That is hard to say."

Smonny made inquiries among the antiquarians and discovered one of the stolen documents. It was part of a lot sold off by a collector named Floyd Swaner. Smonny traced him down but it was too late; Floyd Swaner was dead. His heir and grandson Eustace Chilke was said to be something of a ne'er-do-well, always on the move, here and there, far and wide. His present whereabouts were unknown.

On Rosalia, labor was scarce. Smonny contracted with Namour for a workforce of indentured Yips, and in such a fashion renewed her connection with Cadwal.

Namour and Smonny evolved a wonderful new scheme. Calyactus, Oomphaw of Yipton, had become old and foolish. Namour persuaded him to visit Rosalia for medical treatments which would renew his youth. At Shadow Valley Ranch Calyactus was poisoned; Titus Zigonie, calling himself Titus Pompo, became Oomphaw in his stead.

Smonny's investigators finally discovered Eustace Chilke working as a tour-bus operator at Seven Cities on John Preston's World. As soon as possible Smonny introduced herself to Chilke and hired him to supervise Shadow Valley Ranch. She finally decided to marry him, but Chilke politely declined the honor. Smonny became peevish and dismissed Chilke from his position. Namour ultimately took him to Araminta Station.

"Smonny and Namour are an amazing pair," wrote Floreste. "Neither have any scruples whatever, though Namour likes to pose as a gentleman of culture, and for a fact is a personable fellow, with many odd competences. He can force his body to obey the steel of his will: think! He has acted the role of complaisant lover for both Spanchetta and Smonny, managing both affairs with aplomb. Namour, if for no other reason than your superb daring, I salute you!

"So little time is left to me! Were I to live I would compose a heroic ballet, for three principals, representing Smonny, Spanchetta and Namour! Ah, the stately evolutions of my principals! I see the patterns clearly; they swing, whirl, come and go, with the awful justice of Fate! The music I hear in my mind's ear; it is poignant indeed, and the costumes are extraordinary! So goes the dance! The three figures project sentience, and conduct their perambulations with care. I see them now: they circle and go, up-stage and down, mincing and preening, each at his proper gait. How shall the finale be resolved?

"It is all a bagatelle! Why should I trouble my poor mind

over such a question? I shall not be here to direct the production!"

Again Bodwyn Wook paused in his reading. "Perhaps we should have allowed Floreste time to complete this last production! It sounds fascinating!"

"I find it tiresome," said Glawen.

"You are either too young or too practical for such appreciation. Floreste's mind seethes with intriguing notions."

"He takes a long time getting to the point: that is certain."

"Aha! Not from Floreste's viewpoint! This is his testament: his entire reason for being. This is not casual frivolity that you hear but a wail of utter grief." Bodwyn Wook returned to the letter. "I shall read on. Perhaps he is now in the mood to recite a fact or two."

Floreste's tone was indeed somewhat flatter. Before Glawen's return to Araminta Station, Floreste had visited Yipton to plan a new round of entertainments. Thurben Island could no longer be used, and another more convenient location must be selected. During a conversation, Titus Pompo, loose-tongued by reason of too many Trelawny Sloshes, revealed that Smonny had at last settled an old score. She had captured Scharde Clattuc, confiscated his flyer, and taken him to her prison. Titus Pompo gravely shook his head. Scharde would pay dearly for the prideful attitudes which had cost Smonny such grief! As for the flyer, it represented partial compensation for the flyers destroyed by the Bureau B raid. After drinking from his goblet, Titus Pompo asserted that it would not be the last flyer so confiscated!

"We will see about that!" said Bodwyn Wook.

Scharde had been taken to the strangest of all prisons, where 'out' was 'in' and 'in' was 'out.' The prisoners were at liberty to attempt escape whenever the mood came on them.

Bodwyn Wook paused in his reading to pour out two mugs of ale.

"That is a strange prison," said Glawen. "Where could it be located?"

"Let us proceed. Floreste is perhaps a bit absent-minded, but I suspect that he will not omit this important detail."

Bodwyn Wook read on. Almost at once Floreste identified the unique prison as the dead volcano Shattorak at the center of Ecce: an ancient cone rising two thousand feet above the swamps and jungles. The prisoners occupied a strip outside the stockade which encircled the summit and protected the prison officials. The jungle grew high up the slopes; the prisoners slept in tree-houses or behind makeshift stockades to avoid the predators from the jungle. By reason of Smonny's vindictiveness, Scharde had not been killed out of hand.

Titus Pompo, now thoroughly drunk, went on to reveal that five flyers were concealed at Shattorak, together with a cache of weapons. From time to time, when Smonny wished to travel off-world, Titus Pompo's Clayhacker space yacht landed upon Shattorak, taking care to avoid the Araminta Station radar. Titus Pompo was quite content with his pleasant routines at Yipton: an amplitude of rich food; sloshes, slings, punches and toddies; incessant massaging and stroking worked upon him by Yip maidens.

"That is all I know," wrote Floreste. "Despite my happy relations with Araminta Station where I had hoped to build my great monument, I felt, rightly or wrongly, that I should not betray Titus Pompo's drunken confidences, for this reason: they would surely be revealed of themselves soon and without my intercession. You may consider this qualm weak-minded and maudlin. You will insist that 'right' is 'right,' and any deviation or skulkery or failure to bear the burdens of virtue are 'not right.' At this moment I shall not disagree.

"To make a feeble demonstration on my own behalf I will point out that I am not utterly faithless. As best I could, I paid my obligation to Namour, who would not have done the same for me. Of all men, he probably deserves consideration the least, and he is no less guilty than I. Still, in my lonely and foolish way, I have kept faith and allowed him time to make good his flight. I trust that he never troubles Araminta Station again, since it is a place dear to my heart,

where I planned the Araminta Center for the Performing
Arts: the new Orpheum. I have transgressed, but so I
justify my peccancies.

"It is too late for tears of penitence. They would not in
any case carry conviction—not even to myself. Still, when
all is said and done, I see that I die not so much for my
venality as for my folly. These are the most dismal words
known to man: 'Ah, what might have been, had only I been
wiser!'

"Such is my apologia. Take it or leave it as you will. I
am overcome by weariness and a great sadness; I can write
no more."

II.

Bodwyn Wook placed the letter carefully down upon his desk. "So much for Floreste. He has declared himself. If nothing else, he knew how to contrive exquisite excuses for himself. But: to proceed. The situation is complex and we must carefully consider our response. Yes, Glawen? You have an opinion?"

"We should strike Shattorak at once."

"Why so?"

"To rescue my father, of course!"

Bodwyn Wook nodded sagely. "This concept is at least simple and uncomplicated: so much can be said for it."

"That is good to hear. Where does the idea go wrong?"

"It is a reflex, prompted by Clattuc emotion rather than cool Wook intellect." Glawen growled something under his breath which Bodwyn Wook ignored. "I remind you that Bureau B is essentially an administrative agency, which has been pressed to perform quasi-military functions only by default. At best, we can deploy two or three dozen operatives: all highly trained, valuable men. There are how many Yips? Who knows? Sixty thousand? Eighty thousand? A hundred thousand? Far too many.

"Now then. Floreste mentions five flyers at Shattorak: several more than I would have expected. We can put at most seven or eight flyers into the air, none heavily armed. Shattorak is no doubt defended by ground weapons. We strike boldly at Shattorak. In the worst case, we could take losses that would destroy Bureau B, and next week the Yips would swarm across to the Foreshore. And in the best case? We must reckon with Smonny's spies. We might storm over to Shattorak, land in force, and discover no fine jail, no flyer depot, nothing but corpses. No Scharde, no flyers, nothing. Just failure."

Glawen was still dissatisfied. "That does not sound like the 'best case' to me."

"Only under the terms of your proposal."

"Then what do you suggest?"

"First, consideration of all our options. Second, reconnaissance. Third, attack, with full stealth." He brought an image to the wallscreen. "There you see Shattorak, a mere pimple on the swamp. It is of course two thousand feet high. The river to the south is the Verles." The image expanded, to provide a view across the summit of Shattorak: a sterile expanse, slightly disk-shaped, surfaced with coarse gray sand and ledges of black rock. A pond of copper-blue water occupied the center. "The area is about ten acres," said Bodwyn Wook. "The picture is at least a hundred years old; I don't think we have been there since."

"It looks hot."

"So it does, and so it is. I will shift the perspective. You will notice a strip about two hundred yards wide surrounding the summit, where the incline begins. The ground is still barren except for a few large trees. These are evidently where the prisoners sleep. Below, the jungle begins. If Floreste is correct, the prisoners reside around the strip, and are free to escape across the swamp whenever they like."

Glawen studied the image in silence.

"We must scout the terrain with care, and only then proceed," said Bodwyn Wook. "Are we agreed?"

"Yes," said Glawen. "We are agreed."

Bodwyn Wook went on. "I am puzzled by Floreste's references to Chilke. It appears that he is here at Araminta Station only by reason of Smonny's scheming to find and control the Charter. I wonder too about the Society on Old Earth: why are they not taking steps to locate the lost documents?"

"There are not many members left, so I am told."

"Are they indifferent to the Conservancy? That is hard to believe! Who is the current Secretary?"

Glawen responded cautiously: "I think that he is a cousin of the Conservator, named Pirie Tamm."

"Indeed! Did not the Tamm girl go off to Earth?"

"So she did."

"Well then! Since—uh, what is her name?"

"Wayness."

"Just so. Since Wayness is present on Old Earth, perhaps she can help us in regard to the missing documents from the Society archives. Write her and suggest that she make a few inquiries into this matter. Emphasize that she should be absolutely discreet, and give out no clue as to her objectives. For a fact, I can see where this might develop into an important issue."

Glawen nodded thoughtfully. "As a matter of fact, Wayness is already making such inquiries."

"Ah ha! What has she learned, if anything?"

"I don't know. I have had no letters from her."

Bodwyn Wook raised his eyebrows. "She has not written you?"

"I'm sure she has written. But I have never received her letters."

"Odd. The doorman at Clattuc House has probably tucked them behind his wine-cooler."

"That is a possibility, though I'm beginning to suspect another person entirely. In any event, I think that as soon as we deal with Shattorak, I should take advice from Chilke, then go to Earth to look for these documents."

"Hmf yes. Ahem. First things first, which means Shattorak. In due course we will talk further on the subject." Bodwyn Wook picked up Floreste's letter. "I will take charge of this."

Glawen made no complaint, and departed the New Agency. He ran back to Clattuc House at a purposeful trot and pushed through the front portal. To the side were a pair of small chambers occupied by Alarion co-Clattuc, the head doorman, together with an antechamber where, if necessary, he could overlook comings and goings. Alarion's duties included receipt of incoming mail, sorting and delivering parcels, letters and inter-House memoranda to the designated apartments.

Glawen touched a bell-button and Alarion appeared from his private rooms: a white-haired man, thin and bent, whose only vanity would seem to be a small goatee. "Good evening, Glawen! What can I do for you this evening?"

"You might enlighten me regarding some letters which should have arrived for me from Old Earth."

"I can only inform you as to what I know of my certain knowledge," said Alarion. "You would not want me to fabricate tales of non-existent parcels and messages engraved on gold tablets delivered by the archangel Sersimanthes."

"I take it that nothing of that sort has arrived?"

Alarion glanced over his shoulder toward his sorting table. "No, Glawen. Nor anything else."

"As you know, I was away from the Station for several months. During this time I should have received a number of letters from off-world; yet I cannot find them. Do you remember any such letters arriving during my absence?"

Alarion said slowly: "I seem to recall such letters. They were delivered to your chambers—even after Scharde met with his accident. As always, I dropped the letters into the door-slot. Then, of course, Arles moved into your rooms for a time, but surely he took proper care of your mail. No doubt the letters are tucked away somewhere."

"No doubt," said Glawen. "Thank you for the information."

Glawen became aware that he was ravenously hungry: no surprise, since he had not eaten since morning. In the refectory he made a hurried meal on dark bread, beans and cucumbers, then went up to his apartments. He seated himself before the telephone. He touched buttons, but in response was treated to a crisp official voice: "You are making a restricted call, and cannot be connected without authorization."

"I am Captain Glawen Clattuc, Bureau B. That is sufficient authorization."

"Sorry, Captain Clattuc. Your name is not on the list."

"Then put it on the list! Check with Bodwyn Wook, if you like."

A moment passed. The voice spoke again. "Your name is now on the list, sir. To whom do you wish the connection?"

"Arles Clattuc."

Five minutes passed before Arles' heavy face peered hopefully into the screen. At the sight of Glawen, the hope gave way to a scowl. "What do you want, Glawen? I thought it was something important. This place is bad enough without harassment from you."

"It might get worse, Arles, depending upon what happened to my mail."

"Your mail?"

"Yes, my mail. It was delivered to my chambers and now it's gone. What happened to it?"

Arles' voice rose in pitch as he focused his mind upon the unexpected problem. He responded peevishly: "I don't remember any mail. There was just a lot of trash. The place was a pig-pen when we moved in."

Glawen gave a savage laugh. "If you threw away my mail, you'll be breaking rocks a lot longer than eighty-five days! Think seriously, Arles!"

"No need to take that tone with me! If there was mail, it probably got bundled up into your other stuff and stored in a box."

"I have been through my boxes and I have found no letters. Why? Because you opened them and read them."

"Nonsense! Not purposely, at least! If I saw mail with the name 'Clattuc' on it, I might have automatically glanced at it."

"Then what?"

"I told you: I don't remember!"

"Did you give it to your mother to read?"

Arles licked his lips. "She might have picked it up, in order to take care of it."

"And she read it in front of you!"

"I did not say that. Anyway, I wouldn't remember. I don't keep a watch on my mother. Is that all you wanted to say?"

"Not quite, but it will do until I find what happened to my letters." Glawen broke the connection.

For a moment he stood in the center of the room brooding. Then he changed into his official Bureau B jacket and cap and took himself down the corridor to Spanchetta's apartments.

A maid responded to the bell and conducted him into the reception parlor: an octagonal chamber furnished with a central octagonal settee upholstered in green silk. In four alcoves four cinnabar urns displayed tall bouquets of purple lilies. Spanchetta stepped into the room. Tonight she had elected to dramatize her majestic big-bosomed torso in a gown of lusterless black, unadorned by so much as a silver button. The hem brushed the floor; long sleeves draped her arms; her hair lofted above her scalp in an amazing pyramidal pile of black curls almost a foot high, and she had toned her skin stark white. For five seconds she stood in the doorway, staring at Glawen with eyes glinting like slivers of black glass, then advanced into the room. "What is your business here, that you come dressed in your toy uniform?"

"The uniform is official and I am here on an official investigation."

Spanchetta gave a mocking laugh. "And of what am I accused on this occasion?"

"I wish to question you, in regard to the purloining and wrongful sequestration of mail—namely, the mail which arrived for me during my absence."

Spanchetta made a scornful gesture. "What should I know of your mail?"

"I have been in communication with Arles. Unless you produce the mail at once, I shall order an instant search of the premises. In this case you will be subject to criminal charges whether the mail is found or whether it is not found, since the testimony of Arles has established that the mail was given into your custody."

Spanchetta reflected a moment, then turned away and started from the room. Glawen followed on her heels. Spanchetta stopped short, and snapped over her shoulder:

"You are invading a private domicile! That is a notable offense!"

"Not under circumstances such as this. I want to see where you have been keeping the letters. Also I don't care to cool my heels an hour or so in the reception parlor while you go about your affairs."

Spanchetta managed a grim smile and turned away. In the corridor she stopped by a tall armoire. From one of the drawers she took a packet of letters secured with string. "This is what you are looking for. I forgot about them; it is as simple as that."

Glawen leafed through the letters, which numbered four. All had been opened. Spanchetta watched without comment.

Glawen could think of nothing to say which could adequately express his outrage. He heaved a deep sigh. "You may be hearing more from me in this matter."

Spanchetta's silence was insulting. Glawen turned on his heel and departed, that he might not say or do anything to compromise his dignity. The maid politely opened the door; Glawen stalked through and out into the corridor.

III.

Glawen returned to his own chambers, and stood in the middle of the sitting room, seething with fury. Spanchetta's conduct was worse than intolerable; it was indescribable. As always, after Spanchetta had performed one of her characteristic offenses, there seemed no reasonable or dignified recourse. Time and time again the rueful remark had been made: "Spanchetta is Spanchetta! She is like a natural force; there is no coping with her! Just leave her be; that is the only way."

Glawen looked down at the letters he clutched in his hand. All had been opened and carelessly re-sealed, with no regard for his sensibilities; it was as if they had been violated and befouled. There was nothing he could do about it, since he could not throw the letters away. He must accept the humiliation.

"I must be practical," said Glawen. He went to the couch and flung himself down. One by one he examined the letters.

The first had been posted from Andromeda 6011 IV, the junction where Wayness would transfer to an Explorer Route packet for the remainder of her voyage to Old Earth. The second and third letters had been mailed from Yssinges, a village near Shillawy on Earth; the fourth from Mirky Porod in Draczeny.

Glawen read the letters quickly, one after the other, then read them more slowly a second time. In the first letter she wrote of her journey along the Wisp to Port Blue Lamp on Andromeda 6011 IV. The second letter announced her arrival upon Old Earth. She spoke of Pirie Tamm and his quaint old house near Yssinges. Little had changed since her last visit, and she felt almost as if she were coming home. Pirie Tamm had been saddened to hear of Milo's death and had expressed deep concern over the state of affairs existent upon Cadwal. "Uncle Pirie is secretary of the Society somewhat against his will. He is not interested in talking Society business with me, and perhaps thinks me too curious, even something of a nuisance. Why, he seems to wonder, should I, at my age, be so concerned with old documents and their whereabouts? At times he has been almost sharp and I must move carefully. It seems to me he wants to sweep the whole problem under the rug, on the theory that if he pretends the problem does not exist it will go away. Uncle Pirie, so I fear, is not aging gracefully."

Wayness wrote guardedly of her 'researches' and the obstacles and barriers she constantly found in her way. Other circumstances she found not only puzzling but also somewhat frightening—the more so that she could not identify them or convince herself of their reality. Old Earth, wrote Wayness somberly, was in many ways as sweet and fresh and innocent as it might have been during the archaic ages, but sometimes it seemed dank and dark and steeped in mystery. Wayness would very much have welcomed Glawen's company, for a number of reasons.

"Don't worry," said Glawen to the letter. "As soon as soon can be, I'll be on my way!"

In the third letter Wayness expressed concern over the lack of news from Glawen. She spoke even more cautiously than before of her 'researches,' which, so she hinted, might well take her into far parts of the world. "The odd events I mentioned still occur," wrote Wayness. "I am almost certain that—but no, I won't write it; I won't even think it."

Glawen grimaced. "What can be happening? Why is she not more careful? At least until I arrive?"

The fourth letter was short and the most despairing of all, and only the postmark, at Draczeny in the Moholc, indicated her activity. "I won't write again until I hear from you! Either my letters or yours have gone astray, or something awful has happened to you!" She included no return address, writing only: "I am leaving here tomorrow, though as of this instant I am not quite sure where I will go. As soon as I know something definite, I will communicate with my father, and he will let you know. I do not dare tell you anything more specific for fear that these letters might fall into the wrong hands."

Spanchetta's hands were certainly wrong enough, thought Glawen. The letters made no specific references which might compromise Wayness' 'researches,' although many of her guarded allusions might well intrigue a person of Spanchetta's cast of mind.

Wayness made a single reference to the Charter, but in connection with the moribund Naturalist Society. A harmless reference, thought Glawen. She wrote sadly of Pirie Tamm's disillusionment with the entire Conservationist concept, whose time, so he felt, had come and gone—at least in the case of Cadwal, where generations of over-flexible Naturalists, in the name of expediency, had allowed circumstances to reach their present difficult stage. "Uncle Pirie is pessimistic," wrote Wayness. "He feels that the Conservationists on Cadwal must protect the Charter with their own strength, since the current Naturalist Society has neither the force nor the will to assist. I have heard him declare that Conservancy, by its innate nature, can only be a transitory phase in the life-cycle of a world such as Cadwal. I tried to argue with him, pointing out that there is no intrinsic reason why a rational administration guided by a strong Charter can not maintain Conservancy forever, and that the current problems on Cadwal arise from what amounts to the sloth and avarice of the former administrators: they wanted a plentiful source of cheap labor and so allowed the Yips to remain on Lutwen Atoll in clear violation of the Charter, and it is this generation which must finally bite the bullet and set matters right. How? Obviously the Yips must be transferred from Cadwal to an equivalent or better off-world location: a hard, costly and nervous process, and at the moment beyond our capacity. Uncle Pirie listens only with half an ear, as if my well-reasoned projections were the babblings of a naive child. Poor Uncle Pirie! I wish he were more cheerful! I wish I were more cheerful! Most of all, I wish you were here."

Glawen telephoned Riverview House, and brought the face of Egon Tamm to the screen. "Glawen Clattuc here. I have just now read the letters Wayness wrote me from Earth. Spanchetta had intercepted them and laid them aside. She had no intention of giving them to me."

Egon Tamm shook his head in amazement. "What a strange woman! Why should she do something like that?"

"It indicates her contempt for anything connected with me or my father."

"It still verges upon the irrational! Every day the world becomes more perplexing. Wayness confuses me; her conduct is beyond my understanding. But she refuses to confide in me, on the grounds that I could not conscientiously keep my mouth shut." Egon Tamm turned a searching gaze upon Glawen. "What of you? Surely you must have some clue as to what is going on!"

Glawen side-stepped the question. "I have no idea where she is or what she is doing. She has had no letters from me—for a very good reason, of course—so she is not writing until she hears from me."

"I have had no recent letters. She tells me nothing in any case. Still, I sense a force, or pressure, pushing her where she really does not want to go. She is much too young and inexperienced for any serious trouble. I am deeply concerned."

Glawen said in a subdued voice: "I have much the same feeling."

"Why is she so secretive?"

"Evidently she has learned something which would cause damage if it were generally known. Indeed, if I might make a suggestion—"

"Suggest all you like!"

"—it might be best if neither of us should so much as speculate regarding Wayness in public."

"That is an interesting idea, which I do not totally understand. Still I will take it to heart—though I am baffled by what could have so aroused the girl and taken her so far away. Our problems are undeniably real, but they are here on Cadwal!"

Glawen said uncomfortably: "I am certain that she has good reasons for whatever she is doing."

"No doubt! Her next letter may supply a few more details."

"And include her current address, or so I hope. Speaking of letters, I imagine that Bodwyn Wook told you of Floreste's final testament."

"He reported its gist and recommended that I study it in detail. In fact—first, let me explain conditions at Riverview House. Every year I must endure official scrutiny of my affairs by a pair of Wardens. This year the two Wardens are Wilder Fergus and Dame Clytie Vergence, whom I think you will remember, and her nephew Julian Bohost is here also."

"I remember them well."

"They are unforgettable. I have other unusual guests— 'unusual,' that is, in the context of Riverview House. They are Lewyn Barduys and his travelling companion—a creature of many distinctions who uses the name 'Flitz.' "

" 'Flitz'?"

"No more, no less. Barduys is a man of wealth, and can afford such frivolities. I know nothing about him, except that he seems to be a friend of Dame Clytie."

"Dame Clytie is her usual self?"

"Even more so. She has elevated Titus Pompo to the stature of a folk hero—a noble and selfless revolutionary, a champion of the oppressed."

"She is serious?"

"Quite serious."

Glawen smiled thoughtfully. "Floreste discusses Titus Pompo in some detail."

"I would like to hear this letter," said Egon Tamm. "My guests might also be interested. Perhaps you would join us for lunch tomorrow and read the letter aloud."

"I will be happy to do so."

"Good! Until tomorrow, then, a bit before noon."

IV.

In the morning Glawen telephoned the airport and was connected to Chilke. "Good morning, Glawen," said Chilke. "What is on your mind?"

"I would like a few words with you, at your convenience."

"One time is as good as another."

"I'll be there at once."

Arriving at the airport, Glawen went to the glass-walled office at the side of the hangar. Here he found Chilke: a man of invincible nonchalance, a veteran of a thousand escapades, some creditable. Chilke was sturdy and heavy-shouldered, of middle stature, with a blunt-featured face, an unruly mat of dust-colored curls and cheeks roped with cartilage.

Chilke stood by a side-table, pouring tea into a mug. He looked over his shoulder. "Sit down, Glawen. Will you have some tea?"

"If you please."

Chilke poured out another mug. "This is the authentic stuff, from the far hills of Old Earth, not just some local seaweed." Chilke settled himself into his chair. "What brings you out so early?"

Glawen looked through the glass panes of the partition and across the hangar. "Can we talk without being overheard?"

"I think so. No one has his ear pressed to the door. That's a feature of glass walls. Any odd conduct makes you conspicuous."

"What about microphones?"

Chilke swung around and turned knobs to bring a wild wailing music from a speaker. "That should jam any microphone within hearing range, so long as you don't try to sing. Now what is it that is so secret?"

"This is the copy of a letter Floreste wrote yesterday afternoon. He says that my father is still alive. He also mentions you." Glawen gave the letter to Chilke. "Read it for yourself."

Chilke took the letter, leaned back in his chair and read. Halfway through he looked up. "Isn't it amazing? Smonny still thinks I own a great hoard of Grandpa Swaner's valuables!"

"It's only amazing if you don't. And you don't?"

"I hardly think so."

"Have you ever made an inventory of the estate?"

Chilke shook his head. "Why bother? It's just refuse cluttering up the barn. Smonny knows this very well; she's burgled the place four times."

"You're sure it was Smonny?"

"No one else has showed any interest in the stuff. I wish she would take herself in hand. It makes me nervous to be the object of her avarice, or affection, or wrath—whatever it is." Chilke returned to the letter. He finished, mused a moment, then tossed the letter back to Glawen. "Now you want to rush out and rescue your father."

"Something like that."

"And Bodwyn Wook is joining you on the mission?"

"I doubt it. He is a bit over-cautious."

"I suspect for good reason."

Glawen shrugged. "He is convinced that Shattorak is defended and that an attack from the air would cost us five or six flyers and half of the staff."

"You call that over-caution? I call it common sense."

"A raid would not need to come down from above. We could land a force somewhere on the slope of Shattorak and attack from the side. He still sees difficulties."

"So do I," said Chilke. "Where would the flyers land? In the jungle?"

"There must be open areas."

"So it might be. First, we would need to alter the landing gear on all our flyers, which would be duly noted by the spies. They would also give notice of our departure and Smonny would have five hundred Yips waiting for us."

"I thought you had chased out all your spies."

Chilke held out his hands in a gesture of helpless and injured innocence. "What happens when I need to hire mechanics? I use what I find. I know I have spies, just like a dog knows it has fleas. I even know who they are. There's one of my prime candidates yonder, working on the carry-all door: a magnificent specimen by the name of Benjamie."

Looking toward the carry-all, Glawen observed a tall young man of superb physique, flawless features, coal-black hair and clear bronze skin. Glawen watched him a moment, then asked: "What makes you think he's a spy?"

"He works hard, obeys all orders, smiles more than necessary, and watches everything which is going on. That's how I pick out all the spies: they work the hardest and give the least trouble — aside from their crimes, of course. If I were a deep-dyed cynic, I might try to hire all spies."

Glawen had been watching Benjamie. "He doesn't look like a typical spy."

"Perhaps not. He looks even less like a typical worker. I've always felt in my bones it was Benjamie who laid the trap for your father."

"But you have no proof."

"If I had proof, Benjamie would not be grinning so cheerfully."

"Well, so long as Benjamie is not watching, this is what I have in mind." Glawen explained his concept. Chilke listened dubiously. "At this end, the notion is feasible, but I can't turn a tap without clearance from Bodwyn Wook."

Glawen gave a sour nod. "That is what I thought you'd say. Very well; I'll go this very minute and put my case to him."

Glawen hurried up Wansey Way to the New Agency, only to be informed by Hilda, the vinegary office manager, that Bodwyn Wook had not yet put in an appearance. Hilda was suspicious and resentful of Glawen, and felt that he enjoyed too many perquisites. "You'll have to wait, just like everybody else," said Hilda.

Glawen cooled his heels for an hour before Bodwyn Wook's arrival. Ignoring Glawen, he stopped by Hilda's desk to mutter a few terse words, then marched past Glawen looking neither to right nor to left.

Glawen waited another ten minutes, then told Hilda: "You may announce to the Superintendent that Captain Glawen Clattuc has arrived and wishes a word with him."

"He knows you're here."

"I can't wait much longer."

"Oh?" demanded Hilda sarcastically. "You have an important engagement elsewhere?"

"The Conservator has invited me to lunch at Riverview House."

Hilda grimaced. She spoke into the mesh of the transceiver. "Glawen is becoming restive."

Bodwyn Wook's voice came as a harsh mumble. Hilda turned to Glawen. "You can go on in."

Glawen marched with dignity into the inner office. Bodwyn Wook looked up from his desk and jerked his thumb toward a chair. "Be seated, please. What is all this about you and the Conservator?"

"I had to tell that woman something; otherwise she would keep me sitting bolt upright all day. It's clear that she dislikes me intensely."

"Wrong!" declared Bodwyn Wook. "She adores you but is afraid to show it."

"I find that hard to believe," said Glawen.

"No matter! Let us not waste time discussing Hilda and her megrims. Why are you here? Do you have something new to tell me? If not, go away."

Glawen spoke in a controlled voice. "I would like to ask your plans in regard to Shattorak."

Bodwyn Wook said briskly: "The matter has been taken under advisement. As of this instant, no decisions have been made."

Glawen raised his eyebrows as if in surprise. "I should think haste would be a priority."

"We have a dozen priorities! Among other incidentals, I would very much like to destroy Titus Pompo's space-yacht—or, even better, capture it."

"But you are planning no immediate action to rescue my father?"

Bodwyn Wook flung his lank arms into the air. "Do I plan a hell-roaring swoop upon Shattorak in full force? Not today, and not tomorrow."

"What is your thinking?"

"Have I not explained? We want to survey the ground with stealth and caution. That is how we do it at Bureau B, where intellect dominates hysteria! Some of the time, at least."

"I have an idea which seems to accord with your plans."

"Ha hah! If it entails a private assault, replete with Clattuc flair and insolence, save your breath. We can spare no flyers for any such madcap excursion."

"I intend nothing rash, sir, and I would not use one of the Bureau flyers."

"You plan to walk and swim?"

"No, sir. There is an old Skyrie utility flyer at the back of the airport. The superstructure is cut away; in fact it is no more than a flying platform. Chilke sometimes uses it to carry freight down to Cape Journal. It is suitable for what I have in mind."

"Which is, specifically, what?"

"I would approach Ecce at sea level, fly up the Vertes River to the foot of Shattorak, secure the Skyrie and proceed up the slope to the prison. There I would reconnoiter."

"My dear Glawen, your proposal is as like to horrid suicide as two peas in a pod."

Glawen smilingly shook his head. "I hope not."

"How can you avoid it? The beasts are savage."

"Chilke will help me equip the Skyrie."

"Aha! So you have taken Chilke into your confidence!"

"Necessarily. We will install floats and a canopy over the front section, also a pair of G-ZR guns, on swivels."

"And after you set down the Skyrie—what then? Do you think you can simply saunter up the hill? The jungle is as evil as the swamp."

"According to the references, the creatures become torpid during the afternoon."

"Because of the heat. You will go torpid, as well."

"I'll load the small swamp crawler on the afterdeck of the Skyrie. It might make the climb up Shattorak easier—perhaps safer."

"Words like 'easy' and 'safe' don't apply on Ecce."

Glawen looked off out the window. "I hope to survive."

"I hope so too," said Bodwyn Wook.

"Then you will approve the plan?"

"Not so fast. Assume you are able to climb Shattorak—what then?"

"I'll arrive at the prison strip outside the stockade. With luck, I'll find my father at once, and we will return down the hill with as little commotion as possible. If his absence is noticed, it will be assumed that he tried to escape across the jungle."

Bodwyn Wook gave a disparaging grunt. "That is the optimum case. You might be detected, or trip some kind of alarm."

"The same would be true of any attempt at reconnaissance."

Bodwyn Wook shook his head. "Scharde is a lucky man. If I were captured, I wonder who would come for me."

"I would, sir."

"Very well, Glawen. I see that you are determined to have your way. Use prudence! Do not challenge unfavorable odds. Clattuc élan is useless on Mount Shattorak. Secondly, if you cannot rescue your father, bring away another person who can supply us with information."

"Very well, sir. What of radio communication?"

"We don't have peepers*; there has never before been any need for such things. You must do without. Now then, what else?"

"You might call Chilke and mention that he is to proceed on the Skyrie."

---

*Peepers: transceivers which first encode a message then compress it into a 'peep' a billionth of a second long, which can be transmitted without fear of detection.

"Very well. Anything more?"

"You should know that Egon Tamm has invited me to Riverview House. He wants me to read Floreste's letter to Dame Clytie Vergence and some of the other LPFers."

"Hmf. You have become quite the society man. I suppose you want a copy of the letter."

"I already have one, sir."

"That is all, Glawen! Be off with you!"

V.

Shortly before noon Glawen arrived at Riverview House, where he was admitted into the shadowy front hall by Egon Tamm himself. In the last few months, so it seemed to Glawen, Egon Tamm had aged perceptibly. Gray dusted the dark hair at his temples; his clear olive complexion had taken on an ivory pallor. He greeted Glawen with more than ordinary cordiality. "In all candor, Glawen, I am not enjoying my present company. I find it difficult to maintain my official detachment."

"Dame Clytie is evidently in good form."

"The best. She is at it now, pacing up and down the parlor, exposing criminals, issuing manifestos, and generally expounding her new pantology. Julian calls out 'Hear, hear!' from time to time and tries one debonair attitude after another, so that Flitz will notice him. Lewyn Barduys listens with half an ear. I cannot guess what he is thinking; his mind is opaque. Warden Fergus and Dame Larica are both staid and proper, and sit in dignified silence. I am not anxious to draw Dame Clytie's fire, so I too am discreet."

"Warden Ballinder is not on hand, then?"

"Unfortunately not. Dame Clytie ranges the field unchallenged."

"Hmf," said Glawen. "Maybe my appearance will distract her."

Egon Tamm smiled. "Floreste's letter will distract her. You brought the letter, I hope?"

"It is in my pocket."

"Come along then. It is almost time for lunch."

The two passed through an arched passage into a large airy parlor with tall windows to south and west overlooking a wide expanse of lagoon. The walls were enamelled white, as was the ceiling save for the ceiling beams which retained their natural age-darkened color. Three rugs patterned in green, black, white and russet lay on the floor; couches and chairs were upholstered in dull green twill. On the back wall shelves and cabinets displayed a marvelous variety of curios, oddments and artifacts representing the collections of a hundred previous Conservators. At the western end of the room a table—against which Julian Bohost leaned in a carefully debonair posture—supported books, periodicals and a bouquet of pink flowers in a bowl glazed pale blue-green celadon.

Six persons occupied the room. Dame Clytie paced the floor, hands clasped behind her back, and Julian leaned against the table. By the window sat a young woman with smooth silver hair and flawless features, absorbed in her own thoughts and paying Julian not the slightest attention. She wore skin-tight silver trousers, a short loose black shirt and black sandals on bare feet. Beside her stood a man of middle stature or a trifle less, short-necked and compact of physique, with narrow pale gray eyes and a short blunt nose on a small bald bony head. Warden Fergus and Dame Larica Fergus sat stiffly on a couch, watching Dame Clytie with the expressions of birds watching a snake. Both were middle-aged, and wore the somber garments of Stroma.

Dame Clytie marched back and forth, head lowered. "—inevitable and necessary! Not everyone will be pleased, but what of that? We have already discounted their emotions. The progressive tide—" She halted in mid-stride to stare at Glawen. "Halloo! What have we here?"

Julian Bohost, leaning against the table, a goblet of wine to his lips, lofted his eyebrows high. "By the nine gods and the seventeen devils! It is Glawen, the brave Clattuc who guards us from the Yips!"

Glawen paid no heed. Egon Tamm introduced first the middle-aged couple. "The Warden Wilder Fergus and Dame Larica Fergus." Glawen bowed politely. Egon Tamm proceeded. "Yonder is Flitz, glistening in the sunlight." Flitz glanced aside from the corner of her eye, then returned to a contemplation of her black sandals.

Egon Tamm continued. "Beside Flitz stands her close friend and business associate Lewyn Barduys. They are currently the guests of Dame Clytie at Stroma."

Barduys gave Glawen a courteous salute. Glawen saw that Barduys was not, after all, bald; that a short fine stubble of flaxen hair covered his scalp. His movements were deft and decisive; he seemed antiseptically clean.

After her first startled comment, Dame Clytie had gone to look stonily from the window. Egon Tamm asked gently: "Dame Clytie, I wonder if you remember Captain Clattuc? You met once before, I believe."

"Of course I remember him. He is a member of the local constabulary, or whatever it is called."

Glawen smiled politely. "Usually it is known as Bureau B. Actually, we are an IPCC affiliate."

"Indeed! Julian, is this your understanding?"

"I have heard something to this effect."

"Odd. It was my understanding that the IPCC imposed stringent standards upon its personnel."

"Your information is correct," said Glawen. "You will be relieved to learn that Bureau B operatives, if anything, are over-qualified."

Julian laughed. "My dear Aunt Clytie, I do believe that you blundered into a trap."

Dame Clytie grunted. "I am singularly indifferent." She turned away.

Julian called out: "What brings you here, Glawen? The main attraction is missing—somewhere on Earth, so we are told. Do you know where?"

"I came to visit the Conservator and Dame Cora," said Glawen. "Finding you and Dame Clytie here is a pleasant surprise."

"Nicely spoken! But you evaded my question."

"In regard to Wayness? So far as I know, she is visiting her uncle Pirie Tamm at Yssinges."

"I see." Julian sipped from his goblet. "Cora Tamm tells

me that you too have been junketing off-world on a holiday."

"I traveled off-world: yes—on official business."

Julian laughed. "Certainly that is how it will be described on the expense vouchers."

"I hope so. I would be outraged if I were asked to pay for what went on."

"Then the trip was not a success?"

"I accomplished my mission and escaped with my life. I discovered that the impresario Floreste had been involved in horrid crimes. Floreste is now dead. My mission was a success."

Dame Clytie demanded: "You killed Floreste, your most noteworthy artist?"

"I did not kill him personally. A lethal vapor was admitted into his cell. As a matter of fact, Floreste made me the trustee of his estate."

"I find that most remarkable."

Glawen nodded. "He explains himself in a letter—which also discusses Titus Pompo in some detail. The two were well acquainted."

"Really! I would like to see this letter."

"I have it with me, as a matter of fact. After lunch I will read it."

Dame Clytie held out her hand. "I will glance at it now, if you please."

Glawen smiled and shook his head. "Certain parts are confidential."

Dame Clytie turned away and once again started to pace. "The letter can tell us nothing we do not already know. Titus Pompo is a patient man, but his patience has limits. A great tragedy is in the offing, unless we take action!"

"Quite right," said Glawen.

Dame Clytie darted him a suspicious glance. "For this reason I will propose a trial or pilot resettlement program, at the next full plenum."

"It would be premature," said Glawen. "Several practical matters stand in the way."

"And these are?"

"First of all, we can't resettle the Yips until we find a world able to accept and absorb them. Transport is also a problem."

Dame Clytie stared incredulously. "You cannot be serious!"

"Of course I am serious. For the Yips it will be a dislocation, but there is no alternative."

"The alternative is settlement along the Marmion Foreshore, to be followed by a system of universal democracy!" She turned to Egon Tamm. "Do you not agree?"

Warden Fergus spoke indignantly: "You are aware that the Conservator must uphold the Charter!"

"We must deal with the facts of life," snapped Dame Clytie. "The LPF insists upon democratic reform; no one of good will can oppose us!"

Dame Larica Fergus responded sharply: "I oppose you, right enough, and I especially deplore Peefer hypocrisy!"

Dame Clytie blinked in angry perplexity. "How then am I a hypocrite? Are not my feelings plain enough?"

"Of course, and why not? The Peefers are already planning the great estates they will claim for themselves once the Charter is broken!"

"That remark is irresponsible and tendentious!" cried Dame Clytie. "Further, it is calumny!"

"Still, it is true! I have heard such talk myself! Julian Bohost, your nephew, has mentioned several areas he considers pleasant."

Julian said smoothly: "Truly, Dame Larica, you make much out of nothing—what is, at worst, idle talk."

Dame Clytie stated: "The point is not germane to the main issue, and should not be raised."

"Why not, when the Peefers intend to destroy the Conservancy? It is no wonder you side with the Yips."

Julian said: "Truly, Dame Fergus, you have it all wrong. Members of the LPF party—not 'Peefers,' if you don't mind—are practical idealists! We believe in first things first! Before we cook soup, we make sure we have a pot!"

"Well spoken, Julian!" declared Dame Clytie. "I have never heard such weird and wonderful accusations!"

Julian performed an airy flourish of the wine glass. "In

a world of infinite choices, anything is possible. All things flow. Nothing is fixed."

Lewyn Barduys looked at Flitz. "Julian is talking high abstraction! Are you confused?"

"No."

"Ah! You are acquainted with these ideas?"

"I wasn't listening."

Julian drew back in shock. "What a pity and what a loss! You have missed several of my most inspirational dictums!"

"Perhaps you will repeat them another time."

Egon Tamm said: "I notice that Dame Cora has summoned us to lunch. She will prefer that we desist from politics during our meal."

The party trooped out upon the tree-shaded terrace: a structure of dark swamp-elm planks built out over the water of the lagoon. On a table laid with pale green cloth, settings of green and blue faience had been arranged, along with tall goblets of swirled dark red glass.

Dame Cora seated her guests with amiable disregard for their antipathies, so that Glawen found himself beside Dame Clytie and across from Julian, with Dame Cora herself at his left.

Conversation was initially tentative, touching on a variety of casual topics, although Dame Clytie for the most part maintained a glum silence. Julian inquired again in regard to Wayness. "When is she expected home?"

"The girl is a total puzzle," said Dame Cora. "She declares herself homesick, still she seems to have no schedule or time-table. Evidently her research is keeping her occupied."

Barduys asked: "Into what kind of research is she involved?"

"I gather she is studying conservancies of the past, trying to learn why some were successful and others failed."

"Interesting," said Barduys. "It would seem a large project."

"That is my feeling," said Dame Cora.

Egon Tamm said: "Still, it can do no harm, and she will

learn a great deal. I feel that everyone who is able to do so should make a pilgrimage to Old Earth during his lifetime."

"Earth is the source of all true culture," said Dame Cora.

Dame Clytie said in a bleak monotone: "I fear that Old Earth is tired, decadent, and morally bankrupt."

"I think you are overstating the case," said Dame Cora. "I am acquainted with Pirie Tamm and he is neither decadent nor immoral, and if he is tired, it is because he is old."

Julian tapped his goblet with a spoon to command attention. "I have arrived at the opinion that anything said about Old Earth is both true and false at the same time. I would like to visit Old Earth myself."

Egon Tamm spoke to Barduys. "What is your opinion?"

"I seldom form opinions about anything, or anyone, or anywhere," said Barduys. "If nothing else, I reduce the risk of issuing absurd pronouncements."

Julian compressed his lips. "Still, experienced travelers know the difference between one place and another. That is known as 'discrimination.' "

"Perhaps you are right. What do you say, Flitz?"

"You may pour me some more wine."

"Sensible, though the message is latent."

Dame Cora asked Barduys: "I gather, then, that you have visited Earth?"

"Yes indeed! On many occasions."

Dame Cora gave her head a wondering shake. "I am surprised that you and, ah, 'Flitz' found your way out to this remote little backwater at the end of the Wisp."

"We are essentially tourists. Cadwal is not without a reputation for the quaint and unique."

"And what sort of business do you generally pursue?"

"In the main, I am an old-fashioned entrepreneur, assisted to a large extent by Flitz. She is highly astute."

Everyone turned to look at Flitz, who laughed, showing beautiful white teeth.

Dame Cora asked: "And 'Flitz,' for a fact, is the only name you use?"

Flitz nodded. "That is all."

Barduys explained: "Flitz has discovered that a single

name meets her needs and sees no reason to burden herself with a set of redundant and unnecessary syllables."

" 'Flitz' is an unusual name," said Dame Cora. "I wonder as to its derivation."

Julian asked Flitz: "Was your name originally 'Flitzenpoof,' or something of the sort?"

Flitz slid a brief sidelong stare toward Julian. "No." She returned to the contemplation of her goblet. Dame Cora addressed Barduys. "Do you have some special area of business in which you are most interested?"

"To some extent," said Barduys. "For a time I was occupied with the logic of public transport, and I became involved in the construction of submarine transit-tubes. Recently I have taken a fancy to what I call 'theme' inns and hostelries."

"We have several of these here and there around Deucas," said Egon Tamm. "We call them 'wilderness lodges.' "

"If time permits I will visit some of these," said Barduys. "I have already examined the Araminta Hotel. Sad to say, it lacks interest, and is even a bit archaic."

"Like everything else at Araminta Station," sniffed Dame Clytie.

Glawen said: "The hotel, for a fact, is something of an outrage. It was put together in bits and pieces, an annex at a time. Eventually, we'll build another, but I expect that the new Orpheum will come first, if only because Floreste collected a good part of the financing."

Egon Tamm said to Glawen: "Perhaps now is as good a time as any to read Floreste's letter."

"Certainly, if anyone is interested."

"I am interested," said Dame Clytie.

"I also," said Julian.

"Just as you like." Glawen brought out the letter. "Some of the material I will omit, for one reason or another, but I think you will find the balance interesting."

Dame Clytie instantly bristled. "Read the letter in its entirety, if you please. I see no reason for truncations. We are all either public officials or persons of the highest integrity."

Julian said gently: "Dear Aunt Clytie, I hope it is not a case of either one or the other."

Glawen said: "I will read as much of the letter as possible." He opened the envelope, removed the letter, and began to read, omitting the sections dealing with Shattorak and all mention of Chilke. Julian listened with a lofty half-smile; Dame Clytie made occasional clicking sounds between her teeth. Barduys listened with polite interest, while Flitz stared off across the lagoon. Warden Fergus and Dame Larica gave occasional small exclamations of shock.

Glawen finished the letter. He folded it and replaced it in his pocket. Warden Fergus turned to Dame Clytie. "And these abominable folk are your allies? You and all the other Peefers are fools!"

"LPFers, if you don't mind," murmured Julian.

Dame Clytie said heavily: "I am seldom mistaken in my appraisals of the human condition! Floreste evidently recorded events incorrectly, or wrote to the order of Bureau B. The letter may well be a bare-faced forgery."

Egon Tamm said: "Dame Clytie, you should not utter such charges without substantiation. In effect, you are slandering Captain Clattuc."

"Hmf. Forgery to the side, the fact remains that the statements in this letter fail to accord with my view of the case."

Glawen asked innocently: "Are you acquainted with either Titus Zigonie or his wife Simonetta—born, I am sorry to say, a Clattuc?"

"I know neither of them personally. Their gallant conduct provides me all the evidence I require. They are clearly fighting the strong and good fight for justice and democracy!"

Glawen turned to Egon Tamm. "Sir, if you will excuse me, I must now be returning to the Station. Thank you, Dame Cora, for lunch." Glawen bowed to the others in the parlor and departed.

CHAPTER II

I.

Midnight was two hours gone; Araminta Station was quiet and dark, save for a few yellow lamps along Wansey Way and the beach road. Lorca and Sing were gone behind the western hills; across the black sky streamed the coruscating sparkling flow of Mircea's Wisp.

In the shadows to the side of the airport hangar there was furtive movement. A door opened; Glawen and Chilke slid out the modified Skyric. The frame had been fitted with floats and a cabin; the swamp crawler had been strapped to the cargo deck; fairings had been attached wherever possible.

Glawen walked around the vehicle and saw nothing to alter his mood. Chilke said: "One last word, Glawen. I have in the office a bottle of very fine very expensive Damar Amber, which we will drink on your return."

"That seems a good idea."

"On second thought, perhaps we should break into it now, just to make sure of it, so to speak."

"I prefer to think that I will be returning."

"That is a more positive approach," said Chilke. "You might as well get going. The way is long and the Skyrie is slow. I'll keep Benjamie hard at it in the warehouse taking inventory, so you should be safe from that direction."

Glawen climbed into the control cabin. He waved his hand at Chilke and took the Skyrie aloft.

The lights of Araminta Station dwindled below. Glawen set off on a westward course which would take him to the side of the high Muldoon Mountains at minimal altitude, across the continent of Deucas, across the great Western Ocean to the shores of Ecce.

The lights became faint and glimmered away in the east; the Skyrie drifted through the night sky at its best speed. With nothing better to do, Glawen stretched out on the seat, wrapped himself in his cloak and tried to sleep.

The lightening sky of dawn aroused him. He glanced from the window to find forested hills below: the Syndics, according to his charts, with Mount Pam Pameijer looming high to the south.

Late in the afternoon Glawen passed the western coast of Deucas: a line of low cliffs with lazy blue swells crumpling into ribbons of white spume at their feet. Cape Tierney Thys jutted west; beyond lay the ocean. Glawen reduced altitude; the Skyrie flew onward, southwest by west, fifty yards above the long blue swells of the Western Ocean. The course should bring him to the east coast of Ecce where the Great Vertes River entered the ocean.

The afternoon passed; Syrene dropped below a clear horizon, leaving dainty white Lorca and pompous red Sing to rule the western sky; two hours later they too sidled down and out of sight and the night became dark.

Glawen checked his instruments, verified his position on the pre-plotted course and again tried to sleep.

An hour before noon of the following day Glawen noted distant clouds rearing into the western sky. An hour later a low dark line appeared at the horizon: the coast of Ecce. Glawen re-verified his position on the chart and was assured that directly ahead lay the mouth of the great Vertes River, at this point perhaps ten miles wide. Exact measurements were impossible, by reason of the vagueness of distinction between water and land of the surrounding swamp.

As Glawen approached the water below changed color, taking on an oily olive-green luster. Ahead the Vertes estuary became evident; Glawen swung somewhat to the north so that he might skirt the northern shore. Dead trees, logs, snags, tangles of brush and reeds floated on the current. Below appeared a bank of slime grown over with reeds; he had arrived at the continent Ecce.

The river flowed through a miasma of swamps, floats of water-logged vegetation, dull blue, green and liver-colored; occasionally fingers of soggy marshland supported a growth of sprawling trees, holding foliage of every shape up toward the sky. Through the air a hundred sorts of flying organisms wheeled and darted, sometimes diving down into the mud to emerge with a writhing white eel, and sometimes into the water, or occasionally one pouncing down upon another. Upstream on the river floated a dead tree. Perched in one of the branches was a disconsolate mud-walker: a gangling half-simian andoril eight feet tall, all bony arms and legs and tall narrow head. Tufts of white hair surrounded a visage formed of twisted cartilage and plaques of horn, with a pair of ocular stalks and a proboscis on its spindly chest. Beside the drifting tree the river surged; a heavy head on a long thick neck rose above the surface. The mud-walker squealed in horror; the proboscis on its chest squirted fluids toward the head, but to no avail. The head showed a gaping yellow maw; it jerked forward, engulfed the mud-walker and sank beneath the surface. Glawen thoughtfully raised the Skyrie so that it flew somewhat higher above the river.

Now was that time of day when the heat reached its oppressive maximum, so that the denizens of Ecce tended to become inactive. Glawen himself grew uncomfortable, as heat penetrated the cabin, taxing the competence of the cooling unit Chilke had installed. Glawen tried to ignore the sweltering conditions and concentrate on what must be done. Shattorak still lay a thousand miles to the west; Glawen could not hope to reach the base before dark, and nighttime would not be optimum for his arrival. He slowed the Skyrie to a hundred-mile-an-hour drift along the river, which allowed him opportunity to survey the unfolding panorama.

For a time the landscape consisted of olive-green river to his left hand and swamps to his right. On the slime, families of flat gray animals slid about on flaps attached to

their six legs. They browsed on young reeds, moving slug-
gishly until a heavy tentacle with an eye at the tip thrust
up from the mud, at which they darted away at astonishing
speed, so that the tentacle struck down into the mud
defeated.

The river embarked on a series of meandering loops,
first far to the south, then back an equal distance to the
north. Glawen, consulting his charts, struck off across the
intervening tongues of land: for the most part dense jungle
choked over with trees. Occasionally a rounded hummock
rose to an elevation of as much as fifty feet. Sometimes the
summits lacked vegetation, in which case each was inhabited by a heavy-headed beast with a lithe slate-gray body:
a creature similar to the bardicant of Deucas, thought
Glawen. As the Skyrie drifted past he noticed that the
summit was cropped clean of vegetation by a band of
waddling russet rodents, bristling with short heavy spines.
The stone-tiger surveyed the troop with a lofty detachment,
and turned itself away, evidently without appetite for the
creatures: a surprise to Glawen; on Deucas the bardicant
devoured anything which came its way with undiscriminat-
ing voracity.

From the west drifted heavy gray banks of clouds,
trailing curtains of rain across the landscape. A sudden
squall struck the Skyrie and buffeted it sidewise, rocking
and sliding, followed a moment later by a freshet of rain, so
that Glawen could no longer see so much as the river below.

For an hour the rain streamed down upon the land,
then drifted away to the east, leaving open sky overhead.
Syrene floated low toward a tumble of angry black clouds;
Lorca and Sing pursued their own erratic dance off to the
side. To the west and slightly north, Glawen made out the
silhouette of Shattorak: a dim brooding shadow on the
horizon. Glawen took the Skyrie down at a slant to the river,
to fly close beside the right bank, almost grazing the surface, to make the Skyrie as inconspicuous as possible to
any detectors which might be active on the summit of
Shattorak.

Glawen flew on while Syrene sank into a welter of
clouds. The river channel, at this point, was two miles

wide. Tremulous fields of gray slime to either side supported tufts of black reeds tipped with pompons of blue
silk, spongy dendrons holding aloft a pair of enormous
black leaves. Along the surface ran multiple-legged skim-
mers in search of insects and mud worms. Beneath the
slime another sort waited, invisible save for a periscopic
eye barely protruding above the surface, or sometimes
concealed among the reeds. When an unwary skimmer
ventured near, the tentacle lifted high and darted down to
seize the victim and then drag it below the surface. The
torpid interval had passed; the inhabitants of Ecce were
out in full force: feeding, attacking, fighting or fleeing, each
to its particular habit.

Troops of mud-walkers climbed through the trees, or
strode across the slime on feathery feet, prodding the muck
with long lances in order to gaff and retrieve a mud worm
or some other morsel. Such creatures were representative
of a more or less andromorphic genus prevalent everywhere, in many aspects and species, across Cadwal. These
'mud-walkers' stood seven feet tall on spindly double-
jointed legs. Their high narrow heads were surmounted
with caste-markers of colored fronds; black fur grew in
tufts and blotches from hard hides which shone with a
luster sometimes lavender, sometimes golden-brown.
Despite a seeming contempt for discipline, they went with
vigilance, inspecting the terrain before venturing in any
direction. When they noticed a periscopic eye they chittered
in outrage and pelted the organ with mud-balls and sticks
or squirted it with repellant fluids from their chest probos-
ces, until the eye sullenly retreated into the mud. Coming
upon large predators they showed what seemed reckless
audacity, throwing branches, prodding the creature with
their lances, then darting aside from its lunges on great
high-legged jumps, sometimes even running up and down
a massive back, shrilling and chittering in glee, until the
beleaguered creature submerged in the river or the slime,
or fled pounding into the jungle.

So went the affairs of Ecce, as Glawen flew through the
dark yellow light of late afternoon. Syrene sank; Lorca and
Sing cast a weird pink illumination over the river, and as

they too approached the horizon, Glawen neared the closest approach of the Vertes to Shattorak.

Across the river Glawen noted a low bald hummock, which upon investigation revealed no stone-tiger in residence. Glawen cautiously set down the Skyrie and erected a surrounding electric fence with enough potential to kill a stone-tiger and stun or disable anything larger.

Glawen stood out in the dusk of Ecce for a few moments, listening, breathing the air, feeling the oppression of the humidity and heat. The air carried an acrid stink, which presently began to cause him nausea. If this were the ordinary air of Ecce, then he must be sure to wear a respirator. But a breeze from the river blew past, smelling only of dank swampwater, and Glawen decided that the stench was resident upon the hummock itself. Glawen retired into the cabin of the Skyrie, and insulated himself against the outside environment.

The night passed. Glawen slept fitfully, and was disturbed only once, when some sort of creature brushed against the electric fence. Glawen was awakened by the thud of the discharge, followed by a muffled explosion. He turned on a high floodlight to illuminate the area, and looked through the window. On the cropped turf lay a ruptured corpse from which drained a yellow ooze: one of the lumpish bristle-backed creatures he had seen browsing on another hummock. Steam created by the electric energy had burst the creature's heavy gut; nearby a dozen other such creatures grazed undisturbed by the incident.

The fence had not been damaged; Glawen returned to his makeshift couch.

Glawen lay for a few moments listening to the night. From far and near came a variety of sounds: long low eery moans, coughing grunts and hoarse snarling grinding noises; cackles and squeaks, whistles and fluting cries uncannily similar in timbre to the human voice ... Glawen dozed, and woke only to the light of Syrene rising in the east.

Glawen made a perfunctory breakfast of packaged rations, and sat for a few moments wondering how best to conduct his mission. Beyond the river rose the mass of

Shattorak: a low cone shrouded in jungle two-thirds of the way to the summit.

Glawen disarmed the electric fence and stepped from the cabin to fold it into a bundle. He was instantly struck with a stench of such immoderate proportions that he jerked back into the Skyrie, gasping and wheezing. At last he gained his composure and looked respectfully out toward the corpse. The usual plague of carrion-eaters: insects, birds, rodents, reptiles and the like, was nowhere in evidence; had all these creatures been repelled by the stench? Glawen reflected for a few moments, then consulted the taxonomic almanac included in the flyer's information system. The dead creature, so he discovered, belonged to a small but distinct order, unique and indigenous to Ecce, and was known as a 'sharloc.' According to the index, the sharloc was notorious for 'an odorous exudation secreted by bristles along the dorsal integument. The odor is both repulsive and vile.'

After a moment or two of reflection, Glawen donned his 'jungle-suit': a garment of laminated fabric which insulated him from exterior heat and humidity by means of a flowing film of cool air from a small air-conditioning unit. He stepped outside and with a machete hacked the sharloc corpse into four segments, grateful that the filters in his air-conditioning unit excluded all but a trace of the stench. One of the segments he tied to the forward end of the Skyrie's frame with twenty feet of light cord; he similarly tied a second gobbet to the after end of the frame. The other two pieces he gingerly caught up in a bag and loaded upon the bed of the flyer.

Syrene now stood an hour high in the east. Glawen looked to the north across the river, here two miles wide and marked only by drifting snags and detritus. Before him, at the back of swamp and jungle, rose the bulk of Shattorak, gloomy, brooding and sinister.

Glawen climbed into the Skyrie, took it aloft, and flew at low altitude back across the river with the two gobbets of sharloc dangling below. Where swamp impinged upon the river he saw a tribe of mud-walkers, hopping and sliding, leaping and marching, from tuft to tuft, running high-legged across the slime with great finesse and style, pausing to thrust down their lances in hopes of harpooning a mud-slug. Glawen saw that they were being stalked by a flat black many-legged creature which slid across the slime with stealthy movements. Here, thought Glawen, was a good test of his theory. He changed course, to drift over the flat black predator, the segments of sharloc hanging low. The predator writhed forward suddenly, but the mud-walkers had fled in bounds and jumps; and now, from a distance, inspected the Skyrie with astonished attitudes.

The test, thought Glawen, had been indecisive. He flew on, toward the dark line of dendrons and water-logged trees where swamp merged with jungle. In one of the trees he noticed a monstrous serpent forty feet long and three feet in diameter, with fangs at one end and a scorpion's sting at the other. It slid slowly along a branch, head dangling toward the ground. Glawen flew close above; it writhed and coiled and flailed its sting into the air and then slid rapidly away.

In this case, thought Glawen, the trial had seemed to yield positive results.

Skimming the treetops Glawen searched the area below and presently noticed a large hammer-headed saurian directly ahead. He lowered the Skyrie slowly above the mottled black and green back, until the sharloc segments dangled only three feet from the saurian's head. It became agitated, lashed its heavy tail, roared and charged a tree; the tree fell crashing to the ground. The saurian pounded onward, whipping its tail to right and left.

Once again the test might be interpreted positively, but whatever the case, Glawen deemed it prudent to delay his expedition up the side of Shattorak until mid-day, when—so it was said—the beasts of Ecce became torpid. In the meantime, he must find cover for the Skyrie, to keep it safe from molestation. He approached the edge of the jungle, and landed in a small open area.

The mud-walkers had been watching with curiosity and a constant interchange of rattles and squeaks. With grotesque celerity they scampered around to the windward side of the Skyrie, and slowly approached, beating on the ground with their lances and extending red ruffs to signal displeasure. Fifty feet from the Skyrie they halted and began to hurl mud-balls and twigs. In exasperation Glawen took the Skyrie into the air and flew back toward the river. A half-mile upstream he found a cove shaped by the current and dropped the Skyrie into the water, so it floated on its pontoons. He took it to a tuffet of thorn but was deterred from mooring the flyer by a horde of angry insects, oblivious to the submerged chunks of sharloc—of questionable efficacy in any case, after submersion.

Glawen let the flyer drift on the current to a stand of black dendrons, all pulp, punk and scaly bark, but adequate for the mooring of the flyer, or so it would seem.

Glawen made fast the flyer and took stock of the situation—which was neither the best nor the worst. The sky was overcast; the afternoon rains would shortly be upon him, but these could not be avoided. As for the predators, stinging and biting insects, and other dangers endemic to the country, he had prepared himself to the best of his ability, and now must take his chances.

Glawen unclamped the swamp crawler from its chocks. The evidence seemed to indicate that sharloc stench was repellent, Glawen tied the remaining two segments to front and rear of the crawler, then winched it off the deck into the water, where it floated on its own pontoons. He loaded aboard his backpack and such equipment as he deemed useful, climbed aboard the crawler, and churned toward the shore.

To Glawen's annoyance the tribe of mud-walkers had arrived on the scene, where they watched his approach in agitation, ruffs displaying the bright red of displeasure and threat. Glawen steered so as to arrive at shore upwind, where he hoped that they might be dissuaded from approach by the stench of sharloc. He did not wish in any way to harm them: an act of incalculable consequence were it to occur regardless of precautions. They might either be driven away in terror or their furious vengeful hostility incurred, against which, in the depths of the jungle, Glawen might have no control. He halted the crawler a hundred yards from shore and let it drift. As he had hoped, the putrid sharloc appeared to dissuade the mud-walkers from further hostile behavior. They turned away with a final barrage of insults and mud-balls and wandered off. Of course, thought Glawen, they may simply have become bored.

Cautiously Glawen approached the shore. Syrene was now halfway up the sky and the heat would have been debilitating save for the jungle-suit. A dead hush fell over the swamp, broken only by the whir and buzz of insects. Glawen noted that they seemed to veer away from the crawler, which saved him the necessity of activating the insecticide fogger.

Glawen arrived at the first banks of slime; the crawler churned doggedly forward. He made ready the guns at each side of the crawler, setting the range of response at thirty yards, and setting the mode to 'automatic,' and not a moment too soon. From the slime only twenty feet to the right of the crawler an optic tentacle reared high. Instantly the gun responded, aiming at the motion and destroying the tentacle with a burst of energy. The slime heaved and sucked as the creature below tried to decide what had happened to it. At a distance of a hundred yards the mud-walkers watched in awe, and presently set up a screeching outburst of vituperation, and threw sticks which fell far short and which Glawen ignored.

The crawler slid across the slime and without further incident entered the first fringes of the jungle, and now Glawen was faced with a new problem. The crawler capably negotiated thickets and bushes, tangles of vines, and was even able to push over a small tree. However, when trees with dense and heavy trunks grew so closely as to deny the crawler access, then Glawen was forced to choose a new route, which was often a time-consuming procedure. He discovered, to his discomfiture, that neither the time of torpidity, nor the sharloc stench, nor the automatic gun, nor all three together were enough to protect him from harm. By chance he noted on a branch under which he was about to pass a crouching black creature all maw, fangs, claws, and sinew. It poised immobile and the gun failed to detect its presence. If the crawler had proceeded below, the creature could have dropped directly upon him. Its bulk alone would crush him, even though the automatic gun by that time would have killed it. Glawen destroyed the thing with his handgun and thereafter proceeded in a much more cautious state.

Up the slope of Shattorak went the crawler, occasionally finding an easy avenue for fifty or sixty yards, but more often Glawen was forced to dodge right or left, squeeze through narrow gaps, sidle along declivities, moving far more slowly than he liked.

The afternoon rains came, and thrashed down upon the jungle. Glawen's visibility was much reduced, as was his margin of safety. At last, toward middle afternoon, he arrived at a gully choked with a growth too dense for the crawler to penetrate. At this point the summit was visible, less than a mile upslope. With resignation Glawen alighted from the crawler, slipped into his backpack, made sure of his weapons, and set off on foot: scrambling through the gully, killing a hissing gray bewhiskered creature which sprang at him from the dank shadows, fogging a nest of stinging insects, and finally arriving breathless at the uphill side of the gully. The slope thereafter became less difficult, with vegetation less fecund and with longer perspectives of visibility.

Glawen climbed across outcrops of decayed black rock, through copses of giant fuzzball trees, around solitary horsetail ferns sixty feet tall and barrel trees with boles ten to twenty feet in diameter.

As Glawen approached the summit, ledges of the rotten black stone began to appear; and presently, halting behind a copse of mitre dendrons, he looked out on a strip of open hillside a hundred yards wide, isolated from the flat summit by a stockade of posts woven with saplings and branches ten feet high. Along the strip a number of rude huts could be seen, either built into the crotch of a barrel tree or on the ground. These were protected by makeshift stockades of their own. Some were in use as habitations; others were dilapidated and rapidly decaying to the onslaughts of rain and sun. A few plots of ground had been brought under desultory cultivation. Here, thought Glawen, was the

Shattorak jail; prisoners could escape any time the desire
came upon them. Now then: where was Scharde?

Most of the huts were clustered about a gate through
the stockade: the more distant from the gate, the more
dilapidated their condition.

Glawen moved through the shadows, to station himself
as close to the gate as he dared.

There were six men within range of his vision. With the
afternoon overcast providing relief from the direct rays of
Syrene, one man mended the roof of his tree hut. Two
worked dispiritedly in their gardens; the others sat with
their backs to the boles of the barrel trees, eyes focused
upon nothing. Five of the prisoners seemed to be Yips. The
man who worked on the roof of his hut was tall, gaunt,
black of hair and beard, hollow-cheeked, with a pale ivory
complexion which seemed to show a lavender undertone
around the eye-sockets.

Scharde was nowhere to be seen. Might he be in one of
the huts? Glawen inspected each in turn, but discovered
nothing significant.

Rain suddenly struck down on Shattorak, producing a
muffled drumming sound that filled all the horizons. The
prisoners without haste went to their huts and sat in the
doorways with the rain sluicing from the thatch in front of
their faces and into collection pots. Glawen took advantage
of the rain to slip furtively across the slope to one of the
deserted huts, which provided a degree of shelter. Nearby
he noted a hut perched thirty feet high in the first crotch of
a huge barrel tree; this would provide him an even better
vantage point. He darted through the downpour to the
ladder and clambered up to the rickety porch of the tree
hut. He looked through the door, and finding no one, took
refuge within.

The hut afforded good visibility indeed: over the walls
of the stockade and across the width of the summit. The
rain blurred details but Glawen thought to see a group of
ramshackle structures built of posts, branches and thatch,
much like the tree huts. The structures were to his right,
on the eastern side of the summit. To the left, the ground
humped up in a series of rocky ledges. A pond fifty yards

wide occupied the center of the area. No living creature could be seen.

Glawen made himself as comfortable as possible and set himself to wait. Two hours passed; the rain stopped; the low sun flashed for a few instants through the clouds. The time of torpidity had ended and no longer deterred the creatures of Ecce; once again they set forth upon their missions: to attack and rend, to sting, kill and devour, or to avoid such an eventuality by whatever desperate tactics served them best. From his perch in the tree Glawen could see far and wide over the jungle, over the bends and loops of the mighty Vertes River and far to the south across the swamps of Ecce. From below came a variety of sounds, some muted, some ominously close at hand: choking, gurgling roars; staccato grunts; ululations and screams; hoots and resonant drumming sounds.

The gaunt dark-haired man descended from his tree hut. With an air of purpose he went to the gate which led into the summit compound. Putting his hand through an aperture he manipulated a latch; the gate opened and he stalked through, crossed the compound to a nearby shed, into which he disappeared. Odd, thought Glawen.

Now that the rain had stopped, his view across the central compound was unhindered, but he saw nothing markedly different than before, except on the highest point of the ground to the left a low structure had been built which, in Glawen's estimation, would seem to house a radar installation, to provide warning of approaching aircraft. Glawen noted no movement through the windows; the installation would seem to be automatic. Glawen studied the area with care. According to Floreste, five flyers, or perhaps more, were stored here on Shattorak. They were nowhere evident—an eminently reasonable situation, thought Glawen. The shacks, the stockade and the huts of the prisoners would never be noticed by any but the most careful observation; the textures and irregularities would function as camouflage—but where could five flyers be hidden?

Glawen noticed that the terrain at the western edge of the area showed a rather unnatural conformation, and it might well be that storage space had been carefully roofed over with imitation soil and stone. As if to validate his theories, a pair of men came briskly into sight from over the side of the western slope and climbed to the small hut which Glawen assumed to be a radar transceiver. These men seemed not to be Yips, although as he watched, four Yips appeared from the far side of the summit and came to the shed which the black-haired man had entered. These Yips, Glawen noted, wore handweapons at their waists, though they seemed oblivious to the prisoners out on the strip.

Half an hour passed. The two men remained in the observation station. The four Yips returned the way they had come: across the summit and out of Glawen's sight.

The two occupants of the observation tower now came down to stand beside the pond, looking into the northern sky.

Several minutes passed. Low in the sky to the north a flyer appeared, approached and settled to a landing beside the pond. Two men alighted, a Yip and another: this one slight of physique, dark of complexion, with a scruff of dark beard. The two brought from the flyer a third man with arms shackled behind his back and a loose hood over his head. The three were joined by the two from the observation tower; the entire group of five went to the largest of the sheds, the prisoner hunching disconsolately along, propelled by a man to either side of him.

Half an hour passed. The Yip and the bearded non-Yip emerged from the shed, went to the flyer and departed into the northern sky. The remaining two brought out the prisoner, led him across the summit and out of sight past the rock outcrops.

Another half hour passed. From the near structure, which Glawen now thought to be the cook shed, came the gaunt dark-haired man, whom Glawen identified as the cook. He carried several buckets though the gate and out upon the prison strip. He set the buckets upon a table near the gate, and struck the table three times with a stick, by way of signal. The prisoners approached the table, bringing with them pannikins. The cook served them from the buckets, then returned through the gate to the cook shed.

Five minutes later the cook emerged once more, carrying two smaller buckets. He took these across the summit, in the direction the prisoner had been taken, and disappeared from Glawen's sight behind the first ledge of rock. Five minutes later, he returned to the cook shed.

The time had progressed to late afternoon. From the far side of the summit came other men in groups of two or three. Glawen thought that the total number might be nine or ten. After consuming their supper in the cook shed, they returned the way they had come.

Syrene sank in the west; Lorca and Sing cast a rosy twilight murk over the swamps and jungles, which abruptly dimmed as clouds again swept over the sky, and again rain thundered down upon Ecce. Glawen at once descended from his vantage, ran through the downpour, and climbed to another of the tree huts, where he waited.

Half an hour passed; the rains ceased as suddenly as they had come, leaving a heavy darkness, broken only by a few soft yellow lights within the compound and the glow of three bulbs at the top of the stockade which illuminated the prison strip. From the cook house came the gaunt darkhaired cook. He crossed the compound, opened the gate, stood for a moment surveying the strip to make sure that it harbored no savage beasts, then closed the gate and walked swiftly to the tree which supported his hut. He climbed the ladder, pushed through the opening which gave on the little porch in front of the hut, closed the trap door and secured it against intruders. Turning, he started to enter his hut only to stop short.

Glawen said: "Come into the hut. Make no disturbance."

The cook spoke in a strained reedy voice: "Who are you?" And then, more sharply: "What do you want?"

"Come inside and I will tell you."

Step by unwilling step the cook came forward, to halt warily just within the open doorway, where the wan illumination of the stockade cast black shadows on his long face. He tried to speak in a firm voice: "Who are you?"

"My name would mean nothing to you," said Glawen. "I have come for Scharde Clattuc. Where is he?"

The cook stood rigid a moment, then jerked his thumb toward the stockade. "Inside."

"Why is he inside?"

"Hah!"—a bitter laugh. "When they want to punish someone, he is put down in a doghole."

"What might that be?"

Lights and shadows shifted along the cook's face as he grimaced. "It is a pit eight feet deep and five feet square, with bars on top, open to both sun and rain. Clattuc has so far survived."

For a moment Glawen was silent. Then he asked: "And who, then, are you?"

"I am not here by my own choice: I assure you!"

"That was not my question."

"It makes no great difference; nothing is changed. I am a Naturalist from Stroma. My name is Kathcar. Every day it becomes more difficult to remember that other places exist."

"Why are you here at Shattorak?"

Kathcar made a dreary guttural sound. "Why else? I ran afoul of the Oomphaw, and a cruel trick was played upon me. I was brought here and given a choice: working at the cook house or sweltering in a doghole." Kathcar's voice rang with bitterness. "Is it not preposterous?"

"Yes, of course. The Oomphaw is preposterous. But for the moment, how best can we rescue Scharde Clattuc from the doghole?"

Kathcar started to blurt out a protest, then reconsidered and fell silent. After a moment he spoke, in a somewhat different tone of voice and his head tilted to the side. "You are planning, I gather, to free Scharde Clattuc and take him away?"

"That is correct."

"How will you cross the jungle?"

"A flyer is waiting below."

Kathcar pulled at his beard. "It is a dangerous project: a true doghole affair."

"I expect that it is. First, there will be killing, of anyone who hinders me—or raises an alarm."

Kathcar gave a wincing jerk of the head, and turned a nervous glance over his shoulder. He spoke in a cautious voice: "If I help you, you must take me out as well."

"That is reasonable."

"This is your guarantee?"

"You may count on it. Are the dogholes guarded?"

"Nothing and everything is guarded. The compound is small. Folk are irritable and on edge. I have seen some strange sights."

"Then when is the best time to act?"

Kathcar considered a moment. "For the doghole, one time is as good as another. The glats come up from the jungle in an hour or two, and then no one dares stir from the trees, since glats merge with the shadows and one never knows they are near until it's too late."

"Then we had best go now for Scharde."

Again Kathcar seemed to wince, and again he looked over his shoulder. "There is no real reason to wait," he said hollowly. He turned and stepped furtively out on the little porch. "We must not be seen by the others; they might raise an outcry out of pure anger." He peered right and left along the strip, among the huts: there was nothing to see, neither movement nor flicker of light. Heavy overcast smothered the sky and every trace of starlight. Humid air reeked with the odors of jungle vegetation. Away from the dim glow of the stockade lamps the shadows were opaque and absolute. Kathcar, at last reassured, descended the ladder, with Glawen coming close behind.

"Be quick now," said Kathcar. "The glats sometimes come early. Do you carry a gun?"

"Of course."

"Hold it ready." At a crouching bent-kneed lope Kathcar ran to the gate. He reached through the port, worked the latch mechanism. The gate swung open, just far enough to allow a man to pass. Kathcar peered through the opening, then spoke in a husky whisper: "No one seems to be out. Come, to the rock yonder." He sidled along beside the stockade, seeming to merge with the texture of the materials. Glawen followed, and joined Kathcar in the dense shadow behind a rock ledge. "That was the risky part. We could have been seen from the high hut had anyone looked."

"Where are the dogholes?"

"Just yonder, up and around that shoulder of rock. Now we had best go on hands and knees." He set off crawling through the shadows. Glawen followed. Kathcar suddenly dropped flat. Glawen inched up beside him. "What is the trouble?"

"Listen!"

Glawen listened, but heard nothing. Kathcar whispered: "I heard voices."

Glawen listened, and thought to hear a mutter of conversation, which presently became still.

Kathcar moved off through the shadows, crouching low. He stopped, turned his face down, spoke softly: "Scharde Clattuc! Do you hear me? Scharde? Scharde Clattuc?"

A husky response arose from the doghole. Glawen crawled forward. He felt horizontal bars under his hands. "Father? It is Glawen."

"Glawen! I am alive, or so I believe."

"I have come for you." He looked to Kathcar. "How do we lift the bars?"

"At each corner is a rock. Move it aside."

Glawen groped along the bars and found a pair of heavy rocks, which he pushed aside, while Kathcar did the same on the opposite side. The two lifted the barred frame aside; Glawen reached down into the pit. "Give me your hands."

A pair of hands reached up; Glawen grasped and pulled. Scharde Clattuc emerged from the doghole. He said: "I knew that you would come. I only hoped that I would be alive at the time."

Kathcar spoke in a reedy whisper: "Come; we must put the bars back in place, along with the rocks, so that no one will notice."

The doghole was covered once again and the rocks put back in place. The three crawled away: first Kathcar, then Scharde and Glawen. In the shadow of the ledge they paused to rest and to assess the compound. A glimmer of light fell on Scharde's face; Glawen stared unbelieving into the haggard countenance. Scharde's eyes seemed to have sunk into his head; the skin of his face stretched taut over bone and cartilage. He felt Glawen's eyes upon him and grinned a ghastly grin. "No doubt I look in poor case."

"In very poor case indeed. Are you fit to walk?"

"I can walk. How did you know where to find me?"

"It is a long story. I only arrived home a week or so ago. Floreste supplied the information."

"Then I must thank Floreste."

"Too late! He is dead."

Kathcar said, "Now: to the gate, along beside the stockade, as before."

Like flitting shadows the three arrived at the gate without challenge, and sidled out upon the strip, where wind blowing through the trees created a mournful sound. Kathcar searched the terrain, then gave a signal. "Quick then! To the tree!" On long strides he ran to the tree and started up the ladder. Scharde came next, at a hobbling trot, followed by Glawen. Kathcar gained the porch and looked over as Scharde climbed a painful step at a time. Kathcar reached through the opening and pulled Scharde up on the porch. He called urgently down to Glawen: "Hurry; a rackleg is running this way!"

Glawen scrambled through the opening; Kathcar slammed down the trap door. From below came a rasping thump, a hiss, a jar. Glawen looked to Kathcar. "Shall I kill it?"

"No! The carrion would bring all manner of things; let it go its way. Come into the hut."

Inside the hut the three composed themselves to wait. A glimmer from the stockade lamps entered the hut, to illuminate Scharde's face; once again Glawen was appalled by his father's wasted countenance. "I returned to the Station only about a week ago—and I have much to tell you—but no one knew where you were. Floreste gave us the facts and I came as quickly as I could; I am sorry it could not have been sooner."

"But you came, as I knew you would."

"What happened to you?"

"I was lured and trapped, neatly and cleverly. Someone at the Station betrayed me."

"Who was it, or do you know?"

"I don't know. I went out on patrol and over the Marmion Brakes I noticed a flyer, heading east. It was not one of ours and I was sure it had come from Yipton. I dropped low and followed at a distance, where I would not be noticed.

"The flyer flew east, around the Tex Wyndom Hills and out over Willaway Waste. It descended and landed in a small meadow. I came in low and circled, looking for a place to land where I would not be observed. My intent was to capture the flyer and the passengers, and to learn what was going on, if possible. I found a perfectly situated landing area about half a mile north, behind a low ridge of rock. So I landed, armed myself and set off to the south, toward the ridge. The route seemed easy: too easy. As I passed a jut of rock, three Yips dropped down on me. They took my gun, tied my arms, and brought me and my flyer to Shattorak. It was a neat and clever trick. Someone at the Station who had access to the patrol schedules is a spy, and perhaps a traitor."

"His name is Benjamie," said Glawen. "At least, that is my guess. What happened then?"

"Not a great deal. They put me into the doghole, and there I stayed. After two or three days someone came to look down at me. I could not see clearly: no more than a silhouette. The person spoke; it was a voice I instantly loathed, as if I had heard it before—a heavy chuckling voice. It said: 'Scharde Clattuc: here you are and here you shall bide. Such is your punishment.'

"I asked: Punishment for what?

"The answer came: 'Need you ask? Consider the wrongs you have done to innocent victims!'

"I said nothing more, since I had nothing to say. Whoever it was went away, and that is my last contact with anyone."

Glawen asked: "Who do you think spoke to you?"

"I don't know. I have not thought about it."

Glawen said: "I will tell you what happened to me, if you like. It is a long story; perhaps you would rather rest."

"I have been doing nothing else. I am tired of rest."

"Are you hungry? I have dry rations in my pack."

"I am hungry for something other than porridge."

Glawen brought out a packet of hard sausage, biscuits and cheese, and passed them over to Scharde. "Now then — this is what happened after Kirdy Wook and I left the Station."

Glawen spoke for an hour, ending his narrative with a description of Floreste's letter. "I would not be surprised if the person who spoke to you were not Smonny herself."

"It might be so. The voice was odd."

Rain had started to fall, drumming down upon the roof in what seemed a solid sheet of water. Kathcar looked out the doorway. "This storm goes on and on, worse than usual."

Scharde gave a grim laugh. "I am happy to be out of the doghole. Sometimes it would fill up to my hips with water."

Glawen turned to Kathcar. "How many dogholes are there?"

"Three. Only one was occupied, by Scharde Clattuc, until this afternoon, when they brought in another prisoner."

"You took food to him; who was he?" asked Glawen.

Kathcar made a fluttering gesture of the hand. "I pay no attention to such things; to save my own neck I obeyed orders; no more."

"Still, you must have taken note of the prisoner."

"Yes; I saw him." Kathcar hesitated.

"Go on. Did you recognize him, or hear his name?"

Kathcar responded grudgingly: "As a matter of fact, they spoke his name in the cookhouse, and they were all laughing together, as if at some great joke."

"Well then — what was the name?"

"Chilke."

"Chilke! In the doghole?"

"Yes. That is correct."

Glawen went to look out the door. The rain obscured his vision; he could see nothing but the stockade lamps. He thought of Bodwyn Wook and his cautious plans; he calculated risks and compared them to the impulses of his emotions, but the entire process required less than a minute. He gave one of his guns to Scharde. "The crawler is down the hill, across the first gully. There is a flame-thrower tree just beyond. Directly below, where the river bends you will find the flyer. This in case I do not come back."

Scharde, without comment, took the gun. Glawen signaled to Kathcar. "Come."

Kathcar held back. He cried out: "We should not presume upon our luck! Do you not agree? Our lives deserve to be cherished; let us not ponder lost opportunities from the dogholes!"

"Come." Glawen started down the ladder.

"Wait!" cried Kathcar. "Look first for beasts!"

"There is too much rain," said Glawen. "I can't see them. Nor can they see me."

Cursing under his breath, Kathcar followed down the ladder. "This is senseless and reckless!"

Glawen paid no heed. He ran through the rain to the stockade. Kathcar followed, still crying out complaints which went unheard in the storm. He opened the stockade gate; the two passed through.

Kathcar spoke into Glawen's ear: "In the rain they might think to activate their motion sensor, so we had best go the same way as before. Are you ready? Come along then! To the rock!"

The two ran crouching beside the stockade, with the rain hissing around their ears. Under the rock they halted. "Down low!" Kathcar ordered. "As before! Follow close, or you will lose me."

On hands and knees the two scuttled through the muck, past the first doghole, up and around a ledge, down into a rocky hollow. Kathcar halted. "We are here."

Glawen felt for the bars. He called down into the blackness: "Chilke! Are you there? Can you hear me? Chilke?"

A voice came from below. "Who's calling for Chilke? It's a waste of time; I can't help you."

"Chilke! It's Glawen! Stand up; I'll pull you out."

"I'm already standing, so that I don't drown."

Glawen and Kathcar moved aside the bars and pulled Chilke to the surface. "This is a glad surprise," said Chilke.

Glawen and Kathcar replaced the bars; the three crawled across the compound to the stockade, ran crouching to the gate, passed through. For a moment the rain seemed to diminish its force; Kathcar peered up and down the strip. He gave a startled hiss. "There's a glat! Quick! To the tree!"

The three ran to the tree and scrambled up the ladder. Kathcar secured the trap door just as something heavy slammed against the tree.

Kathcar spoke to Glawen in dour tones: "I hope no more of your friends are captives?"

Glawen ignored the remark. He asked Chilke: "What happened to you?"

"Nothing at all complicated," said Chilke. "Yesterday morning two men jumped me, threw a bag over my head, taped my arms, stowed me aboard our new J-2 flyer and flew away. Next thing I knew I was here. One of the men, incidentally, was Benjamie; I could smell the fancy pomade he wears in his hair. When I get back to the Station, he is out of a job, since he cannot be trusted."

"Then what happened?"

"I heard some new voices. Someone led me into a shack and pulled the bag from my head. Certain peculiar things happened next which I am still sorting out. Afterwards I was conducted to the doghole and dropped in. This gentleman here brought me a bucket of porridge. He asked me my name, and mentioned that it looked like rain. After that I was left alone, until I heard your voice, which I was glad to hear."

"Odd," said Glawen.

"What will we do now?"

"As soon as we can see, we leave. We won't be missed until they come to the cookhouse for breakfast and find no Kathcar."

Chilke peered through the dark. "Your name is Kathcar?"

"That is correct." Kathcar spoke stiffly.

"You were right about the rain."

"It is a terrible storm," said Kathcar. "The worst I have seen."

"You have been here long?"

"Not too long."

"How long?"

"About two months."

"What was your crime?"

Kathcar responded tersely: "I am not sure in my own mind why I am here. Apparently I offended Titus Pompo, or something of the sort."

Glawen told Chilke and Scharde: "Kathcar is a Naturalist from Stroma."

"Interesting!" said Scharde. "How is it that you are acquainted with Titus Pompo?"

"It is a complicated matter, not presently relevant."

Scharde said nothing. Glawen asked him: "Are you tired? Do you wish to sleep?"

"I am probably stronger than I look." Scharde's voice drifted away. "I think I'll try to sleep."

"Give your gun to Chilke."

Scharde gave over the gun, crawled across the hut and stretched out on the floor. Almost at once he dozed.

The rain waxed and waned: slowing for a few minutes as if passing over, then suddenly striking down in new fury. Kathcar marveled anew: "This storm is incredible!"

Chilke said: "Scharde has been here about two months. Who came first: you or Scharde?"

Kathcar appeared to dislike questions. As before, he answered curtly: "Scharde was here when I arrived."

"And no one explained why you were here?"

"No."

"What of your family and friends at Stroma? Do they know of your whereabouts?"

Bitterness tinged Kathcar's voice. "As to that, I cannot guess."

Glawen asked: "Were you an LPFer at Stroma, or a Chartist?"

Kathcar surveyed Glawen sharply. "Why do you ask?"

"It might cast light on why you were imprisoned."

"I doubt it."

Chilke said: "If you have run afoul of Titus Pompo, you must be a Chartist."

Kathcar spoke frostily: "Like the other progressives of Stroma, I endorse the ideals of the LPF party."

"Very strange!" declared Chilke. "You were clapped into jail by your best friends and good clients: I refer, of course, to the Yips."

"No doubt there was a mistake, or a misunderstanding," said Kathcar. "I do not care to dwell on the matter, and I will let bygones be bygones."

"You Peefers are a high-minded group," said Chilke. "As for me, I crave revenge."

Glawen asked Kathcar: "You are acquainted with Dame Clytie Vergence?"

"I am acquainted with this woman."

"And Julian Bohost?"

"I know him. At one time he was considered an influential member of the movement."

"But no longer?"

Kathcar spoke in measured terms. "I differ with him on several important points."

"What of Lewyn Barduys? And Flitz?"

"I am not acquainted with either. And now, if you will excuse me, I too will try to rest." Kathcar crawled away.

A few moments later the rain stopped, leaving a silence broken only by the plash of drops falling from the trees. Imminence charged the air.

Purple-white dazzle fractured the sky. A second of tense silence and another—then an explosion of thunder, dying in a sullen rumble. Across the jungle came a response of grinding chatters, angry roars and bellows.

Silence again, and the pressure of imminence, then a second burst of lightning, and for an instant every detail of the compound was illuminated in brilliant lavender light, followed as before by another clap of thunder. After a moment the rain started again, in a new torrent.

Glawen asked Chilke: "What happened in the shed that was so peculiar?"

"I live a very peculiar life," said Chilke. "If you think of it like this, the business in the shed is just a typical incident, even though the average man might be astounded."

"What happened?"

"First, a Yip in a black uniform took the bag from my head. I saw a table with some documents arranged in a neat pile. The Yip told me to sit down, which I did.

"It seems that I was under surveillance from a lens across the room. A voice came from the speaker: 'You are Eustace Chilke, native to Big Prairie on Earth?'

"I said, yes, that was the case, and to whom was I talking?

"The voice said: 'Your single concern at the moment must be the set of documents you see in front of you. Sign them where indicated.'

"The voice was harsh and distorted, and not at all friendly. I said: 'I suppose it is pointless to complain of the outrage represented by this kidnapping.'

"The voice said: 'Eustace Chilke, you have been brought here for good and sufficient reason. Sign the documents and be quick about it!'

"I said: 'It sounds like Madame Zigonie talking, but not in a kindly voice. Where is the money you owe me for six months work?'

"The voice said: 'Sign the papers at once, or it will be the worse for you.'

"I looked the papers over. The first deeded all my property, without exception or reservation, to Simonetta Zigonie. The second was a letter to whom it might concern authorizing the delivery of my property to the bearer. The third, which I liked the least, was my will, bequeathing everything I owned to my friend Simonetta Zigonie. I tried to protest. 'I'd like to think things over, if you don't mind. I suggest that we go back to Araminta Station and settle the matter like ladies and gentlemen.'

" 'Sign the papers,' said the voice, 'if you value your life!'

"I saw that there was no reasoning with the woman. I said: 'I'll sign if you like, but it's all a great puzzle, since I own little more than the shirt on my back.'

" 'What of the articles you inherited from your grandfather?'

" 'They don't amount to much. The stuffed moose is a bit shabby. There is a small rock collection, with bits of gravel from a hundred planets, a few oddments of bric-a-brac including some purple vases, and probably more junk of the same sort out in the barn. I seem to remember a rather nice stuffed owl with a mouse in its beak.'

" 'What else?'

" 'That's hard to say, since the barn has been so thoroughly burgled that I almost feel ashamed offering the stuff to you.'

" 'Let us have no more delay. Sign the papers, and be quick about it.'

"I signed the three documents. The voice then said: 'Eustace Chilke, you have saved your life, which henceforth shall be spent repenting your fleering and cavalier attitudes, and your disregard for the sensitivities of those who might have wished to befriend you.'

"I decided that Madame Zigonie was referring to my stand-offish conduct at Shadow Valley Ranch. I told her I didn't mind apologizing if it would do any good, but she said that it was too late for that, and what must be, must be. I was taken out and dropped into the doghole, where I instantly got busy repenting. I assure you I was glad to hear your voice."

Glawen asked: "You have no idea what she is looking for?"

"It must be that some of Grandpa Swaner's belongings have more value than I supposed. I wish he had let me know while he was still alive."

"Someone must know something. Who could it be?"

"Hmf. Hard to say. He dealt with lots of strange people—junk dealers, thieves, antiquarians, book dealers. I remember one chap in particular, who was Grandpa's friend, colleague, rival and accomplice, all at the same time. I think they were both members of the Naturalist Society. He traded Grandpa a set of exotic bird feathers and three Pandango soul masks for a parcel of old books and papers. If anyone knew Grandpa's affairs inside-out, it would be this chap."

"Where is he now?"

"I couldn't say. He got into trouble over some illicit tomb-robbing and fled off-planet to evade the authorities."

Glawen, chancing to look over his shoulder, saw the pale glimmer of Kathcar's face, much closer than he had realized. It was evident that Kathcar had been listening to the conversation.

The rain returned in another drumming downpour, and persisted until a hint of wet gray light indicated the coming of dawn.

Light seeped into the sky, and the length and breadth of the prison strip became visible. The four men departed the tree hut and started downhill through the dripping jungle. Glawen went first, followed by Chilke, both with guns at the ready. Presently they arrived at the gully, to find it hip deep in running water, which could not be waded because of the presence of ·water-snappers. Glawen selected a tall tree, sheared its trunk with energy from his gun and dropped it across the gully to create a slippery bridge.

The men found the crawler as Glawen had left it; they clambered aboard and headed down the slope—slowly to avoid sliding out of control. Almost at once they were attacked by a splay-legged creature twenty feet long, with eight clashing mandibles and tail curled forward that it might project a noxious fluid at its prey. Chilke killed it even as it aimed its tail, and the creature fell to the side, mandibles gnashing and the tail waving back and forth, discharging a dark fluid into the air.

A few moments later Glawen halted the crawler, the better to select a route and in the silence an ominous sound could be heard through the underbrush. Scharde gave a croak of alarm; Glawen looked up to see a triangular head six feet across, split into a gaping fanged maw, descending through the foliage at the end of a long arching neck. Glawen fired his gun by reflex, destroying the head. A moment later something bulky toppled and crashed into the jungle.

As best he could Glawen guided the crawler downhill the way he had come. The slope at last began to flatten and the jungle foliage became thin. The vehicle began to splash through water where the river had overflowed the slime. A tribe of mud-walkers watched from across the swamp, hooting and screaming. The water deepened; the crawler began to lose contact with the slime and float on the swirling water.

Glawen halted the crawler. He turned to his three companions and pointed to a clump of vegetation. "This is where I left the flyer, tied to a tree in that clump yonder. The tree must have broken away last night in the storm and carried the flyer away."

"That is bad news," said Chilke. He looked eastward along the face of the swollen river. "I see lots of snags and dead trees, but no flyer."

Kathcar gave a hollow groan. "We were better off at the prison."

"You, perhaps, were better off," said Glawen. "Go on back if you like."

Kathcar said no more.

Chilke spoke ruminatively: "With a few tools and a few materials I could contrive a radio. But there are neither on the crawler."

"It is disaster!" lamented Kathcar. "Sheer disaster!"

"Not just yet," said Scharde.

"How can you say differently?"

"I notice that the current moves about three miles an hour, no more. If the tree fell in the middle of the night—let us say, six hours ago—it will have drifted eighteen miles or less. The crawler can move five or six miles an hour in the water. So if we set off now, we should overtake the tree and the attached flyer in three or four hours."

Without further words Glawen started up the crawler and set off downstream.

The crawler floated across a wilderness of water, through a swelter of heat and glare reflected from the surface, humidity which seemed to stifle the breath and make every movement an effort of monumental proportion. As Syrene rose, the heat and glare became actively painful. Glawen and Chilke rigged an awning using branches and foliage salvaged from the stream, after first shaking away the insects and small serpents which might be clinging to the leaves. The awning provided a large measure of relief. From time to time great heads or ocular process rose from the water with evident intent to attack; constant vigilance was necessary to avoid sudden overwhelming disaster.

For three hours the crawler churned down the river, passing by dozens of snags, dead trees, rafts of detritus, floating reed tussocks. Despite earnest and anxious search, the Skyrie failed to show itself. Kathcar at last asked: "And what if we go another two hours and still don't find the flyer?"

"Then we start thinking very carefully," said Chilke.

"I have already been thinking carefully," said Kathcar sourly. "I do not believe thinking is helpful in this case."

The river widened; Glawen steered a course keeping the left shore always within range of vision, with the main sweep of the river to the right.

Another hour passed. Ahead appeared a spot of white: the Skyrie. Glawen heaved a great sigh and sank down on the bench, feeling an extraordinary emotion mixed of lassitude, euphoria and an almost tearful gratitude for the favorable workings of Destiny. Scharde put his arm around Glawen's shoulders. "I cannot find words for what is in my mind."

"Don't be too grateful too fast," said Chilke. "It looks like we have pirates aboard the craft."

"Mud-walkers!" said Glawen.

The crawler approached the flyer. The tree to which it had been moored apparently had been caught in an eddy and swung into a bank of muck, where it lodged. A tribe of mud-walkers, fascinated by the curious floating object, had run across mud and water and climbed through tangles of debris to approach the craft. At the moment they were prodding at the bag of animal segments Glawen had left on deck, and pushed it into the river.

A vagrant breeze wafted the odor to the crawler, prompting an exclamation from Chilke. "What in the world is that?"

"The odor is from a bag of bad-smelling animal pieces," said Glawen, "which I left on the deck to keep mud-walkers off." He went to the front of the crawler and waved his arms. "Go away! Get off! Go!"

In response the mud-walkers screamed in fury and

threw mud-balls at the crawler. Glawen aimed his gun at the tree and blasted away a great branch. With startled outcries the mud-walkers ran off across the mud, spindly legs pumping furiously, knees held high. At a safe distance they halted and attempted another barrage of mud-balls, without success.

The four men climbed aboard the flyer. Glawen threw buckets of water along the deck hoping to allay the lingering stink of the sacked animal parts and to wash overboard the litter left by the mud-walkers. The crawler was hauled aboard and made secure. "Goodbye, Vertes River," said Glawen. "I have had all I want of you." He went to the controls, took the flyer aloft and flew downriver at a low altitude.

At dusk the four dined on the provisions Glawen had stowed aboard. The river broadened and spilled into the ocean. Lorca and Sing disappeared and the Skyrie flew across the Western Ocean through the starlight.

Glawen spoke to Kathcar: "I am still not clear in my mind as to why you were brought to Shattorak. You must have done something to annoy Smonny, since Titus Pompo himself apparently counts for little."

Kathcar said coldly: "The matter is over and done with, and I do not wish to go into it any further."

"Nevertheless, we are all interested, and there is ample time for you to go into full detail."

"That may be," said Kathcar. "Still, the affair is personal and private."

Scharde said gently: "Under the circumstances, I don't think you can expect to keep affairs of this sort private. It is much too close to all of us, and we are justifiably interested in what you can tell us."

Chilke said: "I must point out to you that both Scharde and Glawen are Bureau B personnel, and their questions have an official tinge to them. As for me, I want to find out how best to make Smonny pay, and also Namour and Benjamie and anyone else who thought that I might not resent being dropped into a doghole."

"I resent it as well," said Scharde. "I am working to keep my rage under control."

"Everything considered," said Glawen, "you had better explain to us what we want to know."

Kathcar was mulishly silent. Glawen prompted him. "You are a member of the LPF faction at Stroma. How did you become acquainted with Smonny Clattuc, or Madame Zigonie—or whatever else she may call herself?"

"It is nothing to marvel at," said Kathcar with great dignity. "The LPF is concerned with conditions at Yipton, and wishes to bring Cadwal into modern times, and out of the sleep of centuries."

"So. You traveled to Yipton?"

"Naturally. I wished to observe the factual state of conditions."

"You went alone?"

Kathcar again became testy. "What possible difference does it make with whom I went?"

"Identify these persons, and allow us to be the judge."

"I went with a deputation from Stroma."

"Who was in the deputation?"

"Several members of the LPF."

"Was Dame Clytie one of them?"

Kathcar was silent a long ten seconds. Then he made a furious gesture of frustration. "If you must know, yes!"

"And Julian?"

"Naturally," said Kathcar with a sniff. "Julian is energetic and insistent. I have even heard him described as a bit bumptious, though perhaps I should not characterize him in this fashion."

"We are discreet, and will not report your condemnation to Julian," said Scharde with a grin. "So what happened at Yipton?"

"You must understand that, while the LPF uniformly and unanimously agrees on the need for progressivism, there are several concepts as to which direction the changes must go. Dame Clytie speaks for one of these philosophies and I represent another, and our conferences are not always harmonious."

Glawen asked: "How do your views differ?"

"It is mainly a matter of emphasis. I favor a carefully structured leadership organization for the new Cadwal and

I have designed the system in careful detail. Dame Clytie, I fear, is a bit impractical and imagines a new society of happy peasants, singing at their toil, dancing and playing tambourines up and down the village commons every night. Everyone will be story-teller or musician; everyone will take joy in producing beautiful artifacts. How is the new community to be governed? Dame Clytie endorses a concept where everyone, young and old, male and female, dolt and sage, all alike are supposed to debate issues at conclaves, then agree by glad hurrahs and vocal acclamations. In short, Dame Clytie opts for a democracy in its purest, most basic and amorphous form."

Glawen asked: "And the native beasts? What happens to them?"

Kathcar spoke airily. "The wild animals? Dame Clytie is not over-interested in the problem. They must learn to live with the new order. Only the truly nasty and repellent creatures will be driven away or exterminated."

"And your views are different?"

"Very much so. I call for a structured centrality, with authority to formulate policy and establish regulations."

"So then, you and Dame Clytie composed your differences and went together to Yipton?"

Kathcar draw back his lips in a sardonic grimace, half-smile, half-sneer. "The junket to Yipton was not my idea. I don't know for certain where the idea originated, but I suspect that Julian, who is always in favor of intrigue, the more devious the better, evolved the notion. I know that he consulted a certain Namour during one of his visits to Araminta Station, and then possibly broached the idea to Dame Clytie. Whatever the case, the plans were made. When I learned how the wind was blowing, I insisted upon joining the deputation, to ensure that my point of view be made known.

"We flew to Yipton. I knew nothing of Simonetta or her status; I thought that we would be conferring with Titus Pompo, and so I was astounded when we went into conference with Simonetta. Neither Julian nor Dame Clytie showed the same surprise, and I am sure that Namour briefed them in advance as to what to expect. I was naturally offended by what I considered a breach of diplomatic courtesy, and I resolved to make my displeasure clear at the first opportunity.

"In any event, Namour took us into an office with a floor of woven bamboo mat, walls of split bamboo, and a ceiling of intricately carved wood, evidently smuggled in from the mainland. We waited fifteen minutes before Simonetta chose to show herself—a delinquency which irritated Dame Clytie, so I could see.

"Simonetta at last condescended to appear, and I was amazed, as I have already indicated. Instead of the earnest, just and dignified Titus Pompo of my expectations, here was a woman as massive and strong as Dame Clytie herself. Simonetta, I must say, is a strange-looking woman. She wears her hair in a massive pile atop her head, like a coil of old rope. Her skin is like white wax. Her eyes glitter like amber beads. There is a sense of wildness and unpredictability about her that is most disturbing. She is clearly a woman of a hundred passions, which she disciplines as much as needful, but no more. Her voice is somewhat harsh and peremptory, but she can pitch it almost to a musical softness when she chooses. She seems to be guided by an instinctive or subconscious shrewdness, rather than formal intelligence; like that of Dame Clytie. On this occasion neither woman wasted any affability on the other, and there was only a cursory attempt at simple and ordinary courtesy. But no matter: we had not come to Yipton for the exchange of pleasantries but, rather, to discover how best to coordinate our efforts toward the common goal.

"I regarded myself as the senior member of the delegation, and started to speak, that I might express the philosophy of the LPF, as I saw it, in an orderly, coherent and definite manner, so that Simonetta should be under no illusions as to our basic point of view. Dame Clytie, however, conducted herself with absolutely vulgar and unforgivable rudeness, interrupting my remarks and shouting me down when I remonstrated and pointed out that I spoke with the authoritative voice of the LPF. Dame Clytie, using her most bluff and boisterous manner, pretended to regard

Simonetta as a comrade-in-arms, and a stout paladin in the cause of virtue and truth. Once again I tried to bring the discussion back to its proper channels, but Simonetta instructed me to hold my tongue, which I considered absolutely egregious and insulting conduct. Dame Clytie, rather than taking note of the insult, made offensive remarks of her own, something like: 'Excellent! If Kathcar will stop his braying for a few moments, we will get on with our business.' Something on that order.

"In any event Dame Clytie began to speak. Simonetta listened for a few moments, then once more became impatient. She said: 'I will be quite candid! I have been done grievous wrongs by the folk of Araminta Station, and the whole thrust of my life is retribution. I intend to sweep down on Deucas like an angel of wrath, and I shall be Mistress of Araminta Station. My revenge will be so sweet as to transcend all other pleasures I have known! All shall know the sting of my fury!'

"Dame Clytie found it necessary to chide her, though she tried to be judicious. 'This is not quite the emphasis or the thrust of the LPF. We intend to break the tyranny of the Charter, and allow the human spirit scope to flourish and grow!'

" 'So it may be,' said Simonetta. 'Still, eventually the Charter will be replaced by the Monomantic Credence, which will guide the future of Cadwal.'

"Dame Clytie said: 'I know nothing about this "Credence," and I would deplore the introduction of some freakish cult.'

" 'This an unkind description,' said Simonetta. 'The Monomantic Credence is the Ultimate Pansophy: the Way of Existence and the Vital Perfection!'

"At this, Dame Clytie became a trifle bleak. Julian leapt into the breach. He discoursed upon the new Cadwal and stated that, where true democracy was the watchword, every person's beliefs must be and should be sacred. He declared that he, personally, would defend such a precept to the death, or some such blather. Simonetta tapped her fingers on the table and barely listened. I saw the way the wind was blowing, directly toward recriminations and bad feelings. I decided to set matters straight, once and for all. I pointed out that absolute democracy—sometimes known as 'nihilism'—is equivalent to utter confusion. Further, everyone knew that rule by committee was only slightly less chaotic than rule by a mob. For true progress, authority must be exercised by a single resolute man of unquestioned quality and judgment. I announced that, while I had no overweening lust for power, the exigencies of the situation demanded that I take on this great responsibility, with all its challenges and trials. I felt that at this very moment we should agree to this program and proceed with full dedication in this direction.

"Simonetta sat staring at me. In a pleasant voice she asked if I were definitely convinced that the person in authority should be a man.

"I answered affirmatively. This, I said, was the lesson of history. Women were valuable adjuncts to society, with unique functions and irreplaceable instinctive skills. In men however resided that peculiar quality composed of wisdom, strength, persistence and charisma necessary for leadership."

"Simonetta asked: 'And what function do you plan for Dame Clytie in your new kingdom?'

"I saw that perhaps I had spoken too expansively, and had stated my case a trifle too earnestly. I replied that 'kingdom' was perhaps not quite the correct terminology, and that certainly I had full and great respect for both the ladies on hand. Dame Clytie might well be in charge of arts and crafts and Simonetta perhaps might do well as Minister of Education—both highly important posts."

Chilke laughed. "Kathcar, you are a marvel."

"I stated what I considered to be no more than universally accepted truisms."

"So you did," said Chilke. "But that made the cheese no less binding."

"In retrospect, I see that I exceeded caution. I had assumed both Dame Clytie and Simonetta to be rational and realistic persons, aware of the fundamental facts of history. I was wrong."

"Quite so," said Chilke. "What happened next?"

"Julian said that he thought that all of us had expressed our views, and now we must reconcile what seemed to be relatively minor differences. Our mutual goal was to throw off the dead weight of the Charter, and it was not an easy task. Simonetta seemed to agree and suggested that we adjourn for lunch. We went out on a terrace overlooking the lagoon, and here we were served a lunch of mussels, fish paste, a bread of seaweed flour and kelp, along with wine from Araminta Station. Apparently I drank more wine than usual, or perhaps the wine was drugged. In any event, I became drowsy and fell asleep.

"I awoke to find myself in a flyer. I assumed that I was returning to Stroma, though neither Dame Clytie nor Julian were on hand. It seemed a very long flight, which ended, to my utter astonishment, on Shattorak. I protested with great indignation; nevertheless, I was taken to a dog-hole and immured. Two days passed. I was told I could either become station cook or remain in the doghole, and I became cook. That is essentially all there is to tell."

"Where are the flyers kept?"

Kathcar grimaced. "These are not my secrets. I am reluctant to discuss such matters."

Scharde spoke in a measured voice. "You are a reasonable man, are you not?"

"Of course! Have I not made this clear?"

"There will be an attack on Shattorak by such forces as we can muster at the Station. If you have failed to provide us exact and detailed information, and any of our personnel is killed, you will be deemed guilty of murder by default, and you will be executed."

"That is not just!" cried Kathcar.

"Call it whatever you like. At Bureau B we interpret justice as loyalty to the terms of the Charter."

"But I am LPF and a progressive! I consider the Charter an archaic piece of rubbish!"

"We will consider you not only a Peefer but also a renegade and a murderer and execute you with no remorse whatever."

"Bah," muttered Kathcar. "It makes little difference one way or the other. The flyers are in an underground hangar on the eastern slope of Shattorak, where a lava cave was enlarged."

"How are they guarded?"

"I cannot tell you, since I never ventured in that direction, nor do I know how many flyers are in the hangar."

"How much staff is on hand?"

"A dozen or so."

"All Yips?"

"No. The best mechanics are off-world folk. I don't know much about them."

"What about Titus Pompo's space yacht? How often does that appear?"

"Twice during my time."

"Have you seen Namour since you went with Dame Clytie to Yipton?"

"No."

"And Barduys—what is his function?"

Kathcar responded haughtily: "As I stated, I know nothing of this person."

"He seems to be a friend of Dame Clytie."

"So it may be."

"Hmf," said Glawen. "Dame Clytie may not be quite so democratic as she would like us to believe."

Kathcar was puzzled. "Why do you say that?"

"In this new society of equals, Dame Clytie no doubt intends to be more equal than anyone else."

"I do not altogether grasp your meaning," said Kathcar with dignity. "Still, I suspect that you derogate the LPF."

"Possibly so," said Glawen.

II.

The Skyrie approached Araminta Station from the southwest, flying very low to avoid observation, and landed in a wooded area south of the River Wan.

Shortly after sunset Glawen approached Riverview House, and knocked at the front door. He was admitted into the reception hall by a maid-servant, who announced him to Egon Tamm. "You have returned in good health! How went your mission?" Egon Tamm's welcome was almost effusive.

Glawen glanced toward the maid, who was still in the room. Egon Tamm said: "Come; we will talk in my office. Will you take some refreshment?"

"I would be happy for a cup of strong tea."

Egon Tamm instructed the maid and took Glawen into his office. "So—were you successful?"

"Yes. I rescued not only Scharde, but also Chilke and another prisoner, a Naturalist named Kathcar. They are waiting outside in the dark. I did not want to bring them in, and show them to your guests."

"They left yesterday, I am happy to say."

"I would like you to notify Bodwyn Wook and ask him to come here to Riverview House; otherwise he will be offended and sarcastic when he sees me."

Egon Tamm spoke into his telephone and was answered by Bodwyn Wook. "Glawen is here," said Egon Tamm. "Everything seems to have gone well, but he asks that you come to Riverview House to hear his report."

"I will be there at once."

The maid entered with tea and biscuits. She placed the tray on the table. "Will there be anything more, sir?"

"Nothing; you may retire for the evening."

The maid departed. Glawen looked after her. "She may be innocent and honest, or she might be one of Smonny's spies. Apparently they are everywhere. It is important that Smonny is not notified that Scharde, Chilke and Kathcar have escaped Shattorak."

"Surely she knows they are gone by now!"

"But she cannot be sure that they simply did not try their luck in the jungle, or perhaps are hiding, hoping to seize one of the flyers."

"You may bring the three around the side of the house into the door at the end of the hall. I will make sure that Esmé is not where she can observe them."

Bodwyn Wook arrived and was admitted by Egon Tamm, who conducted him to the office. He looked from face to face. "Scharde! I am happy to see you alive, though I must say that you look a bit peaked. Chilke, you as well. And who is this gentleman?"

"He is a Peefer from Stroma," said Glawen. "His name is Rufo Kathcar, and he represents a faction somewhat at odds to Dame Clytie."

"Interesting, indeed! Well then: let us hear the news."

Glawen spoke for half an hour. Bodwyn Wook turned to Scharde. "What, in your opinion, should we do next?"

"I believe that we should strike, as quickly as possible. If Smonny receives a hint that her secret is known, it will be too late. In my opinion, we cannot act soon enough."

"Is Shattorak defended?"

Glawen turned to Kathcar. "What can you tell us?"

Kathcar tried to control the peevishness in his voice. "You put me in a most uncomfortable position. Even though I was treated badly by Simonetta, I cannot claim that my interests run parallel to yours. At the basis I intend to throw off the tyranny of the Charter, while you intend to prolong it as best you can."

"It is true that we hope to maintain the Conservancy,

villains that we are," said Bodwyn Wook. "Well, I can see a single solution which is fair to all parties. You need tell us nothing, and we will return you to Shattorak and leave you as we found you. Chilke, how many flyers can we put into the air?"

"Four new flyers, three trainers, two carry-alls, and the Skyrie. Our problem is espionage. Smonny will hear of the first move we make and be ready for us. Which reminds me, I want to seek out Benjamie this very instant, and there will be one spy the less to concern us."

Bodwyn Wook spoke to Egon Tamm: "Kathcar must also be regarded as an adversary, and he must be confined until we take him back to Ecce."

"I will lock him in the shed," said Egon Tamm. "He will be secure. Come, Kathcar; this is the necessity which circumstances have thrust upon us."

"No!" cried Kathcar desperately. "I do not wish to be locked up and I certainly do not want to return to Shattorak. I will tell you what I know."

"As you wish," said Bodwyn Wook. "Where are the Shattorak defenses?"

"There are a pair of guns at either side of the communications shed. There are two more to either side of the hangar. If you approach the summit by the route Glawen took, flying up the river, then up the slope at very low altitude, you should escape detection and be able to destroy the communications shed with no risk of damage from the guns. That is the best I can do for you, since I know no more."

"Very good," said Bodwyn Wook. "We will not return you to Shattorak, but you must be confined until our return, for obvious reasons."

Kathcar expostulated further but to no avail; Egon Tamm and Glawen led him away and locked him into a storage shed to the side of Riverview House.

Bodwyn Wook, meanwhile, dispatched a squad of Bureau B personnel to take Benjamie into custody, but, to Chilke's disappointment, Benjamie could not be found and, indeed, had departed Araminta Station aboard the spaceship *Dioscamedes Translux*, bound down the Wisp toward the junction city Watertown, on Andromeda 6011 IV. "Alas," said Chilke. "Benjamie has the danger tendrils of a Tancred firefox. I doubt if we shall ever lay eyes on Benjamie again."

III.

During the darkest quietest hours between midnight and dawn four patrol flyers departed Araminta Station, armed with such weaponry as the armory was able to provide. At high speed they darted around the curve of the world: across Deucas, over the Western Ocean, then slanted down so as to approach Ecce at low altitude. Up the Vertes River they flew, barely skimming the surface of the water, the better to evade whatever detectors might be operating on the summit of Mount Shattorak.

Where Glawen had landed the Skyrie, the raiding party veered away from the river to fly low over the swamp and up the slope of the volcano, and so arrived at the summit.

Twenty minutes later the operation was over. The communications shed had been destroyed, along with a gun emplacement. The hangar sheltered seven flyers, including the two most recently captured from Araminta Station. The base personnel offered no resistance; twelve captives were taken: nine Yips of the elite police corps — 'Oomps,' attired in black uniforms. The remaining three were hired technicians from off-world. How was it that they had been surprised and captured so easily? None of the Yips would supply an answer, but one of the off-world technicians reported that the escape of Scharde and Chilke, along with the disappearance of Kathcar, had aroused neither suspicion, alarm nor any attempt at increased vigilance; the personnel felt secure in their isolation, and the perils of escape were considered insurmountable. The raid, so he remarked, had preceded a Yip occupation of the Marmion Foreshore by only a week or two, and orders had arrived to arm all the flyers with such weapons as were at hand. In short, the raid could not have occurred at a more opportune time.

IV.

At Araminta Station the Conservator, in company with Bodwyn Wook and Scharde Clattuc, subjected Kathcar to a long and careful inquisition.

Egon Tamm thereupon summoned the six Wardens of Stroma to Riverview House, to confer upon a matter of grave importance.

The meeting took place in the parlor at Riverview House, immediately upon arrival of the six Wardens. Also present at the meeting were Bodwyn Wook, Scharde and Glawen, at the insistence of Egon Tamm. Wardens Ballinder, Gelvink and Fergus sat to one side, facing Dame Clytie Vergence, Jory Siskin—both LPFers—and Lona Yone, who professed neutrality, on the other.

The Conservator, wearing formal robes, called the meeting to order. "This is perhaps the most important session you will have ever attended," he told the Wardens. "A disaster of enormous dimension had threatened us, which we have averted, but only for the nonce. I refer to an armed attack by Yips upon Araminta Station, followed by an invasion of the Marmion Foreshore by thousands of Yips, which of course would signal the end of the Conservancy.

"As I say, we thwarted this action, and captured seven Yip aircraft along with a quantity of weapons.

"In this connection, I am sorry to report that one of your number is guilty of conduct which is very close to traitorous, though I am sure that she will claim that her acts are motivated by idealism. Dame Clytie Vergence is the person in question, and I now expel her from the Board of Wardens."

"That is impossible and illegal as well," snapped Dame Clytie. "I am duly elected by the people's vote."

"Nevertheless, the office is established by the Charter. You cannot work to destroy the Charter and derive your franchise from it at the same time. The same considerations apply to Jory Siskin, also an LPFer; I order his immediate resignation from the Board. And now, Warden Yone, I must ask if you support the Charter without reservation, in all of its aspects. If not, then you too must resign. We can no longer afford the luxury of divisiveness and controversy. The Charter is in danger, and we must act with decision."

Lona Yone, a tall thin woman of late middle years, with white hair cut short to frame a sharp bony face, said: "I dislike the authoritarian posture you have assumed, and I resent the need for defining what I consider my private habits of thought. However, I appreciate that this is not a normal occasion and that I must range myself either to one side or the other. Very well, then. I consider myself independent and uncommitted to partisan intrigue, but I state with conviction that I support the Charter and the concept of Conservancy. I believe, however, that the precepts of the Charter are not being rigorously applied, nor has this ever been more than approximately the case."

Lona Yone drew a deep breath and was about to speak further, but Egon Tamm intervened. "That is good and sufficient."

Dame Clytie spoke with scorn: "You can issue as many fiats as you like. The fact remains that I represent a large constituency of Naturalists, and we defy your harsh and ultimately inhumane principles."

"Then I must warn you and your constituents that if you attempt to interfere with, or circumvent, the implementation of Conservancy law, you all will be considered criminals. This includes consorting with Simonetta Zigonie, and any facilitation of her activities."

"You cannot dictate my choice of companions."

"She is a kidnapper and worse. Scharde Clattuc, who

sits yonder, is one of her victims. Your associate Rufo Kathcar is another."

Dame Clytie laughed. "If she is such a villain, why do you not apprehend her and bring her to justice?"

"If I could extricate her from Yipton without violence or bloodshed, I would do so on the instant," said Egon Tamm. He turned to Bodwyn Wook: "Do you have any ideas on the subject?"

"If we start deporting Yips to Chmanita Planet where their labor is in demand, sooner or later we will come upon Smonny."

"That is a heartless statement," said Dame Clytie. "How will you persuade the Yips to leave Yipton?"

" 'Persuasion' perhaps is the wrong word," said Bodwyn Wook. "Incidentally, where is your nephew? I expected to find him among those present."

"Julian is off-world, on important business."

"I advise both of you to obey the Charter," said Bodwyn Wook. "Otherwise, you too will be persuaded off-world."

"Bah!" sneered Dame Clytie. "First you must demonstrate that this decrepit old shibboleth has a real existence, and is not merely a rumor."

"Eh? That is easy enough. Look over at the wall yonder. That is a facsimile of the Charter. There is one in every household."

"I will say no more."

V.

Evening had come to Riverview House. The Wardens and ex-Wardens had made departure for Stroma. Rufo Kathcar had wished also to return to Stroma, but Bodwyn Wook was not yet satisfied that Kathcar had revealed all he knew, and certainly not all of what he suspected.

In the dining room Bodwyn Wook, Scharde, Glawen and the Conservator lingered at the table over wine, discussing the events of the day. Bodwyn Wook mentioned that Dame Clytie had shown no great agitation at the turn of affairs. "And, certainly, very little remorse."

"The position of 'Warden' is a largely symbolic honor," said Egon Tamm. "There are few real benefits. Dame Clytie was one of the Stroma Wardens because she seemed to define the post; also, it regularized her penchant for meddling into everyone else's affairs."

"She made a rather curious remark," said Scharde. "I have the impression that she said more than she intended, but could not resist the thrust."

Egon Tamm frowned in puzzlement. "Which remark was this?"

"She implied that the Charter was imaginary: a rumor, a legend, a disembodied shibboleth—whatever that might be."

Bodwyn Wook grimaced and poured wine down his scrawny throat with a grand flourish. "This extraordinary woman seems to believe that she can expunge the document from existence by the sheer exercise of her will."

Glawen started to speak, then fell silent. He had undertaken to reveal nothing of Wayness' discovery that the Charter had disappeared from the Society vault, but now it appeared that the knowledge was not as secure as Wayness had hoped. Smonny's efforts to gain control of Chilke's property and now Dame Clytie's angry remarks suggested that the news was secret only from the loyal Conservationists themselves.

Glawen decided that the Station's best interests would be served if he now shed light on the situation. He spoke in a tentative voice: "It may be that Dame Clytie's remarks are more significant than you suspect."

Bodwyn Wook glanced at him sharply. "Indeed! What do you know of the situation?"

"I know enough to find Dame Clytie's remarks troublesome. I worry even more to find that Julian Bohost has taken himself off-world."

Bodwyn Wook sighed. "As usual, all the world revels in full knowledge regarding dire emergencies and imminent disasters, save only the dozing Bureau B officials."

Egon Tamm said: "Allow me to suggest, Glawen, that you explain to us what is going on."

"Certainly," said Glawen. "I have not done so previously because I was pledged to secrecy."

"Secrecy from your own superiors?" roared Bodwyn Wook. "Is it your theory that you know better than the rest of us?"

"Not at all, sir! I simply agreed with my informant that secrecy was to everyone's advantage."

"Aha! And who is this infinitely cautious informant?"

"Well, sir, it is Wayness."

"Wayness!"

"Yes. She is now on Earth, as you know."

"Proceed."

"To make a long story short, she discovered, during a previous sojourn on Earth with Pirie Tamm, that the Charter and the Grant in Perpetuity was nowhere to be found. Sixty years before a certain Secretary of the Society named Frons Nisfit quietly plundered the Society and sold everything of value to document collectors—including, so it seems, the Charter. Wayness hoped to trace the sale of the Charter, and thought that she could function better if no one knew that the Charter was missing."

"That seems reasonable enough," said Scharde. "But is she not taking a great responsibility upon herself?"

"Rightly or wrongly, that was her decision. But it appears that Smonny is also aware of the situation, and perhaps knows more about it than does Wayness."

"Why do you say that?"

"A collector by the name of Floyd Swaner might have ended up with some of the Society documents. He died and left everything to his grandson, Eustace Chilke. Smonny traced down Chilke and took him to the planet Rosalia. Namour brought him here, and Smonny meanwhile attempted to find where either Chilke or Grandpa Swaner had hidden the Charter; she had no success. Smonny then ordered Chilke kidnapped, took him to Shattorak and forced him to sign over all his possessions. It seems that Smonny and her allies, the Yips, are serious."

"So then—what of Dame Clytie? How would she know?"

"I suggest that we talk once again to Kathcar," said Glawen.

Egon Tamm summoned the maid and instructed her to fetch Kathcar from the room which had been put at his disposal.

Kathcar presently appeared and for a moment stood in the doorway, appraising the persons in the room. He had carefully trimmed his black hair and his beard and had dressed himself in somber black and brown garments, in the conservative style of old Stroma. His black eyes darted back and forth, then he came forward. "What is it now, sirs? I have told you everything I know; any further questioning is sheer harassment."

Egon Tamm said: "Sit down, Rufo; perhaps you will take a glass of wine?"

Kathcar seated himself but brushed away the wine. "I consume very little vinous liquor."

"We are hoping that you may illuminate a puzzling circumstance in relation to Dame Clytie."

"I can't imagine what more I could tell you."

"When she conferred with Smonny Zigonie, did the subject of Eustace Chilke arise?"

"The name was not mentioned."

"What of the name 'Swaner'?"

"I heard no such name."

"Odd," said Bodwyn Wook.

Glawen spoke: "Either Dame Clytie or Julian Bohost made contact with Smonny's sister Spanchetta, here at Araminta Station. Were you aware of this?"

Rufo Kathcar showed a petulant frown. "Julian spoke with someone at the Station; I am not certain as to whom it might have been. He reported the occurrence to Dame Clytie and I seem to recall that he used the name 'Spanchetta.' His mood was one of excitement, and Dame Clytie said: 'I think you should investigate this matter; it might prove of the greatest importance' or words to that effect. Then she noticed that I was within earshot and said no more."

"Anything else?"

"Julian went off somewhere immediately afterward."

"Thank you, Rufo."

"Is that all you wish?"

"For now, yes."

Kathcar stalked from the room. Glawen told the others: "Spanchetta showed Julian the letters Wayness wrote me. She did not refer to the Charter directly but she probably said enough to set Spanchetta thinking."

Egon Tamm asked: "Why should Spanchetta show the letters to Julian? This is a puzzle."

Scharde said: "If Spanchetta had wanted to inform Smonny she would have notified Namour. She might well prefer Dame Clytie's plans for the future to those of her sister."

Glawen rose to his feet. He addressed Bodwyn Wook. "Sir, I request a leave of absence starting now."

"Hmf. Why this sudden whim?"

"It is not sudden, sir. The Shattorak operation has been successful and I am anxious to see to another matter."

"Your request is denied," said Bodwyn Wook. "I am assigning you to a special mission. You must proceed to

Earth at best speed and there clarify this matter we have been discussing to the best of your ability."

"Very good, sir," said Glawen. "I withdraw my request."

"Quite so," said Bodwyn Wook.

CHAPTER III

I.

Wayness arrived at the Grand Fiamurjes Spaceport on Old Earth aboard the starship *Zaphorosia Naiad* and went directly to Fair Winds, the residence of her uncle Pirie Tamm at Yssinges, near the village Tierens, fifty miles south of Shillawy.

Wayness approached the entrance to Fair Winds in a mood of uncertainty, not quite sure of what might be the current circumstances, nor even what kind of welcome she might expect. Her recollections, from a previous visit, were vivid. Fair Winds was an ancient manor built of dark timbers, commodious, comfortably shabby, surrounded by a dozen massive deodars. Here lived Pirie Tamm, a widower, with his daughters Challis and Moira: both older than Wayness and active in county society. Fair Winds had resounded with comings and goings, luncheons, garden fêtes, dinner parties and an annual masquerade ball. Pirie Tamm at that time had been a large hearty man, erect and stalwart, brisk and positive, punctiliously correct in his manners. Milo and Wayness had found him a generous host, if somewhat formal.

Arriving this second time at Fair Winds, Wayness discovered many changes. Challis and Moira had married and moved away; Pirie Tamm now lived alone, save for a pair of servants, and the vast old house seemed unnaturally silent. Pirie Tamm, meanwhile, had become thin and white-haired; his once-ruddy cheeks were waxen and hollow; his bluff positive mannerisms were muted and he no longer walked with a brisk confident stride. He maintained a stiff reticence on the subject of his health, but Wayness eventually learned from the servants that Pirie Tamm had fallen from a ladder, broken his pelvis, and owing to complications had lost much of his strength and was incapable of prolonged exertion.

Pirie Tamm greeted Wayness with unexpected warmth. "What a pleasure to see you! And how long will you stay? You will be in no hurry to leave, or so I hope; Fair Winds is much too quiet nowadays!"

"I have no definite schedule," said Wayness.

"Good, good! Agnes will show you to your room where you can freshen up before dinner."

Wayness remembered from her last visit that dinner at Fair Winds was always a formal occasion. She dressed accordingly in a pale brown pleated skirt, a dark gray-orange shirt and a square-shouldered black jacket: garments which admirably suited her dark hair and pale olive complexion.

When she appeared in the dining room, Pirie Tamm looked her up and down with grudging approval. "I remember you as a pretty young lass; you certainly have not altered for the worse—though I doubt if anyone would describe you as 'buxom.' "

"I lack a bit here and there," said Wayness demurely. "But I make do with what I have."

"It might well be enough," said Pirie Tamm. He seated Wayness at one end of the long walnut table and took himself to the other.

Dinner was served in ritual fashion by one of the maids: a rich rosy pink lobster bisque, a salad of cress and sweet parsley dressed with cubes of chicken marinated in garlic oil, cutlets of wild boar from the Great Transylvanian Preserve. Pirie Tamm inquired after Milo and Wayness told of the terrible manner of Milo's death. Pirie Tamm was shocked. "It is particularly disturbing that such deeds should be done on Cadwal, a conservancy and, theoretically, a place of tranquility."

Wayness laughed sadly. "That does not sound like Cadwal."

"Perhaps I am an impractical idealist; perhaps I expect too much of my fellow men. Still I cannot avoid a profound disappointment whenever I look back across the years of my life. Nowhere do I discover the fresh, or the clean, or the innocent. Society is in a condition of rot. I cannot even trust the shopkeepers to give me my correct change."

Wayness sipped wine from her goblet, not quite sure how to respond to Pirie Tamm's remarks. It seemed as if the years might have affected Pirie Tamm's mental processes as well as his physical condition.

Pirie Tamm, apparently expecting no comment, sat brooding off across the room. After a moment Wayness asked: "What of the Naturalist Society? Are you still Secretary?"

"I am indeed! It is a thankless task, in the most literal sense of the words, since no one either appreciates my efforts or tries to assist me."

"I am sorry to hear that! What of Challis and Moira?"

Pirie Tamm made a curt gesture. "They are caught up in their own affairs, to the exclusion of all else. I suppose that it is the usual way of things—though I could wish for something different."

Wayness asked cautiously: "Did they marry well?"

"Well enough, I suppose, depending upon one's point of view. Moira picked herself a pedant, impractical as they come. He teaches some footling course at the university: 'The Psychology of the Uzbek Tree Frog,' or perhaps it's 'Creation Myths of the Ancient Eskimos.' Challis did no better; she married an insurance agent. None of them have set foot off the planet Earth, and none care a counterfeit coprolite for the Society. They titter and change the subject when I mention the organization and its great work. Varbert—that's Moira's husband—calls it a 'geriatric mumble-club.' "

"That is not only unkind but foolish, as well!" declared Wayness indignantly.

Pirie Tamm hardly seemed to hear. "I have discussed their parochialism at length, but they do not even trouble to disagree, which I find most exasperating. As a consequence I see little of them nowadays."

"That is a pity," said Wayness. "Evidently none of their activities interest you."

Pirie Tamm gave a grunt of disgust. "I have no taste for trivial banter nor excited discussion of some celebrity's misconduct, nor would I wish to waste the time. I must research my monograph, which is a tedious business and I must also keep up with Society business."

"Surely there are other members who might be willing to help you?"

Pirie Tamm laughed sourly. "There are barely half a dozen members left, and most are senile or bedridden."

"No new members apply?"

Pirie Tamm laughed again, even more bitterly. "That is a joke. What can the Society offer to attract new members?"

"The ideas are as relevant now as they were a thousand years ago."

"Theories! Murky ideals! Glorious talk! All meaningless when strength and will are gone. I am the Society's last secretary and soon—like me—it will be no more than a memory."

"I am sure that you are wrong," said Wayness. "The Society needs new blood and new ideas."

"I have heard such proposals before." Pirie Tamm indicated a table across the room on which rested a pair of earthenware amphorae, formed of a ruddy orange body, banded with black slip. The ceramist had scratched through the slip to create representations of ancient Hellenic warriors engaged in combat. The urns were about two feet tall and, in the opinion of Wayness, extremely beautiful.

"I had the pair for two thousand sols: a great bargain, assuming that they are genuine."

"Hm," said Wayness. "For a fact, they don't look very old."

"True, and that is a suspicious circumstance. I had them from Adrian Moncurio, a professional tomb robber. He agrees that they are well preserved."

"Perhaps you should have them authenticated."

Pirie Tamm looked dubiously toward the two urns.

"Perhaps. It is an uncomfortable dilemma. Moncurio states that he took them from a secret site in Moldavia where by some miracle they had rested undisturbed for millennia. If so, the circumstances are irregular and I am harboring a pair of illegal and undocumented treasures. If they are fakes, I own a pair of legal, handsome and very expensive garden ornaments. Moncurio himself lacks all qualms and is probably off plying his trade at this very moment."

"It would seem an adventurous occupation."

"Moncurio is the man for it. He is strong, keen and quick and totally lacks scruples, which makes him difficult to deal with."

"How is it, then, that he sold the amphorae so cheaply?"

Pirie Tamm again showed a dubious expression. "He was at one time a fellow of the Society, and spoke of rejoining."

"Did he actually do so?"

"No. I feel that he lacked true Naturalist dedication. We agreed that the Society needed revitalization, even though, as he pointed out: 'There is precious little to revive.' And he added: 'The Cadwal Charter and the Grant-in-Perpetuity are demonstrably secure, of course?' "

"What did you say to that?"

"I told him that we need not consider Cadwal at the moment, that all our best efforts must be devoted to repairing the Society here on Earth.

" 'First,' said Moncurio, 'you must alter the public image you now project, of a few tremulous octogenarians in musty clothes, dozing away the afternoons.'

"I tried to remonstrate, but he went on: 'You must place yourselves squarely at the node of the general culture; you must set up a program of entertaining events which would capture the attention of the average man. These events might be somewhat peripheral to Society goals, but they would generate enthusiasm.' He spoke of such activities as dancings, feasts of exotic dishes, recreations of dramatic adventures, contests and promotions to exploit the touristic potential of Cadwal.

"I stated, somewhat stiffly, I fear, that his proposals

failed to enhance either the short- or the long-term goals of the Society.

" 'Nonsense!' Moncurio declared. 'Further, you might organize a grand beauty pageant, with pretty girls recruited from as many worlds as possible. They would be named "Miss Naturalist-Earth" and "Miss Naturalist-Alcyone," "Miss Naturalist-Lirwan" and so forth.'

"I rejected the proposal as tactfully as I could. 'Such pageants are no longer considered chic.'

"Moncurio contradicted me again. 'Not so! A well-turned ankle, a proper buttock, a graceful gesture—these will never be anything less than chic, so long as the Gaean Reach endures!'

"I said wryly: 'For a man of your age and a tomb robber to boot, you are vehement in this regard.'

"Moncurio became indignant. 'Never forget: a beautiful girl is no less a part of Nature than a bottle-nosed blind worm from the caves of Procyon IX.'

" 'Your point is well-taken,' I told him. 'Still, I suspect that the Society will plot out its future course in less tangential directions. Now then, if you wish to join, you may pay me fourteen sols and fill out the questionnaire.'

" 'I have every intention of joining the Society,' said Moncurio. 'Indeed, this is why I am here. But I am a cautious man, and I wish to look over the accounts before I join. Will you be so good as to show me the ledgers, and also, most importantly, the Cadwal Charter and the Grant?'

" 'That would be inconvenient,' I told him. 'These documents are customarily kept in a bank vault.'

" 'I have heard rumors of depredation and embezzlement. I must insist upon seeing the Charter and the Grant before I join.'

" 'Everything that needs doing is being done,' I told him. 'You must support the Society as a matter of principle, not because of an old paper or two.'

"Moncurio said that he would take the matter under advisement, and so departed."

Wayness said: "It sounds to me as if he suspected that the Charter and Grant were gone."

"I assumed that he had come upon items of the seques-

tered goods, — and this is still the most likely explanation."
Pirie Tamm chuckled sadly. "A year ago, when Moira and
Challis were here with their husbands, I mentioned
Moncurio and his notions for enlarging the Society. All four
thought that Moncurio's ideas were eminently sensible. Ah
well, no matter." Pirie Tamm fixed his gaze on Wayness.
"What of you? Are you a member?"

Wayness shook her head. "At Stroma we call ourselves
'Naturalists,' but it is just a name. I suppose we think of
ourselves as honorary members."

"Ha! No such category exists. You are a member when
you apply and are accepted by the secretary, and when you
have paid your dues."

"That is simple enough," said Wayness. "I now apply for
membership. Am I accepted?"

"Certainly," said Pirie Tamm. "You must pay the initiation
fee and a year's dues in advance: a total of fourteen sols."

"I will do so immediately after dinner," said Wayness.

Pirie Tamm gave a gruff chuckle. "I am obliged to warn
you that you are buying into an indigent organization. A
secretary named Frons Nisfit sold everything he could lay
his hands on, then took the money and disappeared. The
Society now lacks both property and assets."

"You have never tried to find the Charter?"

"Not seriously. The job seemed hopeless. After so many
years the trail is cold."

"What of the secretaries who came after Nisfit: they did
nothing?"

Pirie Tamm gave a grunt of disgust. "Nils Myhack succeeded Nisfit, and held office for forty years. I suspect that
he never realized the documents were gone. Kelvin Kilduc
was next in office, and I am almost certain that he was
unaware of the loss. Kilduc never mentioned any doubt of
the Charter's presence in the vault to me. On the other
hand, I don't believe he was a truly dedicated secretary."

"So — if either Secretary Myhack or Secretary Kilduc
tried to recover the Charter, you know nothing about it?"

"Nothing whatever."

"Somewhere it must still exist. I wonder where."

"There is no way of knowing. If I were wealthy, I might

hire a trustworthy private investigator and put him on the case."

"It is an interesting idea," said Wayness. "Perhaps I shall look into the matter myself."

Pirie Tamm frowned down the table. "You, a slip of a girl?"

"Why not? If I found the Charter and the Grant, you would be delighted!"

"That goes without saying, but the concept is extraordinary. Almost grotesque."

"I can't see why."

"You are not trained in investigative procedures!"

"It seems mainly a matter of persistence, as well as a modest degree of intelligence."

"True enough! But such work is frequently coarse and not altogether genteel. Who knows where such a search might take you? This is a job for a tough, resourceful man, not a vulnerable innocent girl, no matter how persistent or intelligent. Danger still exists on Old Earth—sometimes in subtle and unusual forms."

"I hope that you exaggerate, since I am something of a coward."

Pirie Tamm frowned down the table. "I believe that you are truly in earnest."

"Yes, of course."

"How do you propose to pursue this investigation?"

Wayness considered. "I suppose that I will make a list of likely places to look—museums, collections, dealers in ancient documents—and work down the list."

Pirie Tamm gave his head a disparaging shake. "My dear young lady, there must be hundreds of such places, on Earth alone."

Wayness nodded thoughtfully. "It does seem to be a large job. But who knows? I might find clues along the way. Also, is there not a central directory where ancient archives are indexed and cross-referenced?"

"Of course! The university has access to such information banks. There is also the Library of Ancient Archives at Shillawy." Pirie Tamm rose to his feet. "Let us adjourn to the study for a cordial."

Pirie Tamm took Wayness along the hall and into his study: a large room, with a fireplace at one end and a pair of long tables at the other. Books and pamphlets crammed the shelves; both tables were littered with papers; between them was a swivel chair. Pirie Tamm indicated the tables. "So goes my life these days. I dwell in a swivel chair. I sit in one direction to work on my monograph; I am jerked to attention by a sudden recollection, swing about in the chair to plunge into Society business, then back again to my monograph." Wayness made sounds of commiseration. "No matter," said Pirie Tamm. "I am only happy that I have no more than two tables and two occupations; with three, or four, I would be whirling like a dervish. Come; let us sit by the fire." Wayness settled herself into a tall old chair of baroque design upholstered in moss-green plush. Pirie Tamm poured dark red cherry cordial into small goblets, one of which he handed to Wayness. "This is the finest Tincture of Morella, and is guaranteed to bring the bloom of health to your cheeks."

"I will drink cautiously," said Wayness. "Blooming red cheeks would not become me, and even less a red nose."

"Drink without fear! Red nose or not, your company is most welcome. I seldom entertain these times; in truth I have few acquaintances and fewer friends. Challis tells me that I am widely regarded as a martinet and an ogre, but I suspect that she is only echoing the complaints of her husband. Moira holds similar views, and tells me that I must learn to keep my opinions to myself." Pirie Tamm gave his head a gloomy shake. "Perhaps they are right. Still, I cannot pretend to be happy with the way the world is going. 'Ease' is now the watchword and no one troubles to do his job correctly. Things went differently when I was young. We were taught to take pride in our achievements, and only 'Excellent' was good enough." He glanced sidewise at Wayness. "You are laughing at me."

"Not really. On Cadwal, even during my own life, I have noticed changes. Everyone knows that something terrible is about to happen."

Pirie Tamm raised his eyebrows. "How could that be? I

thought that Cadwal was a place of bucolic languor, where nothing ever changed."

"That notion is quite out of date," said Wayness. "On Stroma half the folk abide by the Charter; the other half consider it obsolete and want to change everything."

Pirie Tamm said gloomily: "They realize, of course, that they would destroy the Conservancy."

"That is their dearest hope! They are restless and believe that the Conservancy has lasted long enough."

"Absurd! Young folk often want change simply for the sake of change, that they may bring significance and identity to their own lives. It is an ultimate form of narcissism. In any case, on Cadwal the Charter is the law and cannot be violated."

Wayness gave her head a slow sad shake. "All very well, but where is the Charter? That is why I am here on Old Earth."

Pirie Tamm refilled the goblets. For a long moment he stared into the fire. "You should know this," he said at last. "There is at least one other person who knows that the Charter and Grant are not in our possession."

Wayness leaned back in her chair. "Who else knows?"

"I will tell you how it happened. It is a curious story, and I can't pretend to understand it. As you know, there have been only three secretaries since Nisfit: Nils Myhack, Kelvin Kilduc and myself. Myhack became Secretary immediately after Nisfit's departure."

Wayness interrupted. "Let me ask you this. Why did the new Secretary, this Myhack, fail to notice immediately that the Charter was missing?"

"For two reasons. Myhack was an amiable chap, but a bit vague and careless in his thinking, and inclined to take things at their face value, so to speak. The Charter and Grant were bound into a folder, which was contained in a stout envelope, thoroughly sealed and tied with red and black ribbons. This envelope reposed at the Bank of Margravia among other documents, and those few financial instruments which Nisfit had been unable to convert into cash. Upon taking the first needful inventory, Myhack found the envelope safe, sealed, securely bound with black and red ribbons, and correctly labeled. He can be forgiven for assuming that the Charter was safe.

"Nils Myhack, after many years as Secretary, finally became something of an invalid, with failing eyesight. His work was done by a succession of more or less capable assistants, the last being a formidable female, originally from off-world, who joined the Society, then made herself so helpful to Myhack that at last he employed her as Assistant Secretary. It seemed to be a labor of love for her, and she let it be known that she would gladly become official Secretary whenever Myhack decided to retire. Her name was Monette; she was a large bustling woman, grim, competent and something of a virago. I personally found her unsympathetic; she had a fishlike stare which tended to make a person uneasy. Myhack however had no complaints, and was always singing her praises: 'Monette is truly invaluable!' and 'The office could not function without Monette!' and one day: 'Monette has an eye like an eagle! She has found an inconsistency in the ledgers and insists that we take inventory of the vault, to assure ourselves that all is in order. I am not up to such a deadly task, so I will send her tomorrow, with the keys and a note, to the bank manager.'

"Kelvin Kilduc and I both made vehement protests, and declared that such an act was grossly improper. Myhack pulled a long face but at last agreed that we should all go to the bank together. So went the program, and obviously to Monette's displeasure; she came in with a face like a storm cloud, and everyone was careful to treat her politely.

"The vault was opened, and Monette made a list of the contents: some financial records, a few paltry bonds and the envelope purportedly containing the Charter, still well sealed and tied in festoons of black and red ribbon, so that everyone was satisfied. All except Monette. Before we could interfere, she had ripped off the ribbons, broken the seals, pulled out the folder. Kilduc cried out: 'Here, here! What are you doing?' Monette answered in a barely patient voice: 'I want to make sure of what is in the folder; that is what I am doing.' She opened the folder, looked inside, then closed the folder and tucked it back in the envelope. Kilduc asked:

'Well Monette? Are you satisfied?' 'Yes,' said Monette. 'Completely.'

"She tied the folder up in its ribbons and tossed it back into the box. Nothing more was said; apparently all was as it should be.

"The next day Monette was gone, without a word of explanation and was seen no more. Kelvin Kilduc became Secretary, and so matters stood until his death, and I was forced to take up the job. You and I went to the Bank of Margravia and opened the vault. I investigated the folder and to my utter shock found not the Charter, but a commercial copy, and no sign of the Grant.

"I thought back across the years to Monette. I am now convinced that her purpose was to make sure of the Charter. If she had found the original and the Grant secure in the vault, she would have succeeded Myhack as Secretary and then appropriated the Charter and Grant to her own uses. She must have been shocked to discover nothing but the copy; I marvel at her ability to hold a straight face.

"That is the story. Monette knew long ago that the Charter was missing. What she did next I cannot guess."

Wayness sat silently, looking into the fire.

After a moment Pirie Tamm went on. "That means that Nisfit sold the Charter, along with the other documents of antiquarian value. The present owner has not thought to register the Grant in his own name, as he would be entitled to do, with all legality. And yet another disturbing factor looms over the near horizon."

"Which is?"

"The Grant must be validated and re-endorsed at least once each century; otherwise the original claim lapses and the Grant is nullified."

Wayness stared aghast. "I knew nothing of this! How much time remains to us?"

"Ten years or so. There is no immediate emergency, but the Grant must be found."

"I shall do my best," said Wayness.

II.

In the morning Wayness arose early. She dressed in a short blue skirt, dark blue knee-length stockings, and a pullover blouse of soft gray-tawny stuff, at once light, warm and complimentary to her pale olive complexion.

Wayness left her room and descended the stairs. At this hour Fair Winds seemed unnaturally quiet. During the night odors had seeped from the fabric of the house: a recollection of countless floral bouquets, curios carved from camphorwood and sanuchi, furniture polish and wax, ancient rugs, along with a hint of lavender sachet.

Wayness went to the morning room and seated herself at the breakfast table. Tall windows overlooked a landscape of green meadows, trees and hedges, with the tile roofs and chimneys of Tierens in the distance. This morning the weather seemed somewhat unsettled. Small clouds raced eastward across the sky on an upper wind, causing the sunlight to brighten, go dim, then brighten again, all in the space of seconds. The light of Sol, thought Wayness — especially here in the Middlelands — shone pale and hazy, notably different from the golden glare of Syrene. The light of Sol appeared to enhance and enrich blues and greens, and perhaps too the muted colors of cloud shadows, while Syrene evoked the inner fire of reds, yellows and oranges.

The maid Agnes looked in from the kitchen and presently served Wayness sliced fruit, a boiled egg, buttered scones with strawberry preserves and rich brown coffee.

A short while later Pirie Tamm appeared, wearing an

old tweed jacket, a striped black and gray shirt, loose
breeches of brown twill: attire more casual than he might
have favored in times gone by. Despite all, he still managed
to project an air of brusque decorum. For a moment he
stood in the doorway, surveying Wayness with the crisp
detachment of a military officer inspecting his troops. Wayness said mildly, "Good morning, Uncle Pirie. I hope I
haven't disturbed you by jumping out of bed so early."

"Of course not," declared Pirie Tamm. "Early rising is a
virtue to which I have subscribed every day of my life." He
came forward, seated himself and unfolded his napkin.
"Mathematics tells the tale. One hour of oversleeping each
day destroys a year of life each twenty-four years. Across
the span of a hundred years, an extra hour of sloth will
excise four years of existence. Think of it! When already I
fear that my life will be far too short to fulfill even my
minimal ambitions. Who was it who said: 'Sleep when you
are dead'?"

"Baron Bodissey, most likely. He seems to have said
most everything."

"Clever girl!" Pirie Tamm gave his napkin a flap and
tucked the corner into his shirt. "You seem bright and alert
this morning—even cheerful."

Wayness shrugged. "At least bright and alert."

"But not cheerful?"

"I can't say that Monette and her activities came as a
happy surprise."

"Ah well, the episode occurred many years ago and who
knows what happened to the woman? I suspect that she
has long since forgotten the affair."

"I hope so."

"Remember, the grant has never been re-registered."
Pirie Tamm looked down the length of the table. "I see that
you have not let your concern spoil your appetite. I detect
eggshells, what once might have been a plate of scones,
and what else?"

"Sliced oranges."

"Excellent. A proper breakfast, which will nicely fortify
you until luncheon. Agnes? Where the devil are you?"

"Here, sir, ready with your tea."

"Tell Cook I'll have a parsley omelet, with a bit of mushroom ketchup. Scones, as well. Mind you, not a hint of leather to the eggs!"

"I'll tell Cook, sir." Agnes hurried from the room. Pirie Tamm looked into the teapot and gave a disdainful sniff. "I suppose it's no weaker than usual." He poured tea into a cup, sipped, blinked, then returned his attention to Wayness, who placed fourteen sols upon the table and pushed them toward Pirie Tamm. "Last night I forgot. Am I now a member of the Naturalist Society?"

"As soon as I verify your identity and note your name into the rolls. The verification will go smoothly, since I will cite myself as your guarantor."

Wayness smiled. "I have heard that on Old Earth good connections count for everything."

"Regrettably, in the main, this is true. I, however, am almost without such advantages, and must go hat in hand like anyone else when I want something done. My sons-in-law hold me in contempt on this account. Well, no matter. I suppose you have been considering the project we discussed last night?"

"Yes. It was at the top of my mind."

"And now—very sensibly, I must say—you have had second thoughts and are giving up the idea?"

Wayness looked at him in astonishment. "Why should you think that?"

"The circumstances are obvious!" snapped Pirie Tamm. "The task far exceeds the capacities of a young girl, no matter how pretty and persuasive."

"Look at it this way," said Wayness. "There is one lost Charter and one of me. We start on equal terms."

"Bah! I am in no mood for sophistries. In fact, I find myself greatly frustrated by the physical infirmities which inhibit my own efforts along these lines. Ah well! Here is my omelet. Let us see how Cook has managed the job. All seems to be in order. Amazing how often a confection of such simplicity defies the best efforts of a well-paid specialist. Now then, what were we talking about? Ah yes, your proposal. My dear Wayness, the task is monumental! It is simply beyond your scope!"

"I don't believe so," said Wayness. "If I intended to walk from here to Timbuctoo, I would start by taking one step, then another, and another, and soon I would be crossing the Niger River by the Hamshatt Bridge."

"Aha! You omit the area between the third step and the last—which is to say, the garden at Fair Winds and the Niger River, which lies across the Sahara Desert. Along the way you might be given wrong directions, or robbed, or fall into a ditch, or be attacked or married or divorced."

"Uncle Pirie! You are far too imaginative!"

"Hmf. I wish I could imagine some nice safe program by which you might learn what you want to know."

"I already have a plan," said Wayness. "I will look through Society archives, especially those dated during Nisfit's tenure, and perhaps find some clue which will lead us further."

"My dear young lady, that is a formidable task in itself! You'll become bored and sad; you'll long to be out in the sunlight, meeting other young folk and enjoying yourself! One day you'll throw up your hands, scream, and run from the house, and that will be the last of the great project."

Wayness tried to keep her voice even. "Uncle Pirie, you are not only imaginative; you are a pessimist."

Pirie Tamm peered at her from the side of his face. "You are not discouraged?"

"I have heard only what I expected to hear, and I have already taken it into account. I must find the Charter and the Grant; I can think of nothing else. If I succeed, my life will have been useful. If I fail, at least I have tried my best."

Pirie Tamm sat for a moment, then a brief wintry smile crossed his face. "Succeed or fail, your life is precious; there is no question as to that."

"I want to succeed."

"Just so. I will do what I can to help you."

"Thank you, Uncle Pirie."

III.

Pirie Tamm led Wayness into a small high-ceilinged room to the side of his study. A pair of tall narrow windows admitted light filtered by the foliage of grape vines trailing from a balcony. Shelves and cases were crammed to bursting with a disorderly clutter of books, pamphlets, tracts and folders. Walls elsewhere displayed hundreds of photographs, drawings, charts and miscellaneous oddments. A desk with a four-foot information screen occupied an alcove. "This is my old den," said Pirie Tamm. "I worked here while the family was at home, using my study for a social center, despite my protests and hints. This room was known as 'the Ogre's Junkyard.' " Pirie Tamm gave a grim chuckle. "I once overheard Varbert, Moira's husband, use the term 'Old High-Arse's Hideaway.' "

"That was not at all respectful."

"In this regard, we agree. In any event, when I closed the door, I was allowed a modicum of privacy."

Wayness looked around the walls. "Things do seem, well, a trifle disorganized. Could the Charter be tucked into one of those trays or folders?"

"No chance of that," said Pirie Tamm, "if only for the fact that the thought also occurred to me and I methodically examined every article of paper on the premises. I fear that your quest will not have so simple a resolution."

Wayness went to examine the desk and the control system. Pirie Tamm said: "It is quite standard and should give you no difficulty. At one time I had a simulator focused

on the desk yonder, which Moira happily used to model new
styles on herself."

"Ingenious!" said Wayness.

"In a sense, yes. One night when Moira was about your
age we hosted a formal dinner party. Moira wore an elegant
gown and was conducting herself with all possible dignity,
but after a bit we began to wonder where all the young men
had taken themselves. We finally found them in here, with
a four-foot replica of Moira in the nude frisking about on
the table. Moira was intensely annoyed and to this day
suspects that Challis imparted a sly hint to the young
men."

"Was Varbert among the group? If so, he must have
liked what he saw."

"He said nothing to me, one way or the other." Pirie
Tamm shook his head sadly. "Time goes by quickly. Try the
chair. Is it comfortable?"

"Just right. Where do I find the Society archives?"

"If you enter 'ARC,' you will be provided a comprehen-
sive index. It is quite simple."

"All of the Society correspondence is on record?"

"Every last jot, jog, item and tittle—for two reasons:
compulsive pettifoggery and because recently we have had
nothing better to do. I guarantee that you will find precious
little of interest, and now I will leave you to it."

Pirie Tamm departed the room. Wayness gingerly set
herself to exploring the records of the Naturalist Society.

By day's end she had learned the scope and organization of the records. A very large proportion of the material
pertained to events of the distant past. These Wayness
ignored, and started her investigation with the arrival of
Frons Nisfit on the scene. She learned the date upon which
Nisfit's delinquencies became known. She reviewed the
subsequent tenures of Nils Myhack, Kelvin Kilduc and Pirie
Tamm. For a time she ranged through the files almost at
random, skimming through financial statements, minutes
of the annual conclaves, and membership rolls. Each year
the dues-paying membership decreased in numbers and
the message was plain to be read: the Naturalist Society
was near upon extinction. She skimmed the files of corre-

spondence: requests for information, memoranda of dues owing and dues collected; death notices and changes of address; scholarly tracts and essays submitted for inclusion into the monthly journal.

Late in the afternoon, with the sun low in the sky, Wayness leaned back from the desk, surfeited with the Naturalist Society. "And it is only a start," she told herself. "Evidently both fortitude and persistence will be very useful before this project is ended."

Wayness left the dim study and went to her room. She bathed, dressed in a dark green gown appropriate to the formality of dinner at Fair Winds. "I must find myself some new clothes," she told herself. "Otherwise, Uncle Pirie will think I am coming down to dinner in a uniform."

Wayness brushed her dark hair and tied it with a length of fine silver chain. She descended to the drawing room, where she was presently joined by Pirie Tamm. He greeted her with his usual punctilio. "And now: in accordance with the invariant ritual of Fair Winds: the Sundowner. Will you try my brave sherry?"

"Yes, if you please."

From a cupboard Pirie Tamm brought a pair of little pewter goblets. "Notice the subtle hint of green in the patina, which to some degree indicates their age."

"How old are they?"

"Three thousand years, at least."

"The shapes are extraordinary."

"Not by accident! After initial forming, they were heated to soften the metal, then bent, crumpled, flared, compressed, distorted and finally given a comfortable lip. No two are alike."

"They are fascinating little objects," said Wayness. "The sherry is good too. A similar wine is produced at Araminta Station, but I suppose that this is better."

"I should hope so," said Pirie Tamm with a sour smile. "After all, we have been at it for a considerably longer time. Shall we step out upon the verandah? The evening is mild, and the sun is setting."

Pirie Tamm opened the door; the two went out on the verandah and stood by the balustrade. After a moment

Pirie Tamm said: "You seem pensive. Are you discouraged by the scope of the job you have taken on?"

"Oh no. For the moment, at least, I had put both Nisfit and the Society out of my mind. I was admiring the sunset. I wonder if anyone has ever made a formal study of sunsets as they appear on different worlds. There must be many interesting varieties."

"Without a doubt!" declared Pirie Tamm. "Off the top of my head I can cite half a dozen striking examples! I particularly recall the sunsets of Delora's World, at the back of Columba, where I went to research my treatise. Each evening we were treated to marvelous spectacles, green and blue, with darts of scarlet! They were unique; I would recognize a Delora sunset instantly among a hundred others. The sunsets of Pranilla, which are filtered through high-altitude sleetstorms, are also memorable."

"Cadwal sunsets are unpredictable," said Wayness. "The colors seem to explode from behind the clouds and are often garish, though the effect is always cheerful. Earth sunsets are different. They are sometimes grand, or even inspiring, but then they wane quietly and sadly into the blue dusk and create a melancholy mood."

Pirie Tamm gave the sky a frowning inspection. "The effect you mention is real. Still, the mood never lasts long and disappears completely by the time the stars come out. Especially," he added, by way of afterthought, "when a jolly meal at a well-laid table is in the offing. The spirits soar under these conditions like a lark on the wing. Shall we go in?"

Pirie Tamm seated Wayness at the massive walnut table and took his own place opposite. "I must repeat that it is a pleasure having you here," said Pirie Tamm. "That is a charming frock you are wearing, incidentally."

"Thank you, Uncle Pirie. Unfortunately it is my only dinner gown, and I must find some new clothes, otherwise you will quickly become bored with me."

"Not on that account, certainly. Still, there are two or three good shops in the village, and I'll take you in whenever you like. By the way, Moira and Challis know that you are here. I expect them to drop by in a day or so, to look you over. If they decide that you are not too gauche, they might introduce you into local society."

Wayness made a wry face. "When I was here before, neither Moira nor Challis liked me very much. I overheard them talking about me. Moira said that I looked like a Gypsy boy dressed in girl's clothes. Challis was amused but felt that the description was too lenient; that in her opinion I was just a moony little prude with a face like a scared kitten."

Pirie Tamm uttered an exclamation of mild astonishment. "My word, those girls have sharp tongues! How long ago was this?"

"Five years, more or less."

"Hmf. I can relate similar incidents. One day I overheard Varbert describe me as 'an unlikely hybrid of screech-owl, heron and wolverine.' On another occasion Ussery spoke of me as the 'house-devil' and wanted someone to give me a chain to rattle as I walked through the halls."

Wayness, with difficulty, restrained a grin. "That was a rude remark."

"I thought so too. Three days later I called both families over on the pretext of asking for advice. I was changing my will, I told them, and could not decide whether too leave everything to the Naturalist Society, or to the Coalition for the Protection of the Screech-owl and the Heron. There was silence in the room. Challis finally said, very tentatively, that surely other possibilities must exist. I said no doubt she was right and I'd give the matter some thought when I had the leisure to do so, and I rose to my feet. Moira asked me why I dangled a length of chain from my belt. I said that I liked to rattle it as I walked up and down the halls." Pirie Tamm chuckled. "Varbert and Ussery have since become noticeably more polite. They expressed enthusiasm upon hearing of your arrival, and spoke of introducing you to suitable young people—whatever that means."

"It means they'll look me over and decide I'm still a frump and pair me off with a dog-breeder's assistant, or a very tall divinity student, or perhaps a junior underwriter from Ussery's office. I will be asked how I liked Old Earth, and where, exactly, is Cadwal—of which none will have ever heard."

Pirie Tamm gave a bark of laughter. "Not unless you have met a Society member, which is unlikely, since there are only eight left."

"Surely there are nine, Uncle Pirie! Don't forget to count me!"

"I counted you, never fear! But as of today we must omit Sir Regis Everard from the count, since he has died."

"That is depressing news," said Wayness.

"So it is." Pirie Tamm looked over his shoulder. "Something dark stands back there in the shadows counting on its fingers."

Wayness peered into the shadows. "You are giving me the shudders."

"Ha hum," said Pirie Tamm. "Indeed. Ah, well; we must learn to deal impersonally with the topic. Never forget, the institution provides a livelihood for multitudes of the living. Reckon them up! Priests, mystics, grave diggers, composers of odes, paeans and eulogies; also doctors, hangmen, mortuary attendants, tomb builders and tomb robbers—which prompts me to ask if you have come across the name Adrian Moncurio? Not yet? The name will surface sooner or later, since he was a former member. As you may recall, it was Moncurio who presented me with the beautiful amphorae."

"A tomb robber is a good friend to have," said Wayness.

IV.

Two weeks went by. One evening Pirie Tamm entertained his daughters Moira and Challis, with their husbands Varbert and Ussery, at dinner. For the occasion Wayness wore one of her new costumes: a high-collared dark mulberry pullover blouse with a skirt of soft mulberry, dark blue and dark red stripes which clung to her hips, then hung in soft lines almost to her ankles. When she descended the stairs, Pirie Tamm was moved to exclaim: "Upon my soul, Wayness! You've become a full out-and-out three-masted smasher!"

Wayness kissed his cheek. "You'll make me vain, Uncle Pirie."

Pirie Tamm gave a snort of amusement. "I'm sure that you have no illusions about yourself!"

"I try to be practical," said Wayness.

The guests arrived and were received at the door by Pirie Tamm. For a time there was a flurry of greetings and counter-greetings, then a new set of exclamations as Wayness was discovered. Moira and Challis gave her quick head-to-toe inspections, followed by a spate of enthusiastic comments: "My, how you have grown! Challis, would you have recognized the child?"

"It's hard to think back to that funny little waif who found Earth such a strange and frightening place!"

Wayness smiled pensively. "Time works changes, for better or worse. You both seem far older than as I remember you."

"They are relentless socialites and have led fast hard lives," said Pirie Tamm.

"Father! What a thing to say!" cried Moira.

"Pay no attention, Wayness dear!" said Challis. "We are quite ordinary upperclass folk."

Varbert and Ussery came forward and were introduced: Varbert, tall and lean as a pickerel with a beak of a nose, ash-blond hair, a receding chin; Ussery somewhat shorter, plump of cheek, soft of midriff, with a mellow voice and a sententious style of speaking. Varbert used the critical manner of a discriminating aesthete who could be satisfied with nothing less than perfection; Ussery, somewhat more tolerant in his judgments, was both easy and jovial in his remarks. "So this is the notable Wayness: equal parts tomboy and bookworm! I say, Varbert! She is not at all what I expected!"

"I try to avoid preconceptions," said Varbert indifferently.

"Aha!" said Pirie Tamm. "That is the mark of a disciplined mind!"

"Quite so. I am thereby ready for anything, at all times and on all occasions, and who knows what might blow in from the outer worlds?"

Wayness said: "Tonight, since it is a special occasion, I am wearing shoes."

"What an odd girl!" murmured Varbert to Moira, just at the edge of audibility.

"Come," said Pirie Tamm briskly. "Let us all have a glass of sherry before dinner."

The party trooped into the drawing room, where Agnes served sherry and where Wayness again became the focus of attention.

"Why are you visiting Earth this time?" asked Moira. "Is there any special reason?"

"I'm doing some research on the early Naturalist Society. I may also take a few trips here and there."

"Alone?" demanded Challis, eyebrows raised. "It's not wise for an inexperienced young girl to travel alone on Earth."

Ussery said in reasonable tones: "She probably won't be alone for very long."

Challis chilled her over-jovial husband with a glance. "Moira is quite right. This is a wonderful old world, but for a fact we breed some strange creatures in the dark places."

"I see them often," said Pirie Tamm. "They hide in the Faculty Club at the University."

Varbert felt impelled to remonstrate. "Come now, Pirie! I'm at the Faculty Club every day! We have a distinguished membership!"

Pirie Tamm shrugged. "I may be a trifle extreme in my views. My friend Adrian Moncurio is far more uncompromising. He asserts that all the honest folk are gone from Earth, leaving a residue of deviates, freaks, nincompoops, hyper-intellectuals and sweet-singers."

"That's utter nonsense," snapped Moira. "None of us fit these categories!"

Ussery spoke mischievously: "Speaking of music, are you performing at the lawn party?"

Moira spoke with dignity: "I have been asked to participate in the program, yes. I shall do either 'Requiem for a Dead Mermaid' or 'Bird Songs of Yesteryear.' "

"I especially like your 'Bird Songs,' " said Challis. "The piece is ever so plaintive."

"It seems that we are in for a treat," said Ussery. "I believe I will have another taste of that excellent sherry. Challis, have you invited Wayness to the party?"

"Naturally, she is welcome to come. But there won't be any young people on hand, and I doubt if she'll find much excitement, or anyone to interest her."

"No matter," said Wayness. "If I wanted excitement, or interesting company, I could have stayed home on Cadwal."

"Really!" said Moira. "I thought Cadwal was a nature preserve, where the only activity was nursing sick animals."

"You should visit Cadwal and see for yourself," said Wayness. "I think that you would be surprised."

"No doubt, but I am not up to such adventures. I have little tolerance for discomfort and bad cooking and nasty insects."

"I share your sentiments," said Varbert. "One could make a nice philosophical case that the outer worlds were never intended for our habitancy, and that the Gaean Reach is an unnatural construct."

Ussery gave a jocular laugh. "If nothing else, we Earthlings avoid a number of very picturesque diseases, such as Daniel's Number Three Dengue and the Big-eye, Shake-leg and Chang-chang."

"Not to mention pirates and slavers and all the wild things that happen Beyond."

Agnes appeared in the doorway. "Dinner is served."

The evening ended on a note of careful politeness. Ussery gallantly reiterated his invitation to the lawn party, but before Wayness could respond, Challis snapped: "Ussy, have mercy! You must allow the poor girl to make up her own mind. If she wants to come, I'm sure she will let us know."

"That seems a sensible arrangement," said Wayness. "Goodnight to all!"

The guests departed; Pirie Tamm and Wayness were left alone in the drawing room. "They are not bad people," said Pirie Tamm gruffly, "and not even typical Earth folk—but don't ask me to define this typical creature since he is far too variable, and sometimes surprising. Also, he can be gloomy and dangerous, as Moira hinted. Earth is an old planet, with pockets of rot here and there."

Days passed, and weeks. Wayness read documents of every description, including the Society's by-laws, along with those amendments which had been added across the centuries. The by-laws were almost naive in their simplicity, and seemed to be based on a hypothesis of universal altruism.

Wayness discussed the by-laws with Pirie Tamm. "They are wonderfully quaint, and almost seem to urge the secretary to become a swindler. I marvel that anything was left for Nisfit."

"The Secretary is, first of all, a member of the Society," said Pirie Tamm in lofty tones. "Almost by definition he is a gentleman and a person of probity. We Naturalists, now and always, have considered ourselves an elite element of the general population. We were never mistaken in this belief—until Nisfit."

"Something else puzzles me. Why has interest in the Society declined so dramatically over the years?"

"There has been a great deal of soul-searching done on this point," said Pirie Tamm. "Many reasons have been advanced: complacency, a failure of new ideas with an attendant waning of enthusiasm. The public began to think of us as a group of fusty old bug-collectors, and we did nothing adventurous or startling to dispel the idea, nor did we make membership any easier or any more appealing. A candidate needed the endorsements of four active members, or failing this—as might be the case of a candidate from off-world—he must submit a thesis, a biographical précis, and a police report attesting to his identity, correct name and lack of criminal record. A discouraging route."

"I wonder that Nisfit was accepted as a member."

"On this occasion the system failed us."

Wayness continued her research. She came upon a list of the items Nisfit had sold. The list had been compiled by the new secretary Nils Myhack, and included the comment: "The rascal has hoodwinked us in fine style! What in the name of everything naughty is 'Engenderments adapted into Asset-assignment Account BZ-2'? I could laugh if it were not a crying shame! Luckily, Charter and Grant are safe in the vault "

Here, thought Wayness, was probably the source of the mysterious Monette's conviction—perhaps more accurately, hope—that the Charter still resided in the bank vault.

The properties sequestered by Nisfit were various: drawings and sketches created by Naturalists during off-world expeditions; curios, objects of virtu or aesthetic consequence fabricated by non-Gaean life forms, including tablets in the still undeciphered Myrrhic script, statues from a world at the back of Ursa Minor; vases, bowls and other receptacles found among the Ninarchs. There were collections of small life forms; a case of a hundred magic stone spheres and tablets wrought by the banjees of Cadwal; trinkets worn by the bog-runners of Gemini 333 IV. In another category were Society archives of interest to

collectors of ancient documents, in folders, folios, and
fused black litholite, incised in microscopic symbols;
ancient books and photographs, all manner of chronicles,
notations, biographical records.

The purloined material, in its entirety, thought Wayness, would not be conveniently salable to a single individual or institution. With careful attention she studied
Nisfit's letters. She found membership applications, memoranda of delinquent dues and expulsion notices; correspondence in connection with cases at law; scholarship
funds; expeditions and research projects; the endowments
and investments which provided the income for many Naturalists of Stroma.

The sheer mass of material was almost overwhelming.
Initially Wayness sampled items from all the categories,
then concentrated upon the items she found most provocative. Using a search procedure which sought references
to the word 'Charter,' she discovered nothing of interest.

As something of an afterthought, she subjected the
entire set of files accumulated during Nisfit's tenure to the
search, and at last, among much that was inconsequential,
came upon a case which aroused her interest.

The occasion was the annual conclave during the last
year of Nisfit's office. The minutes of the conclave recorded
a dialogue between Jaimes Jamers, Chairman of the Activities Committee and Frons Nisfit, Secretary.

> Jamers: Mr. Secretary, this is admittedly not
> my official province, so I address you in the hope
> that you will clarify some items which I find puz-
> zling. What for instance is a 'Supersessive'?
> Nisfit: Simple enough, sir. It is an article whose
> use or value to the Society has been superseded.
> Jamers: Your verbiage here, I find to be abso-
> lute jargon. I wish you would express yourself
> more intelligibly.
> Nisfit: Yes, sir.
> Jamers: For example, what does this mean—
> 'Engenderments to Asset Group-potentials'?

Nisfit: Much of the terminology, sir, is derived from Accountancy nomenclature.

Jamers: But what does it mean?

Nisfit: In the broadest sense, funds derived from disposal of excessive or unnecessary materials are consigned to a fund of versatile activity. Endowments, scholarships, emergency procedures and the like. Also, payment of taxes and fees, like the annual Stipulative Charge for the Cadwal Charter, which must carefully be observed.

Jamers: I see. You have been scrupulous in this respect?

Nisfit: Of course, sir.

Jamers: And why is the Cadwal Charter not in its usual place?

Nisfit: I transferred it to the Bank of Margravia, along with other documents.

Jamers: Somehow this all seems a bit loose and untidy. I think that we should have an inventory taken of our properties, so that we know where we stand.

Nisfit: Very good, sir. I will arrange for such an inventory.

During the following week Nisfit vacated his office and was seen no more.

A thought came into Wayness' head which excited her curiosity. Frons Nisfit had become a member of the Society with little regard for the traditional Society stringencies. Who had proposed him for membership? Wayness investigated the files and discovered names which meant nothing to her. What of Monette, who had joined the Society thirty years later? Again Wayness scrutinized the records.

During the relevant period there was no Society member with the surname 'Monette.'

Odd! thought Wayness. She set herself to an even more diligent study, and so made a startling discovery.

Later in the day she reported her findings to Pirie

Tamm. " 'Monette,' as you mentioned, was an off-worlder; when she applied for membership she was required to provide a certified identification, which went into the files. The name was 'Simonetta Clattuc.' "

V.

Wayness told Pirie Tamm what she remembered from Glawen's casual anecdotes regarding Simonetta Clattuc. "Apparently she was notorious for her hot temper, and any small slight incurred her furious revenge. When she was still a young woman, she was frustrated in a love affair and almost at the same time ejected from Clattuc House because of low status. She left Araminta Station in a state of rage and was never heard from again."

"Until she became Nils Myhack's assistant," said Pirie Tamm. "I wonder what she had in mind? She could not have known that the Charter and the Grant were missing."

"That is why she wanted to investigate the bank vault."

"Of course—but she found nothing there or anywhere else, since there is no record of the Grant being re-registered."

"That, at least, is a comfort. On the other hand, she must have searched the files just as I am doing—and probably to the same effect."

"Not necessarily! She would not trouble to search the files if she expected that the Charter and Grant were in the bank vault."

"I hope that you're right," said Wayness. "Otherwise I'm wasting my time searching where she has already searched."

Pirie Tamm made no comment; clearly he felt that, in either case, Wayness was wasting her time.

Wayness nevertheless continued her work, but as

before found nothing in the Society files which cast even a feeble illumination upon Nisfit's dealings.

Days passed, and weeks. Wayness began to encounter moods of discouragement. Her most interesting discovery was a photograph of Nisfit which depicted a thin blond man of indeterminate age, with a high narrow forehead, a trifle of a mustache and a thin down-drooping mouth. It was a face to which she took an instant dislike, representing, as it did, the cause of her frustration.

Further weeks went by, and Wayness could not suppress the conviction that her energies might more profitably be applied elsewhere. Nevertheless, she persevered and every day examined new documents: letters, invoices, receipts; suggestions, complaints, inquiries, reports. All to no purpose; Nisfit had efficiently covered his tracks.

Late one afternoon, her eyelids drooping and her mood close to dejection, Wayness came upon a short passage which evidently had escaped Nisfit's vigilance. The passage occurred toward the end of a routine letter from a certain Ector van Broude, resident of the city Sancelade, two hundred miles to the northwest. He wrote in regard to a special assessment, but added, as a post-script:

"My friend Ernst Faldeker, employed by the local firm Mischap and Doorn, has commented upon the substantial transactions which you, as Secretary of the Society, have initiated. I seriously question the wisdom of this policy; is it truly far-sighted, and in the best interests of the Society? Please explain to me the reasons for these unusual transactions." In high excitement Wayness ran to Pirie Tamm and told him of her discovery.

"That is interesting information," said Pirie Tamm. "Mischap and Doorn at Sancelade, eh? I think I have heard the name, but I cannot place it offhand. Let us consult a directory."

In his study, he instituted a search and presently was accorded information. " 'Mischap and Doorn: Brokerage, Consignment and Commission Sales.' The firm is still extant, and they are still situated in Sancelade. So there you have it."

CHAPTER IV

I.

"Perhaps we can resolve the problem within the next five minutes," said Pirie Tamm. He telephoned the offices of Mischap and Doorn, at Sancelade. The screen flared into luminosity, displaying the red and blue 'Mischap and Doorn' insignia across the top and, in the lower right quadrant, the head and shoulders of a thin-faced young woman with a long thin nose and short blonde hair cut squarely around her head in an uncompromising and rather eccentric style, or so thought Wayness. Her eyes glittered and danced with nervous vitality, but she spoke in the flattest of flat voices: "Please state your name, occupation, connection and present concerns."

Pirie Tamm identified himself, and cited his connection with the Naturalist Society.

"Very well, sir; what is your business with us?"

Pirie Tamm frowned, displeased with the receptionist's manner. Still, he responded politely. "A certain Ernst Faldeker was a member of your firm some forty years ago. I expect that he has retired?"

"As to that, I can't say. He certainly is not with us now."

"Perhaps you will inform me as to his present address."

"Just a moment, sir." The young woman's face disappeared.

Pirie Tamm growled aside to Wayness: "Amazing, is it not? These functionaries think of themselves as angels

reclining on clouds, while far below the human ruck sup-
plicates from the mire."

"She seems very self-possessed," said Wayness. "I suppose that if she were over-sentimental, she might find it a
handicap in her work."

"Possible, possible."

The young woman's face returned. "I find that I am not
authorized to issue this sort of information."

"Well then—who is?"

"Berle Buffums is our present office manager. Would
you care to speak with him? He has nothing better to do at
the moment."

An odd remark, thought Wayness. "Please connect me,"
said Pirie Tamm.

The screen blanked. A moment passed. The agile and
vivacious face returned. "Mr. Buffums is in conference at
the moment and cannot be disturbed."

Pirie Tamm gave a grunt of annoyance. "Perhaps you
can tell me this much. Your firm handled some business
for the Naturalist Society—let me think—it must have been
over forty years ago. I am anxious to learn the disposition
of the goods involved."

The receptionist laughed. "If I let slip a hint of such
information, Bully Buffums would have my gizzard. He
is—shall we say—obsessive in regard to confidentiality. I
could easily be bribed, were it not that Bully Buffums locks
away the Confidential files."

"A pity. Why is he so careful?"

"I don't know. He explains his fiats to no one—least of
all me."

"Thank you for your courtesy." Pirie Tamm broke the
connection. Slowly he turned to Wayness. "It seems a
curious firm, even for Old Earth. It is perhaps because they
are based in Sancelade, an extraordinary city in itself."

"At least we have a clue, or a lead-in, or whatever it
should be called."

"True. It is a start."

"I will go at once to Sancelade. Perhaps, one way or
another, I can persuade Berle Buffums to release his
information."

Pirie Tamm heaved a sad sigh. "With all my heart I curse this damnable ailment, which distresses me more than you can know! My manhood is lost; I feel like a frail old goblin creeping and limping about the house, while you, a slip of a girl go forth on the work I should be doing!"

"Please, Uncle Pirie! Don't say such things. You do what you can and I do what I can, and that is the way it shall be."

Pirie Tamm patted Wayness' head: one of his few expressions of affection. "I will say no more. Our goal is larger than either of us. Still, I don't want you to be threatened, or hurt, or even so much as frightened."

"I am quite cautious, Uncle Pirie. Most of the time, anyway. Now I must go to Sancelade and learn what I can from Mischap and Doorn."

"So it would seem," said Pirie Tamm, though without conviction. "I need not point out that you will face a number of challenges—among them Berle Buffums."

Wayness gave a nervous laugh. "I hope to escape with my life, at least, and—who knows?—maybe the Charter."

Pirie Tamm made a gruff sound. "I must reiterate that Sancelade is a peculiar place, with a remarkable history." Pirie Tamm went on to provide Wayness with a few salient facts. The old city, he told her, had been completely destroyed during the so-called 'Alienate Convulsion'*. For two hundred years it remained a desolate waste, until the autocrat Tybalt Pimm ordained a new city for the site. He specified every aspect of the new Sancelade in exact detail, using a variant of the same complicated architecture for each of the six districts.

At the time Tybalt Pimm's great scheme evoked mockery and jeers, but in due course the derision became muted, and in the end Sancelade was considered the masterwork of a genius gifted in equal parts with imagination, energy and unlimited funds.

Pimm's theories and proscriptions were long enforced,

---

*Off-world repatriates, unable to mesh comfortably into the society of Old Earth, suddenly gave way to a mass psychosis. Forming hysterical gangs, they indulged themselves in a frenzy of savage destruction, in order to punish the environment which they felt had mistreated them.

though at times they became a trifle blurred. The Kyprian Quarter, for instance, which Pimm had designated as the district for light industry, trade schools, inexpensive restaurants and social halls, instead became the resort of artists, musicians, vagabonds and mystics ensconced among a thousand cafés, bistros, studios, small shops for the purchase of oddments, and the like. In the end Sancelade became known as a place where one could live high or low, strait or wide, and in general do as he pleased, so long as he was discreet, or even if he were not discreet.

II.

Wayness rode by surface transit to Shillawy, across a countryside of small farms and villages, where nothing had changed since the dawn of time. From Shillawy she rode the underground slideway which two hours later delivered her to the Central Station at Sancelade.

A cab took her to the hotel Pirie Tamm had recommended: the Marsac, situated at the edge of the prestigious Gouldenerie, hard by the Kyprian Quarter. The Marsac was a sprawling old structure of many wings, three restaurants and four gilded ballrooms on the banks of the River Taing. Wayness found herself enveloped in an atmosphere of casual elegance, muted and quite unself-conscious, of a sort to be discovered nowhere else in the Reach. She was conducted to a high-ceilinged chamber, with walls enamelled a faded beige. A soft Marocain rug pattered in brown, black, dark red and indigo enlivened the gray terrazzo floor; bouquets of fresh flowers had been placed upon tables at each side of the bed.

Wayness changed into a neat dark brown suit, the better to represent her businesslike intentions, then returned to the lobby. The city directory instructed her that the offices of Mischap and Doorn were located in Flavian House on Alixtre Square, at the far side of the Gouldenerie.

The time was now an hour into the afternoon. Wayness lunched in the Waterview Grill and watched the River Taing flow by, meanwhile trying to fix upon her best course of action.

In the end she decided to pursue a plan both simple and direct; she would present herself at the offices of Mischap and Doorn, ask to see Mr. Buffums and in her very nicest manner ask for a few trifles of information. "Mischap and Doorn was a long-established and reputable firm," she told herself. "They would have no reason to deny such a small request."

After lunch she crossed the Gouldenerie to Alixtre Square—a formal garden surrounded by four-story structures, no two alike, but all built in exact accordance with Tybalt Pimm's aesthetic precepts.

Mischap and Doorn occupied the second floor of Flavian House, on the north side of the square. Wayness climbed to the second floor and entered a court planted with ferns and palms. A directory listed Mischap and Doorn's various offices and departments: Executive Offices, Personnel, Accounting, Appraisals, Exchanges, Extra-terrestrial Properties, and several others. Wayness went to the Executive offices. The door slid aside to her touch. She entered a large room, furnished as if to accommodate a working force of perhaps eight persons, but now occupied only by two women. The thin-faced young receptionist sat at a desk in the exact middle of the room. A plaque announced her name and rank: GILJIN LEEPE Assistant to the Executive Manager. At a table to the far right an elderly woman, squat, gray-haired, large of feature, heavy of bone and ample of flesh, sat with trays, books, tools and optical instruments engrossed in the study of a set of small objects.

Giljin Leepe was perhaps half a dozen years older than Wayness and an inch taller, engagingly angular, with a taut thin body and breasts which were little more than hints. Her sea-blue eyes, when wide, made her seem innocent and guileless; when she lowered her lids she became comically crafty and sly. Still, her face, under a thatch of short dusty-blonde hair, cut in a pudding-bowl crop, was far from unattractive. An odd creature, thought Wayness, and definitely one to be dealt with cautiously. Giljin Leepe surveyed Wayness with equal interest, raising her eyebrows as if to ask herself: "What in the world do we have here?" Aloud she said: "Yes, Miss? These are the offices of Mischap and Doorn; are you sure that you have come to the right place?"

"I hope so. I want a bit of information, which perhaps you can supply."

"Are you buying or selling?" Giljin Leepe handed Wayness a pamphlet. "These are the properties we are currently handling; maybe you'll find what you want here."

"I am not a customer," said Wayness apologetically. "I am trying to trace some properties which you handled forty or so years ago."

"Hm. Didn't someone call on this matter yesterday?"

"Yes, I suppose so."

"I am sorry to say that nothing has changed, except that I am a day older. Nelda never changes, but then she dyes her hair."

"Ha ha!" said Nelda. "If so, why should I choose the color of dirty soapsuds?"

Wayness could not help but be fascinated by Giljin Leepe's mouth, which was thin, wide, pink, and in constant movement: curling, twisting first up one corner and down the other, wincing and compressing, or drooping at both corners together.

"In any case," said Giljin Leepe, "Bully Buffums remains as usual."

Wayness looked toward the door in the back wall, which evidently led into Mr. Buffums' private office. "Why is he so careful?"

"He has nothing better to do. Mischap and Doorn runs itself, and the directors have warned Bully Buffums not to interfere. So he busies himself with his art collection—"

Nelda interposed. "Art, did you say? I know what I call it."

"Bully occasionally sees an important customer, and sometimes shows his art collection if he thinks he can shock him—or her."

"Would he oblige me, do you think, if I explained what I wanted and why?"

"Probably not. You can try."

Nelda said: "Warn the girl, at least."

"There isn't much to warn against. He can of course be a bit tiresome."

Wayness looked dubiously toward Mr. Buffums' door. "What is 'tiresome,' and how much is a 'bit'?"

"I betray no confidences when I mention that Bully is not always happy in the company of pretty girls. They make him feel insecure. But he has his moods."

Nelda said: "They come on him when he eats too much rare meat."

"The theory is as good as any," said Giljin Leepe. "For a fact, Bully Buffums is unpredictable."

Wayness again looked toward the door at the back of the room. "You may announce me. I will be as nice as I can and maybe Mr. Buffums will like me."

Giljin Leepe gave an uninterested nod. "Who shall I announce?"

"I am Wayness Tamm, Assistant Secretary of the Naturalist Society."

The door at the back of the room had slid aside. A large man stood in the opening. He called out sharply: "What is going on, Giljin? Have you nothing better to do than entertain your friends?"

Giljin Leepe spoke in her most neutral voice: "This is not a friend; she represents an important client, and wants a trifle of information in regard to some dealings."

"Who is the client, and what are the dealings?"

"I am Assistant Secretary of the Naturalist Society. I am inquiring about a transaction conducted quite some time ago, by a former secretary."

Mr. Buffums sauntered forward: a tall plump man well into his early maturity, with a round flushed face and over-long ash-blond hair parted in the middle and combed so as to hang past his ears in the so-called 'pack-saddle' style. "Most odd!" he said. "A woman came to the office — how long ago? Ten years? Twelve years? — wanting the same information."

"Really!" said Wayness. "Did she announce her name?"

"Probably, but I have forgotten."

"Did you give her the information?"

Mr. Buffums raised dark eyebrows, in distinctive contrast with his ash-blond hair, and considered Wayness with round pale eyes. He said in a pedantic and somewhat nasal voice: "I consider all my dealings confidential. This is sound business policy. If you care to consult me further, you may step into my office." Mr. Buffums turned away. Wayness looked sidewise at Giljin Leepe, and was not encouraged by her rueful shrug. Shoulders sagging, step after slow step, like a prisoner on his way to the gallows Wayness followed behind.

Mr. Buffums slid shut the door and, selecting a thin sliver of metal on a key-ring, locked the door.

"Old fashioned locks are best, don't you think?" asked Mr. Buffums cheerfully.

"I suppose so," said Wayness. "That is, when they are needed in the first place."

"Ah! I see what you mean! Well, perhaps I am a bit over-precise. When I conduct a business conversation, I do not care for intrusions, and I am sure that you are of the same mind. Am I right?"

Wayness reminded herself that she must be nice to Mr. Buffums, so that he should not feel insecure. She smiled politely. "You have had far more experience than I, Mr. Buffums; undoubtedly you know best."

Mr. Buffums nodded. "I can see that you are a shrewd young lady, and I have no doubt but what you will be a great success."

"Thank you, Mr. Buffums; I am glad to hear you say so, and I will be grateful for your help."

Mr. Buffums made a large gesture. "Of course! Why not?" He went to lean against his desk. He did not seem particularly insecure, thought Wayness; was that a good or a bad sign? He was certainly a most puzzling person, definitely of a volatile temperament, one moment cantankerous, the next arch and facetious. She looked around the office. To the left a sliding partition closed off a section of the room; to the right was a desk, chairs, table, communicator, shelves, files and other office paraphernalia. Four narrow windows overlooked a garden court.

"You find me at a slack moment," said Mr. Buffums. "I am—if I say so myself—an able administrator, which means that the work of the company proceeds without my constant guidance. This is all to the good, since it leaves me more time for my private interests. By any chance, have you studied the philosophy of aesthetics?"

"No, not at any length."

"It happens to be one of my own interests. I specialize in one of the most profound and universal aspects of the subject, even though, for one reason or another, it commands little serious or scholarly attention. I refer, of course, to erotic art."

"Fancy that!" said Wayness. "I wonder if you are acquainted with the Naturalist Society?"

Mr. Buffums seemed not to hear. "My collection of erotic curiosa is naturally not exhaustive, but I flatter myself that its overall quality is superb. I occasionally show it to persons with an intelligent and sympathetic attitude. What of yourself?" He watched her closely.

Wayness spoke carefully: "I have never studied the subject and, for a fact, I know next to nothing—"

Mr. Buffums interrupted her with a wave of the hand. "No matter! We will consider you an interested amateur, with many latent potentialities."

"I'm sure of that, but—"

"Look." Mr. Buffums touched a switch; the partition dividing his office split, folded and disappeared, to reveal an extensive area which Mr. Buffums had converted into a sort of museum of erotic art, symbols, artifacts, adjuncts, representations, statues, statuettes, miniatures and an unclassifiable miscellaneity. Nearby stood a marble statue of a nude hero in a state of acute priapism; across the room another statue depicted a woman preoccupied with the attentions of a demon.

Wayness glanced about the collection, her viscera squirming from time to time, but her most urgent impulse was laughter. Such a reaction would surely offend Mr. Buffums, and she carefully blanked away all expression from her face, showing only what she felt to be polite interest in the exhibits.

Evidently this was not enough. Mr. Buffums was watching her through half-closed eyes and showing a frown of dissatisfaction. Wayness wondered where she had gone wrong. A new idea entered her mind: "Of course! He is an exhibitionist! If I show shock or distress or so much as lick my lips, he will be stimulated." She brooded a moment. "Naturally I want to be nice to Mr. Buffums and put him into a good mood." But not in this particular way; it was beneath her dignity.

Mr. Buffums spoke in a rather pompous voice: "In the Great Mansion of Art there are many chambers, some large, some small, some swimming in rainbow fluxes; others which reveal themselves in colors more subtle and muted and rich; others still are revealed only to the truly discriminating. I am one of those latter and my special field is erotica. I have roamed its near and far shores; I know every permutation and extravagance."

"That is impressive. In regard to my own concerns—"

Mr. Buffums paid no heed. "As you can see, I am cramped for space. I can give only cursory attention to the amatory musics, the postures, the provocative scents and odors." Mr. Buffums glanced at her sidewise, brushing aside a lock of the ash-blond hair which had fallen forward over his eye, and which made so striking a contrast with his dark eyebrows. "Still, if you like, I will anoint you with a drop of what the legendary Amuille called her 'Summons to the Hunt.' "

"I don't think it would be convenient today," said Wayness. She hoped that Mr. Buffums would not be put off by her evasiveness. "Perhaps some other time."

Mr. Buffums gave a terse nod. "Perhaps. What do you think of my collection?"

Wayness spoke judiciously: "From the limits of my own experience, it would seem exhaustive."

Buffums looked at her in reproach. "No more? Nothing else? Let me show you around; persons of imagination are often fascinated, or even excited."

Wayness smilingly shook her head. "I must not impose upon you."

"No imposition whatever! I find it hard to restrain my enthusiasm." He went to a table. "For instance, these articles here, so common, so ordinary, so often misunderstood."

Wayness glanced down at the table. She searched for

something to say, since Mr. Buffums clearly expected an intelligent comment. "I don't quite see how anyone could misunderstand. They seem most assertive."

"Yes, possibly so. They lack all subtlety and they do not dissemble. Perhaps this is their charm. Did you say something?"

"Nothing of consequence."

"They are what best might be called 'folk art,' " said Mr. Buffums. "They pervade every era of history, and all classes of society, and serve many functions: puberty rituals, voodoo curses, fertility rites, buffoonery and pranks, and other more workaday purposes. The best are carved from wood. They come in all sizes, colors and degrees of tumescence."

Mr. Buffums waited for Wayness' comment. She said cautiously: "I don't think I would call such things 'folk art.' "

"Oh? What would you call them?"

Wayness hesitated. "Now that I think about it, 'folk art' is as good a name as any."

"Just so. These raffish little articles often do yeoman service for folk who must be considered aesthetic vulgarians. At such times thongs or straps are inserted through these holes to make them fit—" Mr. Buffums took up one of the objects and, smiling modestly, held it against himself "—in this fashion. What do you think of it?"

Wayness examined him critically. "It does not go well with your complexion. The pink one yonder would suit you better. It is larger and more conspicuous, but is probably in better taste."

Frowning, Mr. Buffums put the article aside and turned petulantly away. Wayness saw that she had annoyed him, despite all efforts to be tactful.

Mr. Buffums took a few quick steps toward his desk, then halted and swung about. "Well then, Miss Whatever-your-name—"

"I am Wayness Tamm, and I am here on behalf of the Naturalist Society."

Mr. Buffums arched his dark eyebrows high. "Is this a joke? To my clear understanding the Naturalist Society is defunct."

"The local chapter is somewhat inactive," Wayness

admitted. "However, there are plans to renew the Society. For this reason we are trying to trace certain records which were consigned to Mischap and Doorn by the then-Secretary, Frons Nisfit. If you could inform us about these documents, we would be most grateful."

Mr. Buffums went to lean against his desk. "That is all very well, but for seven generations we have nurtured a reputation for confidentiality which affects each transaction, large or small. Nothing has changed. We cannot risk any conduct which might involve us in litigation."

"But there is no reason for such concern! Nisfit was authorized to dispose of Society assets and certainly no one questions Mischap and Doorn's conduct."

"That is gratifying news," said Mr. Buffums wryly.

"As I mentioned, we are only trying to recover some of the Society memorabilia."

Mr. Buffums gave his head a slow shake. "These objects will now have been scattered far and wide; at least, such is my opinion."

"That is the worst case," said Wayness. "It is just possible that everything is in the hands of a single collector."

"Your arguments are persuasive," said Mr. Buffums.

Wayness could not contain a gush of optimistic emotion. "Oh, I hope so! I do indeed!"

Mr. Buffums leaned back, smiling his faint smile. "How badly do you want this information?"

Wayness' heart sank. She stared into Buffums' amused face. She said: "I came all the way to Sancelade to speak with you, if that is what you mean."

"Not quite. What I mean is this. If I do a favor for you, then you must do a favor for me. Is that not fair?"

"I'm not sure. What kind of favor do you have in mind?"

"I must explain that I am by way of an amateur dramatist, of not inconsiderable skill, if I say so myself. Already I have several nice little pieces to my credit."

"So then?"

"At the moment I am creating a pastiche of various elements which when merged, scored and edited will generate a most delicious mood. Now then. There is a certain short sequence which so far has resisted my ingenuity. I think that you can help me with it."

"Oh? What must I do?"

"It is simple enough. I take my theme from an old myth. The nymph Ellione falls in love with a statue portraying the hero Leausalas and tries to bring the marble image to life through the fervor of her caresses. Yonder you will notice a marble statue which will serve well enough for a rehearsal. Ignore its priapic condition. Optimally, Leausalas should first seem relaxed, to be gradually aroused by Ellione's attentions. No doubt I will find a way to deal with the problem. In the end, Ellione is encouraged—but enough for the moment. We will begin with the first sequence. If we are agreed, you may disrobe on the dais yonder, while I use the camera."

Wayness tried to speak, but Mr. Buffums paid no heed. He pointed. "Just step up on the dais and slowly remove your clothes. You will quickly become accustomed to the camera. When you are nude, I will issue further instructions. The camera is ready; let us begin the sequence."

Wayness stood stiff and still. She had long been aware that during her quest options of this sort, or even more basic, might be offered her, and she had never precisely defined how far she would go before feeling impelled to draw back. In this case, she found Mr. Buffums offensive and not at all amusing, her response came promptly:

"I'm sorry, Mr. Buffums. I would like to be a great actress and dance in the nude, but my mother and father would disapprove, and of course there is no more to be said."

Mr. Buffums tossed his head, so that his long pale hair flew back. He made an angry sound. "Tschah, but are we not the haughty one? Well then, just so, and let it be! I wish you no misfortune, but I cannot abide vapidity. Leave me, please; you have wasted enough of my time!" He strode to the door, unlocked it and slid it aside. "Our Miss Leepe will show you out." He called through the doorway: "Miss Leepe, this young woman is leaving; I will not see her again, at any time." Mr. Buffums retreated; the door slid shut with a thud.

Wayness marched into the outer office, teeth clenched.

She stopped by Giljin Leepe's desk, looked back over her shoulder, started to speak, but thought better of it.

Giljin Leepe made an airy gesture. "Say anything you like; you won't hurt our feelings. Everyone who knows Bully Buffums wants to kick him at least three times a day."

"I'm so furious I can't think of anything."

Giljin Leepe put on a wise expression. "The interview did not go well?"

Wayness shook her head. "Not at all well. He showed me his art collection, and hinted that he might give me the information I wanted, but first I must dance in the nude. I guess I did everything wrong. When I told him that I was not a good dancer he became surly and sent me away."

"There is no such thing as a typical interview with Bully Buffums," said Giljin Leepe. "Each is unique, and everyone comes away marveling at Bully's behavior."

Nelda spoke from her table across the room. "He is almost certainly impotent."

"Naturally, neither Nelda nor I can cite any direct evidence," said Giljin Leepe.

Wayness heaved a deep sigh and stared bleakly back toward Mr. Buffums' office. "I've probably made a serious mistake. I can't afford to be squeamish. Still, I don't know whether I could bear to disrobe in front of that man or not. It makes me squirm just to look at him."

Giljin Leepe surveyed Wayness with bright inquisitive eyes. "Would you do so if there was no other way of getting your information?"

"I suppose so," said Wayness. "After all, jumping around in my bare skin for a few minutes would not kill me." She paused. "I am not sure it would end there. I suspect that he wanted me to, well, make love to a statue."

"And there you would draw the line?"

Wayness hunched her shoulders. "I don't know. Five minutes? Ten minutes? It's what bad dreams are made of. There must be another way."

"I know the statue," said Giljin Leepe. "It is even a handsome statue. If I wanted to look at it again, I could do so easily." She pulled open the top drawer of her desk. "I have here the key to Bully's office. He thinks he lost it.

Notice! It has a black tip—not that you are at all interested."
She glanced at a clock. "Nelda and I will be leaving in about
half an hour. Bully usually leaves shortly afterwards."

Wayness nodded. "This, of course, is of no interest to
me."

"Of course not. What were you trying to learn from
Bully Buffums?"

Wayness explained what she needed to know.

"Forty years ago? That would be in Bully's CON-A files,
under the code 'OB' for old business. Then 'N,' for 'Naturalist.' It should not be hard to find. Now then—" Giljin Leepe
rose to her feet "—I am about to visit the lavatory. Nelda, as
you can see, has her back turned and is absorbed in her
work. When I return, I will assume that you have left the
premises—though I must point out that if you were standing in the shadows at the back of the bookcase yonder, I
would notice nothing. So now—I will bid you goodbye and
good luck."

"Thank you for your advice," said Wayness. "Thank
you, Nelda."

"You may start toward the door, so that, if Bully should
ask, I can assert that I saw you on your way out."

III.

Giljin Leepe and Nelda were gone. The office was silent. Half an hour passed before Mr. Buffums emerged from his inner chamber. He slid shut the door behind him and carefully locked it, using one of twenty keys dangling from his key ring. Swinging around, he marched across the office to the outer door and was gone. The thud of his footsteps diminished and became part of the silence. The premises were vacant.

Not quite vacant. In the shadows something stirred and shifted. Ten minutes passed and the shape seemed to become restless. Nonetheless it composed itself for a further period of waiting, lest Mr. Buffums, discovering that he had forgotten an important document, should return to repair the lack.

Another fifteen minutes passed. Wayness stole furtively from the shadows. "It is no longer Wayness Tamm the Naturalist," she told herself. "It is now Wayness Tamm the burglar. Still, burgling is better than dancing for Mr. Buffums." She moved to Giljin Leepe's desk and availed herself of the key with the black tip. She noted the telephone switch panel at the side of the desk and resisted the whimsical impulse to call her Uncle Pirie and announce her new avocation. Wayness became vexed with herself. "I am starting to be giddy. It is probably nervous hysteria. I must put a stop to it."

Wayness went to the door at the back of the room. She fitted the key and eased open the door: inch by inch by inch. With skin tingling she listened but heard only silence; the collection, no matter how rich, dark and heavy its essences, could create no sound.

Wayness slipped into Mr. Buffums' office. Taking the key from the lock, she slid the door shut and went briskly to Mr. Buffums' desk, sparing a single wary glance toward the marble statue.

Wayness seated herself before the communicator. She studied the keyboard a moment; all seemed standard. She indicated CON-A, then 'OB,' to bring an alphabetical directory to the screen. She struck 'N,' to elicit another directory. She wrote 'Naturalist Society' and was provided a tabular listing, which included as categories: 'Correspondence,' 'Parcels, Description,' 'Parcels, Disposition' and finally: 'Subsequences.'

Wayness looked into 'Parcels, Description,' and almost at once discovered the notation pertaining to Frons Nisfit and his dealings. The items listed were numerous, and ended with 'Miscellaneous Papers and Documents.'

A box at the bottom of the listing, labeled 'Comments,' contained the remark: 'I have notified Ector van Broude, fellow of the Society, in regard to these transactions, which seem notably unwise. E. Faldeker.'

Wayness brought to the screen the category 'Parcels, Disposition.' The information she sought was contained in a single sentence: 'This entire lot has been consigned to Gohoon Galleries.'

Wayness stared at the words. So there she had it! 'Gohoon Galleries'!

She jerked her head around: what was that? A tremor, a near-inaudible thud? Wayness sat stiff, head tilted to listen.

Silence.

A sound from outside, thought Wayness. She turned back to the screen and brought up the contents of the 'Subsequences' file.

She discovered two entries. The first was dated twelve years previously: "Request to view made on this date by off-world woman identifying herself as Violja Fanfarides. No conflict of interest perceived; request granted."

The second entry bore the current date and read: "Request to view made on this date by off-world young woman, identifying herself as Wayness Tamm, Assistant Secretary of the Naturalist Society. Circumstances suspicious; request denied."

Wayness stared at the remark, infuriated anew. Again she jerked her head around to listen. This time there was no mistake. Someone was at the door. In a single movement Wayness switched off the screen and dropped to her knees behind the desk.

The door slid open; Mr. Buffums entered the chamber, carrying a large parcel in his arms. Wayness shrank down, making herself as inconspicuous as possible. If he approached, she would surely be discovered.

Incommoded by the parcel, Mr. Buffums had left the door open; Wayness tensed herself, ready to dash for the outer office. But Mr. Buffums had turned in the opposite direction. Peering around the desk Wayness saw that he had carried his parcel to a table in the left part of the chamber and had started to remove the wrappings.

Wayness watched covertly. His back was turned. She rose from behind the desk; on stealthy feet she tiptoed to the door and with vast relief passed through. Noticing Mr. Buffums' key ring dangling from the lock, Wayness gently closed the door and locked it with a double turn so that it could not be opened from within. It seemed a fine prank to play on Mr. Buffums. She hoped that he would be extremely inconvenienced and very much puzzled.

Wayness went to Giljin Leepe's desk, where she replaced the key with the black tip. Again she glanced at the telephone switch-panel and studied it for a moment. She pushed two toggles, and turned a switch; Mr. Buffums would now be denied the use of his telephone and would be unable to call anyone for assistance. Wayness laughed aloud. It was, all in all, a good day's work.

Wayness returned to the Marsac Hotel. She immediately telephoned Giljin Leepe, using a blank screen.

"Giljin here," said a cheerful voice.

"This is an anonymous call. You may be interested to know that by some peculiar accident Mr. Buffums has locked himself into his office, with his keys on the outside of the door. Hence he cannot get out."

"Yes," said Giljin Leepe. "I consider that interesting news. I will stop answering my telephone, and I will suggest to Nelda that she do the same; otherwise he will insist that one or another of us come to liberate him!"

"There is more interesting news. By accident his telephone has been connected to the instrument on Nelda's desk, and he will be unable to make his wishes known until someone arrives in the morning."

"What a strange situation!" said Giljin Leepe. "Mr. Buffums will surely be perplexed and probably annoyed, for he is not a stoic person. He suspects no intruder?"

"Not to my knowledge."

"Good. In the morning I will carefully put everything to rights, and Mr. Buffums will be more bewildered than ever."

IV.

After her call to Giljin Leepe, Wayness consulted the hotel's directories and learned that 'Gohoon Galleries' was still a viable concern, that its business was auctioneering, and that its offices were located in Sancelade, readily accessible to her inquiries, which she would continue tomorrow.

The time was late afternoon. Wayness sat in a corner of the hotel lobby, flipping through the pages of a fashionable journal. She became restless and, slipping into her long gray cloak, went out to walk along the promenade which bordered the River Pang. A breeze from the west, where the sun was setting, flapped the fabric of her cloak, rustled leaves in the plane trees, and sent a million little waves scurrying across the water.

Wayness walked slowly and watched the sun drop behind the far hills. With the coming of twilight, the breeze died to a whisper and then was gone; the wavelets on the river disappeared. A few other folk were abroad: elderly couples, lovers who had made rendezvous along the riverbank, occasionally a person as solitary as herself.

Wayness paused to look out across the river, where the pale lavender-gray sky was reflected along the moving surface. She tossed a stone into the water and watched the black whorls dissipate. Her mood was unsettled. "I have had some success, true. I am not altogether ineffectual, which I suppose is good news. But after that—" The name 'Violja Fanfarides' suddenly intruded. "I wonder ..." Wayness grimaced. "Odd. I feel queasy inside, as if I were coming down sick." She brooded for a few moments, then put the name aside. "I suspect that Mr. Buffums and his 'curiosa' have affected me more than I might have liked. I hope there will be no lasting effect upon my personality."

Wayness went to sit on a bench and watched the afterglow fade from the sky. She remembered her conversation with Pirie Tamm on the subject of sunsets. Surely on Cadwal she had known sunsets as mild and serene as this! Perhaps. That particular shade of twilight gray, after all, was not absolutely unique. Still, one would be a thing of Earth and the other of Cadwal, and so they would be distinct.

The stars began to appear. Wayness looked around the sky, hoping to find the racked 'W' of Cassiopeia, which would guide her toward Perseus, but the foliage of a nearby plane tree blocked her view.

Wayness rose to her feet and started back toward the hotel. She found herself in a more practical frame of mind. "I will bathe and change into something frivolous, and then it will be time for dinner, and I am already beginning to feel hungry."

V.

In the morning Wayness dressed once again in her dark brown suit and after breakfast rode the slideway to Gohoon Galleries, in Clarmond, at the western edge of Sancelade. Here a few of Tybalt Pimm's most rigorous tenets had been relaxed. The buildings surrounding Beiderbecke Circus rose to heights of ten or twelve stories. In one of these structures Gohoon Galleries occupied the first three floors.

At the entrance a pair of uniformed guards, one male, the other female, photographed Wayness from three sides, and took note of her name, age, home and local address as stated on her identification papers. Wayness inquired the reason for such precautions.

"It is not arbitrary nuisance-mongering," she was told. "We display much valuable merchandise for viewing prior to the auctions. Some of these articles are small and easily purloined. Cameras record such acts, and we can instantly identify the offenders and regain our property. The system, while strict, is efficient."

"Interesting," said Wayness. "I had not planned to steal anything; now the thought is farther from my mind than ever."

"That is the effect we are trying to achieve!"

"As it happens, I have come only for information. Where must I apply?"

"Information regarding what?"

"A sale conducted here some years ago."

"Try the Office of Records, on the third floor."

"Thank you."

Wayness ascended to the third floor, crossed a foyer and passed through a wide archway into the Office of Records: a room of considerable extent, divided down the middle by a counter. A dozen persons stood by the counter, studying large black-bound tomes, or waiting to be served by the single attendant: a small crooked man of advanced years, who nevertheless moved with alertness and dexterity: listening to requests, disappearing into a back room to emerge with one or more of the large black tomes. Another attendant, a woman almost as old, issued from the back room from time to time pushing a cart, which she loaded with books no longer in use and returned them into the back room.

The white-haired old clerk scuttled back and forth at a run as if he were fearful of losing his job, though it seemed to Wayness that he was doing the work of three men. She went to stand at the counter and was presently approached by the clerk. "Yes, Miss?"

"I am interested in a consignment from Mischap and Doorn, which was subsequently auctioned off."

"And what would be the date?"

"It would be quite some time ago, perhaps forty years or more."

"What was the nature of the consignment?"

"Material from the Naturalist Society."

"Where is your authorization?"

Wayness smiled. "I am Assistant Secretary of the Society, and I will write you out one at once, if you like."

The clerk raised his tufted white eyebrows. "I see that I am dealing with an important personage. Your identification will suffice."

Wayness displayed her official papers, which the clerk examined. "Cadwal, eh? Where is that?"

"It's out beyond Perseus, at the tip of Mircea's Wisp."

"Fancy that! It must be a fine thing to travel far and wide! But then, a man can't be everywhere at once." Twisting his head sidewise he cocked a bright blue eye at Wayness. "And, do you know, sometimes I find it hard to be anywhere at all." He scribbled a few words on a slip of

paper. "Let me see what I can find." He scuttled off. Two
minutes later he reappeared, carrying a black-bound tome
which he placed in front of Wayness. From a pocket inside
the front cover he brought a card. "Sign your name, if you
please." He tendered her a stylus. "Briskly now; the day is
not long enough for all I must do."

Wayness took the stylus and looked down the names on
the card. The first few were unfamiliar. The last name, signed
after a date twelve years old, was: 'Simonetta Clattuc.'

The clerk tapped his fingers on the counter; Wayness
signed the card. The clerk took card and stylus and moved
to the next person waiting.

With nervous fingers Wayness turned the heavy pages
of the volume, and in due course came upon the page
labeled:

Code: 777-ARP; Sub-code: M/D;
Naturalist Society/Frons Nisfit, Secretary.
Agent: Mischap and Doorn.
Three parcels:
(1) Art Goods, Drawings, Curios.
(2) Books, texts, references.
(3) Miscellaneous documents.
Parcel (1), itemized.

Wayness let her eyes slide down the page, and the next
page, on which were catalogued a large number of oddities,
art objects and curios, each tagged with the price it had
brought at the auction, the name and address of the buyer,
and sometimes a coded notation.

On the third page Parcel (2) was similarly summarized.
Wayness turned to the fourth page, where the items of
parcel (3) would be catalogued, but the goods offered for
auction were stated to be the estate of a certain Jahaim
Nestor.

Wayness turned the page back, read carefully, searched
through pages back and forth. To no avail. The page
describing 'Parcel (3), Miscellaneous Documents' was gone.

Wayness, looking closely, saw where a sharp blade had

excised the page at its inner border, after which it had been removed.

The clerk came trotting past; Wayness signaled him to a halt. "Yes?"

"By any chance, are duplicate records available?"

The clerk produced a whinny of sardonic laughter. "Now why would you be wanting reiterations of the very same matter which is here before your eyes?"

Wayness said meekly: "If these records were incorrect, or disordered, then a duplicate set might have them right."

"And I would be running twice as far and twice as fast, with everybody wanting two books instead of one. And should we find a difference then we have the grandest farraw of all, with one claiming one way and another claiming the opposite. Never and by no means! A mistake in the text is like a fly in the soup; the clever man simply works his way around it. No, Miss! Enough is enough! This is an Office of Information, not Dreamy Cuckoo-land."

Wayness looked numbly down at the book. The trail had come to an end and she had nowhere to go.

For a space Wayness sat motionless, then she straightened and stood upright. Nothing more could be said; nothing more could be done. She closed the book, left a sol for the comfort of the over-worked clerk, and departed.

CHAPTER V

I.

"A most discouraging denouement to your quest," said Pirie Tamm. "Still, there is a positive element to the situation."

Wayness made no comment. Pirie Tamm elucidated. "On this basis. Monette, Violja Fanfarides, Simonetta Clattuc—whatever she calls herself—gained important information, but it has brought her no perceptible benefit, since the grant has not been re-registered. This must be regarded as a good omen."

"Omen or not, there was only a single trail, and she wiped it out of existence."

Pirie Tamm took a pear from the bowl at the center of the table and began to peel it. "So now," he mused, "you will go back to Cadwal?"

Wayness burnt her uncle Pirie with a brief smoldering glance. "Of course not! You know me better than that!"

Pirie Tamm sighed. "So I do. You are a most determined young lady. But determination by itself is not enough."

"I am not totally without resources," said Wayness. "I copied the pages pertaining to Parcels One and Two."

"Indeed! Why so?"

"At the time I was not thinking clearly, and perhaps my subconscious was in charge. Now it occurs to me that someone who bought from Parcels One or Two might also have bought from Parcel Three."

"A clever idea, though the odds are not good. It has

been a long time and many of the individuals at the sale
will be hard to find."

"They would be my last resort. Five institutions were
represented at the sale: a foundation, a university and
three museums."

"We can make inquiries in the morning by telephone,"
said Pirie Tamm. "It is but, at best and at worst, a forlorn
hope."

II.

In the morning Wayness consulted the World Directory and discovered that, of the five institutions she had listed, all were still functional. She called each in turn, on the telephone, and in each case asked to be connected to the officer in charge of special collections.

At the Berwash Foundation for the Study of Alternate Vitalities, she was informed that the collections included several compendiums produced by Fellows of the Naturalist Society, all descriptive and anatomical studies of nonterrestrial life forms, and also three rare works by William Charles Schulz: THE LAST AND FIRST EQUATION AND EVERYTHING ELSE; DISCORD, GRINDING AND SLOPE: WHY MATHEMATICS AND THE COSMOS MAKE POOR FITS; and the PAN-MATHEMATIKON. The curator asked: "The Naturalist Society is perhaps preparing to make another donation?"

"Not at the present time," said Wayness.

The Cornelis Pameijer Museum of Natural History owned a set of six volumes describing a variety of alien homologues created by the dynamics of parallel evolution. The six volumes had been designed and published by the Naturalist Society. The Museum supported no other collection of Society documents or papers.

The Pythagorean Museum owned four monographs upon the abstruse subject of nonhuman music and sonic symbolism, by Peter Bullis, Eli Newberger, Stanford Vincent and Captain R. Pilsbury.

The Bodleian Library owned a single volume of sketches depicting the generation of the quasi-living crystals of the world Tranque, Bellatrix V.

The Funusti Memorial Museum at Kiev, at the edge of the Great Altaic Steppe, lacked a formally designated information officer, but after consultation between museum functionaries, Wayness was transferred to a somber young curator with a long pallid face, coal-black hair which he wore brushed severely back from his high narrow forehead. While clearly of an earnest disposition, he seemed to find Wayness agreeable, in both semblance and conduct. He listened with careful attention to her questions and was able to provide information at once. Yes, the Museum's extensive collections included several treatises produced by members of the Naturalist Society, analyzing various aspects of non-terrestrial communication. He mentioned in passing, almost as an afterthought, a separate collection of antique papers, still incompletely collated, but which definitely included records, registers and other documents from the files of the ancient Naturalist Society. The collection was generally not open to public inspection, but it was impossible to include an officer of the Naturalist Society in this category, and Wayness would be allowed to study the collection at her convenience.

This would be immediately, said Wayness, since she wished to compile a general bibliography of all such material for the use of the rejuvenated Society. The curator approved of the idea, and identified himself as Lefaun Zadoury. Upon her arrival he would give Wayness every possible assistance, so he assured her.

"Let me ask one last question," said Wayness. "Within the last twelve years has a woman by the name of Simonetta Clattuc, or possibly Violja Fanfarides, or Monette, looked over this material?"

Lefaun Zadoury, thinking the question a trifle odd, arched his black eyebrows, then turned aside to consult his records. "Definitely not."

"That is good news," said Wayness, and the discussion ended on a cordial basis.

III.

Almost effervescent with hope, Wayness took herself far to the north and east, over mountains, lakes and rivers and finally down upon the great Altaic Steppe and the ancient city Kiev.

The Funusti Museum occupied the grandiose precincts of the old Konevitsky Palace on Murom Hill, at the back of Kiev's Old Town. Wayness took lodging at the Mazeppa Hotel, and was shown into a suite of rooms paneled in pale brown chestnut, decorated with red and blue floral designs. Her windows overlooked Prince Bogdan Yurevich Kolsky Square: a roughly pentagonal area paved with slabs of pink-gray granite. On three sides, two cathedrals and a monastery, lovingly restored or perhaps reconstructed in the ancient style, held aloft dozens of onion-domes, gilded with gold foil, or painted red, blue, green, or in spiral stripes.

Wayness read from a pamphlet she found on a nearby table: "The structures to be perceived at various sides of Kolsky Square are exact replications of the original structures, and have been rebuilt with careful attention to the Old Slavic style, using traditional materials and methods.

"To the right is Saint Sophia's Cathedral with nineteen domes. At the center is Saint Andrew's Church of eleven domes, and to the left is Saint Michael's Monastery, with only nine domes. The cathedral and the church are lavishly decorated with mosaics, statues and other bedizenment of gold and jewels. Old Kiev suffered many devastations, and

Kolsky Square has witnessed many awful incidents. But today, visitors from across the Gaean Reach come only to marvel at the inspiring architecture and at the power of priests who were able to wring so much wealth from a land at that time so poor."

The wan sunlight of mid-afternoon illuminated the old square; many folk were abroad, clasping their coats, mantles and cloaks tightly about themselves against the gusts of wind which blew down from the hills. Wayness started to telephone the Funusti Museum, then thought better of it; nothing could be gained by calling so late in the day. Lefaun Zadoury had already been extremely helpful and she did not want him to suggest that he meet her somewhere and show her the sights of the city.

Wayness went out alone on the square and looked into Saint Sophia's Cathedral, then dined at Restaurant Carpathia on lentil soup, wild boar with mushrooms and hazelnut torte.

Leaving the restaurant, Wayness discovered that twilight had fallen over the city. Old Kolsky Square was windy, dark and deserted; she crossed to the Mazeppa Hotel in complete solitude. "It is as if I were sailing across the ocean in a small boat," she told herself.

In the morning she telephoned Lefaun Zadoury at the Funusti Museum. As before, he seemed to be wearing a voluminous black gown, which Wayness thought rather odd and fusty. "Wayness Tamm here," she told the long somber face. "If you remember, I called you from Fair Winds, near Shillawy."

"Of course I remember! You are here more quickly than I had expected. Are you coming to the museum?"

"If it is convenient."

"One time is as good as another! I shall look forward to seeing you; in fact, I will try to meet you in the loggia."

Lefaun Zadoury's enthusiasm, muted as it was, assured Wayness that her decision not to call Funusti Museum the previous afternoon had been correct.

A cab took Wayness north along Sorka Boulevard with the Dnieper River to the right and a row of massive apartment blocks of concrete and glass to the left, with tier upon tier of other apartment blocks ranged along the hills behind. The cab at last turned up a side road, wound up the hillside and halted in front of a massive structure, overlooking the river and the steppe beyond.

"The Funusti Museum," said the cab driver. "Once the palace of Prince Konevitsky, where the lords dined on fine meats and honeycakes by day and danced the fandango by night. Now it is quiet as the grave, a place where everyone walks on tiptoe and wears black. And should one dare to belch one must crawl under a table to hide. Which, then, is better: the joys of splendor and grace, or the black shame of pedantry and mingering? The question supplies its own answer."

Wayness alighted from the cab. "I see that you are something of a philosopher."

"True! It is in my blood! But first and foremost, I am a Cossack!"

"And what is a Cossack?"

The driver stared incredulously. "Can I believe my ears? But now I see that you are an off-worlder. Well then, a Cossack is a natural aristocrat; he is fearless and steadfast, and cannot be coerced. Even as a cab driver he conducts himself with Cossack dignity. At the end of a journey, he does not calculate his fare; he announces the first figure that comes into his head. If the passenger does not choose to pay, well then: what of that? The driver gives him a single glance of contempt and drives off in disdain."

"Interesting. And what fare are you calling out to me?"

"Three sols."

"That is far too much. Here is a sol. You may accept it or drive off in disdain."

"Since you are an off-worlder, and do not understand these things, I will take the money. Shall I wait? There is nothing here of interest; you will be in and out in a trice."

"No such luck," said Wayness. "I must pore over some tiresome old papers and I cannot guess how long I will be."

"As you wish."

Wayness crossed the front terrace and entered a marble-floored loggia which seemed alive with echoes. Gilded pilasters stood along the wall; above hung an enormous chandelier of ten thousand crystals. Wayness looked here and there but saw no sign of Lefaun Zadoury the curator. Then, as if from nowhere, a tall gaunt figure appeared, marching across the loggia at a bent-kneed lope, his black gown fluttering behind. He halted and looked down at Wayness, lank black hair, black eyebrows and black eyes at stark contrast to his white skin. He spoke in a voice without accent: "The chances are good that you are Wayness Tamm."

"Quite good. And you are Lefaun Zadoury?"

The curator responded with a measured nod. He studied Wayness from head to toe, then back to head. He gave a gentle sigh and shook his head. "Amazing."

"How so?"

"You are younger and less imposing than the person I might have expected."

"Next time I will send my mother."

Lefaun Zadoury's long bony jaw dropped. "I spoke incautiously! In essence—"

"It is no great matter." Wayness looked around the octagonal loggia. "This is an impressive chamber. I had not imagined such grandeur!"

"Yes, it is well enough." Lefaun Zadoury glanced about the room as if seeing it for the first time. "The chandelier is absurd, of course—a behemoth of large expense and little illumination. Someday it will fall in a great splintering jangle and kill someone."

"That would be a pity."

"Yes, no doubt. In general, the Konevitskys lacked good taste. The marble tiles, for example, are banal. The pilasters are out of scale and of the wrong order."

"Really! I had not noticed."

"The museum itself transcends such deficiencies. We have the world's finest collection of Sassanian intaglios, a great deal of absolutely unique Minoan glass, and we own the complete sequence of the Leonie Bismaie miniatures. Our Department of Semantic Equivalences is also considered excellent."

"It must be inspiring to work in such an atmosphere," said Wayness politely.

Lefaun Zadoury made a gesture which might have meant anything. "Well then—shall we look to our own business?"

"Yes, of course."

"Come, if you please. We must fit you into a proper gown, like my own. This is the uniform of the museum. Don't ask me to explain; all I know is that you will be conspicuous otherwise."

"Whatever you say," Wayness followed Lefaun Zadoury into a side chamber. From a rack he selected a black gown which he held up against Wayness. "Too long." He chose another gown. "This will serve well enough, though both material and cut leave much to be desired."

Wayness draped herself in the gown. "I feel different already."

"We will pretend that it is of the finest Kurian weave and the most stylish cut. Would you like a cup of tea and an almond cake? Or do you want to go directly to work?"

"I am anxious to look at your collections," said Wayness. "A cup of tea later, perhaps."

"So it shall be. The material is on the second floor."

Lefaun Zadoury led the way up a sweeping marble staircase, along several tall corridors lined with shelves, at last into a room with a long heavy table at the center. Black-gowned curators and other museum personnel sat at the table, reading documents and making notes; others occupied small alcoves working at information screens; still others padded here and there carrying books, portfolios, a variety of other small articles. The room was silent; despite so much activity, nothing could be heard but the rustle of black cloth, the sound of paper sliding across paper, the pad of soft slippers upon the floor. Zadoury took Wayness into a room to the side and closed the door. "Now we can talk without disturbing the others." He gave Wayness a sheet of paper. "I have listed the articles in our Naturalist collection. It comprises three categories. Perhaps if you explained your interest and what you were looking for, I could help you more efficiently."

"It is a complicated story," said Wayness. "Forty years ago a secretary of the Society disposed of some important papers, including receipts and proofs of payment, which have now come into question. If I could locate these papers, the Society would benefit greatly."

"I understand completely. If you can describe these papers, I will help you look."

Wayness smilingly shook her head. "I will know them when I see them. I'm afraid that I must do the work myself."

"Very well," said Lefaun Zadoury. "The first category, as you can see, consists of sixteen monographs, all devoted to semantic research."

Wayness recognized this to be the parcel which the museum had bought at the Gohoon auction.

"The second category deals with the genealogy of the Counts de Flamanges.

"The third category, 'Miscellaneous Documents and Papers,' has never been collated and, so I suspect, will interest you more. Am I right?"

"You are right."

"In that case, I will requisition the materials and bring them here. Compose yourself for a few minutes, if you please."

Lefaun Zadoury left the room, and in due course returned, pushing a cart. He unloaded three cases to the table. "Do not be alarmed," he told Wayness, his manner almost jocular. "None of the cases are full to the brim. And now, since you reject my help, I will leave you to yourself."

At the door Lefaun Zadoury touched a plaque and a small red light appeared. "I am required to activate the monitors. We have had some unfortunate experiences in the past."

Wayness shrugged. "Monitor all you like; my intentions are innocent."

"I'm sure of it," said Lefaun Zadoury. "But not everyone demonstrates your many virtues."

Wayness darted him a speculative glance. "You are very gallant! But now I must go to work."

Lefaun Zadoury left the room, obviously pleased with himself. Wayness turned to the table. She thought: "I might not be so innocent and many-virtued if I caught sight of the Charter or the Grant. We shall see."

The first of the cases contained thirty-five neatly bound pamphlets, each a biographical study of one of the founders of the Naturalist Society.

"Sad!" mused Wayness. "These tracts should be back in the care of the Naturalist Society. Not that anyone would ever read them."

Certain of the volumes, so Wayness noticed, showed signs of hard usage, and their pages in some cases were annotated.

The names involved were meaningless; Wayness gave her attention to the second case. She found several treatises dealing with the genealogy and connections of the Counts de Flamanges across a span of two thousand years.

Wayness gave her mouth a twitch of disappointment and turned to the third case, though she had lost hope of finding anything significant. The contents of the third case were miscellaneous papers, newspaper clippings and photographs, all relating to the proposed construction of a spacious and beautiful edifice, to house the general offices of the Naturalist Society. Within the structure ample space existed for a College of Naturalistic Science, Art and Philosophy; a museum and monstratory; and possibly even a variety of vivaria, where life forms of far worlds might be studied in a near-native environment. Advocates of the scheme spoke of the reputation which would accrue to the Society; opponents decried the vast expense and wondered as to the need for such an expansive facility. Many pledged large sums to the proposal; Count Blaise de Flamanges offered a tract of three hundred acres from his estates in the Moholc.

Enthusiasm for the project climaxed a few years before Frons Nisfit's arrival on the scene, but the fervor waned, when full financial support for the scheme was not forthcoming, and finally Count Blaise de Flamanges withdrew his offer of land and the concept was abandoned.

Wayness stood back in disgust. She had come upon not so much as a mention of either Cadwal, the Cadwal Charter or the Grant. Once again the trail had met a dead end.

Lefaun Zadoury reappeared. He looked from Wayness to the cases. "And how go your researches?"

"Not well."

Lefaun Zadoury went to the table, glanced into the cases and opened a few of the books and pamphlets. "Interesting—or so I suppose. This sort of stuff is not my specialty. In any case, the time for refreshment has arrived. Are you ready for a cup of good yellow tea and perhaps a biscuit? Such small pleasures enhance our existence!"

"I am ready for some enhanced existence. Can we leave these documents in the open? Or will I be scolded by the monitor?"

Lefaun Zadoury glanced toward the red light, but it could no longer be seen. "The system has gone awry. You could have stolen the moon and no one would have noticed. Come along, all the same; the documents will be safe."

Lefaun Zadoury escorted Wayness to a small noisy lunch room where Museum personnel sat at spindly little tables drinking tea. Everyone wore black gowns and Wayness saw that she would have been conspicuous indeed in her ordinary clothes.

The dismal garments affected neither the volume nor the pace of conversation; everyone talked at once, pausing only long enough to swallow gulps of tea from earthenware mugs.

Lefaun Zadoury found a vacant table and they were served tea and cakes. Lefaun looked to right and left apologetically. "The splendor and the luxury, as well as the best cakes, are reserved for the big-wigs, who use Prince Konevitsky's grand dining room. I have seen them at it. Each uses three knives and four forks to eat his herring, and wipes the grease from his face with a napkin two feet square. The riffraff like ourselves must be content with less, though still we pay fifteen pence for our snack."

Wayness said gravely: "I am an off-worlder and perhaps naive, but it seems not all so bad. For a fact, in one of my cakes I found no less than four almonds!"

Lefaun Zadoury gave a dour grunt. "The subject is complex and yields only to careful analysis."

Wayness had no comment to make and the two sat in silence. A young man of frail physique, so that he seemed almost lost inside his black gown, came up to mutter into

Lefaun Zadoury's ear. Untidy wisps of blond hair fell over his forehead; his eyes were watery blue and his complexion was bad; Wayness wondered if he might not be in poor health. He spoke with nervous intensity, tapping the fingers of one hand into the palm of the other.

Wayness' thoughts wandered, into regions of gloom and discouragement. The morning's work had produced no new information and the trail which had led by fits and starts from the Society to the Funusti Museum had come to a dead end. Where next? In theory, she could try to trace each of the names on the Gohoon listings, on the chance that one had possibly bought from the third parcel, but the work was so immoderately large and the chances of success so small that she put the project out of her mind. She became aware that Lefaun Zadoury and his friend were discussing her, each in turn murmuring into the other's ear. After delivering his opinion, each would turn a surreptitious glance toward her, as if to verify his remark. Smiling to herself, Wayness pretended to ignore them. She reflected upon the scheme to erect a magnificent new headquarters for the Naturalist Society. A pity that the project had come to naught! Almost certainly Frons Nisfit would never have found such easy scope for plunder. She mused further and a new idea began to tick in her mind.

Lefaun Zadoury's friend went his way; Wayness watched him sidle off across the lunchroom, arms and elbows jerking erratically to the side.

Lefaun Zadoury turned back to Wayness. "A good fellow, that! His name is Tadiew Skander; have you ever heard of him?"

"Not that I know of."

Lefaun Zadoury gave his fingers a condescending fillip. "There are —"

Wayness interrupted him. "Excuse me a moment, please. I must check a reference."

"Of course!" Leaning back in his chair Lefaun Zadoury folded his hands on his chest, and watched Wayness with dispassionate curiosity.

Wayness looked into a pocket of her shoulder-bag and extracted the pages she had copied at Gohoon Galleries, listing the items in Parcels One and Two. She glanced under her eyelashes toward Lefaun Zadoury, his gaze was as impassive as ever. Wayness twisted her mouth into a crooked wince and shifted her position in the chair; the scrutiny was causing her skin to crawl. She frowned, twitched her nose and thereafter ignored Lefaun Zadoury as best she could.

Wayness carefully studied the lists, one after the other, and was gratified to find that her memory had been accurate: none of the three cases she had studied in the museum workroom were represented on the Gohoon list: no works of genealogy, nor biographical studies, nor yet documents pertaining to a new headquarters for the Naturalist Society.

Odd, thought Wayness. Why was there no correspondence?

The implications of the discovery suddenly struck Wayness. She felt a tingle of excitement. Since the material had not come from Gohoon, it had come from somewhere else.

Where, then?

And of equal importance: when? Since if the Funusti's acquisition had been made before Nisfit's tenure, then the whole question became moot.

Wayness tucked the lists back into her shoulder-bag and considered Lefaun Zadoury, who met her gaze with the same imperturbable expression as before.

"I must get back to my work," said Wayness.

"As you like." Lefaun Zadoury rose to his feet. "There were no extras. You need pay thirty pence only."

Wayness darted him a quick glance but made no comment and placed three coins on the table. The two returned to the workroom. Lefaun Zadoury made a grand gesture toward the table. "Notice, if you please! It is as I said! Nothing has been disturbed!"

"I am relieved," said Wayness. "If anything were amiss, I might be held responsible and severely punished."

Lefaun Zadoury pursed his lips. "Such incidents are rare."

"I am lucky to have the benefit of such expert advice,"

said Wayness. "Your knowledge would seem to be compre-
hensive."

Lefaun Zadoury said judiciously, "At the very least I try
to function with professional competence."

"Would you know how and when the Museum acquired
this material?"

Lefaun Zadoury blew out his cheeks. "No. But I can find
out in short order, if you are interested."

"I am interested."

"Just a moment, then." Lefaun Zadoury stalked into
the adjoining room and seated himself in one of the alcoves
before an information screen. He worked the controls,
studied the screen, gave his head a jerk, signalizing the flux
of information from the screen into his brain. Wayness
watched from the doorway.

Lefaun Zadoury rose to his feet and returned to the
workroom. Carefully he closed the door, and stood as if
mulling over a set of complicated ideas. Wayness waited
patiently. At last she asked: "What did you learn?"

"Nothing."

Wayness tried to keep her voice from becoming a
squeak. "Nothing?"

"I learned that the information is not available, if that
suits you better. We are dealing with the gift of an anonymous donor."

"Ridiculous!" Wayness muttered. "I can't understand
such secrecy!"

"Neither the Funusti Museum nor the universe at large
is an inherently logical place," said Lefaun Zadoury. "Are
you finished with this material?"

"Not yet. I must think."

Lefaun Zadoury remained in the room, standing half-
expectantly, or so it seemed to Wayness. What could he be
waiting for? She put a tentative question: "Is the information known to anyone at the museum?"

Lefaun Zadoury raised his eyes toward the ceiling. "I
should think that one of the pombahs in the GEP—that's
the Office of Gifts, Endowments and Procurements—keeps
a compendium of such information. It would be highly
inaccessible, of course."

Wayness said thoughtfully: "I myself might offer a small endowment to the museum if I were supplied this trifling bit of information."

"Even impossible things are thinkable," said Lefaun Zadoury. "But now we are dealing with persons in high places, and they hardly turn their heads to spit for less than a thousand sols."

"Ha! That is totally out of the question. I can endow a sum of ten sols, with another ten to you for your expert counsel: twenty sols in all."

Lefaun threw up his hands in shock. "How could I mention a sum so paltry to the exalted personage whom I would need to consult?"

"It seems very simple to me. Point out that a few words and ten sols is better than dead silence and no sols."

"True," said Lefaun. "Well then, so be it. In view of our friendly association I will risk making a fool of myself. Excuse me for a few minutes." Lefaun Zadoury departed the room. Wayness went to the table and surveyed the three cases. Biographies of thirty-five early Naturalists, genealogical data, and documents relating to the construction of palatial new headquarters for the Society: nothing she cared to re-examine at the moment.

Ten minutes passed. Lefaun Zadoury returned to the room. For a few seconds he stood appraising Wayness with a faint smile which she found unsettling. Finally she told herself: "In anyone else that would be considered a saturnine, or cynical, leer, but I believe that Lefaun Zadoury is merely trying to present an affable, debonair image." Aloud she said: "You seem pleased. What did you learn?"

Lefaun came forward. "I was right, of course. The official sneered at me and asked if I had been born yesterday. I told him no, that I was trying to oblige a charming young lady, and with that he relented, though he insisted that the entire endowment, all twenty sols, be paid into his control. Naturally, I had no choice but to agree. Perhaps you will wish to make an adjustment." He waited, but Wayness said nothing. Lefaun's smile slowly drained away, leaving his face as morose as ever. "In any case, you must now pay the stipulated sum over to me."

Wayness stared in wonder. "Really, Mr. Zadoury! That is not the way things are done!"

"How so?"

"When you bring me the information, and I verify it, then I will make the endowment."

"Bah!" grumbled Lefaun. "What is the use of so much rigmarole?"

"Simple enough. Once money is paid over, no one is ever in any hurry, and meanwhile I sit waiting in the Mazeppa Hotel for days on end."

"Hmf," sniffed Lefaun. "Why is the name of this donor so important?"

Wayness patiently explained. "In order to renew the Society, we need the help of old Naturalist families."

"Are these names not listed among Society records?"

"The records were damaged some time ago by an irresponsible Secretary. Now we are trying to repair this damage."

"To destroy records is a crime against reason! Luckily, everything that has been written once has probably been written ten times."

"I hope so," said Wayness. "It is why I am here."

Lefaun pondered for a moment, then spoke, somewhat abruptly: "The situation is more complicated than you might think. The information will not reach me until this evening."

"That is inconvenient."

"Not necessarily!" declared Lefaun in a sudden burst of enthusiasm. "I will take advantage of the occasion to show you the sights and sounds of Old Kiev! It will be an important evening, which you will never forget!"

Wayness, feeling the need for support, leaned back against the table. "I would not think of putting you to so much trouble. You might bring the information to my hotel, or I will come to the museum early tomorrow."

Lefaun held up his hand. "Not another word! It will be my great pleasure!"

Wayness sighed. "What do you have in mind?"

"First, we shall dine at the Pripetskaya, which specializes in reed-birds on the spit. But first: a dish of jellied eels dressed with caviar. Nor will we neglect the Mingrelian venison, in currant sauce."

"All this sounds expensive," said Wayness. "Who is paying?"

Lefaun Zadoury blinked. "It occurred to me that since you are spending Society funds—"

"But I am not spending Society funds."

"Well then, we can share expenses. This is my usual habit when I dine in company with my friends."

"I have an even better idea," said Wayness. "I seldom eat much for dinner; certainly not eels and birds and wild animals. So we shall each settle our own account."

"On second thought, we will go to Lena's Bistro, where cabbage rolls are both cheap and tasty."

Wayness told herself philosophically that, after all, she had nothing better to do. "Whatever you like. When and where do we receive the information?"

" 'Information'?" Lefaun was momentarily puzzled. "Ah yes. At Lena's; that will be the place."

"Why Lena's? Why not here and now?"

"These things must be arranged. It is a delicate business."

Wayness made a dubious sound. "It seems most peculiar. In any case, I must be back early at my hotel."

Lefaun spoke with heavy jocularity: "Do not kill the bull before the cow is fresh! Let us see what we shall see!"

Wayness compressed her lips. "Perhaps it will be better, after all, if I simply come here tomorrow morning; then you may stay out as late as you please. Remember, I need verification, unless you bring me a print-out copied from official Museum records."

Lefaun bowed with exaggerated deference. "I will call for you at your hotel early this evening—shall we say eight o'clock?"

"That is late."

"Not at Kiev. The town is barely astir. Well then, shall we say seven?"

"Very well. I would like to be back at nine."

Lefaun made an ambiguous sound, and looked around the room. "I must attend to my regular affairs. When you are done with these files, please notify someone in the outer chamber, and he or she will call the porter. Until seven, then."

Lefaun Zadoury departed the room on long strides, black gown fluttering behind him. Wayness turned and looked at the three cases. Biography, genealogy, a projected new Society headquarters. They were elements of a single parcel; so Lefaun Zadoury had informed her and the code printed on each case was the same.

Wayness pondered a moment, then went to the door and looked into the outer chamber. It was now half-empty, and many of those who remained were preparing to leave.

Wayness closed the door. She returned to the table and copied the code which marked each of the three cases.

From far and wide across the city came the sound of a hundred great bells, tolling the hour of noon. Wayness leaned against the table and waited: five minutes, ten minutes. Once again she went to the door and looked out into the workroom, where everyone except a few preoccupied curators had gone off to lunch. Wayness went to a nearby alcove and seated herself in front of the information screen. She activated 'Search' and 'Naturalist Society.' The screen yielded information regarding two parcels: semantic and linguistic references purchased from Gohoon Galleries and a second parcel comprising the three cases identified by the code she had only just copied. The indicated donor was: 'Aeolus Benefices,' situated in the city Croy. The donation had been made fifteen years before.

Wayness copied the address, and ended the 'Search' program. She sat a moment thinking. Was the operation she had just completed beyond the imagination of Lefaun Zadoury? She thought not.

Wayness turned away from the alcove. "I do not want to become a cynic," she told herself, "but until I find a more useful philosophy I see that I must abide by the rules of the jungle." Thinking of Lefaun Zadoury, she could not help but grin. "I have also saved twenty sols, which is a good morning's work."

Wayness approached one of the curators still at work and asked that the porter be notified as to the three cases

in the side room. She was told somewhat ungraciously:
"Notify him yourself; can't you see that I am busy?"

"Notify him how?"

"Push the red button beside the door; the porter may
feel inclined to respond. Or, on the other hand, he may not.
But that is his affair."

"Thank you." Wayness left the workroom, pressing the
red button beside the door as she passed. In the loggia, she
discarded the black gown, which lifted her spirits even
further.

With nothing better to do, Wayness set out on foot:
down the hill to the boulevard beside the Dnieper. At a
wayside cart painted cheerfully red, blue and green, she
bought a hot meat pie and a paper cornucopia filled with
fried potato strings. Sitting on a bench she ate her lunch
and watched the Dnieper flow by. What to do about Lefaun
Zadoury and his no doubt unwholesome plans for the
evening? She could not make up her mind; in spite of
everything, he was amusing company.

Wayness finished her lunch and sauntered back along
the prospect to the old Prince Kolsky Square and the
Mazeppa Hotel. She made inquiries at the travel desk and
learned that there would be no good connections for Croy
until morning. "In that case," thought Wayness, "I will dine
at Lena's Bistro after all, if only to embarrass Lefaun
Zadoury."

Wayness went up to her room with the intention of
telephoning her uncle Pirie Tamm, but she hesitated. There
were arguments which could be made in both directions.
Pirie Tamm was a great one for issuing warnings and citing
dangers.

Wayness caught sight of her reflection in the mirror,
and decided that her hair had become over-long. She
thought of Giljin Leepe and her eccentric thatch, but no, in
fact, definitely not; a style so extreme would only make her
feel self-conscious.

Wayness went down to the hair-dresser's shop on the
ground floor, where her dark curling locks were trimmed so
to hang just to the turn of her jaw.

Wayness returned to her room full of decision and immediately put through a call to Fair Winds.

Pirie Tamm's first questions were indeed somewhat plaintive, and Wayness reassured him as best she could. "I am in a nice respectable hotel; the weather is fine and I am in good health."

"You look somehow drawn and peaked."

"That is because I have just had a haircut."

"Ah! That explains it! I thought that you might have eaten something which upset your stomach."

"Not yet! But tonight I am having cabbage rolls at Lena's Biotro. It is said to be picturesque"

"Often that is merely a synonym for 'dirty.' "

"You must not worry so! Everything is going well. I have not been seduced or robbed or murdered, or dragged screaming down into a cellar."

"So far so good, as you say, but any of these outrages might happen at a moment's notice!"

"Somehow I suspect that seduction might take a bit longer. I am quite shy and I need a few minutes, or even an hour, before I warm up to people."

"You must not joke about such things! They need only happen once, and then it is too late to take care."

"You are right, Uncle Pirie, of course. I should not be so flippant. Let me tell you now what I have learned. It is really quite important. Part of the Society Collection at Funusti Museum came by way of Gohoon Galleries. But another portion was donated fifteen years ago by Aeolus Benefices, of Croy."

"Aha, ahem. That is interesting indeed." Pirie Tamm's tone of voice had changed in a subtle manner. "Incidentally, one of your friends from Cadwal arrived yesterday, and is staying with me."

Wayness' heart bounded. "Who? Glawen?"

"No," said another voice and a second face moved into the screen. "It's Julian."

"Oh my," said Wayness in a husky half-whisper, and then aloud: "What are you doing here?"

"Just what you are doing—looking for the Charter and

the Grant. Pirie and I think that it would be prudent if we joined forces."

Pirie Tamm said in a brassy voice: "Julian is quite right; we are all in this together! The job is too big to be handled by a slip of a girl, which I have been saying since you began."

"I have done quite well so far. Uncle Pirie, send Julian out of the room; I want to talk with you privately."

"My word!" drawled Julian. "Tact is not one of your strong points, is it?"

"I don't know what else to say, in order to get you out of earshot."

"Very well. If that is your wish, I will go."

Pirie Tamm presently spoke. "Well then, Wayness, I certainly am surprised by your attitude!"

"I'm not only surprised at you, Uncle Pirie; I am horrified that you let me pour confidential information into Julian's ear. He is a vehement LPFer; he intends to destroy the Conservancy and let the Yips run loose over all Cadwal! If Julian gets to the Charter and the Grant before I do, you can kiss the Conservancy goodbye!"

Pirie Tamm's voice was subdued. "He indicated that you and he had a, well, romantic attachment, and that he had come to help you."

"He was lying."

"What will you do now?"

"Tomorrow I will leave here for Croy. I can't make any other plans until I see how the land lays."

"Wayness, I am sorry."

"No matter now. Just don't tell anyone else anything—except Glawen Clattuc, in case he should arrive."

"So it shall be." Pirie Tamm hesitated, then said: "Call me again, as soon as you can. I will be more careful; I assure you of this."

"Don't fret, Uncle Pirie. Perhaps it is not so bad, after all."

"That would be my dearest hope."

IV.

Time had passed. Wayness sat slumped in the chair, staring sightlessly across the room. The intensity of her first emotions had brought spasms of shivering and tingling to her arms and legs and viscera; an acrid sensation had risen in her throat.

The physical reactions had passed, leaving her limp and dispirited.

The damage had been done, and done decisively. There was no way she could pretend otherwise. Julian could easily precede her to Croy by a full day or more; ample time to seek out information, and then take steps to deny the same information to Wayness.

The idea aroused her to further spasms of fury. She took herself in hand. Emotion wasted her energies and accomplished nothing. Wayness heaved a deep sigh and sat up in the chair.

Life went on. She considered the evening which lay ahead. The information Lefaun Zadoury planned to sell her was now moot, but the prospect of explaining as much no longer amused her. Likewise, dining on cabbage rolls at Lena's Bistro in company with the morose and frugal curator had lost whatever appeal it might have had. Nevertheless, for want of anything better to do, she rose to her feet, bathed and changed into a knee-length gray frock with a narrow black collar and a long narrow panel of black frogging down the front.

The time was late afternoon. Wayness thought of the

outdoor café in front of the hotel. She went to the window and surveyed the square. Slanting light from the westering sun illuminated the ancient granite flags. Wayness noticed that the cloaks and capes of persons crossing the square flapped to gusts of wind from the steppe. Donning her own soft gray cloak, Wayness went down to the outdoor café in front of the hotel, where she was served green Daghestani wine with bitters.

Despite her best efforts, Wayness could not avoid brooding about Julian Bohost and the deceit he had practiced upon Pirie Tamm. A question gnawed at her mind: how had Julian learned that the Charter and Grant were missing? There was no way of knowing. In any case, the secret was no longer a secret—nor, so she thought, had it been for twelve years.

Wayness sat in the wan sunlight, watching the folk of old Kiev as they went about their affairs. The sun declined and shadows fell across the square. Wayness shivered and retreated into the lobby. She made herself comfortable and presently began to doze. She awoke to find that six o'clock had come and gone. She sat up and looked about the lobby. Lefaun Zadoury was not yet in evidence. She picked up a journal and read of archaeological researches in Kharesm, keeping watch for the gaunt young curator from the corner of her eye.

A tall figure came to stand beside her chair without her noticing; she looked up, half-startled. It was Lefaun Zadoury, but in a new guise which made him almost unrecognizable. He wore long over-tight trousers striped in black and white, a pink shirt with a green and yellow cravat, along with a vest of heavy black twill and a long bottle-green coat open down the front. A low-crowned hat of pale brown canvas pulled down over his forehead.

With difficulty Wayness controlled her amusement. Lefaun Zadoury looked down at her half-suspiciously. "You are nicely turned out, I must say."

"Thank you." Wayness rose to her feet. "I did not recognize you at first; you are out of uniform."

Lefaun's long face twisted into a sardonic half-smile. "Did you expect to see me wearing a black gown?"

"Well no, but I did not expect such a dynamic display."

"Piffle and nonsense! I dress in whatever I pick up first. I am oblivious to style."

"Hm." Wayness looked him up and down, from big feet in black shoes to the soft-brimmed canvas hat. "I'm not so sure of that. You made a choice when you first bought your clothes."

"Never! Everything I wear is plucked from the catch-as-catch-can rack at the fair, and these things were the first I found that would fit. They look well enough to suit me and cover my shanks from the wind. Well then: shall we go?" Lefaun added in a grumbling voice: "You were anxious to be out and in again almost before sunset, so I came a bit early, to show you something more of the town."

"Just as you say."

Outside the hotel Lefaun halted. "First: the square. You have already taken note of the churches, which have been rebuilt a dozen times, probably more. Still, they are said to be quaint. Are you familiar with the history of the far past?"

"Not particularly."

"Are you a student of ancient religions?"

"No."

"The churches will then be meaningless. As for me, I am bored with them, gaudy domes and all. We shall explore elsewhere."

"Such as where? I do not want to be bored either."

"Aha! Have no fear! You will be in my company!"

The two set off at a diagonal across the square, toward the hills of the Old Town. As they walked, Lefaun pointed out items of interest. "These granite flags were quarried in the Pontus and brought here by barge. It is said that each flag represents four dead men." He glanced sidewise with eyebrows raised. "Why are you hopping and jumping like that?"

"I don't quite know where to put my feet."

Lefaun made an extravagant gesture. "Ignore all senti-ment; walk where you will. They were low-class men, in any event. Do you think of dead cows when you eat meat?"

"I try not to do so."

Lefaun nodded. "Yonder, on that contrivance of iron

rods, is where Ivan Grodzny roasted the folk of Kiev for their misdeeds. That was long ago, of course, and the grill is a reconstruction. Directly to the side, in that little kiosk a vendor sells grilled sausages, which I think to be in rather bad taste."

"Yes, quite."

Lefaun came to a halt. He pointed to the crest of a hill behind the Old Town. "Do you see that pillar? It is one hundred feet high. For five years the ascetic Omshats occupied the top of the pillar, from which he declaimed his soliloquies. There are two accounts of his going. Some say he simply disappeared from sight, though many folk were gathered around the base of the pillar at the time. Others claim that he was struck by a monstrous bolt of lightning."

"Perhaps both accounts are correct."

"I suppose that's possible. In any case, we are now at the center of the square. To the left is the Spice-merchants' Quarter; to the right is the Mercery. Both are places of considerable interest."

"But we are going elsewhere?"

"Yes, even though we may encounter certain complexities which you, as an off-worlder, might find incomprehensible."

"So far I understand you very well, or so I suspect."

Lefaun ignored the remark. "Let me try to instruct you. First, the premise: Kiev has a long tradition of intellectual and artistic achievement, as perhaps you are aware."

Wayness made an ambiguous sound. "Proceed."

"That is all in the background. The city has taken a mighty leap to become one of the most advanced centers of creative thought anywhere around the Reach."

"That is interesting to hear."

"Kiev is like a great laboratory where reverence for past aesthetic doctrine crashes headlong into utter contempt for the same doctrine—sometimes in the same individual—and the collision produces a coruscation of wonders."

"Where does all this happen?" Wayness asked. "At the Funusti Museum?"

"Not necessarily, though the Prodromes, a select little society, numbers among its members both Tadiew Skander, whom you met today, and myself. In general, the venue is old Kiev itself, to be seen and heard and felt at places like the Bobadil, and the Nym, and Lena's and Dirty Edvard's, where liver and onions are served from wheelbarrows. At Stone Flower the motif is cockroaches, and there are some truly fine specimens! At the Universo, everyone walks about in the nude and collects as many signatures as possible on his or her bare skin. Some lucky folk were signed last year by the great Zoncha Temblada, and have not bathed since."

"Where are all the wonderful new art forms? So far I have heard mainly of cockroaches and signatures."

"Just so. It was early realized that every possible permutation of pigment, light, texture, form, sound and whatever is left had been achieved, and that to strain for novelty was wasted effort. The single ever-fresh ever-renewing resource was human thought itself, and the gorgeous patterns of its interplay between or among individuals."

Wayness frowned in puzzlement. "Are you referring to 'talk'?"

"I suppose that 'talk' is an appropriate word."

"At least it is inexpensive."

"Exactly—which makes it the most egalitarian of all creative disciplines!"

"I am happy that you explained this to me," said Wayness. "We are on our way to Lena's Bistro, then?"

"Yes. The cabbage rolls are the best, and it is there that we will receive the information you require, although I am not sure when it will arrive." Lefaun glanced down at Wayness. "Why are you looking at me like that?"

"How am I looking?"

"When I was little, my grandmother found that I had dressed our fat pug dog in her best lace cap. I cannot quite describe the expression: a kind of helpless fatalistic wonder as to what other mischief I might have in mind. So—why do you look at me like that?"

"Perhaps I will explain by and by."

"Bah!" Lefaun reached up with both hands to pull his hat down as far as possible across his face. "I cannot understand your conundrums. Do you have the money?"

"All that I shall need."

"Very well. It is not too far now—just under the Varanji Arch and a few paces up the hill."

The two continued across the square, Lefaun marching on long bent-kneed strides, Wayness half-running to keep up: to the side of the Spice-merchants' Quarter, under a squat stone arch and off up the hill by a set of crooked streets, overhung by the second stories of structures to either side, almost to blot out the sky. The way twisted and narrowed, to become a flight of steps, which gave upon a small plaza. Lefaun pointed. "Yonder is Lena's Bistro. Just around the corner is Mopo's, with the Nym just up Pyadogorsk Alley. Here is what has been voted 'the creative node of the Gaean Reach' by the membership of the Pro-dromes. What do you think of that?"

"It is certainly an odd little square."

Lefaun studied her somberly. "Sometimes I feel that you are laughing at me."

"Tonight I might laugh at anything," said Wayness. "If you think of it as hysteria, you might not be wrong. Do you wonder why? It is because this afternoon I have had an appalling experience."

Lefaun considered her with sardonically raised eye-brows. "You spent half a sol by mistake."

"Worse. If I think about it, I start to quiver."

"Too bad," said Lefaun. "But let us go in before the crowd arrives. You can tell me all about it over a flask of beer."

Lefaun pushed open a tall narrow door bound in ara-besques of black iron; the two entered a room of moderate size, furnished with heavy wooden tables, wooden benches and chairs. Tongues of yellow flame from wall sconces, six to each side of the room, provided a soft yellow light, and Wayness reflected that if the building had not caught on fire before, it was not likely to do so tonight.

Lefaun gave Wayness instructions: "Buy tickets from the cashier yonder, then go to the wall and look at the pictures. When you see something you fancy, drop tickets into the proper slot and out will come a tray, metered to the tickets you have paid over. It is simple, and you may dine with great flexibility—grandly, upon pig's feet with sour cabbage and herrings or modestly, on bread and cheese."

"I shall certainly try the cabbage rolls," said Wayness.

"In that case, follow me, and I will show you how it is done."

The two brought their trays to a table, each with cabbage rolls, fried groats and beer. Lefaun said in a grumbling voice: "The time is early; no one of consequence is here and so we must eat alone, as if by stealth."

"I don't feel stealthy," said Wayness. "Are you frightened by solitude?"

"Of course not! I frequently sit alone! Also, I am one of a group known as the Running Wolves. Every year we go out to run across the steppe, ranging far into the wilds and the folk are surprised to see us coursing past. At sunset we sup on bread and bacon which is toasted robber-style from a tripod; then we lie down to sleep. I always look up at the stars and wonder how it is going up yonder in the far places."

"Why not go to see for yourself?" suggested Wayness. "Instead of coming every night to Lena's."

"I do not come here every night," said Lefaun with dignity. "I often go to the Spasm, or to Mopo's or the Convolvulus. In any case, why go elsewhere, since here is the focus of human intelligence?"

"So it may be," said Wayness. She ate the cabbage rolls, which she found tolerable, and drank a pint of beer. Patrons of the café began to arrive in force. Some were Lefaun's acquaintances and joined him at the table. Wayness was introduced to more folk than she could remember: Fedor, who hypnotized birds; the sisters Euphrosyne and Eudoxia; Big Wuf and Little Wuf; Hortense who cast bells; Dagleg who spoke only what he called 'immanences' and Marya, a sexual therapist who, according to Lefaun, had many interesting stories to tell. "If you need advice along these lines, I will call her over and you can ask whatever you like."

"Not just now," said Wayness. "What I don't know are things I don't want to know."

"Hmf. I see."

The bistro became full; all the tables were occupied. Wayness presently told Lefaun: "I have been listening carefully, but so far I have heard no conversation except that of people commenting upon their food."

"The hour is early," said Lefaun. "In due course there will be talk enough." He nudged Wayness with his elbow. "For instance, take note of Alexei who stands yonder."

Wayness, turning her head, saw a portly young man with a round face, yellow hair cut short to a bristle and a short pointed beard.

"Alexei is unique," said Lefaun. "He lives poetry, and thinks poetry, and dreams poetry, and presently he will recite poetry. But you will not understand him, since poetry, or so he claims, is such an intimate revelation that he uses terms intelligible only to himself."

"I discovered that," said Wayness. "I heard him speak a moment ago and could understand not a word."

"Of course not. Alexei has created a language of a hundred and twelve thousand words controlled by an elaborate syntax. This tongue, so he claims, is sensitive and flexible, superbly adapted to the expression of metaphors and allusions. It is a pity that no one can enjoy it along with Alexei, but he refuses to translate a single word."

Wayness said: "It may be all for the best, especially if his poetry is bad."

"Possibly so. He has been accused of both narcissism and ostentation, but he is never offended. It is the typical artist, so he declares, who is mad for acclaim and whose self-esteem depends upon adulation. Alexei sees himself as a lonely man, indifferent to both praise and censure."

Wayness craned her neck. "He is now playing the concertina and dancing a jig, all at the same time. What do you make of that?"

"It is just Alexei in one of his moods; it means nothing." He called across the room. "Hoy there, Lixman! Where have you been?"

"I am fresh down from Suzdal, and glad to be back."

"Naturally! At Suzdal the intellectual climate is as stiff as the weather."

"True. Their best and almost only resort is a place called Janinka's Bistro, where I had a strange experience."

"Tell us about it, but first, would you like a glass of beer?"

"Certainly."

"Perhaps Wayness will buy a flask for us both."

"No, I think not."

Lefaun gave a dismal groan. "I will go presently to make my own purchases—unless someone makes an offer. What of you, Lixman?"

"If you recall, it was you who made the proffer to me."

"Yes, I remember now. What was it you were telling us about Suzdal?"

"While I sat at Janinka's I met a woman who told me that I was accompanied everywhere by the spirit of my grandmother, who was anxious to help me. At the time I was playing at dice, and I said: 'Very well, Grandmother, how shall I bet?' 'She says to bet on the double three!' came the answer. So I bet on the double three and won the stake, I looked around for another hint, but the lady was gone, and now I am unsure and nervous. I dare do nothing of which my grandmother might disapprove."

"That is a curious state of affairs," said Lefaun. "Wayness, what is your advice?"

"I should think that if your grandmother were tactful, she would allow you a few moments of privacy from time to time, especially if you brought the matter up in a respectful fashion."

"I can suggest nothing better," said Lefaun.

"I will give the matter thought," said Lixman and went off across the room.

Lefaun rose to his feet. "It seems that I must buy beer, after all. Wayness, your flask is empty; what of you?"

Wayness shook her head. "The evening is getting on and I must leave Kiev early tomorrow. I can find my own way back to the hotel."

Lefaun's mouth drooped open and his black eyebrows jerked high. "What of the information you wanted? And what of the twenty sols?"

Wayness forced herself to meet the darkling gaze. "I

have been trying to find a way to tell you, without using the words 'swindler' or 'scoundrel.' At noon I would have had no qualms, but now I am dreary and apathetic; today I blurted out everything I knew to my uncle. A man named Julian Bohost was listening—and the consequences may be tragic!"

"Now I understand! Julian is the swindler and the scoundrel."

"Agreed! But in this case I was referring to you."

Again Lefaun was taken aback. "How so?"

"Because you tried to sell me information you could have had in two minutes!"

"Hah! The indications were obvious enough. But facts are facts and guesses are guesses. For which will you pay out your money?"

"Neither! I found the information by myself."

Lefaun seemed more puzzled than perturbed. "I am surprised that it took you so long to form an opinion."

"I worked fast enough when I was able to use one of the information screens in the workroom. You could have done the same, except that you preferred to make a great mystery in order to swindle me to the tune of twenty sols."

Lefaun, closing his eyes, reached up with both hands to pull the hat so far down over his head that it rested on his eyebrows and the tips of his ears. "Ay, ay, ay!" said Lefaun softly. "I am in disgrace, then."

"Very much so."

"Alas! I have prepared a little supper at my flat; I have simmered rose petals in essence of duck; I have wiped the dust from my best bottle of wine. All for your delectation. And now—you will not come?"

"Even for ten bottles of your best wine I would not have come. I lack confidence in 'Running Wolves' and curators as well."

"A pity! But here is Tadiew Skander, my partner in vice. Tadiew, over here! Did you get the information?"

"I did—but it cost more than we had estimated, since I had to deal with Old High-trousers himself."

Wayness laughed. "Well done, Tadiew! The timing was

perfect; the delivery soft as silk, and the poor brainless fool of a girl will pay whatever you ask!"

Lefaun said to Wayness: "Write the information you have discovered on a piece of paper. We shall have a test, to determine whether or not Tadiew is tricking us. It is now twenty-two sols, Tadiew?"

"Twenty-two sols!" cried Tadiew. "The final figure was twenty-four!"

"Now then, Tadiew! You have noted your expensive information in writing?"

"So I have."

"Please place it face down on the table. Now then—have you communicated this information to anyone?"

"Of course not. This is the first I have seen you since noon!"

"Correct."

Wayness watched with curled lip. "I wonder what you are trying to prove."

"Tadiew and I are admitted scoundrels; we admit to bribery and corruption of dignified officials. I want him to break down and admit that he is more vile and more scurrilous than I am."

"I see. But the comparison is of no interest to me. Now, if you will excuse me—"

"One moment! I also want to place a fragment of information upon the table—an intuition I gained from looking into the cases. There! It is done! Three pieces of paper lie before us. Now then—we need an expert arbitrator who is unaware of our discussion, and I see just the person yonder. Her name is Natalinya Harmin, and she is a senior curator at the museum." He indicated a tall woman of imposing physique, keen of eye and massive of jaw, her blonde hair braided and tied in a rope around her head: not a person to trifle with, thought Wayness. Lefaun called out: "Madame Harmin! Be good enough to step over here for a moment."

Natalinya Harmin turned her head; observing Lefaun's signal, she crossed the room to stand looking down at him.

"I am here, Lefaun. Why, may I ask, are you glowering at me in that fashion?"

Lefaun spoke in surprise: "I was wearing what I intended for an agreeable expression."

"Very well! I have seen it and you may relax. What do you want?"

"This is Wayness Tamm, a handsome little creature down from space, who is anxious to explore the marvels of Old Kiev. I must mention that she is headstrong, extremely naive, and suspects everyone of turpitude."

"Ha! That is not naivete, but sound common sense. Above all, young lady, do not go running out on the steppe with Lefaun Zadoury. At the very least, you will suffer sore feet."

"Thank you," said Wayness. "That is good advice."

"Is that all?" asked Natalinya Harmin. "If so—"

"Not quite," said Lefaun. "Tadiew and I are at odds and we want you to arbitrate the point at issue. Am I right, Tadiew?"

"Exactly! Madame Harmin is famous for her forthright candor."

"Candor, is it? Asking me for candor is like opening Pandora's box. You may learn more than you want to know."

"We must take the chance. Are you ready?"

"I am ready. Speak."

"We want you to identify these words fully and exactly." He took the paper from in front of Wayness and handed it to Natalinya Harmin. She read it aloud: " 'Aeolus Benefice, at Croy.' Hmf."

"Are you acquainted with this institution?"

"Naturally, though it is an aspect of Museum policy that we normally do not publicize."

Lefaun told Wayness: "Madame Harmin is telling us that when an anonymous bequest arrives at the museum we state its provenance to be 'Aeolus Benefice of Croy,' in order to forestall inconvenience to ourselves. Am I right, Madame Harmin?"

Natalinya Harmin gave a crisp nod. "In essence, this is correct."

"So that when one looks in the files and finds that a bequest is attributed to 'Aeolus Benefices,' he will understand that the entry is totally meaningless?"

"Exactly. It is our way of writing 'Anonymous Bequest,'." said Natalinya Harmin. "What else do you want to know, Lefaun? You are not getting a raise in pay this quarter if that is the question you are preparing to ask."

Wayness had slumped back into her chair, almost weak with joy. Julian Bohost, whatever the reason for his presence at Fair Winds, had been baited along a false trail, and in a most convincing manner.

"One more question," said Lefaun. "For the sake of argument, if someone wanted to find the true source of an anonymous bequest, how would he go about it?"

"He would be turned away, politely but briskly, and no one would listen to his complaints. This information is considered a sacred trust, and is inaccessible even to me. Is there anything else?"

"No, thank you," said Lefaun. "You have provided us full and exact information."

Natalinya Harmin returned to her own party. "Now then," said Lefaun. "To the next step. I have noted several words upon my paper. There is no mystery about these words. They were formed in my mind by simple processes. This morning, when I first looked into the three cases, I noted that the genealogical studies in the second case traced the lineage of the Counts de Flamanges, with emphasis upon those associated with the Naturalist Society. Among the biographies in the first case the only volume showing signs of use was that concerning the Count de Flamanges. The third case included much material regarding the Count de Flamanges and his offer of three hundred acres to the Naturalist Society. In short, the cases apparently had been donated by someone connected with the de Flamanges." Lefaun turned over his paper. "Therefore 'Count de Flamanges, of Castle Mirky Porod near Draczeny, in the Moholc.' These are the words you will read here." Lefaun tilted his beer mug; finding it empty he set it down with a thud. "I seem to be empty. Tadiew, lend me five tickets."

"Never. You already owe me eleven."

Wayness hastily pushed a number of tickets toward Lefaun. "Take these; I won't need so many."

"Thank you." Lefaun rose to his feet. Tadiew called out: "In that case, bring me another quart!"

Lefaun went to the dispenser and returned with two large mugs brimming with foam. "I take no pride in my deduction; the facts seem to cry out for attention. Now then, Tadiew, what more can you tell us?"

"First, that I am out of pocket fourteen sols and that I have used every trick in my repertory to penetrate the inner files."

Lefaun told Wayness: "It helps a great deal when one has a warm relationship with the secretary to one of our high bashaws."

"Do not deprecate my efforts!" snapped Tadiew. "I went on tenterhooks, I can assure you, and for a time hid behind a desk."

"In the main, it was well done, Tadiew! I personally lack your subtle skills. You may now produce the lightning bolts of surprising information that your work has achieved."

"Don't crow!" With a fretful motion Tadiew turned over his paper, to reveal a name: " 'Countess Ottilie de Flamanges.' The bequest was made about twenty years ago, upon the death of the Count. She still lives in her castle, alone except for servants and dogs. She is said to be somewhat eccentric."

Wayness brought out money. "Here is thirty sols. I understand nothing of your financial arrangements, nor who paid what to whom. You must straighten such matters out between yourselves. And now—" Wayness rose to her feet "—I must return to the hotel."

"What?" cried Lefaun. "We have not yet visited Mopo's nor the Black Eagle!"

Wayness smiled. "Still, I must go."

"Nor have you seen my dinosaur's tooth, nor tasted my special saffronella, nor even listened to the chirping of my pet cricket!"

"I regret these omissions—but they are unavoidable."

Lefaun gave a dismal groan and rose to his feet. "Tadiew, guard my chair; I will be back shortly."

V.

All the way back to the Mazeppa Hotel Wayness was kept busy negating Lefaun's proposals and refuting his arguments, which were both urgent and inventive:

" . . . only a few yards to my flat: the stroll of a quarter-hour through the most picturesque part of Kiev!"

And: "We should never reject what Life decides to offer us! Existence is like a plum pie; the more plums one can find the better!"

And: "I marvel, I stand in awe, I am baffled when I try to calculate the probabilities of our meeting—you, the denizen of a world at the back of nowhere; I, a gentleman of Old Earth!

"It seems an act of Predestination that we ignore, to our sure regret! No matter how one implores the Fates, our neglected opportunities can never be repaired!"

To which Wayness made the following rejoinders:

"Up hill and down dale, hopping culverts and drains, stumbling over cobbles, scuttling through the back alleys like rats: is that it? No, thank you; tonight your cricket must chirp alone."

And: "I don't feel at all like a plum. Think of me, rather, as a green persimmon, or a dead starfish, or a dish of old tripes."

And: "I agree that the odds against our meeting were enormous. It seems that Destiny is trying to tell you something—namely, that your chances of success elsewhere, say with Natalinya Harmin, are far better than with me."

At last Lefaun gave up and let her enter the hotel with no more than a muttered: "Goodnight."

"Goodnight, Lefaun."

Wayness ran across the lobby and went directly up to her room. For a few moments she sat thinking, then telephoned Fair Winds.

Pirie Tamm's bleak face appeared on the screen. "Fair Winds."

"Wayness here. Are you alone?"

"Quite alone."

"Are you sure? Where is Julian?"

"Presumably in Ybarra. He used the telephone this afternoon and immediately told me that though he was sorry to leave Fair Winds so abruptly, he must visit an old friend who was departing Ybarra spaceport in two days, and inside the half-hour he was gone. Not a chap I particularly liked. What is your news?"

"It is tolerably good news," said Wayness. "In effect, we have sent Julian off on a wild goose chase. He has gone to Croy, of course."

"A wild goose chase, you say?"

Wayness explained. "I'm calling now, because I did not want you to worry all night long."

"Thank you, Wayness. I shall sleep better, be assured. And what are your plans?"

"I am not sure yet. I must do some thinking. Perhaps I will go directly to not far from here . . ."

CHAPTER VI

I.

In her room at the Mazeppa Hotel Wayness studied a map. The town Draczeny in the Moholc was no vast distance from Kiev as the crow flew, but connections were anything but direct. The castle Mirky Porod was evidently located in a region of great natural charm, to the side of the usual tourist routes and commercial depots, though it was not indicated on the map.

Wayness pondered her options. Julian had been discomfited, at least temporarily. The chances were slight that he would return to Fair Winds. In the morning, therefore, Wayness flew directly to Shillawy, to arrive at Fair Winds during the middle afternoon.

Pirie Tamm was clearly happy to see her. "It seems as if you have been gone for weeks."

"I feel much the same. But I can't relax just yet. Julian has a bad temper and he hates to be thwarted."

"What can he do? Very little, or so I suppose."

"If he learns that 'Aeolus Benefices' is another way of saying 'Funusti Museum' he can do a great deal. I spent thirty sols for information; Julian might spend forty, but to the same effect. So—I dare not delay."

"What, then, are your plans?"

"At this particular moment I want to learn something of the Counts de Flamanges, so that when I present myself at Mirky Porod, I will not be arriving in a state of total ignorance."

"Most wise," said Pirie Tamm. "If you like, while you are changing for dinner, I will check the references and see what information is available."

"That would be very helpful."

At dinner Pirie Tamm announced that he had assembled a considerable body of information. "Probably as much as you will need. However, I suggest that we postpone the report until after dinner, since I have a tendency toward discursiveness. Notice this tureen! We have been served a truly noble dish: stewed duck with dumplings and leeks."

"Just as you like, Uncle Pirie."

"I will say this much: over the centuries the family has been neither staid nor stolid, but has produced its share of adventurers and eccentrics, as well as several renowned scholars. Naturally there are hints of a scandal or two. At the moment, this particular quality seems to have gone into abeyance. It is an aged woman, the Countess Ottilie, with whom you must deal."

Wayness mulled over the information in silence. A thought occurred to her. "You mentioned that Julian used the telephone before he left?"

"Yes; so he did."

"You have no idea whom he called?"

"None whatever."

"Odd. Julian has never mentioned friends on Earth — and it is just what he would most likely talk about."

"For a fact, he is quite a talker." Pirie Tamm grinned sourly. "He is dissatisfied with Araminta Station and its social and environmental works."

"There is room for criticism; everyone agrees to that," said Wayness. "If the staff had done a better job over the years, there would be no Yips at Yipton, and no problem now."

"Hm. Julian spoke at length of the 'democratic solution.' "

"What he meant is entirely different from what you understood. The Conservationists want to resettle the Yips on another world, and maintain the Conservancy. The LPFers — they hate being called 'Peefers,' though it is much easier—want to let the Yips loose on the mainland, where they would live, so it is claimed, in rustic simplicity, singing and dancing, and celebrating the passage of the seasons with quaint rites."

"That is more or less what Julian implied."

"Meanwhile the Peefers will annex vast estates of choice land for themselves, and become the new landed gentry. When they talk about this, they speak of 'public service' and 'duty' and 'administrative necessities.' But I've seen Julian's plans for the country house he hopes to build someday - using cheap Yip labor, of course."

"He used the word 'democracy' several times."

"He used the Peefer definition. Each Yip has one vote and each Conservationist has one vote. Ah well, enough of Julian. At least, I hope so."

After dinner, the two went to the drawing room and settled themselves in front of the fire. "Now," said Pirie Tamm, "I will tell you something about the Counts de Flamanges. The family is very old—three or four thousand years, at least. Mirky Porod was built on the site of a mediæval castle and for a time functioned as a hunting lodge. The place has a colorful history: the usual tumult of duels by moonlight, intrigues and betrayals, romantic escapades by the hundreds. Nor has there been any lack of the macabre. Prince Pust over a period of thirty years kidnapped maidens and did horrid deeds upon them; his victims numbered over two thousand and his imagination never flagged. Count Bodor, one of the early Flamanges, conducted demoniac rituals, which ultimately became frenzies of the most fantastic sort. I derive this information from a book called UNUSUAL TALES FROM THE MOHOLC. The author tells us that the ghosts at Mirky Porod are therefore of dubious origin, and might derive either from the time of Prince Pust, or of Count Bodor, or possibly other circumstances now forgotten to history."

Wayness asked: "How long ago was this book written?"

"It seems to have been a relatively recent work. I could find it if you became interested in one or another of the cases."

"No. Don't bother."

Pirie Tamm nodded placidly and went on with his remarks.

"In general, the Counts de Flamanges seem to have been of good character, save for the occasional bad hat like Count Bodor. A thousand years ago Count Sarbert was a founder of the Naturalist Society; the family has traditionally been associated with conservationist causes. Count Lesmund offered to donate a large tract of land to the Naturalist Society as a site for a new headquarters, but unfortunately the plan came to naught. Count Raul was a member and a strong supporter of the Society until his death some twenty years ago. His widow, the Countess Ottilie, now lives at Mirky Porod alone. She is childless, and the heir is Count Raul's nephew, Baron Trembath, whose estate is beside Lake Fon, and who operates an equestrian school.

"Countess Ottilie, as I mentioned, lives in seclusion, seeing no one but doctors for herself and veterinaries for her dogs. She is said to be extremely avaricious, though she commands great wealth. There is a hint or two that she is, let us say, eccentric. When one of her dogs died, she beat the attending veterinary with her walking stick and drove him away. The veterinary seems to have been of philosophical disposition. When the journalists asked if he intended to sue, he merely shrugged and said that both beating and biting were accepted hazards of his profession, and there the matter rested.

"Count Raul had been a generous contributor to the Society: a fact which the Countess bitterly resented.

"Mirky Porod itself occupies a splendid site, at the head of a valley, with Lake Jerest only a few yards away. There are wild hills and dense forests at the back and forests to both right and left. It is not uncomfortably large; in fact, I made copies of photographs and the floor plan, if you are interested."

"Very much so."

Pirie Tamm gave her the material in an envelope. He spoke plaintively: "I wish I understood better what you have in mind. The Charter and Grant will never be found at Mirky Porod; that is certain."

"Why do you say that?"

"If these documents had come into the possession of Count Raul, he would certainly have turned them over to the Society."

"So it would seem. Still, there are any number of possibilities why that should not be so. For instance, suppose he were ill when he received the documents and never found time to check them over? Or that these items were mislaid while he was sorting things out? Perhaps Countess Ottilie recognized their value and put them aside? Or, worse, threw them into the fire?"

"As you say, anything is possible. Still, Count Raul did not buy the material at Gohoon's auction; there was a far larger volume of material, and if Countess Ottilie were giving away those relatively personal records, she surely must have included the other material. In other words, it was someone else who bought the Charter and Grant from Gohoon—which means that your searches are not leading you toward the Charter but away from it."

"Not so," said Wayness. "Imagine the Charter as resting on the rung of a ladder. We can find it either by starting at the top and working down, or starting at the bottom and working up."

"That is a fine analogy," said Pirie Tamm. "Its only fault is unintelligibility."

"In that case, I will explain again, but without the analogy. Nisfit stole the goods; they passed through Mischap and Doorn to Gohoon, then to someone we must call A. Simonetta Clattuc learned the identity of A, but either she could not find him or he passed the material on to B, who might have given it to C, who sold it to D, who passed it on to E. Somewhere along this progression she has been brought to a halt. Let us say that the Funusti Museum is F, and Count Raul de Flamanges E, then now we are looking for D. In other words, we must work backward along the line until we reach whoever has the Charter. Simonetta is starting from A, and seems to have met difficulties along the way. Then there is Julian, who is starting from X, which is to say, Aeolus Benefices at Croy. Where he goes from there I can't even guess. In any case, we have no time to delay, and Countess Ottilie may not choose to be helpful."

Pirie Tamm clenched his teeth. "If only I had my strength, how gladly I would take the load from your shoulders!"

"You are already helping enormously," said Wayness. "I could not function without you."

"It is nice of you to say so."

II.

By a variety of modes Wayness traveled from Fair Winds into the deep Moholc: by omnibus to Shillawy, by subterranean slideway to Anthelm and by feedertube to Passau, thence by airbus to Draczeny and by rickety omnibus into the far Moholc, under the loom of the Carnat Mountains.

Late in the afternoon, with the wind blowing in gusts, Wayness arrived at the village Tzem, beside the River Sogor, with steep forested hills close to either side. Clouds raced across the sky; Wayness' skirt fluttered as she stepped down from the bus. She moved away a few steps, then glanced back, to verify that no one had followed her, nor was there any other vehicle approaching from the direction they had come.

The bus had halted in front of the village inn: The Iron Pig, if the sign swinging above the door were to be credited. The main street followed the course of the river, which was spanned by a stone bridge of three arches directly in front of the inn. At the center of the bridge, three old men wearing baggy blue pantaloons and high-cocked hunter's hats stood fishing. To fortify themselves, they took occasional swallows from large green bottles which were kept in tackle boxes at their feet, meanwhile calling back and forth from one to the other, exchanging advice, cursing the perversity of all fish, the impudence of the wind, and whatever else came to mind.

Wayness secured lodging at The Iron Pig, then went out to explore the village. Along the main street she discovered a bakery, a green-grocer's market, a tool shop which also sold sausages, a hair-dresser/insurance agent, a wine shop, a post office and a number of other enterprises of less note. Wayness stepped into a stationer's shop, which was little more than a booth. The proprietress, a jovial woman of middle age, leaned on her counter, gossiping with a pair of cronies who sat on a bench opposite. Here was a sure font of information, thought Wayness. She bought a journal and stood pretending to read but with an ear tuned to the conversation, which presently she was allowed to join. She described herself as a student investigating antiquities of the region. The proprietress told her: "You've come to the right place; there are three of us here, each more antique than the others."

Wayness accepted a cup of tea and was introduced to the company. The proprietress was Madame Katrin; her friends were Madame Esme and Madame Stasia.

After a few moments Wayness mentioned Mirky Porod, and, as she had anticipated, tapped an instant freshet of information.

Madame Katrin gave an exclamation of regret. "It is not now as it was in the old days! Then Mirky Porod commanded our attention, that I'll tell you, what with banquets and balls, and all manner of goings-on! Now it is as dull as ditchwater."

"That was when Count Raul was alive," Madame Esme told Wayness.

"True! He was a man of importance, and there was never any lack of famous folk at Mirky Porod! And not always on their best behavior—that is, if all the stories one heard could be believed."

"Ha ha!" declared Madame Stasia. "I believe them well enough, human nature being what it is!"

"And the famous folk, along with their rank and their wealth, always seem to have more of this 'human nature' than anyone else," observed Madame Katrin.

"Just so," said Madame Esme sagely. "And if it were not so rich and juicy, there would be no scandal!"

Wayness asked: "What of the Countess Ottilie? How did she deal with the scandals?"

"My dear!" exclaimed Madame Stasia. "It was she who created them!"

"The countess and her dogs!" sniffed Madame Katrin. "Between them they drove poor Count Raul to his death!"

"How so?" asked Wayness.

"Of course nothing is certain, but it is said that the count, in one last futile effort, forbade Countess Ottilie to bring her beasts into the dining room. Soon after, he committed suicide by jumping from a window in the North Tower. Countess Ottilie said that he had been driven by remorse for his cruelty to her and her little friends."

The three ladies chuckled. Madame Katrin said: "And now all is quiet at Mirky Porod. Each Saturday afternoon the countess entertains her friends. They play at piquet for small stakes, and if the countess loses more than a few pence, she flies into a rage."

Wayness asked: "If I went to call on the countess, would she receive me?"

Madame Stasia said: "As to that, much depends on her mood."

"For example," said Madame Esme, "do not go on a Sunday after she has lost a sol or two at her game."

"Also, and most important!" said Madame Katrin. "Do not go out accompanied by a dog! Last year her grand-nephew Baron Parter went to call on her, along with his mastiff. As soon as the dogs saw each other it was instant warfare, with yowling and snapping and yelping such as was never heard before! Some of the countess' dearest little friends were discomfited, and young Baron Parter was sent away faster than he had come, along with his mastiff."

"Those are two good hints," said Wayness. "What else?"

Madame Esme said: "There is no harm in telling the truth! The countess is a dragon, and not sympathetic."

Madame Katrin flung her arms into the air. "And stingy? Ah, there has never been the like! She buys my journals, but only after they are a month old, when I sell them at half-price. For this reason, she is always a month behind in her life."

"It is ridiculous!" said Madame Stasia. "If the world

came to an end, Countess Ottilie would not know until a month had passed."

"Time to close up shop," said Madame Katrin. "Now I must see about a bite of supper for Leppold. He has been fishing all day and caught not so much as a sparrow. I'll open a packet of mackerel, which will give him something to think about."

Wayness left her new friends and returned to the inn. There was no telephone in her room and she was obliged to use a booth in the corner of the lounge. She called Fair Winds; Pirie Tamm's image appeared on the screen.

Wayness told of her discoveries to date. "Countess Ottilie seems even more of a termagant than I had expected, and I doubt if she will be helpful."

"Let me think this over," said Pirie Tamm. "I will call you back shortly."

"Very well. Still, I wish—" Wayness looked over her shoulder, as someone came into the lounge. She checked her speech and at Fair Winds her face left the screen.

Pirie Tamm raised his voice. "Wayness? Are you there?"

Wayness' face returned to the screen. "I'm here. For a moment I was—" She hesitated.

"You were what?" Pirie Tamm demanded sharply.

"Nervous." Wayness looked over her shoulder onee again. "I think that when I left Fair Winds I was followed—at least for a time."

"Explain, if you please."

"There isn't much to explain—maybe nothing. When I left Fair Winds a vehicle followed my cab to Tierens, and I glimpsed a face with a black mustache. At Shillawy I doubled back and saw him distinctly: a stocky little man, rather meek-looking, with a black mustache. Afterwards, I did not see him again."

"Ha!" said Pirie Tamm in a dispirited voice. "I can only advise vigilance."

"That is the same advice I have been giving myself," said Wayness. "After Shillawy no one seemed to be following me but I was not at all happy. I remember reading of tags and spy-cells and other such intricate devices, and I began to wonder. At Draczeny I took time to examine my cloak, and for a fact I found something suspicious: a little black shell half the size of a ladybug. I took it into the station restaurant and when I hung up my cloak, I tucked the shell under the collar of a tourist's long coat. I took the omnibus to Tzem and the tourist flew off to Zagreb or some such place."

"Well done! Though I cannot imagine who would be following you."

"Julian—if he were dissatisfied with what he found at Croy."

Pirie Tamm made a dubious sound. "Whatever the case, you seem to have slipped them off handily. I too have been busy, and I think you will approve of my arrangements. You may or may not be aware that Count Raul was a horticulturist of note; indeed, it was for this reason that he became such an ardent Society member. To make a long story short I have ranged far and wide among the few connections I have left, with good result. Tonight Baron Stam, who is Countess Ottilie's cousin, will make an appointment for you. I will have full details later this evening, but, as it stands now, you will be identified as a student of botany, who wishes to look through Count Raul's papers on the subject. If you are able to ingratiate yourself with Countess Ottilie, no doubt you will have an opportunity to put other apparently casual questions to her."

"That sounds reasonable," said Wayness. "When do I present myself?"

"Tomorrow, since he will telephone Mirky Porod this evening."

"And my name is still Wayness Tamm?"

"We saw no good reason for a false identity. However, do not stress your connection with the Naturalist Society."

"I understand."

III.

Halfway through the morning Wayness climbed aboard the rickety old conveyance which connected Tzem with a few even more remote villages to the east. After a ride of three miles up and down hills, through a dark deep forest, for a space beside the River Sogor, Wayness was discharged in front of a massive iron portal which guarded the avenue leading to Mirky Porod. The gates were open and the gatekeeper's lodge was deserted; Wayness set off up the avenue, which after two hundred yards swung around a copse of firs and hemlock to reveal the façade of Mirky Porod.

Wayness had often noticed in old buildings a quality which transcended character to become something close to sentience. She had wondered about this trait: was it real? Had the structure absorbed vitality over the years, perhaps from its occupants? Or was the condition imaginary: a projection of the human mind?

Mirky Porod, basking in the morning sunlight, seemed to demonstrate such a sentience: a reflective and tragic grandeur, enlivened by a certain frivolous insouciance, as if it felt neglected and tired but was too proud to complain.

The architecture—so it appeared to Wayness—neither obeyed nor defied convention, but, rather, seemed innocently oblivious to aesthetic norms. Exaggerations and excesses of mass were countered by playful elongations of form; subtle surprises were everywhere. The towers, north and south, were too squat and too heavy, with roofs too tall and too steep. The roof of the main structure showed three gables, each with its balcony. While the gardens were not impressive, a vast lawn extended from the terrace to a far line of sentinel cypress trees. It was as if someone of a romantic temperament had made a quick sketch on a scrap of paper and had ordained a structure with proportions exactly as sketched, or perhaps the inspiration had been a picture in a child's book of fairy tales.

Wayness pulled at the bell chain. The door was presently opened by a plump young maid, not much older than herself. She wore a black uniform with a white lace cap to confine her blonde hair; Wayness thought that she seemed a trifle surly and out of sorts, though she addressed Wayness politely enough. "Yes, miss?"

"My name is Wayness Tamm. I have an appointment with Countess Ottilie for eleven o'clock."

The maid's blue eyes widened in mild surprise. "Do you now? We haven't had too many visitors of late. The countess thinks that everyone is out to cheat her, or sell her fake jewels, or steal her things. In the main, of course, she is right. That is my view of it, at least."

Wayness laughed. "I've nothing to sell and I'm too timid to steal."

The maid smiled wanly. "Very well, I'll take you to the old creature, for all the good it will do you. Just mind your manners and praise her dogs. What was the name again?"

"Wayness Tamm."

"This way, then. She's taking her elevenses out on the lawn."

Wayness followed the maid across the terrace and down to the lawn. Fifty yards away, solitary as an island in a green ocean, the countess sat at a white table, in the shade of a green and blue parasol. She was surrounded by a band of small fat dogs, all sprawled in attitudes of repose.

Countess Ottilie herself was tall and gaunt, with a long sharp face, haggard cheeks, a long crooked nose with large nostrils, and a long jaw. Her white hair, parted in the middle, had been drawn to the nape of her neck and tied into a knot. She wore an ankle-length blue gown of filmy stuff and a pink jacket.

At the sight of Wayness and the maid the countess cried out: "Sophie! Here at once!"

Sophie made no reply. The countess silently watched them approach.

Sophie spoke in a sullen voice: "This is Miss Wayness Tamm, Your Ladyship. She says that she has an appointment with you."

Countess Ottilie ignored Wayness. "Where have you been? I called you, to no avail!"

"I was answering the door."

"Indeed! You took your time about it! Where is Lenk, who should look after such things?"

"Madame Lenk's back was taken bad this morning. Mr. Lenk is applying a salve."

"That is all pooh-bah! Madame Lenk always chooses to suffer at the most inconvenient times! Meanwhile I am not attended! I might as well be a bird on the fence, or the painting in a picture!"

"Sorry, Your Ladyship."

"The tea was thin and barely warm! What of that?"

Sophie's round face became sulkier than ever. "I did not brew the tea; I only brought it out!"

"Take the pot away, and bring out a fresh pot on the instant!"

"It won't be on the instant," said Sophie grimly. "You'll have to wait, like anyone else, while it steeps."

Countess Ottilie's face became mottled and she prodded the lawn with her cane. Sophie took the tray with the cup and teapot. In so doing, she trod on the tail of one of the dogs, which uttered a shrill cry. Sophie also cried out, jerked backward and dropped the tray; pot and cup fell to the lawn, with a few drops splashing on Countess Ottilie's hand, which caused her to bellow a hoarse curse. "You have scalded me!" She swung her cane but Sophie already had jumped back and twisted her pelvis to the side, so that the cane struck only empty air. "I thought you said the tea was cold!" Sophie called. Countess Ottilie had sprained her wrist, and was more vexed than ever. "Ah, you slut, to stamp poor Mikki, and then feign innocence! It is monstrous! Come here at once!"

"So you can beat me? Never!"

The countess struggled to her feet and swung the cane again, but Sophie, dancing back a safe distance, stuck her tongue out at Countess Ottilie. "That is what I think of you, stupid old crow that you are!"

Countess Ottilie panted, "As of this instant you are discharged! Leave at once!"

Sophie marched off two paces, then, bending, flung up her skirts to show Countess Ottilie the expanse of her buttocks, then strolled triumphantly away.

Wayness stood to the side, shocked, worried and amused. She came cautiously forward, picked up tray, pot and cup and set them on the table. The countess glared at her. "Go! I have no need for you either."

"If you wish, but I had an appointment to see you at this time."

"Hmf." Countess Ottilie settled back into her chair. "Naturally you want something of me, like all the rest!"

Wayness saw that she had not made an auspicious beginning. "It is a pity that you have been disturbed. Should I come back when you have had time to rest?"

" 'Rest'? It is not I who needs rest; it is poor little Mikki, with his sore tail. Mikki? Where are you?"

Wayness peered underneath the chair. "He seems to be doing quite nicely."

"Then that is one worry I am spared." She examined Wayness coldly, with eyes behind folds and layers of loose skin, like the eyes of a turtle. "Now that you are here, what do you want? I think Baron Stam said something about botany?"

"Yes, that is correct. Count Raul, of course, was well known in the field and some of his findings have never been fully documented. With your permission, I would like to look over his papers. I will cause you as little inconvenience as possible."

Countess Ottilie set her lips in a hard line. "Botany was another of Count Raul's expensive triflings. He knew a thousand ways to spend money. They called him a philanthropist, but he was something else: he was a fool!"

"Surely not!" said Wayness, once again shocked.

Countess Ottilie tapped the lawn with her cane. "That is my opinion. You are convinced otherwise?"

"Of course not! But—"

"We were never left in peace because of whiners and solicitors. Each day would see more of them, with their big teeth and unctuous grins. Worst of all was the Nature Society."

"The Naturalist Society?"

"Those are the ones! I detest the sound of the name: They were beggars, thieves, carnivores! They never desisted, never relented; always a plea here and a wheedle there! Would you believe it? One time they wanted to build a grand palace for their comfort upon our ancient lands!"

"Extraordinary!" said Wayness, feeling a hypocrite and a traitor. "Incredible!"

"I set them right, I can tell you! They got nothing!"

Greatly daring, Wayness said thoughtfully: "Count Raul did some very interesting work on Naturalist Society data. Do you know of any papers pertaining to the Naturalist Society?"

"Nothing! Have I not described these people? I emptied the file into a box and sent it away where I will never be reminded of money spent so foolishly."

Wayness smiled in polite agreement. The interview was going poorly. "As for me, I will cost you nothing, and in the end the Count's reputation may well be enhanced."

Countess Ottilie made a scornful sound. "Reputation? A joke! I care nothing for my own, even less for that of Count Raul."

Wayness forged grimly ahead. "Still, Count Raul's name is honored at the university. No doubt he owes much of his stature to your encouragement."

"No doubt."

"Perhaps then I might dedicate my thesis to 'Count Raul and Countess Ottilie de Flamanges'!"

"As you like. If that is all you came for, you may go."

Wayness ignored the remark. "Count Raul kept records of his collections and acquisitions, as well as his researches?"

"Of course. If nothing else, he was meticulous."

"I would like to look through his records, so that I might clear up certain puzzles."

"Impossible. We keep such things locked up nowadays."

Refusal was no more than Wayness had been expecting. "It would of course be in the interests of science, and of course I would be helped in my career. I assure you that I would be no trouble to you."

Countess Ottilie prodded the lawn with her cane. "Not another word! Yonder is the gate; go the way you have come, and at once!"

Wayness hesitated, reluctant to accept so devastating a defeat. "May I come again, when you are feeling better?"

Countess Ottilie stood erect, showing herself to be a woman taller than Wayness had assumed. "Did you not hear me? I want none of you about, prying and picking, always reaching with your fingers, nibbling at my things."

Wayness turned away and marched in a rage of her own to the gate.

IV.

The time was noon. Wayness stood in the road outside the gates to Mirky Porod, waiting for the omnibus which, according to the schedule, passed each hour. She looked up the road; no bus was in sight and no sound could be heard save the singing of insects.

Wayness went to sit on a stone bench. Her circumstances were more or less as she had expected them to be; nevertheless, she felt deflated and depressed.

What now? Wayness forced herself to ponder. Several schemes suggested themselves, all either impractical, illegal, immoral or dangerous. Wayness liked none of them, especially all variations on the theme of kidnapping one or more of the dogs.

Down the avenue from Mirky Porod came Sophie the erstwhile maid, carrying a pair of bulging suitcases. She looked at Wayness. "Here we are again. How did your interview go?"

"Not well."

"I could have told you that from the start." Sophie put down her suitcases and joined Wayness on the bench. "As for me, I am finished, definitely and forever. I have suffered enough from that old reptile and her curs."

Wayness gave rueful assent. "She has an uncertain temper."

"Oh, her temper is certain enough," said Sophie. "It is always bad, and niggardly to boot. She pays as little as she can and she wants attention at all hours. No wonder she has trouble keeping staff."

"How many folk work for her?"

"Let me see. Mr. Lenk and Madame Lenk, a cook and a scullion, four maids, a footman who serves as chauffeur, two gardeners and a boy. I will say this; Mr. Lenk makes sure there's a good table, and no one is truly over-worked. Lenk is sometimes a bit amorous, but he can be controlled by means of a hint to Madame Lenk, who then makes Lenk so miserable that one almost takes pity on the poor man. He is surprisingly quick and one must be agile enough to keep from being backed into a corner, in which case there is often no help for it."

"It would seem that Lenk keeps everyone happy at Mirky Porod."

"He tries his best, for a fact. In the main he is easy enough, and holds no grudges."

"Are there truly ghosts at the castle?"

"That is a serious question. Everyone who has heard them claims that he has heard them, if you get my meaning. As for me, you would not find me anywhere near North Tower when the moon is at the full."

"What does Countess Ottilie say about the ghosts?"

"She says it was ghosts who pushed Count Raul from the window, and I suppose that she would know best."

"So it would seem."

The omnibus arrived and the two rode to Tzem. Wayness went directly to the telephone in The Iron Pig and called Mirky Porod. The face of a middle-aged man, sleek and suave, with plump jowls, lank black hair, drooping eyelids and a neat little mustache appeared on the screen. Wayness asked: "Am I addressing Mr. Lenk?"

From his end of the connection, Lenk observed Wayness' image with approval and touched back his mustache. "True enough! I am Gustav Lenk. How may I oblige you, and be assured that I will make every effort to do so!"

"It is simple enough, Mr. Lenk. I have been talking with Sophie, who has just resigned her position at Mirky Porod."

"That is unfortunately the case."

"I wish to apply for the position, if it is still open."

"It is still open, right enough. I have barely had time to learn of the vacancy myself." Lenk cleared his throat and examined Wayness' image with even greater interest. "You have had experience at this kind of work?"

"Not a great deal, but I am sure that with your help I will have no problems."

Lenk said cautiously: "In ordinary circumstances this would be correct. However, if Sophie had anything to say about Countess Ottilie—"

"She spoke at length, and with emotion."

"Then you must know that the difficulties are not the work itself, but Countess Ottilie and her pets."

"I understand this clearly, Mr. Lenk."

"I must point out, also, that the pay is not large. You would start at twenty sols a week. However, your uniform is furnished, and there are no deductions. If I may say so, the staff is congenial, and all of us realize that dealing with the Countess is difficult. Nevertheless, it must be accomplished, and in fact this is the basis for all our employments."

"That is well understood, Mr. Lenk."

"You have no aversion to dogs?"

Wayness shrugged. "I can put up with them."

Lenk nodded. "In that case, you may come out at once, and we will fit you into the routine with as little delay as possible. Now then: your name?"

"I am—" Wayness reflected a moment "—Marya Smitt."

"Previous employer?"

"I have no references at hand, Mr. Lenk."

"In your case, I think we can make an exception. I will see you presently."

Wayness went to her room. She combed her hair straight back over her scalp, drew it tight and tied it with a black ribbon at the nape of her neck. She inspected herself in the mirror. The change, so she thought, made her seem older and wiser, and definitely more competent.

Wayness departed the inn, rode the omnibus to Mirky Porod and, now full of apprehensions and uncertainty, carried her suitcase up the avenue to the side entrance.

Lenk was rather taller and more ponderous than Wayness had expected, and carried himself with the dignity befitting his position. Still, he greeted Wayness with affability and took her into the servant's lounge, where she met Madame Lenk: a stout woman with graying black hair cut unflatteringly short, strong arms and a brisk decisive manner.

Together, Lenk and Madame Lenk instructed Wayness in regard to her duties. In general, she must attend to Countess Ottilie and her wants, and pay no heed to her cantankerousness, and always be ready to dodge blows of the cane. "It is a nervous reaction," said Lenk. "She only means to convey a mood of dissatisfaction."

"Still, I cannot approve the tactic," said Madame Lenk. "One time I was bending to pick up a journal she had dropped and without so much as a by-your-leave here came the swish of the cane, catching me broad abeam. I was naturally disturbed and inquired why Her Ladyship had struck the blow. 'It was a matter of convenience,' she said. I started to say more but she waved her cane and told me to make a selection on the list of misdeeds for which I had gone unpunished and place a check-mark against the item."

"In short," said Lenk, "be on your guard at all times."

"While we are on the subject," said Madame Lenk, "I will remark that Mr. Lenk himself is often a bit too friendly with the girls, and sometimes he goes so far as to forget his manners."

Lenk made a gallant gesture. "My dear, you exaggerate, and you will alarm poor Marya so that she will flee at the sight of me."

"That is not her only recourse," said Madame Lenk. She addressed herself to Wayness. "If Lenk should ever forget himself and start to take liberties, you need only murmur the words 'Hell on Earth.' "

" 'Hell on Earth'? It is a cryptic message."

"Exactly! But if Lenk does not desist from his efforts, I will explain it to him in detail."

Lenk showed an uneasy smile. "Madame Lenk of course is joking. At Mirky Porod we work in harmony and live at peace with each other."

"Except during our encounters with the countess, of course. You must never cross her or contradict her, no matter what her nonsense, and never despise her dogs, and always clean their horrid little messes cheerfully, as if it were all great fun."

"I will do my best," said Wayness.

Madame Lenk fitted Wayness out in a black uniform with a white apron and a white gauze cap, with wings protruding an inch or so over the ears. Examining herself in the mirror, Wayness was confident that Countess Ottilie would not recognize her for Wayness Tamm the importunate student.

Madame Lenk conducted Wayness about the castle, avoiding only the North Tower. "There is nothing there save disembodied spirits, or so it is claimed. I myself have seen none of these, though truly I have heard odd noises which were probably squirrels or bats. In any event, you need not worry about the North Tower. Now then, here is the library. The double doors lead into Count Raul's old study, which is used but seldom, and the doors are kept locked. Here is the countess; I will introduce you."

Countess Ottilie gave Wayness the briefest of inspections, then went to sit in an upholstered chair. "Marya, is it? Very good, Marya! You will find me an indulgent mistress—far too indulgent, perhaps. I make few demands. Since I am old, I require a good deal of running and fetching, and you must learn where I keep my things. Every day the routine is much the same, except Saturday when I play at cards, and on the first of each month when I ride to Draczeny to visit the shops. You will quickly learn this routine, since it is not difficult.

"Now you must meet my little friends, who are most important to me. There: Chusk, Porter, Mikki, Toop." As she spoke she pointed a crooked forefinger. "There: Sammy, now scratching herself, and Dimpkin, and oh! you naughty Fotsel! You know you should not raise your leg in the house! Now Marya must sop up behind you. Finally, under the chair is Raffis." The countess sat back. "Marya, tell me their names, so that I will know you were attending."

"Hm." Wayness pointed. "That is Mikki, and that is

Fotsel who made the mess; I remember you well enough. Raffis is under the chair. That spotted one is Chusk, I believe, and that one, who was scratching, is Sammy. The others I don't remember."

"You have done quite well," said Countess Ottilie, "even though you have neglected Porter, Toop and Dimpkin: all dogs of reputation and character."

"No doubt," said Wayness. "Madame Lenk, if you will show me the mop and bucket, I will clean up the wet at this moment."

"We find that a sponge is most effective for minor nuisances," said Madame Lenk. "You will find equipment in the closet."

So began Wayness' stint as domestic servant. Every day was different, even though each followed a standard routine. At eight o'clock every morning Wayness entered Countess Ottilie's bedroom to kindle the fire, even though the castle was adequately heated by ergothermic mechanisms. The countess slept in an enormous old bed among a dozen large fluffy pillows of down cased in pink, pale blue and yellow silk. The dogs slept on cushions in boxes ranged along the side wall and woe betide the interloper who chose to test out another dog's cushion.

Wayness was next required to draw back the curtains which the countess insisted should be tightly drawn against any sliver of exterior light; especially she detested moonlight playing through the windows. Wayness next assisted the countess to prop herself up among her cushions, amid curses, objurgations and cries of accusation: "Marya, can you not be careful! You are hurting me with your hauling and yanking! I am not made of iron, or of leather! Now then, you know I am not comfortable in this position! Push that yellow pillow farther down behind my back. Ah! Relief at last! Bring me my tea. Are the dogs all well?"

"All fit and blooming, Your Ladyship. Dimpkin is doing its business as usual in the corner. I think Chusk has taken a dislike to Porter."

"It will soon pass by. Bring me my tea; don't stand there like a ninny."

"Yes, Your Ladyship."

After placing the tea tray on the bed and commenting upon the state of the weather, Wayness next rang for Fosco the footman, who led the dogs away for their feeding and a chance to relieve their bladders and bowels in the side yard.

In due course, Wayness assisted the countess with her own routines of the morning, again to the accompaniment of complaints, threats and recriminations, to which Wayness paid little heed, though keeping a wary eye upon the cane. When the countess had been dressed and seated at her table, Wayness rang down for her breakfast, which was delivered by way of a dumb-waiter.

While the countess consumed her breakfast, she dictated notes in regard to activities of the day.

At ten o'clock Countess Ottilie used her lift to descend to the ground floor, and took herself usually into the library, where she read mail, glanced at a journal or two and then consulted with Fosco in regard to the dogs, whom Fosco had now fed and groomed. Fosco was required to provide an opinion as to the health, vigor and psychological state of each beast, and often the discussions proceeded at length. Fosco never became impatient, nor was there any reason for him to do so, since this was the only task required of him, other than occasionally serving as chauffeur for the countess when she went off upon one of her infrequent short journeys.

During this interval Wayness was free until summoned by the countess. She usually passed the time in the servant's lounge, gossiping and taking refreshment with the other maids and Madame Lenk, and sometimes Lenk himself.

A summons from the countess usually came a few minutes before eleven. If the weather were raw or gusty or wet, the countess remained in the library by the fire. If the day were fine, she went out through the library doors, across the terrace and down upon the lawn.

Depending upon her mood—and Wayness had learned that the countess was a moody person indeed—she might walk out to the table, fifty yards from the terrace, and settle herself: an island of pink flounces and lace and lavender shawls isolated on the face of a smooth green grassy ocean. At other times she might climb aboard an electric cart and fare forth on a voyage of exploration to a far corner of the lawn, with her dogs streaming behind in a line. The most agile first, the oldest and fattest puffing and thumping along at the rear. Wayness was then required to load table, chair and parasol upon another cart, follow, set up the furniture, and serve tea.

On these occasions the countess more often than not desired solitude, and Wayness would be sent back to the library, to await a tone from her wristband which would alert her to the countess' needs.

One day, after Wayness had been so dismissed, she made a detour around to the side of the North Tower, where she had never previously ventured. Behind a hedge of black-green yew she came upon a little cemetery, with twenty, or perhaps as many as thirty, small graves. On some of the tombstones inscriptions had been carved deep into the marble; on others bronze plaques served the same purpose, while still other stones supported marble statues in the likeness of small dogs. To the side grew lilies and clumps of heliotrope. Wayness' curiosity was instantly sated; she backed away and went at a fast walk to the library, to await Countess Ottilie's summons. As always, whenever she had the opportunity, she tested the doors which led into the study; as always they were locked and — as always — Wayness felt a pang of urgency. Time was passing; events were in motion which she could not control.

By this time Wayness knew where to find the keys to the study. One hung from Lenk's key ring, a second from a similar key ring in the possession of the countess. Wayness had taken pains to learn the daily disposition of the keys. By day the countess often carried them with her, sometimes rather carelessly, so that on occasion they were left somewhere she had been sitting. Thereupon the keys were deemed lost, creating a great scurrying search, punctuated by the countess' hoarse outcries, until the keys were found.

At night the countess kept her keys in the drawer of a cabinet beside her bed.

Late one night, with the countess snoring among her down pillows, Wayness crept quietly into the room and made for the cabinet, which was visible in the dim illumination of the night-light. She had started to pull open the drawer when the dog Toop awoke in annoyance and startlement, and began to yelp: a tumult in which the other dogs instantly joined. Wayness scuttled from the room, before the countess could raise up to see what had caused the disturbance. Standing breathless in the adjoining chamber, Wayness heard the countess rasp: "Quiet, you little vermin! Just because one of you farts, must you all celebrate? Not another sound!"

Wayness, discouraged, went off to bed.

Two days later, the footman Fosco resigned his position. Lenk tried to assign the task of dog-grooming to Wayness, who declared that she could spare no time from her regular duties, then to the maid Fyllis, who objected even more definitely: "They can grow hair in a mat two inches thick for all of me! You must do the job yourself, Mr. Lenk!"

Lenk was thus miserably employed for two days until he hired another footman: a handsome young man named Baro, who took to the job with a conspicuous lack of enthusiasm.

For a time Lenk's conduct toward Wayness was irreproachably correct, if somewhat fulsome and urbane. But each day he became a trifle more friendly, until at last he thought to test the waters and patted Wayness on the bottom, playfully, as if in a spirit of camaraderie. Wayness recognized that Lenk's program must be nipped in the bud, and jerked aside. "Really, Mr. Lenk! You are being quite naughty!"

"Of course," said Lenk cheerfully. "But you have a most enticing little bottom, just round enough, and my hand became charged, as it were, with wanderlust."

"Then your hand must be kept under stern control and not allowed to stray."

Lenk sighed. "It was not only my hand that became charged," he murmured, preening his mustache. "In the final analysis, what is a bit of naughtiness between friends, after all? Is that not what friends are for?"

"All this is far too deep for my understanding," said Wayness. "Perhaps we should ask Madame Lenk's advice."

"That is an insipid suggestion," sighed Lenk, turning away.

On occasion, usually in the late afternoon, the countess would fall into one of her special moods. Her face would lengthen and become immobile; she would refuse to speak to anyone. On the first such occasion Madame Lenk told Wayness: "The countess is dissatisfied with the way the universe is run, and she is now considering how best to change things."

Often during such occasions, with little attention to the weather, the countess would go out to her table on the lawn, seat herself, produce a packet of special cards and proceed to play what seemed an elaborate game of solitaire. Over and over the countess played the game, clenching her bony fists, performing wild gestures, peering down in sudden suspicion, hissing and muttering, showing her teeth in what could be either rage or exultation, never desisting until either the cards submitted to her will, or the sun went down and the light failed.

On the second such occasion, a cool wind was blowing and Wayness went out with a robe, but the countess rejected it with a wave of the hand.

At last, in the dying twilight, Countess Ottilie stared down at the cards, whether in triumph or defeat Wayness could not be sure. The countess heaved herself to her feet and the keys fell jingling to the grass. The countess was already moving away and noticed nothing. Wayness picked up the keys and tucked them into the pocket in her skirt. Then she gathered cards, robe and followed the countess across the lawn.

Countess Ottilie did not go directly to the castle, but off at a slant toward the foot of North Tower. Wayness followed ten paces to the rear. The countess paid her no heed.

Twilight had fallen over the landscape, and a cool breeze was blowing through the ancient pines which grew on the hills. Countess Ottilie's destination became clear: the little cemetery beside the North Tower. She entered through a gap in the yew hedge and wandered among the graves, stopping now and again to utter chirrups and little calls of encouragement. Wayness, waiting outside the hedge, heard her voice: "—it has been long, ah how long! But do not despair, my good Snoyard; your loyalty and trust shall be rewarded! And you, Peppin, no less! How you used to romp! And dear little Corly, whose muzzle was so soft! I grieve for you every day! But we shall all meet again, on some happy day! Myrdal, do not whimper; all graves are dark . . ."

In the gloom behind the yew hedge Wayness bestirred herself; it was as if she were involved in a queer dream. She turned and ran through the dusk, one hand pressed against the keys to keep them secure. She halted by the terrace and stood waiting.

A few minutes later she saw the pale form of the countess approaching, moving slowly and leaning on her cane. Wayness waited silently. The countess passed as if she were invisible and, crossing the terrace, entered the library, with Wayness coming after.

The evening went by slowly. While the countess dined, Wayness furtively examined the keys, and found to her satisfaction that each was tagged with a label. There it was: 'Study': the key she had wanted so long and so badly! After a moment's thought she went to the scullery where a few tools and oddments were kept on a workbench and where she previously had noticed a box of old keys. Sorting through the box she found a key of the same general type as the key to the study, and tucked it into her pocket.

A shadow in the doorway! Wayness turned about startled. It was Baro, the new footman: a stalwart young man, black-haired, with expressive hazel eyes and features of perfect regularity. He carried himself with assurance, and spoke with an easy flow of inconsequential language. Wayness, while conceding Baro to be an exceedingly handsome young man, thought him vain and glib, and kept her distance from him—a tendency which Baro instantly noted and interpreted as a challenge. Thenceforth, he began to make easy casual advances toward her, which Wayness as easily and casually avoided. It was now Baro who stood behind her. He spoke, "Marya: princess of all that is delightful! Why are you skulking in the scullery?"

Wayness restrained the first tart response which came to her tongue, and said only: "I was looking for a bit of string."

"Here it is," said Baro. "Right here on the shelf." Reaching past her, he placed a hand on her shoulder and leaned his body against hers, so that she felt his animal warmth. He wore, so she noticed, a pleasant fresh scent, mingled of fern, violet and odd off-world essences.

"You smell nice, but I'm in a bit of a hurry," said Wayness. She ducked under his arm, sidled past his body and gained the freedom of the pantry and then the kitchen beyond. Behind came Baro, smiling a vague bland smile.

Wayness went to sit in the servant's lounge, annoyed and disturbed. Contact with Baro's body had aroused a response in her, and had also sent tingles of fear and revulsion racing along the fibers of her subconscious. Baro entered the room. Wayness became wary, and picked up a journal. Baro came to sit beside her. Wayness paid him no heed.

Baro spoke in a soft voice: "Do you like me?"

Wayness turned him a dispassionate glance. She delayed several seconds before answering. "I haven't given the matter any thought, Mr. Baro. I doubt if I will."

"Poof," said Baro, as if he had received a blow in the solar plexus. "My word, but you are a cool one!"

Wayness, turning the pages of the journal, made no response.

Baro uttered his easy laugh. "If you relaxed just a bit, you might find that I was not such a bad fellow after all."

Wayness gave him another expressionless glance, laid the journal aside and, rising to her feet, went to sit with Madame Lenk, only to be summoned by a tone from her wristband. "Off you go," said Madame Lenk. "It is time for the ball game ... Hoy! Listen to the rain! I must send Lenk to foster the fire."

The countess had gone into the library, along with her dogs. Outside the windows rain thrashed down upon the terrace and across the lawn, where it could occasionally be glimpsed in the instantaneous blue illumination of lightning bolts.

The ball game was played by the countess, who hurled the ball; the eight dogs, who bounded after it, snapping and snarling at each other; and Wayness, who must pull the ball from the jaws of the animal which had gained possession and return the wet ball to the countess.

After ten minutes the countess tired of the game, but insisted that Wayness continue to play in her stead.

At last the countess' attention wandered and she began to doze. Wayness, standing behind her chair, took occasion to detach the key to the study from the key ring, and replace it with the key she had taken from the box in the scullery, switching the label as well. She hid the key ring in the soil of a potted plant to the side of the room, and went to fetch Countess Ottilie's night-time potion from the kitchen: an unpleasant concoction of raw egg, buttermilk and cherry cordial, mixed with a packet of therapeutic powders.

Countess Ottilie awoke from her nap in a querulous mood. She scowled at Wayness. "Where have you been? You must not leave me so! I was about to ring for you!"

"I was fetching the potion, Your Ladyship."

"Hmf. Bah! Give it here then." The countess was only partially mollified. "It is a mystery to me how you flit here and there so carelessly, like a fluff on the wind!"

The countess swallowed her potion. "So now, once more it is bedtime. I have negotiated the trials of another day, despite all! It is not so easy when one is old, especially when one is wise, as well!"

"I'm sure not, Your Ladyship."

"Everywhere—grasping hands and pinching fingers! From all sides the gleam of predatory eyes, like the eyes of wild beasts circling the fire of a lone adventurer! I wage a stark and pitiless battle; greed and avarice are my sworn enemies!"

"Your Ladyship is armed with great strength of character."

"Yes, that is true." Gripping the arms of her chair, the countess struggled to gain her feet. Wayness ran forward to help, but the countess angrily waved her away, and sat back in the chair. "That is unnecessary! I am not an invalid, no matter what they say."

"I have never thought so, Your Ladyship."

"That is not to say that I shall not die some day, and then: who knows?" The countess glanced sharply at Wayness. "You have heard the ghosts in North Tower?"

Wayness shook her head. "I am happier not knowing of such things, Your Ladyship."

"I see. Well, I will say no more. It is time for bed. Help me to my feet, and take care for my poor back! I suffer tremendously when I am jerked about!"

During the intricate routine of preparing for bed the countess discovered the loss of her keys. "Ah! Chife, pox and vomit! Why must these trials so afflict me? Marya, where are my keys?"

"Where Your Ladyship usually keeps them, or so I suppose."

"No, I have lost them! They are out on the lawn, where any thief of the night can come upon them! Call Lenk, at once!"

Lenk was summoned and informed as to the missing keys. "I suspect that I dropped them out on the lawn," said the Countess. "You must find them at once!"

"In the dark? With the rain driving down at a slant? Your Ladyship, that would be impractical."

The countess began to fulminate and pounded her cane into the floor. "It is I who determines what is practical at Mirky Porod! Never be deceived! I have taught this truth to others!"

Lenk turned his head sharply and held up his hand. Countess Ottilie cried out: "What do you hear?"

"I don't know, Your Ladyship. It might have been the cry of a ghost."

"A ghost! Marya, did you hear it?"

"I heard something, but I think it was one of the dogs."

"Of course! There! This time I heard it too. It is Porter, suffering from his catarrh."

Lenk bowed. "As you say, Your Ladyship."

"And my keys?"

"We shall find them in the morning, when we can see."
Lenk bowed again and withdrew. The countess grumbled at
length, but at last went to bed. Tonight she was unusually
testy and Wayness changed and rearranged her down pillows a dozen times before the countess finally tired of the
game and fell asleep.

Wayness went to her room. She removed her white
apron and her white cap, and changed into soft-soled
slippers. Into her pocket she tucked pencil, paper and an
electric torch.

At midnight she left her room. The house was quiet.
Wayness delayed a diffident moment or two, then summon-
ing all her courage, descended the stairs, where she
stopped to listen again.

Silence.

Wayness passed through the library to the doors leading into the study. She worked the key; the door slid ajar
with a faint creak. Wayness studied the lock, making sure
that she could not accidentally lock herself into the study.
In this case, there could be no difficulty. Wayness entered
the study, closed and locked the door. She brought out her
torch and took stock of her surroundings. A large desk,
equipped with a communications screen and a telephone,
occupied the center of the room. Beyond the windows the
rain still fell, though not so heavily as before, with frequent
splashes of blue lightning fracturing the sky. To the side a
stanchion supported a large terrestrial globe. Shelves along
the walls displayed books, curios, oddments, weapons.
Wayness examined the books. None seemed to be ledgers
in which Count Raul might have kept his accounts. She
turned her attention to the desk. The communicator—it
had not been used for many years, and might well be
inoperative.

Wayness seated herself and touched a switch. To her
delight and heartfelt relief, the screen brightened to display
Count Raul's personal emblem: a black double-headed
eagle standing upon a pale blue globe, limned with circles
of latitude and longitude.

Wayness set about her task of discovering where Count
Raul kept the information she sought. The task might have

been easier if the count had been as methodical as he was meticulously all-inclusive.

Half an hour passed. Wayness chased down a dozen blind alleys and dead ends, before chancing upon the file containing the information she sought.

Count Raul had not bought any material from Gohoon Galleries. Furthermore, his collection of Naturalist Society documents had included only the items Wayness had discovered at the Funusti Museum. Here Wayness was disappointed. She had hoped, with a hope so secret that she had not even admitted it to herself, that she might find Charter and Grant in the study, perhaps in a cubbyhole of this very desk.

Not so. Count Raul had derived his material from a dealer named Xantief in the old city Trieste.

It was at this moment that Wayness heard the slightest of noises: a grating sound, of iron scraping on iron. She glanced up in time to see the handle of the door to the terrace move, after it had been tested by someone standing outside.

Wayness pretended not to notice. She altered the name 'Xantief' to 'Chuffe' and 'Trieste' to 'Croy,' and conducted a search to make sure that there was no other mention of the name. Meanwhile, she watched the window. A great spasm of blue lightning shattered the sky. Wayness saw the silhouette of a man standing by the window. His hands were raised; he seemed to be busy with a tool. Wayness rose to her feet without haste and went to the door which led into the library. From outside came an instant thud as if something had been dropped, and another extremely faint sound. Wayness knew that the man had hastened along the terrace, entered the library, and now had stationed himself beside the study door, to intercept her once she stepped out. Or perhaps he would push her back into the study and lock the door behind the two of them, and then who knows what might happen?

Nothing nice, thought Wayness, the skin prickling at the nape of her neck.

She was trapped. She could open the doors out to the terrace but the man would almost certainly catch her as she emerged.

At the study door came an ominous grinding sound, faint and muffled, as the man busied himself at the lock.

Wayness looked wildly around the room. On the shelves were weapons: scimitars, kiris, yataghans, poniards, kopf-nockers, long-irons, spardoons, quangs and stilettos. Unfortunately, all were clamped tightly to the wall. Wayness' eye fell on the telephone.

Wayness picked up the telephone. She ran to the desk and pressed '9.'

After a moment Lenk's voice sounded in the speaker. It was a sleepy cross voice, but to Wayness it sounded sweet indeed. "Mr. Lenk!" she called breathlessly. "It's Marya! I'm on the stairs! I hear noises in the library! Come at once before the countess wakes up!"

"Ah! Yes. Yes, yes! Keep her quiet, by all means! The library, you say?"

"I think it's a prowler; bring your gun!"

Wayness went to the door and listened. Silence from the library, as the burglar, or whoever he might be, had become wary.

Wayness heard sounds from the library: Lenk's voice. "What is going on here?"

Wayness eased the door open. Lenk, carrying a gun, had gone to the outside door and stood looking out across the terrace. Wayness slipped out of the study and closed the door. When Lenk looked around she was standing by the door into the hall. "The danger is over," said Lenk. "The intruder escaped, despite my best efforts. He left a drill. Most unusual."

Wayness said: "Perhaps we should not tell the countess. She would only worry, to no avail, and make life miserable for us all."

"True," said Lenk in a troubled voice. "It would do no good to tell her. She would never let up on the subject of her keys, and how I had brought on the burglary by neglecting her orders."

"I will say nothing, then."

"Good girl! I wonder what the rascal wanted."

"He won't be back! Not after seeing you with your gun!

But I hear Madame Lenk! You had best tell her what has happened while I am here to corroborate the tale."

"No fear this time," said Lenk with a sour grin. "She heard you calling on the telephone. I don't see how you managed it without rousing the countess."

"I spoke softly, if you remember. And she was snoring to outdistance the thunder. There was no problem."

"Yes, of course. Perhaps I should have called Baro; I'm sure he could give a good account of himself."

"Perhaps so. Still, the fewer who know, the better."

In the morning all proceeded according to routine. As soon as possible, Wayness rescued the key ring, restored the proper key to its place, then went out on the lawn. Ten minutes later she returned triumphantly with the keys.

Countess Ottilie was only moderately pleased. "It is what you should have done last night, to save me hours of anxiety. I slept not a wink."

While Baro was occupied grooming the dogs Wayness departed Mirky Porod. She rode the omnibus into Tzem. From the telephone in The Iron Pig she called Mirky Porod. Lenk appeared on the screen and stared slack-jawed at Wayness' image. "Marya? What are you up to?"

"Mr. Lenk, it is a complicated matter and I am sorry to leave you so abruptly, but I received an urgent message which I can't ignore. I have called to say goodbye. Please make my explanations to the countess."

"But she will be shattered! She has come to depend on you, just like all the rest of us!"

"I am sorry, Mr. Lenk, but now I see the omnibus and I must go."

CHAPTER VII

I.

Wayness rode the omnibus from Tzem to Draczeny, and apparently was not followed. At Draczeny she changed to a slideway car and was conveyed at great speed to the west.

Late in the afternoon the car halted at Pagnitz, a transfer station on the route which continued all the way across the continent to Ambeules. Wayness pretended to ignore the stop; then, at the last possible instant, jumped to the station platform. For a moment she stood watching to see if anyone else had altered his or her plans at the last minute, but no one had done so—specifically no plump little man in a dark suit with a black mustache like a smudge across his pallid face.

Wayness took lodging at the Inn of the Three Rivers. From her room she telephoned Pirie Tamm at Fair Winds.

Pirie Tamm spoke cordially: "Aha, Wayness! It is good to hear your voice! Where are you calling from?"

"At the moment I am at Castaing, but I am leaving at once for Maudry and the Historical Library. I will call you as soon as possible."

"Very well; I won't keep you on the line. Until tomorrow."

Half an hour later Wayness placed a second call to Pirie Tamm at the bank in Yssinges.

The circumstances had made him testy. "I never thought I would see the day when I distrusted my own telephone! It's a damned outrage!"

"I'm sorry, Uncle Pirie. I know that I am causing no end of trouble."

Pirie Tamm held up his hand. "Nonsense, girl! You are doing nothing of the sort! It's the uncertainty I find galling! I have had experts in to check out the entire system, but they find nothing. They also guarantee nothing. There are too many ways to tap into a system, so we must continue to take precautions, at least for a time. Now then: what have you been doing?"

As succinctly as possible Wayness told of her activities. "I am now on my way to Trieste, where I hope to find Xantief, whoever he is."

Pirie Tamm gave a deprecatory grunt, the better to mask his feelings. "It seems, then, that you have climbed — or is it 'descended'? — another rung on the ladder. Either way, should we consider this an achievement?"

"I hope so. The ladder is already longer than I might like."

"Hmf, yes indeed. Stand by a moment while I look into the directory. We'll pick up a line on this fellow."

Wayness waited. A minute passed and another. Pirie Tamm's face returned to the screen. " 'Alcide Xantief': this is his name. There is a business address, no more: Via Malthus 26, Trieste Old Port. He is listed as a dealer in 'Arcana,' which means whatever you want it to mean."

Wayness made a note of the address. "I wish I could rid myself of the conviction that I was being followed."

"Ha! Perhaps you are, for a fact, being followed, and this is the basis of your conviction."

Wayness gave a cheerless laugh. "But I don't see anyone. I just imagine things, like dark figures stepping back into the shadows when I turn to look. I wonder if I might not be neurotic."

"I hardly think so," said Pirie Tamm. "You have good reason to be nervous."

"So I keep telling myself. But it is no great comfort. I would prefer to be neurotic, I think, with nothing to fear."

"Certain kinds of surveillance are hard to avoid," said Pirie Tamm. "You probably know of tracer buttons and tags." And he suggested several procedures of avoidance. "Like the telephone experts, I guarantee nothing."

"I'll do what I can," said Wayness. "Goodbye for now, Uncle Pirie."

During the evening, Wayness bathed, washed her hair, scrubbed her shoes, handbag and suitcase in order to remove any radiant substance which might have been sprayed or smeared upon them. She laundered her cloak and outer garments and made sure that no spy cell or tracer button had been affixed to the hem of her cloak.

In the morning she used all the ploys suggested by Pirie Tamm and others of her own contrivance to elude any possible follower or flying spy cell, and at last set off for Trieste by subterranean slideway.

At noon she arrived at the Trieste Central Depot, which served New Trieste, north of the Carso, one of the few remaining urban areas still dominated by the Technic Paradigms: a checkerboard of concrete and glass shapes, rectilinear and identical save for the numbers on the flat roofs. The 'Technic Paradigms' had been applied to New Trieste, and thereafter rejected almost everywhere else on Earth in favor of construction less intellectual and less brutally efficient.

From the Central Depot Wayness rode by subway ten miles south to the Old Trieste Station: a structure of black iron webbing and opal-green glass covering five acres of transit terminals, markets, cafés and a cheerful animation of porters, school children, wandering musicians, persons arriving and departing.

At a kiosk Wayness bought a map, which she took to a café by a pair of flower stalls. While she lunched on mussels in a bright red sauce redolent of garlic and rosemary she studied the map. On the front page the editor had included an instruction:

> 'If you would know the secrets of Old Trieste,
> which are many, then you must come upon them
> reverentially and gradually, not like a fat man
> jumping into a swimming pool, but rather as a
> devout acolyte approaching the altar.'
>
> —A. Bellors Foxtehude.

Wayness unfolded the map and after a puzzled glance or two decided that she was holding it upside down. She turned it about, but nothing was clarified; she had evidently been holding it correctly in the first place. Again she reversed the map, to what must be the proper orientation, with the Adriatic Sea on the right hand. For several minutes she studied the tangle of marks. According to the legend, they indicated streets, major and minor canals, incidental waterways, alleys, bridges, special walkways, squares, plazas, promenades and major edifices. Each item was identified by a printed super- or sub-script, and it seemed that the shortest streets had been assigned the longest names. Wayness looked from right to left in bewilderment and was about to return to the kiosk for a less challenging map when she noticed Via Malthus, on the western bank of the Canal Bartolo Seppi, in the Porto Vecchio district.

Wayness folded the map and looked around the café. She discovered no portly waxen-skinned gentleman with a black mustache, and no one else seemed to be paying her any unusual attention. Unobtrusively she departed the café and the shelter of the station, to find the sun hidden behind scudding gray clouds and a raw wind blowing in from the Adriatic.

Wayness stood for a moment, skirts flapping against her legs, then ran to a cab rank and approached the driver of a three-wheeled cab, of a sort which seemed to be in general use. She showed the driver her map, pointed out Via Malthus and explained that she wanted to be taken to a hotel nearby. The driver responded confidently: "The Old Port is charming! I will take you to the Hotel Sirenuse. You will find it both convenient and agreeable, nor are its charges a confiscation."

Wayness climbed into the cab and was whirled away through Old Trieste: a city of unique character, built half on a narrow apron of land under the stony hills and half on piles driven into the Adriatic. Canals of dark water flowed everywhere, washing the foundations of the tall narrow houses. A dark mysterious city, thought Wayness.

By slants this way and that, by sudden darts over

humped bridges, into the Plaza Dalmatio by the Via Con-
dottiere and out by the Via Strada, went the cab, with
Wayness unable to trace the course on her map, so that if
the driver were inserting a mile or two into his route she
had no sure way of knowing. At last the cab swung into the
Via Severin, crossed the Canal Flacco by the Ponte Fidelius
and into a district of crabbed streets and crooked canals,
below a gaunt skyline of a thousand odd angles and
shapes. This was the Porto Vecchio, hard by the wharves:
a district silent by night but bustling by day with the
movement of the locals and the surge of tourists, in and
out, predictable as tides.

The Way of the Ten Pantologues ran beside the Bartolo
Seppi Canal, and was lined with bistros, cafés, flower
stalls, booths selling fried clams and potatoes in paper
packets. Along the sidestreets dim little shops dealt in
specialty merchandise: curios, off-world artifacts, incu-
nabula; rare weapons and musical instruments pitched in
every key imaginable. Certain shops specialized in puzzles,
cryptography, inscriptions in unknown languages; others
sold coins, glass insects, autographs, minerals mined from
the substance of dead stars. Still other shops purveyed
softer stuff: dolls costumed in the styles of many times and
places, also dolls cleverly programmed to perform acts
which were polite and acts not at all polite. Spice shops
vended condiments and scents, oils and esters, of an interesting sort; confectioneries sold cakes and bonbons available nowhere else on Earth, as well as dried fruits, syrups
and glazes. A variety of shops displayed models of ships,
ancient trains and automobiles; while others specialized in
models of spaceships.

The cab driver took Wayness to the Hotel Sirenuse, a
sprawling old hulk devoid of architectural grace, which had
expanded over the centuries, annex by annex, and now
occupied the entire area between the Way of the Ten
Pantologues and the Adriatic shore. Wayness was assigned
a high-ceilinged chamber at the back of the second floor.
The room was cheerful enough, with pink and blue floral
wallpaper, a crystal chandelier and glass doors giving upon
a small balcony. Another door opened into a bathroom

equipped with fixtures of playfully rococo design. On a buffet Wayness found the telephone screen, several books, including a truncated edition of Baron Bodissey's monumental ten volumes: LIFE; also TALES OF OLD TRIESTE, by Fia della Rema; THE TAXONOMY OF DEMONS, by Miris Ovic. There was also a menu from the hotel restaurant, a basket of green grapes and a decanter of red wine on a tray, along with two goblets.

Wayness ate a grape, poured herself half a glass of red wine and went out upon the balcony. She saw, almost directly below, the rotting old wharf, creaking to the slow Adriatic swells. Half a dozen fishing boats were moored alongside. Beyond was sky and sea, with veils of gray rain sweeping across the water. To the north, her view was circumscribed by a dark blur of shoreline, which disappeared entirely, behind the rain, at the edge of vision. For several minutes Wayness stood on the balcony, sipping the tart red wine. The damp wind blew into her face, bringing the scent of the wharf. This was Old Earth in one of its truest manifestations, she thought. Nowhere out among the stars would there be found a panorama like this.

The wind blew fresh. Wayness drained the goblet, turned back into the room, closed the glass doors. She bathed, changed into gray-tan trousers tight at the hips, loose below the knees, gathered at the ankles, which she wore with a neat black jacket. After consideration, she put through a call to Fair Winds, and half an hour later was speaking with Pirie Tamm at the bank.

"I see you arrived in safety," said Pirie Tamm. "Were you followed?"

"I don't think so. But I can't be sure."

"So—what now?"

"I'll be going off to see Xantief. His shop is not too far away. If I learn anything definite, I will call you. If not, I may wait a bit. Even when I don't say anything, I'm afraid that the call might be traced."

"Hmf," grunted Pirie Tamm. "So far as I know, that is not possible."

"Probably not. I suppose that you have had no word from Julian, or anyone else?"

"Nothing from Julian, but a letter from your parents arrived this morning. Shall I read it?"

"Please do!"

The letter told her of Glawen's homecoming, Floreste's disgrace and execution, and Glawen's absence on a solitary expedition to Shattorak on Ecce, from which, at the time of writing, Glawen had not yet returned.

Wayness was not cheered by the letter. "I worry a great deal about Glawen," she told Pirie Tamm. "He is utterly reckless when he thinks something needs to be done."

"You are fond of him?"

"Very much indeed."

"He is a lucky fellow."

"It's nice of you to say so, Uncle Pirie, but I am lucky too—if he survives."

"At the moment it's better that you worry about yourself. I imagine Glawen Clattuc would agree with me."

"I suppose he would. Goodbye then, Uncle Pirie."

Wayness descended to the lobby. The hotel was busy; folk came and went in a steady stream; others made rendezvous with friends. Wayness looked here and there, but recognized no one.

The time was now three o'clock of a rather dank and misty afternoon. Wayness left the hotel and set out along the Way of the Ten Pantologues. Thin layers of fog floated across the hills and down over the slopes. Wisps, mists and dreary odors rose from the Bartolo Seppi Canal. The landscape was a collage of abstract shapes, black, brown, and gray.

Wayness was gradually diverted from her thoughts by a tickling at the back of her neck. Could it be that once again she was being followed? Either this was so, or she had developed a vexing obsession. She stopped short and pretended interest in the window display of a candlemaker's shop, meanwhile watching sidelong back over her shoulder. As usual, she saw nothing to nourish her suspicions.

Still dissatisfied, she turned and walked back the way she had come, taking note of those whom she passed. No one seemed at all familiar—but still, that plump little man, bald, with the cherubic pink face: could he have worn a black wig, a false mustache and skin-coloring to deceive her? It was possible. And that broad-shouldered young tourist, moon-faced, with the long yellow hair: could that conceivably be the sinister young footman who had called himself Baro? Wayness grimaced. Nowadays anything was possible, and disguise was a fine art, what with flexible masks and lenses which altered not only the color but also the shape of eyes. Recognition no longer counted for much, and the only definite way to identify a follower was by his conduct.

Wayness decided to put her theories to the test. She ducked into a dark little alley, then, ten feet along, stepped into an entry where she was hidden from view.

Time passed: five minutes, then ten minutes. Nothing of importance occurred. No one entered the alley nor so much as paused to look along its length. Wayness began to suspect that her nerves were issuing false alarms. She left her place of concealment and returned to the Way of the Ten Pantologues. A tall spare woman wearing a black gown, with black hair gathered into a tight bun, stood nearby. She took note of Wayness and instantly raised her eyebrows in scorn, then sniffed, swung about and marched away.

Odd! thought Wayness. But perhaps not so odd. The woman might have assumed that Wayness had gone into the alley in order to relieve herself.

There was, to Wayness' knowledge, no correct or approved method for explaining a mistake of this sort. Further, if Wayness had misinterpreted the woman's conduct, the explanations, no matter how delicately put, could very easily become complicated.

Wayness departed the scene at the best speed she could manage with dignity.

Another two hundred yards along, the Way brought her to the conflux of the Bartolo Seppi Canal with the Canal Daciano. A bridge, the Ponte Orsini, conveyed the Way over the Canal Daciano, where the Way met Via Malthus. Wayness turned to her right and walked slowly. Fifty yards along she came upon a dim little shop with a modest sign above the door. On a black ground faded gold cursive script read:

Xantief
ARCANA

The door was locked; the shop was empty. Wayness stood back and compressed her lips in annoyance. "Curse all!" muttered Wayness to herself. "Does he think I have come all this way just to stand outside his door in the rain?" And indeed, the mist had become a drizzle.

Wayness tried to look through the glass panes of the door, but saw nothing. It was possible that Xantief had stepped out for a moment and might soon return. Hunching her shoulders against the drizzle, she glanced at the shop to the right, which sold pomanders compounded from off-world herbs. The shop to the left specialized in jade medallions, about three inches in diameter, or possibly they were buckles.

Wayness sauntered to the far end of the Via Malthus, where it debouched upon the wharf. She paused, looked back along the street. No one seemed interested in her movements. She returned up Via Malthus and halted by the shop which sold the jade medallions. A sign in the door read:

ALVINA IS IN!
Enter

Wayness pushed open the door and went into the shop. At a desk to the side sat a thin middle-aged woman with a jaunty short-billed fisherman's cap pulled down over russet-gray curls. She wore a heavy pullover of dark gray knit, a gray twill skirt; with bright gray-green eyes she glanced sidelong at Wayness. "I see that you are new to Trieste, and never expected the rain."

Wayness gave a rueful laugh. "It took me by surprise. But I came to visit the shop next door, which is closed. Do you know Mr. Xantief's business hours?"

"I do indeed. He opens his shop three times a week at midnight for three hours only. He will be open tonight, in case you are interested."

Wayness' jaw went slack. "What an absurd schedule!"

Alvina smiled. "Not when you know Xantief."

"Surely it can't be convenient for his customers! Or is he merely perverse?"

Alvina, still smiling, shook her head. "Xantief is a man of many fascinating traits. Almost incidentally, he is a crafty shopkeeper. He pretends that he does not want to sell his merchandise, the implication being that it is too good for the common ruck, and that his prices are far too low. This, of course, is nonsense—I think."

"It is his shop, and naturally he can do as he likes with it. Even though people get sopping wet." Wayness spoke in what she thought to be a reasonable voice, but Alvina's sensitive ear caught a nuance of emotion.

"In connection with Xantief, vexation is pointless. He is a patrician."

"I was not planning to create a disturbance," said Wayness with dignity. "Still, I appreciate the advice." She went to look out the door, but the rain had started in earnest.

Alvina seemed in no hurry to be rid of her, so she asked: "Xantief has been here a long time?"

Alvina nodded. "He was born about fifty miles east in a castle. His father, the thirty-third baron, died while Xantief was still a young scholar. Xantief tells how he was called to the deathbed. The old baron told him: 'My dear Alcide, we have enjoyed many years together, but now it is my time to go. I die happy, since I bequeath to you a heritage of incalculable value. First, a discriminating and certain good taste which other men will find enviable. Second, the unthinking and instinctive conviction of worth, honor and excellence, which accompanies your quality as the thirty-fourth baron. Third, you will inherit the physical assets of the barony, with all its lands, holdings and treasures, in fee singular and complete. Now then: I charge you that while my passing should be no occasion for ribaldry and merry-making, neither should you grieve, since, if I am able, I will always be on hand to guard you and keep you in your hour of need.' So saying, the old man died and Xantief became the thirty-fourth baron. Since he already knew of his good taste in wine, food and women, and had never felt any doubts regarding his personal worth, his first step was to reckon up the physical assets. He found that they were not large: the moldering old castle, a few acres of limestone crags, two dozen ancient olive trees and a few goats.

"Xantief made the most of his inheritance. He opened his shop, and originally stocked it with some rugs, hangings, books, paintings and bric-a-brac from his castle, and prospered from the first. That is, at least, the story he tells."

"Hm. You seem to know him well."

"Tolerably well. Whenever he comes by during the day he drops in to look over the tanglets. He is sensitive to them and sometimes I go so far as to take his advice." Alvina gave a short laugh. "This is a curious business. Xantief may touch the tanglets and test their strength, but I am not allowed to do so, nor are you."

Wayness turned to look at the glowing green buckles, or clasps—whatever they were—on display in the window, each on a small pedestal covered with black velvet. Each was similar but notably different from all the rest.

"They are beautiful little things; jade, I suppose?"

"Nephrite, to be exact. Jadeite gives a different feel: somewhat more coarse. These are cold and unctuous, like green butter."

"What are they used for?"

"I use them to sell to collectors," said Alvina. "All authentic tanglets are antiques, and very valuable, since the only new tanglets are counterfeit."

"What were they originally?"

"At first they were hairclasps, worn by the warriors of a far world. When a warrior killed an enemy he took the clasp and wore it on the scalp rope of his hair. In this way tanglets became trophies. The tanglets of a hero are even more; they are talismans. There are hundreds of distinctions and qualities and special terms, which make the subject rather fascinating, when you acquire some of the lore. Only a finite number are authentic tanglets, despite the efforts of counterfeiters, and each one is annotated and named and attributed. All are valuable, but the great ones are literally priceless. A hero's rope of six tanglets is so full of mana it almost sparks. I must take extraordinary care; a single touch sours the sheen and curdles the mana."

"Poof!" said Wayness. "Who would know the difference?"

"An expert: that's who, and on the instant. I could tell you stories for hours on end." Alvina looked toward the ceiling. "I'll tell you just one, about the famous tanglet: Twelve Kanaw. A collector named Jadoukh Ibrasil had coveted Twelve Kanaw for many years, and finally, after complicated negotiations, took possession of Twelve Kanaw. On the same night, his beautiful spouse Dilre Lagoum saw the tanglet and innocently wore it in her hair to a fête. Jadoukh Ibrasil joined his wife, complimented her upon her beauty, then noticed the tanglet in her hair. Witnesses say that he turned white as a sheet. He knew at once what he must do. Courteously he took Dilre Lagoum's arm and led her into the garden and cut her throat among the hydrangeas. Then he stabbed himself. The story is usually heard only among collectors. The general feeling is that Jadoukh Ibrasil did what he had to do, and at this point the talk becomes metaphysical. What do you think?"

"I don't quite know," said Wayness cautiously. "It may be that all collectors are mad."

"Ah, well! That is a truism."

"I should think that work among such temperamental objects would be hard on the nerves."

"Sometimes it is," Alvina admitted. "I find, however, that my high prices are a great solace." Alvina rose to her feet. "I will let you handle a counterfeit, if you like. You can do no damage."

Wayness shook her head. "I think not. I have better things to do than handle counterfeits."

"In that case, I'll make us a pot of tea—unless you are in a hurry?"

Wayness looked out the window, to find that the rain had stopped, at least for the moment. "No, thank you. I think I'll take advantage of the let-up and run back to the hotel."

II.

Wayness stood for a moment in front of Alvina's shop. Out over the Adriatic shafts of sunlight had broken through the clouds. Via Malthus smelled of damp stone mingled with odors from the canal and the everywhere pervasive scent of the sea. Beside the canal an old man wearing a red stocking cap with a tail dangling to his shoulders walked with a small white dog. Diagonally across the street an old woman stood in the doorway of her house, conversing with another old woman who stood on the sidewalk. Both wore black gowns and lace shawls; as they talked, they turned to look with disapproval toward the old man walking stiffly and slowly with his dog; it seemed as if they were disparaging him for reasons beyond Wayness' understanding. None of the three could be considered a threat. Wayness set off at a fast walk up Via Malthus, then to the left along the Way of the Ten Pantologues, keeping an unobtrusive watch over her shoulder. She arrived at the Hotel Sirenuse without incident, and went directly to her room.

The westering sun had banished most of the tattered clouds and had transformed some of the grays and dark grays of the landscape into whites. Wayness stood out upon the balcony for a few minutes, then turning back into the room, settled into an armchair, to reflect upon what she had learned. Most of it, while interesting, seemed irrelevant to her principal concerns. She found herself dozing and stumbled to the bed for a nap.

Time passed. Wayness awoke with a start of urgency, to

find that the time was already middle evening. She changed into her dark brown suit and went down to the restaurant. She dined upon a bowl of goulash with a salad of lettuce and red cabbage and half a carafe of the soft local wine.

Upon leaving the dining room, Wayness went to sit in a corner of the lobby, where with one eye she pretended to read a periodical and with the other she watched the comings and goings.

The time moved toward midnight. At twenty minutes to the hour, Wayness rose, went to the entrance and looked up and down the street.

Everything was quiet, and the night was dark. A few street-lamps stood at infrequent intervals, in islands of their own wan light. On the hillside a thin fog dimmed a thousand other lights so that they seemed no more than sparks. Along the Way of the Ten Pantologues, no one walked abroad, so far as Wayness could see. But she hesitated and went back into the hotel. At the registration desk, she spoke to the night clerk: a young woman not much older than herself. Wayness tried to speak in a matter-of-fact voice. "I must go out to meet someone, on a matter of business. Are the streets considered safe?"

"Streets are streets. They are widely used. The face you look into might be that of a maniac, or it might be the face of your own father. I am told that in some cases they are the same person."

"My father is far away," said Wayness. "I would be truly surprised to see him on the streets of Old Trieste."

"In that case, you are rather more likely to discover a maniac. My mother worries greatly when I am out by night. 'No one is safe even in their own kitchen,' she tells me. 'Only last week the repair man who was called to fix the sink insulted your grandmother!' I said that the next time the repair man is called, Grandmother should go out on the street instead of hanging around the kitchen."

Wayness started to turn away from the desk. "It seems that I must take my chances."

"One moment," said the clerk. "You are wearing the wrong uniform. Tie a scarf over your head. When a girl is out looking for excitement her head is uncovered."

"The last thing I want is excitement," said Wayness. "Do you have a scarf I might borrow for an hour or so?"

"Yes, of course." The clerk found a square of black and green checked wool which she gave to Wayness. "That should be quite adequate. Will you be late?"

"I should think not. The person I must see is only available at midnight."

"Very well. I will wait up for you until two. After that you must ring the outside bell."

"I'll try to be back early."

Wayness tied the scarf over her hair, and set off on her errand. By night the streets of Porto Vecchio in old Trieste were not to Wayness' liking. There were sounds behind the curtained windows which seemed to carry a sinister significance, even though they were almost inaudible. Where the Way crossed the Daciano Canal, a tall woman in a black gown stood on the Ponte Orsini. A cool chill played along Wayness' skin. Could this be the same woman who had glared at her earlier in the day? Might she have decided that Wayness needed further chastisement?

But it was not the same woman and Wayness laughed shakily at her own foolishness. This lady who stood on the bridge was quietly singing, so softly that Wayness, pausing to listen, could barely hear. It was a wistful pretty tune, and Wayness hoped that it might not linger on and on, to haunt her memory.

Wayness turned down Via Malthus, watching behind her more warily than ever. Before she reached Xantief's shop, a man wearing a cloak and hood came springing light-footed around the corner from the Way of the Ten Pantologues. He paused, to peer down Via Malthus, and then followed after Wayness.

With heart in mouth, Wayness turned and ran to Xantief's shop. Behind the windows she saw a faint illumination; she pushed at the door. It was locked. She cried out in distress and tried the door again, then knocked on the glass and pulled at the bell cord. She looked over her shoulder. Down Via Malthus came the tall man, moving on his light springing strides. Wayness turned and huddled back into the shadows. Her knees were loose; she felt apathetic, trapped. Behind her the door opened; she saw a white-haired man, slight of physique and of no great stature, but erect and calm. He moved aside and Wayness half-stumbled, half-fell through the doorway.

The man in the hooded cloak strode lightly past, never so much as troubling to look aside. He was gone: down Via Malthus and into the darkness.

Xantief closed the door and moved a chair forward. "You are disturbed; why not rest for a moment or two?"

Wayness sagged into the chair. Presently she regained her composure. She decided that something needed to be said. Why not the truth, then? It would serve well enough, and had the advantage of needing no fabrication. She spoke, and was surprised to find her voice still tremulous: "I was frightened."

Xantief nodded courteously. "I had reached the same conclusion—though no doubt for different reasons."

Wayness, after considering the remark, was obliged to laugh, which seemed to please Xantief. She straightened herself in the chair and looked around the room: more like the parlor of a private residence than a place of business, she thought. Whatever might be the 'arcana' which were Xantief's stock-in-trade, none were on display. Xantief himself matched the image Wayness had derived from Alvina's remarks. His tendencies were obviously aristocratic; he was urbane and fastidious, with a clear pale skin, features of aquiline delicacy, soft white hair cut only long enough to frame his face. He dressed without ostentation in an easy suit of soft black stuff, a white shirt and the smallest possible tuft of a moss-green cravat.

"For the moment, at least, your fright seems to be under control," suggested Xantief. "What was its cause, may I ask?"

"The truth is simple," said Wayness. "I am afraid of death."

Xantief nodded. "Many people share this dread, but only a few come running into my shop at midnight to tell me about it."

Wayness spoke carefully, as if to an obtuse child: "That is not the reason I came."

"Ah! You are not here by chance?"

"No."

"Let us proceed a step farther. You are not, so to speak, a human derelict, or a nameless waif?"

Wayness spoke with dignity. "I cannot imagine what you have in mind. I am Wayness Tamm."

"Ah! That explains everything! You must forgive me my caution. Here in Old Trieste there is never a dearth of surprising episodes, sometimes whimsical, sometimes tragic. For instance, after a visit like yours, at an unconventional hour, the householder discovers that a baby has been left on the premises in a basket."

Wayness spoke coldly: "You need not worry on that account. I am here now only because you have made these your business hours."

Xantief bowed. "I am reassured. Your name is Wayness Tamm? It fits you nicely. Please remove that ridiculous dust rag, or fly chaser, or cat blanket: whatever it is you are wearing for a scarf. There! That is better. May I serve you a cordial? No? Tea? Tea it shall be." Xantief glanced at her from the side of his face. "You are an off-worlder, I think?"

Wayness nodded. "More to the point, I am a member of the Naturalist Society. My uncle, Pirie Tamm, is secretary."

"I know of the Naturalist Society," said Xantief. "I thought it to be a thing of the past."

"Not quite." Wayness stopped to reflect. "If I told you everything, we would be here for hours. I'll try to be brief."

"Thank you," said Xantief. "I am not a good listener. Proceed."

"A long time ago—I am not sure of the exact date—a secretary of the Society named Frons Nisfit sold off Society assets and embezzled the proceeds.

"The Society is now trying to revive itself, and we need some of the lost documents. I discovered that about twenty years ago you sold some Naturalist material to Count Raul de Flamanges. That, in effect, is why I am here."

"I remember the transaction," said Xantief. "What next?"

"I wonder if you own other Society material, such as documents relating to the Cadwal Conservancy."

Xantief shook his head. "Not a one. It was only a freak that I was involved at all."

Wayness sagged back in the chair.

"Then perhaps you will tell me how the Society materials came to you, so that I can carry my inquiries another step."

"Certainly. As I mentioned, this sort of thing is not in my ordinary line. I took the documents only so that I might transmit them to Count Raul, whom I considered an altruist and a great gentleman and, indeed, a friend. Here is the tea."

"Thank you. Why are you laughing?"

"You are so extremely earnest."

Wayness started to blink, but tears came too fast for her. She wished that she were safe home at Riverview House, snug in her own bed. The idea was far too melting and almost broke through her self-possession.

Xantief had come to stand beside her and was wiping her cheeks with a fine handkerchief smelling of lavender. "Forgive me; I am not usually so insensitive. Clearly you are under a great strain."

"I'm afraid that I've been followed—by dangerous people. I tried to avoid leading them here, but I can't be sure."

"What makes you think you were followed?"

"Just as you opened your door, a man came past. He was wearing a cape with a hood. You must have seen him."

"So I did. He passes by every night about this time."

"You know him?"

"I know well enough that he was not following you."

"Still, I feel eyes watching me, brushing the back of my neck."

"It may be so," said Xantief. "I have heard many strange tales in my time. Still—" He shrugged. "If your followers were amateurs, you could shake them off easily. If they were professionals, you might or might not evade them. If they were dedicated experts, your skin would radiate a set of coded wave-lengths. You would be surrounded by flying spy cells, each no larger than a droplet of water, and when you tried to cut them off by ducking into subway cars, they would already have settled into your clothing."

"Then there may be spy cells in this room right now!"

"I think not," said Xantief. "During my own dealings I am often obliged to take precautions, and I have installed instruments which would warn me of such nuisances on the instant. More than likely, you are suffering from nervous fatigue and imagining a great deal."

"I hope so."

"Now then: as to my involvement with the Naturalist Society papers. It is a strange story in itself. By any chance, did you notice the shop next door?"

"I spoke with Alvina; she told me of your hours."

"Twenty years ago she was approached by a gentleman named Adrian Moncurio, who wished to sell a holding of fourteen tanglets. Alvina called in experts who determined that the tanglets were not only authentic but highly important. Alvina was happy to sell them on a consignment basis. Moncurio, who seems to have been something of an adventurer, went off in search of new merchandise. After a time he returned, with twenty more tanglets. These, however, were declared counterfeit by the experts. Moncurio tried to bluster but Alvina refused to sponsor them for sale. Moncurio snatched up his false talismans and departed Trieste, before the Tanglet Association was able to act.

"For a period nothing was heard of Moncurio, but during this time, posing as a half-demented aged junkdealer he was selling the counterfeits to inexperienced collectors, who thought they were taking advantage of the blundering old fool. Before the Tanglet Association could act, all twenty counterfeits had been sold and Moncurio was seen no more."

"But what of the Naturalist Society documents?"

Xantief made a placid gesture. "When Moncurio first approached Alvina, he also wanted her to sell the Naturalist Society material. She referred him to me. I was interested only in the material concerning Count Raul, but Moncurio insisted on selling all or nothing. So I took the lot for a rather nominal figure, and passed them on to Count Raul for the same sum."

"You found nothing to do with the planet Cadwal? No Charter, for instance? No grant, or deed, or title certificate?"

"There was nothing of that sort whatever."

Wayness slumped back into the chair. After a moment she asked: "Did Moncurio mention the source of the papers? Where he had found them, who had sold them?"

Xantief shook his head. "Nothing definite, as I recall."

"I wonder where he is now."

"Moncurio? I have no idea. If he is on Earth, he is lying low."

"If Alvina sent him money for the first fourteen tanglets, she must have an address where he could be reached."

"Hm. If so, she did not notify the Association—but perhaps she felt that the information had come to her in confidence." Xantief reflected a moment. "If you like, I will have a word with her. She might tell me but hesitate to tell you."

"Oh please do!" Wayness jumped to her feet and spoke in a rush: "I'd like to tell you everything—but mainly this: unless I succeed, Cadwal may be swarmed over and the Conservancy will be gone."

"Aha," said Xantief. "I am beginning to understand. I will call Alvina at once; like myself she keeps late hours." He picked up the black and green scarf and tied it around Wayness' head. "Where are you staying?"

"At the Hotel Sirenuse."

"Goodnight then. If I learn anything useful, I will instantly let you know."

"Thank you very much."

Xantief opened the door. Wayness stepped out into the street. Xantief looked right and left. "All seems quiet. As a rule the streets are safe this time of night, with all proper footpads snug in their beds."

Wayness walked quickly up Via Malthus. At the corner she looked back to where Xantief still stood watching. She raised her hand and waved farewell, then turned into the Way of the Ten Pantologues.

The night seemed even darker than before. On the Ponte Orsini the woman in black no longer sang her soft song. The air carried a chill as well as the dank odors of Old Trieste.

Wayness set off along the street, her footsteps clicking crisply along the pavement. From behind a pair of clamped iron shutters came a mutter of low voices and an undertone of woeful sobbing. Wayness' footsteps faltered an instant, then hurried on past. She came to a place where shadows marked the entrance into a narrow alley descending toward the wharf. As Wayness went by, a man moved forward from the shadows: a tall person wearing dark clothes and a soft black hat. He seized Wayness around the shoulders and forced her into the alley. She opened her mouth to scream; he clasped a hand over her face. Wayness' knees went limp; he half-carried her, half-led her stumbling down the alley. She began to struggle and to bite; he said without emotion: "Stop, or I will hurt you."

Wayness again let herself go limp; then she gave a frantic lurch and broke free; she had nowhere to go but down the alley, and she ran at full speed. To the side a door opened into a yard. She pushed through the door, slammed it shut behind her and shot the latch just as her pursuer thrust against it. The door rattled and creaked. He struck with his shoulder again; the door was a flimsy affair and would not hold him back. Wayness picked up an empty wine bottle from what appeared to be a potting table. The man crashed into the door; it burst open and he came through. Wayness hit him over the head with the bottle; he staggered and fell. She pushed the potting table over on top of him and was away and up the alley as fast as she could run. She arrived at the Way and looked back; her assailant had not appeared.

Wayness moved onward at a trot toward the hotel, slowing to a fast walk the last thirty yards.

In the entrance Wayness paused to look back along the Way and to catch her breath. The full impact of the episode began to work on her. She realized that she had never been so frightened before, though at the time she had felt no particular emotion, save a furious exultation when she had felt the glass bottle strike home. She shuddered to a complex mix of emotions.

Wayness shivered again, this time from the chill. She went into the hotel, and approached the desk. The clerk smiled at her. "You are back in good time." She glanced curiously at Wayness. "Have you been running?"

"Yes, just a bit," said Wayness, trying to bring her breathing under control. She looked over her shoulder. "Actually, I became frightened."

"That is nonsense," said the clerk. "There is nothing out there to be frightened about, especially when you are wearing the scarf properly."

The scarf had slipped back from Wayness' head so that she was wearing it as a neckerchief. "Next time I'll be more careful," said Wayness. She untied the scarf and returned it to the clerk. "Thank you very much."

"It was nothing in particular. I was glad to help."

Wayness went up to her room. She bolted the door and pulled the curtains across the windows. She settled into the armchair, and sat thinking about the episode in the alley. Had the attack been a random sexual assault, or had it been intended upon the life and limb of Wayness Tamm? There was no definite evidence in either direction, but her intuition seemed content to operate without the benefit of evidence. Or perhaps there had been evidence, at the subliminal level. The timbre of his voice had seemed familiar. And, unless she had imagined this, his person had exhaled an almost imperceptible scent, mixed of fern, violet and perhaps a few off-world essences. He had felt young and strong.

Wayness did not care to think any more definitely—not at this time.

Five minutes passed. Wayness rose to her feet and started to undress for bed. The telephone tinkled. Wayness stared. Who could be calling her at this hour. Slowly she went to the telephone, and without activating the screen asked: "Who is it?"

"Alcide Xantief."

Wayness sat down and turned on the screen. Xantief said: "I hope I am not disturbing you?"

"Of course not!"

"I spoke to Alvina. You made a good impression on her. I explained that any help she could give you would be work in a good cause—if for no other reason than the happiness of a rather nice person known as Wayness Tamm. She agreed to do what she could for you, if you arrived tomorrow about noon at her shop."

"That is good news, Mr. Xantief!"

"Before you get your hopes up, she mentioned that she did not know Moncurio's present whereabouts, but only the address he had supplied to her some years ago."

"Anything is better than nothing."

"Exactly. I will bid you goodnight once again. These are my working hours, as you know; in fact, I hear a customer waiting for me now."

III.

In the morning Wayness awoke to find the sun shining brightly down upon the Adriatic. She was served breakfast in her room by one of the blue-uniformed call-boys: an undersized youth named Felix. After a covert appraisal, Wayness decided that Felix might suit her purposes very well. He was deft and agile, with lank black hair and sharp black eyes in a thin knowledgeable face. He readily agreed to perform whatever services Wayness might require, and she gave him a sol to cement the arrangement.

"First and foremost," she told him, "all our dealings must be kept confidential. No one must know. This is very important!"

"Have no fear!" declared Felix. "This is the way I normally do business! I am known to be discretion personified!"

"Good! This is what I want you to do first." She sent Felix out to the shops along the wharf. He returned presently with an old pea jacket, a gray workshirt, dungarees, rubber-soled sandals and a fisherman's cap.

Wayness donned her new garments and surveyed herself in the mirror. She made a not-too-convincing old salt, but at least she was unrecognizable, especially after she darkened her face with skin tone.

Felix echoed her opinions. "I don't know exactly what I'd make of you, but for sure you don't look like what you were before."

At half an hour before noon, Felix led her down the service stairs into the basement of the hotel, then along a dank passage to a flight of stone steps closed off by a heavy timber door. Felix opened the door and they descended still further, finally to jump down upon the shingle of the beach at the far side of the sea wall, under the wharf, with the waters of the Adriatic only fifteen feet to the side.

The two proceeded a hundred yards along the shingle at the base of the sea wall and at last came to a ladder by which they climbed to the face of the wharf. Felix was now ready to turn back, but Wayness protested. "Not yet! I feel safer with you beside me."

"That is an illusion," said Felix. He looked over his shoulder. "No one has followed; if someone did so, and started a row, I should probably run away, for I am a coward."

"Come along anyway," said Wayness. "I do not expect you to lay down your life for what I intend to pay you. My thinking is this: if we are attacked, and if we both run, my chances for survival are doubled over what they would be if I were alone."

"Hmf!" said Felix. "You are even more cold-blooded than I. If I come, I will expect an extra sol, for the danger involved."

"Very well."

Where Via Malthus opened upon the wharf, a small restaurant served dock workers, fishermen, and whoever else felt the need for fish stew, or mussels, or fried fish. Again Felix was ready to turn back but again Wayness would not hear of it. She gave him careful instructions.

"You must go up Via Malthus to a shop with some green buckles in the window."

"I know the shop. It is run by a crazy woman named Alvina."

"Go into the shop and tell Alvina that Wayness Tamm is waiting here, at this restaurant. Make sure no one overhears. If she cannot leave her shop, bring a message."

"First, my pay."

Wayness shook her head. "I was not born yesterday. You will be paid when you return with Alvina."

Felix set off. Ten minutes passed. Alvina entered the restaurant, followed by Felix. Wayness had seated herself in a corner, and Alvina looked here and there in puzzlement. Felix led her to the corner table. Wayness now paid Felix three sols. "Do not mention this excursion to anyone," she told him. "Also, leave the door open at the bottom of the steps, so that I can return the way we came."

Felix departed, not displeased with himself. Alvina gave Wayness a cool inspection. "You are taking careful precautions—although you neglected a black beard."

"I never thought of that."

"No matter. I would never have recognized you as you are now."

"I hope not. Last night I was attacked on my way home from Xantief's shop. I barely escaped."

Alvina raised her eyebrows. "That is disturbing!"

Wayness wondered if Alvina were taking her seriously. Perhaps she thought the disguise over-dramatic.

A waiter in a stained white apron appeared. Alvina ordered a bowl of red fish soup and Wayness did the same.

Alvina asked: "I wonder if you would tell me the background of your search?"

"Certainly. A thousand years ago the Naturalist Society discovered the world Cadwal, and considered it so beautiful, with so many entrancing aspects that they decided to make it into a perpetual Conservancy, safe from human exploitation. At the moment the Conservancy is in serious danger: all because a former secretary sold off Society documents to antique dealers, including the grant in perpetuity to Cadwal and the original Cadwal Charter. These documents disappeared—where, no one knows. But if they are not found, the Society may lose title to Cadwal."

"And how do you enter the picture!"

"My father is Conservator of Cadwal, and lives at Araminta Station. My uncle, Pirie, is secretary of the Society here on Earth, but he is an invalid, and there is no one to do what needs to be done but me. Other folk are also looking for the Grant of Ownership; some of them are wicked, some are simply foolish, but they want to break the Conservancy, and so they are my enemies. I think that some of them tracked me to Trieste despite my best efforts. I fear for my life, I fear for Cadwal, which is vulnerable. If I don't find the documents, the Conservancy cannot survive. I am getting closer and closer. My enemies know this and they will kill me with no compunction whatever, and I am not ready to die just yet."

"I should think not." Alvina drummed her fingers on the table. "You have not heard the news, then?"

Wayness looked up in apprehension. "What news?"

"Last night Xantief was murdered. This morning he was found in the canal."

Time stood still. Everything became blurred except for Alvina's gray-green eyes. Wayness finally managed to stammer: "This is terrible. I had no idea—it must be my fault! I led them to Xantief."

Alvina nodded. "It might have happened that way. Or maybe not; who knows? It makes no great difference, one way or the other."

After a pause Wayness said: "You are right. It makes no difference." She wiped the tears from her face. The waiter brought bowls of red soup. Wayness looked numbly at the bowl.

"Eat," said Alvina. "We have to pay for it, regardless."

Wayness pushed the bowl away. "What happened?"

"I don't like to tell you. It was not nice. Someone wanted information from Xantief. He could give them none because he had none, except what he told you. No doubt he explained this immediately, but they persisted and killed him, and dropped him into the canal." Alvina busied herself with the soup, then said: "It is clear, however, that he did not mention me."

"How so?"

"I came to my shop early today, and no one was waiting for me. Eat your soup. It is pointless to suffer on an empty stomach."

Wayness heaved a deep sigh. She pulled the bowl of soup toward herself and began to eat. Alvina looked on with a grim smile. "Whenever tragedy has dealt me its worst blows, then I go forth and rejoice. I drink fine wine, and

dine on delicacies I can't afford, and perhaps indulge myself
in some sort of worthless new gew-gaw."

Wayness laughed weakly. "Does the program work?"

"No. Still, eat the soup."

After a few moments Wayness said: "I must learn to be
absolutely callous. I cannot let myself be weak."

"I don't think you are weak. Still, are there no others to
help you?"

"Yes, but they are far away. Glawen Clattuc will be here
sometime soon—but I can't wait."

"You carry no weapons?"

"I don't own any."

"Wait here." Alvina left the restaurant, returning a few
minutes later with a pair of small parcels. "These articles
will give you comfort, at the very least." She explained their
use.

"I thank you," said Wayness. "May I pay for them?"

"No. But if you use either upon whoever murdered
Xantief, please let me know."

"I promise that I will." Wayness tucked the articles into
pockets of the pea jacket.

"Now, to business." Alvina brought out a slip of paper.
"I cannot direct you to Moncurio himself, since he is gone
from Earth. Where, I have no idea, but he left me an
address in case money came in from some old accounts
which had never been settled."

Wayness asked doubtfully: "Is this address still useful?"

"It was as of last year. I sent money to the address, and
finally got back a receipt."

"From Moncurio?"

Alvina grimaced and shook her head. "I sent the money
in care of Irena Portils, who is apparently Moncurio's
spouse—formally or informally, I have no idea. She is a
difficult and suspicious woman. Do not expect her to oblige
you, gladly or otherwise, with Moncurio's current address.
She would not even give me a proper receipt for the money;
she said that there must be no linkage between her name
and his. I told her that this was preposterous, since
Moncurio had already made the linkage, and that if she did

not sign the receipt using Moncurio's name and her own as an endorsement, I would void the draught and send her no more money. Ha! Her avarice is even stronger than her nervousness, and she sent the proper receipt, with just enough icy sarcasm to irritate me."

"Perhaps she is nicer when she is not worried," said Wayness without conviction.

"Anything is possible. Still I can't imagine how you will deal with her, much less extract information."

"I must give the matter some thought. Perhaps I will try a subtle indirect approach."

"I wish you luck. Here is the address." She gave over the paper. Wayness read:

>   Sra. Irena Portils
>   Casa Lucasta
>   Calle Maduro 31
>   Pombareales, Patagonia

IV.

Wayness returned to the Hotel Sirenuse the way she had come: along the wharf to the ladder, down to the shingle and beside the sea wall to the stone steps, then up and through the timber door into the nether regions of the hotel. Here she lost her way and for a time groped back and forth along damp dark passages smelling of must, old wine, onions and fish. Finally, behind a door she had forgotten, she found the service stairs, and so climbed thankfully to the second floor, where she hurried back to her room. She threw off her disguise, bathed and dressed in her ordinary clothes. Then she sat looking out across the sea, pondering the new realities of her life.

Outrage and anger served no purpose; they were only a frustration. Fear was equally profitless—though fear was hard to control.

Wayness became restless. There was too much to think about, and too many complexities. While she thought, she was static and vulnerable; she could protect herself only by activity.

Wayness went to the telephone and called Fair Winds. Agnes appeared, then went to summon Pirie Tamm from the garden. "Ah Wayness!" He spoke guardedly. "I was on my way out; I have an errand at the bank in Tierens. Do you wish to call back in half an hour or so?"

"If you can spare me a minute, I'll talk to you now." Wayness tried to sound easy and casual, but her voice seemed strained, even to her own ears.

"I can spare a minute or two. What is your news?"

"It is both good and bad. I spoke with a certain Alcide Xantief yesterday. He knew nothing himself but in passing he mentioned a repository in Bangalore. I telephoned there this morning and they have the documents we are seeking, and they would seem to be quite accessible."

"Amazing!" said Pirie Tamm, blinking in perplexity.

"It is that and more, when I think of what I have gone through to get this information. I have written to you, to my father and to Glawen, so that the information will not be lost in case something happens to me."

"Why should anything happen to you?"

"Last night I had a rather frightening experience. It might have been mistaken identity, or romance Adriatic style: I can't be sure. But in any case I escaped."

Pirie Tamm gave an exclamation of outrage. "That is damnable! I like this expedition of yours less and less! It's not right that you should be tackling a man's job!"

"Right or wrong, the job must be done," said Wayness. "And there is no one to do it but me."

"Yes, yes," grumbled Pirie Tamm. "We've been over these arguments before."

"Be sure that I am taking all precautions, Uncle Pirie, and now I will let you go on your errand. If you are indeed stopping by the bank, please ask after a remittance I am expecting from home."

"I'll do that, certainly. But what now for you?"

"I'm off for Bangalore, by the best connection, or even the worst, so long as I get there fast."

"And when will I hear from you next?"

"Soon; from Bangalore, most likely."

"Goodbye then, and take care of yourself."

"Goodbye, Uncle Pirie."

Half an hour later Wayness called the bank in Tierens from the public telephone in the hotel lobby. Pirie Tamm's face again appeared on the screen. "Now then! Perhaps we can talk more freely."

"I hope so, since I distrust even the telephone in my own room. I am certain that I have been followed to Trieste." Wayness decided not to mention the murder of Xantief.

"I gather then, that Bangalore will not be your next destination?"

"You gather correctly, Uncle Pirie. If I can send someone off on a wild goose chase, so much the better."

"So what have you achieved in Trieste?"

"I have descended another step on the ladder, and you will be surprised to learn whom I found there."

"Oh? Who might this be?"

"It is your tomb-robbing friend Adrian Moncurio."

"Ha!" said Pirie Tamm after a moment's reflection. "I am surprised, to be sure—though maybe not as much as I might be!"

"Do you have any inkling as to his present address?"

"None whatever."

"What of mutual friends?"

"We have none. Since I have not heard from him, I suspect that he is either off-world or dead."

"In that case I must continue my inquiries. They may possibly take me off-world."

"Off-world where?"

"I don't know yet."

"Then where are you going from Trieste?"

"I am afraid to tell you, for fear the information will somehow leak out. Even now I am using the hotel's public telephone, on the chance that the telephone in my room has been tapped."

"You are quite right! Trust nothing and no one!"

Wayness sighed, thinking of Xantief, his clarity and honor. "Another matter, Uncle Pirie. I did not send you down to the bank for nothing. I am carrying about three hundred sols, but if I must go off-world, it won't be enough. Can you spare me a thousand or so?"

"Of course! Two thousand, if you like!"

"It is twice as good as a thousand. I will accept with thanks, and return whatever is left as soon as possible."

"You need not concern yourself with money; if for nothing else, this is money spent for the Conservancy!"

"That is my opinion too. Ask the officer which bank at Trieste is their correspondent, and send me two thousand sols which I will pick up at once."

"You can't imagine how you worry me," growled Pirie Tamm.

Wayness cried: "Stop, Uncle Pirie! For the moment at least I am safe, since I have sent everyone off to Bangalore! They will be very irritable when they find it is just a prank, but by that time I will be far away."

"So when will I hear from you again?"

"At the moment I can't even guess."

V.

Wayness settled her account at the front desk, then returned to her room. The events at Trieste had been helpful in more ways than one. Wayness' concepts of evil had altered from the abstract to the real. She now knew with grisly certainty the quality of her opponents. They were persistent, cruel, smilingly callous. They would kill her if they caught her, and this would be a tragic event indeed—from her point of view. It would mean the cessation of that quick and lively intelligence known as Wayness, with its special little graces and quirks and affectionate good nature and wry sense of humor. Tragedy indeed!

Wayness debated changing into her disguise of the morning, and compromised, by shrouding herself in the pea jacket and pulling the cap down over her dark curls. She accoutered herself with the weapons Alvina had given her, and felt greatly comforted.

Wayness was now ready to leave. She went to the door, opened it a slit and looked along the hall. It was not at all unlikely for someone to be waiting, to overwhelm her as she opened the door and bear her back into the room, where she could be dealt with at leisure. Wayness grimaced at the idea.

The hall was empty. Wayness departed the hotel by the back stairs and the timber door which opened upon the strip of shingle under the wharf.

VI.

For three days and three nights Wayness practiced every tactic of evasion, concealment and dissimulation that her imagination could contrive, including traps against mobile spy cells and tattletags. She made quick sorties through crowds, doubling back on her tracks, over and over, watching to see whom she might be confusing. She boarded an omnibus and when it halted for an instant at a village traffic stop, she jumped out and was quickly out of town on a van transporting farm laborers. At Lisbon on the Atlantic coast she boarded the northbound slideway, only to debark at the first stop, then to return aboard, to sequester herself in the women's restroom until the next stop, where again she debarked and slipped aboard a car traveling in the opposite direction, which she rode all the way to Tanjer. Here she changed her semblance, discarding her green travel cape and the blonde wig she had acquired, to join a group of young wanderers, all dressed alike in dungarees and gray pullovers. She spent a night in the Tanjer hostel. The next morning she booked passage on the trans-Atlantic skytrain and six hours later was discharged at the sprawling city Alonso Saavedra, on the Rio Tanagra. She was by this time certain that she had eluded pursuit; but she continued to set traps for spy cells, hide in secret places to watch for trackers and to change vehicles unpredictably. In due course she arrived by skycoach at the provincial capitol Biriguassu, then flew south and west across the pampas to the mining town Nambucara. She

spent the night at the Stella d'Oro Hotel, and dined on a
steak of startling proportions, served with fried potatoes,
avocado sauce, and a roast bird—possibly a small long-
legged chicken—to the side.

Pombareales lay still far to the south, with catch-as-
catch-can travel connections. In the morning Wayness
somewhat dubiously climbed aboard an airbus of vener-
able vintage, which rose with a lurch and groan, then flew
heavily south, wallowing to gusts of wind. The other passengers seemed to take the vehicle's alarming peculiarities
for granted, and showed concern only when one of the
lurches caused them to spill their beer. A gentleman sitting beside Wayness described himself as a steady patron
who long ago had abandoned fear. He explained that since
the vehicle had been flying back and forth from north to
south and north again for many years, there was no
reason to suppose that on this day of all days it would
collapse in mid-air and fail to do its duty. "In sheer point
of fact," he told Wayness, "the vehicle becomes safer each
day it flies, and I can prove this point by mathematics,
which of course is infallible. You speak with a good accent;
may I assume that you are skilled in the use of logic?"

Wayness modestly admitted that this was the case.

"Then you will follow my reasoning without difficulty.
Assume that the vehicle is new. Let us say that it flies safely
for two days, then crashes on the third day. Its safety record
is not good: one crash in three trips. If, however, the vehicle
flies ten thousand days, as has this one, its safety record is
at least one in ten thousand and one, which is very good!
Furthermore, each succeeding day that passes without
incident, the risk becomes smaller, so that by an equal
increment the passenger's sense of security should
increase."

The vehicle was struck by a particularly vicious gust of
wind; it jerked and plunged and from somewhere came a
wrenching tearing sound, which the gentleman ignored.
"We are probably safer here than if we were sitting at home
in an easy chair, at the mercy of a rabid dog."

"I appreciate your explanation, which is very clear,"

said Wayness. "I still feel a bit nervous, but now I do not know why."

Late in the afternoon the airbus landed at the town Aquique, where Wayness disembarked, after which the airbus took off once again for Lago Angelina, to the southeast. Wayness discovered that she had missed the triweekly connection to Pombareales, still another hundred miles to the southwest, almost in the shadow of the Andes. She could either lay over two days at Aquique, or she could proceed by surface omnibus on the following day.

Aquique's best hotel was the Universo, a tower of concrete and glass five stories high adjacent to the airport. Wayness was assigned an airy room on the top floor, overlooking all Aquique: several thousand concrete and glass blocks arranged on a rectilinear grid concentric about the central plaza. Beyond, the pampas spread away to the edge of vision.

During the evening, Wayness felt lonely and homesick, and spent an hour writing letters to her father and mother, with an insert for Glawen, if he were still at Araminta Station. "I have given up expecting any word from you. Julian showed up at Fair Winds and did nothing to make himself popular; to the contrary. However, he mentioned that you had gone off somewhere to help your father, and as of now, I don't know whether you are alive or dead. I hope alive, and I wish you were here with me now, as this enormous tract of wasteland is on the whole depressing. I find that I have only so much energy to devote to intrigues and plots, and then I start feeling miserable. Still, I will survive. I have an enormous amount to tell you. This is a strange countryside, and sometimes I forget that I am traveling Old Earth and believe myself off-world. In any case, I send you all my love, and I hope that we will be together soon."

In the morning Wayness boarded the omnibus, and was transported south and west across the pampas. She relaxed into the seat and covertly appraised her fellow passengers: a routine which by now had become almost reflexive. She saw nothing to arouse her suspicion; no one showed any interest in her, save a young man with a narrow forehead and a wide big-toothed smile, who wanted to sell her a religious tract.

"No, thank you," said Wayness. "I am not interested in your theories."

The young man produced a paper sack. "Would you care for some candy?"

"No, thank you," said Wayness. "If you plan to eat it yourself, please move to another seat, as the smell will make me sick, and I will vomit on your religious tract."

The young man moved to a different seat and ate his candy in solitude.

The bus moved across a desolation of low hills, outcrops of rotten rocks, tufts of bracken, willow and aspens in the dips and declivities, a few low cypress trees bedraggled by the wind. The environment was not without its own bleak beauty. Wayness thought that had she been required to paint the landscape, she could have done so with a very limited palette. There would be several tones of gray: dark for the shadows, grays tinted with umber, ocher and cobalt for rocks and outcrops; dun, olive drab and dusty tan; copper-green and splotches of black-green for the cypresses.

As the bus proceeded, the mountains loomed higher into the sky, and a wind striking down from the west gave vitality and movement to the landscape.

The sun, rather pale by reason of high haze, moved toward the zenith. In the distance appeared a clutter of low white structures: the town Pombareales.

The bus drove into the town square and stopped in front of the rambling three-story Hotel Monopole. Wayness thought that the town seemed much like Nambucara, on a somewhat smaller scale, with the same central plaza, the same surrounding grid of streets lined with white rectilinear structures. It was a town of no obvious attraction, thought Wayness, except that it might be the last place on Earth where agents of the Tanglet Association might come seeking a wrongdoer.

Wayness carried her bag into the cavernous lobby of the Hotel Monopole. The clerk at the registration desk offered her a room overlooking the square, or a room not overlooking the square, or if she chose a corner suite both overlooking and not overlooking the square. "We are not busy," said the clerk. "The price is the same: two sols per day, which includes breakfast."

"I will try the suite," said Wayness. "I have never before been allowed so much room."

"In this part of the world 'room' is a plentiful resource," said the clerk. "You may have all you like at no great charge, with the wind and a panoramic view of the Andes included."

Wayness found the suite adequate in all respects. The bathroom functioned properly; the bedroom contained a large bed, smelling faintly of antiseptic soap; the sitting room was furnished with a heavy oak table, a large blue rug, several massive chairs, a couch, a desk with a cabinet, and a telephone. Wayness resisted the temptation to call Fair Winds and went to sit in one of the chairs. She had made no plans; they seemed pointless in the absence of information. She must reconnoiter, and discover what there was to be known about Irena Portils.

The time was half an hour before noon: too early for lunch. Wayness went down to the lobby and approached the desk clerk. Discretion and subtlety were now of prime importance; for all she knew, he might be Irena Portils' brother-in-law. She approached the object of her inquiry at an oblique angle. "A friend wants me to look up someone on Via Madera. Where would that be?"

"Via Madera? There is no Via Madera in Pombareales."

"Hm. I should have made a note of the name. Could it be Via Ladera? Or Baduro?"

"There is the Calle Maduro, and the Avenida Onyx Formadero."

"I think it was Calle Maduro: a house with two black granite balls marking the gateway."

"I don't recall such a house, but Calle Maduro is yonder." He pointed his pencil. "Go three blocks south along Calle Luneta, and you will come to the intersection with Calle Maduro. Here you must make a choice. If you turn left and walk several blocks you will come to the poultry cooperative. If you turn to the right, you will eventually arrive at the cemetery. Choose for yourself; I cannot advise you."

"Thank you." Wayness turned toward the door. The clerk called her back. "The way is long and the wind blows dust; why not ride in style? There is Esteban's cab: the red vehicle parked directly outside the door. His charges will not be an outrage if you threaten to patronize his brother Ignaldo, who drives a green cab."

Wayness went out to the red cab. In the front seat sat a small man, all arms and legs, with weathered brown skin and a long droll face. At the sight of Wayness he cried out: "On the instant!" and flung open the door.

Wayness asked: "Is this Ignaldo's cab? I am told that his rates are fair—in fact, very fair."

"Utter nonsense!" said Esteban. "Your innocence has been abused. Sometimes he pretends to offer low rates, but he is a sly devil and cheats his passengers double in the end. Who should know better than I, who compete with him."

"For this reason you might well be biased in your judgment."

"Not so. Ignaldo knows no conscience. If your dying grandmother were rushing to reach the church before the priest went home, Ignaldo would take her on a long detour through the country and become lost, until either she had died, whereupon his rates for transporting corpses came into effect, or until, for the sake of her soul, the dying woman agreed to his larceny!"

"In that case, I will give you a trial, but first you must reveal your own rates."

Esteban threw his hands high in impatience. "Where do you want to go?"

"Here and there. You may take me up Calle Maduro for a start."

"That of course is possible. Do you wish to look at the cemetery?"

"No. I want to look at the houses."

"On Calle Maduro there is little to see, and my charges will be minimal. For one half hour the fare will be one sol."

"What! That is double Ignaldo's rate!"

Esteban made a sound of disgust and gave in so readily that Wayness knew that her outcry had been justified. "Very well; I have nothing better to do. Climb in. The rate is one sol per hour."

Wayness stepped primly into the cab. "Mind you, I am not hiring the cab for an hour. For one-half hour, I pay one-half sol, and this rate must include the gratuity."

Esteban roared: "Why do I not just give you the cab and all my miserable belongings and walk from the town a pauper?"

Esteban's emotion was so genuine that Wayness knew they had arrived at his ordinary rate.

Wayness laughed. "Calm yourself! You cannot hope for sudden wealth every time some poor innocent enters your cab."

"You are not so innocent as you look," grumbled Esteban. He closed the door and the cab set off up the Calle Luneta. "Where do you want to go?"

"First, let us drive up Calle Maduro."

Esteban gave a nod of comprehension. "You have relatives in the cemetery, so it seems."

"I don't know of any."

Esteban raised his eyebrows. What kind of odd conduct was this? "There is little to see from one end of town to the other; even less along Calle Maduro."

"Do you know the folk who live along the street?"

"I know everyone in Pombareales." Esteban turned the cab into Calle Maduro, which had been hard-surfaced a very long time ago and was now pocked with potholes. Only about half of the lots had been developed; houses stood in isolation at intervals of twenty yards or more. Each was surrounded by a yard, where occasionally a few sickly shrubs or a wind-beaten tree indicated someone's attempt at a garden. Esteban pointed to a house which showed blank windows to the street, and patches of thistle in the yard. "There is a house you might buy at the cheap."

"It looks rather dismal."

"That is because it is haunted by the ghost of Edgar Sambaster, who hanged himself one night at midnight when the wind blew down from the mountains."

"And no one has lived there since?"

Esteban shook his head. "The owners have gone off-world. A few years ago a certain Professor Solomon became involved in a scandal and hid there for a few weeks, and no one has heard from him since."

"Hm. Has anyone looked in the house to see whether he might be hanging there too?"

"Yes, that was considered, and the constables made an inspection, but found nothing."

"Odd." The cab had drawn abreast of another house, which was like any of the others except for a pair of life-size statues in the front yard, representing nymphs with their arms raised in benediction. "Who lives there?"

"That is the house of Hector Lopez, who works as gardener at the cemetery. He brought home the statues when a tract of graves was relocated."

"They make an interesting decoration."

"So it may be. There are some who think that Hector Lopez is putting on airs. What is your opinion?"

"I don't find them offensive. Could it be that the neighbors are envious?"

"Possible, I suppose. There you see the house of Leon Casinde, the pork butcher. He is a great singer and may often be heard, drunk or sober, in the cantina."

The cab proceeded up the Calle Maduro, Esteban warmed to his task and Wayness learned much of the lives and habits of those in the houses along the way. Presently they came to No. 31, Casa Lucasta: a house of two stories, somewhat larger than others along the street, with a stout fence enclosing its yard. A garden of sorts grew along the north side of the house, in an angle protected from the wind, where the sun shone its brightest. There were geraniums, hydrangeas, marigolds, a lemon verbena, a ragged clump of bamboo. To the side were miscellaneous pieces of inexpensive outdoor furniture: a table, a bench, several chairs, a lawn swing, a large sandbox, another wooden box containing oddments of hardware. In this area a boy of about twelve and a girl two or three years younger were occupied, each absorbed in his private concerns.

Noticing Wayness' interest, Esteban slowed the cab. He

tapped his forehead significantly. "Both mental cases; very hard for the mother."

"So I should think," said Wayness. "Stop here for a moment if you please." She watched the children with interest. The girl sat at the table, busy with what might have been a puzzle; the boy knelt in the sandbox, building a complicated edifice from damp sand, which he had moistened with liquid from a bucket. Both children were thin: slender rather than frail, long of leg and arm. Their chestnut hair was cut short without affectation of fashion, as if no one cared much how they looked, much less themselves. Their faces were thin, with cleanly modeled features, gray eyes, pale tan skin almost imperceptibly warmed with pink and orange. They were rather attractive children, thought Wayness, though clearly not native to the locality, The girl's face showed more animation than that of the boy, who worked with thoughtful precision. Neither of the two spoke. Each, after a single disinterested glance toward the cab, paid no further heed.

"Hm!" said Wayness. "Those are the first children I have seen along the street."

"No mystery here," said Esteban. "Other children are at school."

"Yes, of course. What is wrong with these two?"

"That is hard to say. The doctors come regularly, and all leave shaking their heads, while the children continue to do as they see fit. The girl goes wild with rage if she is thwarted in any way and falls into a foaming fit, so that everyone fears for her life. The boy is sullen and won't say a word, though he is said to be clever in certain ways. Some say that they need no more than a few good switchings to bring them around; others say it is all a matter of hormones, or some such substance."

"For a fact, they don't look deficient, or slack-witted. Usually the doctors can cure such folk."

"Not these two. The doctor comes up every week from the Institute at Montalvo, but nothing seems to change."

"That's a pity. Who is the father?"

"It is a complicated story. I mentioned Professor Solomon, who was involved in a scandal. He is off-world now, and no one seems to know where, though quite a few folk would like to find him. He is the father."

"And the mother?"

"That would be Madame Portils who goes about proud as a countess, even though she's a local. Her mother is Madame Clara, who was born a Salgas, and is common as dirt."

"How does Madame Portils support herself?"

"She works at the library mending books, or some such footling job. With two children and her own mother in the household she receives a public stipend, which brings her the necessities of life. No cause for vanity there; still she tilts her nose to everyone, even the upper class folk."

"She would seem to be a peculiar woman," said Wayness. "Perhaps she has secret talents."

"If so, she is as jealous with them as if they were crimes. Ah well, it is sad, all the same."

Down from the hill came a gust of wind, blowing dust and litter along the road, hissing among the brambles of the waste. Esteban indicated the girl. "Look! The wind excites her!"

Wayness saw that the girl had jumped to her feet, to face the wind, with feet somewhat apart, swaying and nodding her head to some slow inner cadence.

The boy paid her no heed and continued with his work. From the house came a sharp call. The girl's body lost its tension. Reluctantly she turned toward the house. The boy ignored the call, and continued his work, molding damp sand into a structure of many complications.

From the house came a second call, even sharper than before. The girl halted, looked over her shoulder, went to the sandbox and with her foot obliterated the boy's handiwork. He froze into rigidity, staring at the devastation. The girl waited. The boy slowly turned his head to look at her. As best Wayness could see, his face was blank of expression. The girl turned away and with head drooping pensively, went to the house. The boy followed, slowly and sadly.

Esteban set the cab into motion. "Next we will inspect the cemetery, which must be considered the climactic event for anyone who like yourself has chosen to explore Calle Maduro. To do a proper job, we must count upon investing at least half an hour, or even better—"

Wayness laughed. "I have seen enough for now. You may take me back to the hotel."

Esteban gave a fatalistic shrug and started back down Calle Maduro. "You might enjoy a drive along the Avenida de las Floritas, where the patricians reside. Also, the park is well worth a visit, what with the fountain and the Palladium, where the band performs each Sunday afternoon. You would enjoy the music, which is played freely, for the ears of all. You might well meet a handsome young gentleman or two—who knows?—or even end up with a fine husband!"

"That would be a wonderful surprise," said Wayness.

Esteban pointed to a tall lean woman approaching along the sidewalk. "There is Madame Portils herself, on her way home from work."

Esteban slowed the cab. Wayness watched Irena Portils marching swiftly along the sidewalk, head bent, leaning forward into the wind. At first glance and from a distance she seemed comely; almost instantly the illusion shattered and vanished. She was dressed in a well-worn skirt of russet tweed and a tight-fitting black jacket. From beneath a small shapeless hat, lank black hair hung down past her cheeks. Middle age was close upon her and the years had not treated her kindly. Black eyes in dark sockets were set too closely beside a long pinched nose; her complexion was pasty and ravaged by the deep lines of stress and pessimism.

Esteban turned his head to watch her as the cab passed by. "Strange to say, she was a handsome piece of goods when she was young. But she went off to actor's school and next we heard she had joined a troupe of comic impressionists or dramaturgists—whatever these groups are called, and the word came that she had gone off-world with the troupe and no one thought of her again until one day she returned and then she was married to Professor Solomon, who called himself an archaeologist. They only stayed a month or two and were gone off-world again."

Esteban had arrived at a long low concrete building shaded by a half dozen eucalyptus trees. Wayness said: "This is not the Hotel Monopole!"

"I took a wrong turning," Esteban explained. "This is the poultry cooperative. Now that we are here, perhaps you will want to look at the chickens. No? Then I'll take you to the hotel, at best speed."

Wayness settled back into the seat. "You were telling me about Professor Solomon."

"Ah, yes. The Professor and Irena returned a few years ago, with the children. For a time Professor Solomon was well-regarded, and considered a credit to the community, being a scientist and a man of education. He occupied himself exploring the mountains and looking for prehistoric ruins. Then he claimed he had found some buried treasure and involved himself in a terrible scandal, so that he was forced to take himself off-world. Irena claims she knows nothing of his whereabouts, but no one believes her."

Esteban guided the cab from Calle Luneta to its previous place beside the hotel. "And that is the state of affairs along Calle Maduro."

VII.

Wayness sat in a corner of the hotel lobby, eyes half-closed, notebook in her lap. Under the heading 'Irena Portils' she had started to organize a few ideas, but the topic was baffling and her thinking blurred. Her mind needed rest. A few tranquil hours might clarify her problems. Wayness settled back into the chair and tried not to think.

A soothing murmur permeated the lobby. It was an enormous room, with massive wooden beams supporting a high ceiling. Furnishings were heavy: leather upholstered chairs and couches, long low tables whose tops were single slabs of chiriqui. In the far wall an archway opened into the restaurant.

A party of ranchers entered from the square and seated themselves to drink beer and discuss business before moving into the restaurant for lunch. Wayness found that their joviality, loud voices and sudden claps of hand on leg interfered with her efforts not to think. Also, one of the ranchers boasted a very large bushy black mustache, at which Wayness could not avoid staring, even though she began to fear that the rancher might notice and come over to ask why she was looking at his mustache.

Wayness decided that it was time for her own lunch. She went into the restaurant and was seated where she could overlook the square, though at this time of day nothing of consequence was happening.

According to the menu, one of the daily specials was ptarmigan: an item which intrigued Wayness, since she had never seen it offered on a menu before. Well then, she thought: why not? She so placed her order, but in the end found the ptarmigan too gamy for her taste.

Wayness lingered at the table over dessert and coffee. The afternoon lay before her, but she decided not to attempt another period of serenity, and once again she took up the matter of Irena Portils.

The basic problem was straightforward: how to induce Irena to reveal the whereabouts of the man known as 'Professor Solomon'?

Wayness brought out her notebook and examined the entries she had inscribed earlier in the day.

Problem: Find Moncurio.

—*Solution 1:* Make a full explanation to Irena and request cooperation.

—*Solution 2:* Similar to No. 1, but offer of money—perhaps considerable money.

—*Solution 3:* Hypnotize or drug Irena Portils, and so extract the information from her.

—*Solution 4:* While house is unoccupied, search for clues.

—*Solution 5:* Question Irena's mother and/or children. (???)

—*Solution 6:* None of above.

Wayness was not encouraged by her review of the notes. Solution 1, the most reasonable, would almost surely embroil her in an emotional confrontation with Madame Portils and cause her to become more intractable than ever. The same could be said for Solution 2. Solutions 3, 4, and 5 were almost equally impractical. Solution 6 was clearly the most feasible of the group.

Wayness returned to the lobby. The time was a few minutes after two o'clock, with the balance of the afternoon still ahead. Wayness went to the desk, where the clerk directed her to the public library.

"It is a five-minute walk," said the clerk. He pointed his pencil. "Go along Calle Luneta a single block, to Calle Basilio; on the corner you will find a large acacia tree. Turn to the left and walk a block, which will bring you to the library."

"That seems simple enough."

"Just so. Do not neglect the collection of primitive pottery on display in the reference department. Even here in Patagonia, where the gauchos once roamed, we honor the ideals of high culture!"

A door of bronze and glass slid aside; Wayness entered a foyer equipped with the usual amenities. Halls to left and right led to the various special departments.

Wayness wandered here and there, at all times covertly watching for Irena Portils. She had formed no plan; still it seemed certain that these particular premises might be the best, perhaps the only, environment in which to make Irena's acquaintance. She paused to examine a rack of periodicals, pretended to consult the information banks, stopped to ponder the schedule of library hours, as posted on a sign. Nowhere did she so much as glimpse Irena, who perhaps had gone home for the day.

In the Art and Music room Wayness came upon the collection of primitive pottery to which she had been recommended by the clerk at the hotel. The pieces were displayed upon the shelves of a glass-fronted cabinet. There were a dozen bowls, some high, some low, and as many other utensils. Most had been broken and restored; a few showed rudimentary decoration: patterns of stippling or scratches. The ware had been formed either by pressing slabs of clay into baskets, then firing basket and all; or by the hand-forming of slabs into the shape desired.

A placard attributed the pieces to 'the Zuntil folk': semi-barbarian hunters and gatherers resident in the area many thousands of years before the coming of the Europeans. The pieces had been discovered by local archaeologists at sites along the Azumi River, a few miles north and west of Pombareales.

Wayness frowned at the collection, which had just inserted a rather good idea into her mind. She considered the idea from all angles, but could find no flaws. Of course she would be required to become a liar, a sneak and a hypocrite. But what of that? To make an omelette one must break eggs. She turned to the librarian who sat at a nearby desk: an angular young man with soft sandy hair, a wide thinker's forehead, a high-bridged beak of a nose, a bony jaw and chin. He had been watching Wayness from the side of his face. Meeting her gaze, he blushed and looked hurriedly away, then could not resist another glance.

Wayness smiled at him, and approached his desk. She asked: "Did you arrange the showing of this collection?"

The librarian grinned. "So I did, in part, at any rate. I did none of the digging. That was the work of my uncle and his friend. They are the diggers, and very keen. I don't fancy it all that much, myself."

"You miss most of the fun!"

"Perhaps," said the librarian. He added, in a thoughtful voice: "Last week my uncle and his friend Dante went out on a dig. My uncle was stung by a scorpion. He jumped into the river. During the afternoon his friend Dante was chased by a bull. He jumped into the river too."

"Hm." Wayness considered the collection of pots. "Did they go out again this week to dig?"

"No. They went to the cantina instead."

Wayness had no comment to make.

Beside the collection several maps of the region were posted. One of these marked the location of the Zuntil sites; another, on a larger scale, displayed the reach of the various Inca Empires: the Early, the Middle and the Late. Wayness said: "Apparently the Incas never ranged quite so far south as Pombareales."

"They probably sent war parties out from time to time. But no one has ever found any authentic sites closer than Sandoval, which might well have been nothing more than a trading post."

Wayness spoke offhandedly: "I think that is what the leader of our expedition wants to establish, one way or the other."

The librarian gave a wry chuckle. "There have been more expeditions at Sandoval than ever there were Incas." He appraised Wayness anew. "You are an archaeologist, then?"

Wayness laughed. "After this year in the field and three more years in the laboratory sorting out bones—ask me again." She looked around the room. "You are not too busy to talk?"

"Definitely not. Today is always a slack day. Sit down, if you like. My name is Evan Faures."

Wayness demurely seated herself. "I am Wayness Tamm."

The conversation proceeded. Wayness presently inquired about caves in the mountains and legends of Inca gold. "It would be fun to find a great box of treasure."

Evan looked over his shoulder. "I wouldn't dare mention Professor Solomon if Irena Portils were within hearing distance. But I think she has gone home for the day."

"Who is Professor Solomon and who is Irena Portils?"

"Aha!" said Evan. "There you touch upon one of our most notorious scandals."

"Tell me about it. I like scandals."

Evan once again looked over his shoulder. "Irena Portils is part of the staff. As I understand it, she was once a dancer or some such thing, and went off-world with a troupe of entertainers. She returned married to an archae-ologist named Professor Solomon, who declared himself to be famous everywhere. He made a good impression and became one of the town dignitaries.

"One evening, at a dinner party with friends, Professor Solomon seemed to become convivial and perhaps a trifle indiscreet. In strict confidence he told his friends he had come upon an old map which located a secret cave in which the conquistadores had hidden a treasure of newly minted gold doubloons. 'Probably just a mare's nest,' said Professor Solomon, 'but interesting all the same.'

"A day or two later Professor Solomon slipped away into the mountains. His friends, as soon as they learned of his absence, put discretion aside and told everyone of Professor Solomon's gold.

"A month passed, and Professor Solomon returned. When his friends pressed him for information, he reluc-tantly showed them four gold doubloons, and said that he needed a few special tools to dig away the debris which now covered the chest. Shortly thereafter he disappeared again. The news of his discovery excited a great deal of interest and also avarice. When Professor Solomon returned with four hundred doubloons, he was besieged with offers from collectors. He allowed several of the doubloons to be assayed, which diminished their value, so no one was surprised when he refused to test any of the others. One day at noon precisely he sold the doubloons. Swarms of excited collectors came sweating and screaming and waving their money in the air. Professor Solomon sold the doubloons in parcels of ten, and all four hundred were gone before the hour was over. Then Professor Solomon thanked the collectors for their interest, and said he was off to explore another cave which might yield an even greater treasure of Inca emeralds. He departed, amid acclaim and congratulations. This time he took Irena Portils with him.

"Peace returned to Pombareales—but not for long. A few days later it became known that the collectors had all paid very large sums for doubloons stamped from lead, then plated over with a thin wash of gold. Their value was negligible.

"Collectors are not a fatalistic lot. Consternation gave way to outrage and fury even more intense than the previous enthusiasm."

"So what happened?"

"Nothing. If Professor Solomon had been dragged from his hiding place, pelted with stones, hanged, drawn, quartered, then burnt alive at the stake, and afterwards whipped to within an inch of his life, and finally crucified upside down and forced to pay back all his debts at compound interest, the emotions might have been soothed. But he was nowhere to be found, and to this day no one has suggested amnesty for Professor Solomon. As for Irena Portils, she returned after a few years with her two children. She claimed that Professor Solomon had deserted her. Further, she declared that she knew nothing of the swindle, and she wanted only to be left alone. No one could prove her complicity, though they tried hard enough. After a while Irena came to work at the library. The years went by and that is how things stand today."

"And where is Professor Solomon? Do you think she keeps in touch with him?"

Evan smiled a chilly half-smile. "I don't know. I would never dare to ask. She keeps herself to herself."

"Has she no friends?"

"None, so far as I know. At the library, she does her work, she manages to speak politely when necessary, but she seems only half-focused, as if her thoughts were far away. Sometimes her tensions are so strong that everyone near becomes edgy. It's as if great storms were raging inside her, and she were holding herself together only with effort."

"How odd."

"Very odd. I would not like to be near if ever she lets go."

"Hm." Evan's remarks were discouraging. Irena Portils was her only link to Adrian Moncurio and by one means or another must be cultivated. Wayness said tentatively: "If I come to the library tomorrow, perhaps I will meet her."

It was the wrong thing to say. Evan looked at her in surprise. "Why would you want to meet her?"

"I suppose I am interested in unusual people," said Wayness lamely.

"She doesn't come in tomorrow. It's the day the doctor calls on her children. He sees them every week. Also, Irena works in the back room. You would not meet her in any case."

"It is no great matter."

Evan smiled wistfully. "I could hope that you would be coming back regardless of Irena."

"Possibly," said Wayness. It seemed likely that she would in the end need someone's help. Evan? It would be cruel to exploit him. Still, as she had already noted, to make an omelette, at least one egg must be broken.

"If I have the opportunity, I'll come by again."

Wayness returned to the hotel. The outdoor café fronting on the square was now animated with young business folk, groups of upper class matrons, ranchers and their spouses in town for an afternoon's shopping. Wayness seated herself at a vacant table and ordered tea and nutcake. The wind had died; the sun shone warm. By raising her head and looking far off toward the west, she could see the loom of the Andes. Had it not been for her concerns, Wayness would have found the occasion very pleasant.

For want of any better occupation, Wayness pushed the teapot to the side, brought out paper and pen, and wrote another letter to her father and mother.

She concluded: "I find myself involved in a gigantic game of paper chase, played to occasionally unpleasant rules. At the moment I am hard against a certain Irena Portils, who stands between me and Adrian Moncurio (an old friend of Uncle Pirie, by some strange chance, or perhaps it is not so strange after all). This information, incidentally, is highly confidential, and must not be discussed with anyone but Glawen, for whom I hopefully enclose another note. Sooner or later I suppose I will discover what has been happening."

In her note to Glawen, she again mentioned Irena Portils. "I don't know how to approach her. She seems to be hyper-neurotic, whatever that means.

"I wish this business were over. I find myself continually confused and baffled; I am walking around inside a kaleidoscope.

"But I am not really complaining. When I look back I can actually find cause for encouragement. Step by step, inch by inch, I make progress. I must repeat that I am not at all pleased with Julian. He may or may not be a murderer, but he is many other things.

"In regard to Irena Portils, I must use my ingenuity, and find some way to make her acquaintance. I don't think that the library provides any real opportunity, but this seems to be her only contact with the outside world. Except for the doctor who visits her children every week. I wonder if something could be effected from this direction. I must think about this. As always, I wish you were here with me, and I also hope that you receive this letter."

In this hope Wayness would be denied. By the time the letter arrived at Araminta Station, Glawen had already departed and was on his way to Earth.

Wayness took the letters to the nearby post office, returned to the hotel and went up to her room. She bathed;

then, thinking to resuscitate her morale, she dressed in one of her most attractive evening costumes: a soft black tunic and a skirt striped black and mustard-ocher. With her mood only slightly improved, she went down to the hotel restaurant for her dinner.

Wayness dined without haste on lamb chops and asparagus. By the time she had finished, twilight had arrived, to bring the young folk of Pombareales out for the evening promenade. Girls strolled clockwise around the square; the young men went counter-clockwise, the groups exchanging salutes and repartee as they passed each other. Some of the young men issued compliments; others feigned heart attacks or a convulsion in response to the impact of so much beauty. The most fervent bravos of all uttered passionate outcries, such as: "Ay-yi-yi!" or "Ahay! I am turning inside out!" or "What exquisiteness!" or "Caray! I have been ravished!" The girls ignored such excesses, sometimes with disdain, but none desisted from the promenade.

Wayness went out to the café and seated herself at a table in the shadows. She ordered coffee and watched the moon rise into the Patagonian sky. Her presence did not go unnoticed; she was approached several times by socially inclined young men. One proposed that they visit the Cantina La Dolorosita for music and dancing; another wanted to order a pitcher of pisco punch so that they might drink and talk philosophy; a third invited Wayness to go riding with him in his fast car. They would speed across the pampas in the light of the full moon. "You will be intoxicated by the freedom and space!" he told her.

"That sounds nice," said Wayness. "But what if the car broke down, or you became ill, or something else happened and I had to walk back to Pombareales?"

"Bah!" growled the young man. "The most practical females are also the most dull; present company excepted, of course."

Wayness politely extricated herself from the invitation. She went up to her room and went to bed. She lay awake an hour, perhaps longer, looking up at the ceiling, thinking of places far and near, of persons she loved and others whom she hated. She reflected upon life, which was so new and dear to her, and which someone had already tried to destroy, and of death, which presented little scope for serious analysis. Her thoughts returned to Irena Portils. She had seen the haggard face, with its clenched narrow jaw and lank loose hair a single time, but already she felt the quality of Irena's personality.

Through the open window the sounds of the promenade dwindled as the good obedient girls went home, and the others, perhaps, went for rides in the moonlight.

Wayness became drowsy. She had decided upon an avenue of approach to Irena Portils. It was an uncertain method which, at best, had perhaps one chance in three of getting off the ground. Still, it was better than nothing and Wayness felt a comforting intuition that she might succeed.

In the morning Wayness rose early, dressed in a gray tweed skirt, a white shirt and a dark blue jacket: a neat unobtrusive costume which might have been worn by a lesser bank clerk, or a junior teaching assistant, or even a university student of conservative views.

Wayness left her rooms and descended to the ground floor. She took her breakfast in the restaurant, then left the hotel.

The day was clear but windy, with sunlight of a pale cool color slanting into the square from the northeast. Wayness walked briskly along Calle Luneta, wind flapping at her skirt, dust swirls racing down the middle of the street. She turned up Calle Maduro and proceeded until Casa Lucasta was visible only a hundred yards ahead. Here she paused and took stock of the surroundings. Directly opposite she saw a small white house, dilapidated and untenanted, the glass broken from its windows so that they gazed out upon the street with the bleary blank gaze of a drunkard. Wayness looked right and left, up and down the street. No one was watching. She waited for the passage of a wind-swept plume of dust, then, wrinkling her nose, ran across the street. After another furtive glance to right and left, she jumped up to the porch of the vacant house and drew back into the shadows of a shallow curtain wall. Here, sheltered from the wind, she could lurk unseen while watching to discover who approached along the street.

Wayness composed herself to wait: all day if need be, since she had no idea at what time the doctor might make his call at Casa Lucasta.

The time was close upon nine o'clock. Wayness made herself as comfortable as possible. A vehicle came along the street: a delivery truck loaded with building materials, evidently on its way to the cemetery. Another small vehicle appeared: a baker's van, delivering bread and other goods to houses along the street. A young man rode past on a motorcycle; the delivery truck returned from the cemetery. Wayness sighed and changed her position. The time was now five minutes before ten o'clock. A car of medium size painted an institutional white and black turned into Calle Maduro. This was almost certainly the car she was expecting. Jumping down from the porch, she ran to the sidewalk and as the car drew near, stepped out into the street and made urgent signals. The car slowed and halted. Wayness was relieved to find that the inscription on the side read:

INSTITUTE OF PUBLIC HEALTH
— Montalvo —
ADAPTATIONAL SERVICES

She had not stopped the wrong car.

The driver and Wayness examined each other. She saw a dark-haired man of medium stature, aged perhaps thirty-three or thirty-four, sturdy of physique, with a square resolute face. Wayness thought him quite good-looking, and she also thought that he seemed reasonable and open-minded, which was good, although the rather grim set of his mouth might imply a lack of humor, which was bad. He was dressed casually, in a green pullover and tan twill trousers, indicating a lack of institutional formality, which again, from Wayness' point of view, was good. On the other hand, his expression, as he looked her over, was impersonal and analytical, which was bad, since she would be unable to melt him with an appealing smile and a bit of flirtation. Such being the case, she must accept the more difficult task of using her intelligence.

"Yes, miss?"

"You are the doctor?"

He looked her up and down. "Are you sick?"

Wayness blinked. Humor? If so, it was sardonic. She saw that she had her work cut out.

"I am quite well, thank you. But still I have something important to say to you."

"That sounds a bit ominous. Are you sure you have the right person? I am Dr. Armand Olivano; please do not shoot me by mistake."

Wayness held up her empty hands. "You are safe. I only want to make a suggestion which I hope you will consider wise and necessary."

Dr. Olivano deliberated a second or two, then gave an abrupt shrug. "Since you put it like that, I can hardly refuse to listen." He opened the door. "I have an appointment up ahead, but it can wait a few minutes."

Wayness climbed into the car. "Perhaps you'll be kind enough to drive somewhere and park where we can talk."

Dr. Olivano made no protest. He turned the car about, drove back down Calle Maduro and parked in the shade of the eucalyptus trees beside the poultry cooperative. "Is this satisfactory?"

Wayness nodded. She spoke carefully: "Since I want you to take me seriously, I must start with some facts. My name is Wayness Tamm, which of course will mean nothing to you. But let me ask this: are you a conservationist, philosophically or even emotionally?"

"Of course. Who isn't?"

Wayness made no direct response. "Are you acquainted with the Naturalist Society?"

"There I draw a blank."

"No great matter. There is very little left now. My uncle, Pirie Tamm, is Secretary. I am Assistant Secretary. There are three or four very old members, and that's about all. A thousand years ago the Society was an important organization. It became trustee of the world Cadwal, at the end of Mircea's Wisp at the back of Perseus, and established a permanent Conservancy. I was born on Cadwal; my father, in fact, is the Conservator."

Wayness spoke on for several minutes. As briefly as possible she described the crisis on Cadwal, her discovery that the Charter and the Grant had been lost and her attempts to find them again. "I have traced them this far."

Dr. Olivano was surprised. "Here? To Pombareales?"

"Not exactly. The next rung on the ladder is Adrian Moncurio, a professional tomb robber. At Pombareales he is known as Professor Solomon, and is famous for his lead doubloons."

"Ah! Now I am beginning to understand! We are closing in on Casa Lucasta!"

"So we are. Irena Portils may be Moncurio's legal spouse—though I suspect not. Still, she is probably the only person on Earth who knows where to find him."

Dr. Olivano nodded. "What you have to say is interesting, but you may accept, as an article of faith, that Irena Portils will tell you nothing."

"That was my own feeling, after I saw her walking along the street. She seems a determined woman and under great strain."

"That is an understatement. I took her some forms to be filled out—routine inquiries regarding the family situation. The law insists upon knowing the father's address, but Madame Portils would reveal nothing. Not name, age, birthplace, occupation, or current address of her missing spouse. I pointed out that if she persisted the law might take away her children and put them in an institution. She became very agitated. 'Such information is important to no one but me. He is off-world; that is enough for you to know. If you take my children I will do something terrible.' I believed her, and said that perhaps it was not necessary after all. Later I wrote in a false name and address, and everyone was satisfied. But it's clear that Madame Portils herself is a borderline case. She hides behind a mask as best she can, especially when I come to call, since I represent the awful majesty of the Institute. I know that she hates me; she can't help herself—especially since the children seem to like me."

"Can they be cured?"

"That's hard to say, since no one can define their

affliction. They fluctuate; sometimes they seem almost normal; a few days later they are lost in their reveries. The girl is Lydia; she is often rational—unless she is put under stress. The boy is Myron. He can glance at a printed page and then reproduce it in any scale, large or small, letter by letter, word for word. The drawing is exact, and he seems to derive satisfaction in finishing the job—but he can't read, and he will not speak."

"Can he speak?"

"Lydia says that he can, but is not so sure after all that it was not the wind talking to her, as it often does. If the wind blows at night, she must be watched or she will climb from her window and run through the dark. This is when she becomes difficult, and must be sedated. They are a fascinating pair, and I am in awe of them. One day I set up a chess board in front of Myron. I explained the rules and we started to play. He barely glanced at the board and trounced me in twenty moves. We played again. He looked at the board only long enough to move his piece and beat me with contemptuous ease in seventeen moves. Then he became bored and lost interest."

"He does not read?"

"No, nor does Lydia."

"Someone should teach them."

"I agree. The grandmother lacks skill and Irena is devoid of patience and far too capricious. I would suggest a tutor, except that they can't pay."

"What about me?"

Olivano nodded slowly. "I thought it might be coming to something like that. Let me place the issues before you. First, I believe that you are sincere, and that you deserve all the help I can legitimately give you—but my first duty is to the two children. I can't be an accomplice to any program which might be to their harm."

"I would not harm them," said Wayness. "I only want to get a status in the household so that I can discover Moncurio's address."

"This is clear." Dr. Olivano's voice had taken on a quality Wayness could describe only as "institutional." Despite her best efforts, her own voice rose in pitch: "I don't want to sound over-dramatic, but the destiny of an entire world and thousands of people weigh on me."

"Yes. So it would seem." Dr. Olivano paused, and chose his words with delicacy. "If, in fact, your assessment of the situation is correct."

Wayness looked at him sadly. "You don't believe me?"

"Consider my position," said Dr. Olivano. "In the course of a year I speak with dozens of young women whose delusions are on the whole more convincing than your recital. This is not to say that you are not telling me the truth, as you see it—or even, for that matter, as it actually exists. But from this particular vantage, I have no way of knowing, and I must consider your proposal for a day or two."

Wayness looked bleakly up the road. "Apparently you want to verify what I have told you. If you call Pirie Tamm at Fair Winds the call will be intercepted. I will be traced to Pombareales and probably killed."

"That, in itself, would seem an obsessional remark."

Wayness could not restrain a short rueful laugh. "I have already escaped one attack in Trieste. I dropped an urn or something of the sort on the man's head. I think his name is 'Baro.' A shopkeeper named Alcide Xantief who gave me information was not so lucky. He was murdered and dropped into the Canal Daciano. Are these obsessions? You can call the police at Trieste. Even better, if you will come with me to the hotel, I will call Pirie Tamm at his bank, and you may ask him whatever you like about me and the Conservancy."

"No point in trying now," said Dr. Olivano. "It would be the middle of the night." He straightened in the seat. "It would also be unnecessary. Today, I had made up my mind to do something, even if it was wrong. I cannot justify taking the children away; Irena apparently does not abuse them; she feeds them and keeps them clean, and they are not unhappy—at least, not overtly so. But what of twenty years from now? Would we find Lydia still sorting out pieces of colored paper and Myron building five-dimensional castles in the sandbox?"

Olivano spoke on, looking out past the eucalyptus trees

and across the desolate pampas. "The next thing I know, you appear. Despite everything, I don't believe you are crazy, or delusional." He turned her a brief glance. "Today I will take you to Casa Lucasta, and introduce you as a junior case worker who has been assigned to assist with the children for a short period, as an experiment."

"Thank you, Doctor Olivano."

"I think, on the whole, that it would be better if you did not live in the house."

"I think so too," said Wayness, remembering Irena Portils' desperate face.

"I suppose you know nothing of psychotherapy?"

"Nothing, really."

"No matter. You will not be required to do anything complex. You must give Lydia and Myron sympathetic companionship, and try to bring their attention up from within themselves. This means that you must contrive activities which they will enjoy. Unfortunately, it is hard to know what they like and what they do not like, since they make a mystery of everything. Above all, you must be patient, and never show scorn or vexation, since if you do, they will withdraw and cease to trust you, so that all your work will be lost."

"I will do my best."

"Above all else, including life, death, honor, reputation, truth, is—need I say it?—discretion. Do not involve the Institute in a scandal. Do not let Irena find you rummaging through her drawers, or examining her mail."

Wayness grinned. "I won't let her catch me."

"One difficulty remains. You are not a convincing social worker. I think I should better introduce you as a student in the School of Psychotherapy, working as my assistant. Irena won't think this at all strange, as I have introduced such folk before."

"Do you find her difficult to work with?"

Olivano grimaced and gave no direct response. "She keeps her composure, but only, it seems, after great effort, which puts me on tenterhooks. I feel she is always dancing along the edge of a cliff, and I can never really come to grips with her. As soon as I touch upon something sensitive, she starts to fidget, and I must desist, or risk an outburst of some sort."

"What of the grandmother?"

"That is Madame Clara. She is sharp and shrewd, and notices everything. The children baffle her and she is brisk with them. I think that she stings their bottoms with a length of cane when it suits her. She resents me and surely will distrust you. Ignore her as best you can. You will get no information from her. She probably has none to give. Well then, are you ready?"

"I am ready, and also nervous."

"No reason for that. Your name shall be Marin Wales, since there is a student of that name who is not in residence at the moment."

Olivano turned the car around and drove back up Calle Maduro to Casa Lucasta. Wayness looked dubiously at the two-story white house. She had been worried as to how she might gain admittance; now that the means was opened to her, she worried more than ever. Yet—what was there to fear? If she knew, she told herself, perhaps she might not feel so queasy. Well, there was no help for it. Olivano had already alighted and was waiting for her with a faint smile on his face. "Don't be nervous. You are a student and not expected to know anything. Stand to the side and observe; nothing more is expected of you at the moment."

"But later?"

"You will be playing with two interesting if abnormal children, who will probably like you—which is truly my principal fear, that they may learn to like you too much."

Wayness gingerly stepped from the car, noticing as she did so Irena's face watching from an upper window.

The two crossed the yard to the front door, which was opened by Madame Clara. "Good morning," said Olivano. "Madame Clara, this is my assistant Marin."

"Yes, come in then," said Madame Clara in a flat rasping voice and stood back: a small nervously active woman, somewhat heavy and hunched in the shoulders so that her head hung forward. Her gray hair—which did not seem overly clean—was gathered in an untidy bun; her eyes were black and sharp; her mouth, by reason of a stricture or a damaged nerve, was frozen into an up-curving wince, molding her face into a cast of chronic cynical suspicion, as if she knew and was amused by everyone's ugly secrets.

Wayness looked into the dining room, to the side of the entry hall and discovered the children sitting bolt upright and wide-eyed at the table, unnaturally quiet and decorous, each with an orange clutched in thin fingers. They looked incuriously toward Olivano and Wayness, then returned to their private concerns.

Down the stairs came Irena Portils on long bony legs. She wore a green and yellow blouse with a russet-taupe skirt. It was an unbecoming outfit. The colors were not at all kind to her complexion; the blouse was too short, the skirt rose too high at the waist, emphasizing her rather wide abdomen. Nevertheless, when she first appeared at the head of the stairs, Wayness again thought to glimpse a tragic beauty, so fragile as to disappear at the instant of perception like a bursting bubble, leaving behind the reality of her despoiled and desperate features.

Irena looked at Wayness with surprise and no great pleasure. Doctor Olivano paid no heed, and spoke in a businesslike voice: "This is Marin Wales. She is an advanced student in the field and is functioning as my assistant. I have asked her to work with Myron and Lydia on an intensive basis, in order to accelerate the therapy, which does not seem to be going anywhere under present conditions."

"I don't quite understand."

"It is simple enough. Marin will be here every day, for at least a certain period."

Irena said slowly: "That is very nice, but I am not sure that this is the best of ideas. It may cause a derangement of the household."

"In this case we must proceed as I have outlined. We cannot let the years go by and do nothing."

Both Irena and Madame Clara turned to examine Wayness more closely. Wayness attempted a smile but it was evident that she had made an unfavorable impression.

Irena turned back to Olivano. She asked coldly: "Exactly what is involved in this inconvenient scheme?"

"It will not be all that bad," said Olivano. "Marin will spend as much time as possible with the children. She will in effect be their companion and try to engage their interest, using whatever tactics she thinks appropriate. She will bring her own meals and will cause you no extra work. I want her to observe the children's daily routines, from the time they leave bed to the time they retire."

"That seems a gross intrusion into our privacy, Doctor Olivano."

"As you wish. Your privacy will be respected. I will remove Lydia and Myron to the hospital for the regimen we had in mind. If you will pack some things for the children, I will take them with me now, and you need not be exposed to any inconvenience whatever."

Irena stood stock-still staring miserably at Olivano. Madame Clara, smiling her meaningless half-grin, turned and padded from the room and into the kitchen, as if divorcing herself from the proceedings. Lydia and Myron watched from the dining room. Wayness thought they seemed as vulnerable and defenseless as baby birds in a nest.

Irena looked slowly at Wayness, taking her measure. She muttered, "I don't know what to do. The children must stay with me."

"In that case, if you will leave us alone, I will introduce them to Marin."

"No. I will stay. I want to hear what you tell them."

"Then please take a seat in the corner and do not enter the conversation."

VIII.

Three days had passed; the time was early evening. Following instructions, Wayness telephoned Dr. Olivano at his home near Montalvo, thirty miles east of Pombareales. The face of a pretty blonde woman appeared on the screen. "Sufy Jirou here."

"I am Wayness Tamm, calling for Dr. Olivano."

"One moment, please."

Olivano's face came to the screen. He greeted Wayness without surprise. "You have just met my wife," he told her. "She is a musician, and lacks all interest in abnormal psychology. Speaking of which, what is the news from Casa Lucasta?"

Wayness gathered her thoughts. "It depends upon whom you ask. Irena would say 'Bad.' Clara would say: 'I have no news; I just do my work and hate every minute of it.' As for me, I have discovered nothing—not even the best place to look. I expect no confidences from Irena; she has barely spoken to me and clearly resents my presence."

"I am not surprised. What of the children?"

"There the news is good—so far. They seem to like me, although Myron is very dignified. Lydia is probably not quite so clever, but she is mercurial and demonstrative, and her sense of humor is always unexpected. She laughs at things which seem quite staid to me: a crumpled piece of paper, or a bird, or one of Myron's odd sandhouses. She is delighted when I tickle Myron's ear with a blade of grass;

this is the best joke of all, and even Myron allows himself to be amused."

Olivano showed his faint smile. "You don't seem to be bored with them."

"Not at all. But I can't say that I like Casa Lucasta. At some deep level the house frightens me. I am afraid of Irena and Madame Clara; they seem like witchwomen in a dark cave."

"You express yourself in colorful language," said Olivano dryly.

Sufy's voice sounded from off-screen. She seemed to muse: "Life is perceived as a flux of color." He turned his head away from the screen. "Sufy? I see that you have a remark to make."

"It is of no great consequence. I thought that I might mention that life is perceived as a flux of colors, but this is well known, and solves no mysteries."

"That is a pity," said Wayness. "There are a number of mysteries at Casa Lucasta. I could not estimate how many, since some may be parts of the same mystery."

"Mysteries—such as?"

"There is Irena herself. She goes off in the morning composed, neat and cold as an iceberg. She returns in the afternoon in a terrible mood, her face haggard and mottled."

"I have noticed something similar. Under the circumstances, I did not care to speculate. It may be just a minor problem."

"As for the children, I am surprised how they have changed in just the few days I have been with them. I can't be sure, but they seem more aware of their surroundings, more responsive, more alert. Lydia speaks when the impulse moves her and I understand her—I think. She knows what she means, at least. Today, and I consider it a real triumph, she answered a few of my questions, quite sensibly. Myron pretends not to notice, but he observes and thinks. In the main, he prefers his blissful detachment and his freedom to roam his private worlds. Occasionally though, I see his attention focus on our activity, and if it is interesting enough, he might be tempted to join us."

"What does Irena think of all this?"

"I spoke to her today and told her more or less what I have told you. She merely shrugged and told me that they often went through phases and that they must not be over-stimulated. Sometimes I feel that she wants to keep them as they are: submissive and unable to complain."

"It is not an uncommon attitude."

"Yesterday I brought out paper and pictures, and pencils, and started to teach them to read. Myron grasped the idea instantly, but became bored and couldn't be bothered. Lydia wrote 'CAT' when I showed her a picture of a cat. Myron did the same, after I insisted, and with an air of contemptuous indifference. Irena says it's a waste of time, since they have no interest in reading.

"We made a kite and flew it, which both found exciting. Then the kite crashed and they were mournful. I said that we would make another kite soon, but that they must learn to read first. Myron gave a morose grunt: the only sound I have heard from him. When Irena came home, I wanted Lydia to read for her, but Lydia became engrossed in other affairs. This is when Irena said I was wasting my time. Then she told me that since tomorrow was Sunday, Clara would be away on her own errands. This being the case, Irena would be busy with the children all day: giving them their baths, serving their Sunday dinner, and so forth. She said that I would be in the way, and need not come to Casa Lucasta."

Olivano spoke in surprise. "Baths? Sunday dinner? That is not a lengthy program. Two or three hours, and the rest of the day alone with them, and no Marin on hand to see what goes on." Olivano rubbed his chin. "She can't be receiving a special visitor; the whole town would know about it. Most likely, she simply doesn't want you on hand any more than necessary."

"I don't trust Irena, and I doubt if she is their natural mother; they don't resemble her in the least."

"An interesting thought. We can quite readily get at the truth." Olivano rubbed his chin. "We have taken blood samples from the children in order to check for genetic deviations. We found nothing, of course; their affliction is still a mystery—among all the others. You are calling from the hotel?"

"Yes."

"I will call you back in a few moments."

The screen darkened. Wayness went to the window and looked out across the square. On Saturday night all the folk of Pombareales, from high quality to low, had dressed themselves in their best and come out to promenade. For the young men, fashion dictated tight black trousers, shirts striped with dark rich colors: maroon, deep sea green, gamboge, dark blue, with waistcoats carefully echoing one of the colors present in their shirts: such were the stringencies of the style. The most gallant bravos wore low-crowned black hats with broad brims, rakishly slanted to reflect the wearer's mood. The young women wore short-sleeved ankle-length gowns, with flowers in their hair. From somewhere beyond the range of her vision came the sound of cheerful music. Wayness thought that it all seemed like great fun.

A chime called Wayness to the telephone. Olivano's face, now somewhat somber, appeared. "I have spoken with Irena. She gave me no convincing reason for keeping you away. I explained that the time you could spend at Casa Lucasta was limited, and that I wanted you with the children as much as possible. She said that since I held this opinion she must withdraw her opposition. Therefore you may keep to your usual routine."

In the morning Wayness presented herself at Casa Lucasta at her usual time. Irena opened the door.

"Good morning, Madame Portils," said Wayness.

"Good morning," said Irena, in a cool clear voice. "The children are still in bed; they are not feeling well."

"That is too bad! What do you think is wrong?"

"They seem to have eaten something which disagreed with them. Did you treat them to sweets or pastries yesterday?"

"I brought them some coconut puffs; yes. I ate some too, and I feel fine today."

Irena only nodded her head, as if in vindication. "They will not be too active today; I am sure of that. It is a great nuisance."

"I wonder if I should look in on them?"

"I see no benefit they could derive from your visit. They had a fitful night, and now they are sleeping."

"I see."

Irena moved back into the doorway. "Doctor Olivano mentioned that your time here was limited. When, exactly, will you be leaving?"

"Nothing is settled yet," said Wayness politely. "Much depends upon the progress of my work."

"It must be a dreary routine for you," said Irena. "It certainly is for me. Well then, I will let you go. They may be feeling well enough tomorrow for you to resume your work."

Irena drew back into the shadows; the door closed. Wayness slowly turned away, and went back to the hotel.

For half an hour Wayness sat in the lobby, fidgeting, frowning, wanting to call Dr. Olivano, yet reluctant to do so, for a number of reasons. First of all, it was Sunday morning, when Dr. Olivano might not wish to be disturbed. Secondly— well, there were other reasons.

Despite all, Wayness finally felt impelled to call Olivano, only to be notified by a dispassionate voice that no one was at home. Wayness turned away in both frustration and relief, together with a new and illogical flush of anger toward Irena.

On Monday evening Wayness once again called Olivano. She told him of her visit to Casa Lucasta on Sunday morning and Irena's statements. "When I went there this morning I did not know what to expect —but certainly not what I found. The children were out of bed, dressed and sitting at their breakfast. They seemed listless, almost comatose, and only barely looked at me when I greeted them. Irena was watching me from the kitchen; I pretended to notice nothing unusual, and sat with them while they finished their breakfast. Ordinarily they are anxious to go outside, but this morning they did not seem to care one way or the other.

"We went outside at last. I spoke to Lydia but she barely glanced at me; Myron sat on the edge of the sandbox, making marks in the sand with a stick. In short, they

had lost what they had gained and more, and I can't
understand it.

"When Irena came home, she was expecting me to
comment but I only said that they still seemed to be a bit
under the weather. She agreed to this, saying: 'They are
prone to peculiar moods, which I have learned to ignore.'
That is the news from Casa Lucasta."

"Curse all!" muttered Olivano. "You should have telephoned me yesterday morning."

"I did, but you were not home."

"Of course not; I was at the Institute! Sufy was with her
students."

"I'm sorry. I thought that I might be disturbing you,
since it was Sunday morning."

"You have disturbed me, right enough. But still, we
have learned something. What it is, I don't know." Olivano
reflected. "I will make my usual Wednesday visit. You keep
to your routine, and telephone me tomorrow night, if there
is anything worth reporting. In fact, call anyway."

"Just as you say."

Tuesday went quietly at Casa Lucasta. Wayness
thought that the children seemed less leaden and dismal,
but a quality which she had started to perceive in them—
vitality? immediacy?—had been suppressed.

The afternoon was cool, with a hazy overcast obscuring
the sun and a chilly wind blowing down from the mountains. The children sat on the couch in the sitting room,
Lydia holding a rag doll, Myron twisting a length of string.
Madame Clara went out to the utility room with a basket of
soiled clothes; she would be occupied for at least five
minutes, maybe longer. Wayness jumped to her feet and
ran silently upstairs. The door to Irena's room was closed;
with thudding heart Wayness opened it and peered within.
She saw furnishings of no distinction: a bed, chest of
drawers, a desk. Wayness went at once to the desk. She slid
open a drawer, surveyed the contents, but dared make no
detailed investigation; time was passing too quickly. With
each second the tension grew, until it could no longer be
supported. With a hiss of frustration, Wayness closed the
drawer and ran back the way she had come. Myron and

Lydia watched her incuriously; there was no clue as to what might be going on in their minds: perhaps no more than a colored daze. She dropped upon the couch and picked up one of their picture books, her heart still pounding and her whole being heavy with resentment. She had dared to venture into forbidden territory and it had all gone for naught.

Fifteen seconds later Madame Clara came to look into the sitting room. Wayness paid her no heed. Madame Clara, showing her wincing suspicious grin, looked sharply around the room, then turned away. Wayness drew a deep breath. Had Madame Clara heard sounds? Had she merely sensed that something was amiss? One thing was certain: no efficient search of Casa Lucasta could be accomplished with Madame Clara on the premises.

During the middle evening Wayness telephoned Dr. Olivano at his home near Montalvo. She reported that Myron and Lydia, while still apathetic, were somewhat improved. "Whatever happened to them Sunday seems to be dissipating, but very slowly."

"I will be interested to see them tomorrow."

IX.

On Wednesday morning Dr. Olivano made his routine call at Casa Lucasta, arriving an hour before noon. He found Wayness, with Myron and Lydia, in the side yard. The children were occupied with modeling clay, each molding what at first glance appeared to be an animal of some sort, using as their models pictures in books Wayness had propped in front of them.

Olivano approached. The children glanced at him and went on with their work. Lydia was modeling a horse and Myron a black panther. Olivano thought that both had performed creditably, though neither showed much zest.

Wayness greeted him. "As you see, Lydia and Myron are hard at work. I think that they feel just a bit better this morning. Am I right, Lydia?"

Lydia raised her eyes and showed the ghost of a smile, then returned to the clay. Wayness went on: "I would ask Myron the same question, but he is too busy just now to answer. Still, I think he feels better too."

"They are doing good work," said Olivano.

"Yes. But not as good as they are capable of doing. In the main, they are just pushing the clay back and forth. As soon as they feel better, we will see some really interesting things. Both Myron and Lydia are determined not to let themselves go all dreamy again." Wayness heaved a deep sigh. "I feel as if I have been giving them artificial respiration."

"Hmf," said Olivano. "You should see some of the types

I deal with ten times a day. These two are like flowers in the spring." He looked toward the house. "Irena is at home, I assume."

Wayness nodded. "She is home. To be exact, she is watching us from the window now."

"Good. Then I will show her something worth her interest," said Olivano. He opened his medical case and brought out a pair of small transparent envelopes. He pulled a hair from Lydia's head, to her startlement, and another from Myron, who showed only resignation. Olivano dropped the hairs into the envelopes, which he labeled.

Wayness asked: "Why are you torturing poor Myron and Lydia."

"It is not torture; it is science," said Olivano.

"I always thought that there was a difference."

"There is in this case, at least. Hairs grow in layers, absorbing various materials from the blood as they do so; they become, in effect, stratigraphic records. I will have these hairs analyzed."

"Do you think you will discover anything?"

"Not necessarily. Certain types of substances are either not absorbed or make no distinct strata. Still, it is worth trying." Olivano turned to look toward the house. Through the window they saw Irena's shape move back, as if she were reluctant to be discovered.

Olivano said: "It is time for a conference with Irena."

Wayness asked: "Shall I come?"

"I think your presence would be helpful."

The two went to the front door and Olivano sounded the chime. After a pause Irena opened the door. "Yes?"

"May we come in?"

Irena turned and led the way into the sitting room. She remained standing. "Why were you taking hair from the children?"

Olivano explained the process and its rationale. Irena was clearly not pleased. "Do you think that such a procedure is necessary?"

"I won't know for certain until I see the results of the analysis."

"That is not very informative."

Olivano laughed and gave his head a rueful shake. "If I had definite information, you would be the first to know. Now then, there is another matter, related to general hygiene. You may or may not have heard that the polyvirus XAX-29 was discovered in Pombareales last week. It is not overly dangerous but may be uncomfortable if a person lacks the proper antibodies. I can easily make the determination with a blood sample. If you will permit—" Olivano brought out a small instrument. "You will feel nothing." He stepped forward and before Irena could protest or draw back, he had pressed the instrument against her forearm. "Very good," said Olivano. "I will have results for you tomorrow. In the meantime, don't worry, as the chances of infection are slight, but it is better to be safe than sorry."

Irena stood rubbing her arm, eyes glittering black in her wasted face.

Olivano said politely: "I think that is all for now. Marin has her instructions—essentially, more of the same."

Irena said with a sniff: "She seems to spend a great deal of time playing with the children."

"That is precisely what they need: they should not be allowed to brood and daydream and recede into their private worlds. They seem to have had something of a setback, but they are coming out of it and I want to make sure that it does not happen again."

Irena had nothing to say, and Olivano took his leave.

The week passed. On Friday evening Olivano telephoned Wayness at the hotel. "What is the news from Casa Lucasta?"

"Nothing, except that the children are almost back to where they were. Lydia is talking again and Myron gives his indescribable signals. They are both reading: Lydia goes at it casually; Myron seems to read at a glance."

"Such skill has been recorded before."

"There is something else, most curious. We went for a walk out on the pampas and Lydia found a pretty white stone. This morning she could not find it; I had packed it into a box of oddments by mistake. Lydia looked everywhere, but could not find her stone. Finally she told Myron:

'It is my white stone: gone!' Myron looked around, and went directly to the box and tossed the stone to Lydia. She seemed not at all surprised. I asked her: 'How did Myron know the stone was in the box?' She only shrugged and went back to her picture book. Later, when they had gone into the house for their lunch, I hid Myron's red pencil under the sand in a corner of the sandbox. After lunch they came back into the yard. Myron started to draw but found that his red pencil was missing. He looked around the yard and went directly to the sandbox and found his pen Then he looked at me with a most peculiar expression: puzzled, amused, wondering if I had lost my mind. I found it hard not to laugh. So—there you have it. Myron, who can do all manner of remarkable deeds, is also clairvoyant."

Olivano said: "That faculty is mentioned in the literature—guardedly. It is said to maximize at puberty, then dwindle away." He thought for a few seconds. "I don't think I want to involve myself in this matter, and I would prefer that you keep your findings to yourself. We don't want to make Myron any more of a freak than he is."

Wayness could not let Olivano's remarks, no matter how cool and dispassionate—in fact, they were too cool and too dispassionate—go unchallenged. "Myron is in no sense of the word a freak! Despite all his odd little quirks and funny attempts at dignity, he is gentle and cooperative and really a sweet little boy!"

"Aha! I wonder who has got whom wrapped around their little finger!"

"Yes, I fear so."

"Then you may be interested to know that, while Myron and Lydia are siblings, Irena is not their mother. They have no congruent genetic material."

"It is no more than I suspected," said Wayness. "What do the hair samples tell you?"

"I have not had the results yet, but I should have them by Wednesday. I don't know whether or not I deceived Irena about the virus, but I might as well play out the game and tell her it is no longer a threat. I will also advise her that I want you on hand Sunday, and that the next time the children show any sign of illness, no matter how trivial, that I must be called, since I want no recurrence of the previous ailment which set them back psychologically."

The weekend passed without untoward incident. On Wednesday morning Dr. Olivano arrived at Casa Lucasta as usual. It was another chilly day with wan sunlight seeping through a high overcast and a wind blowing down from the Andes. Despite the weather Wayness with Lydia and Myron were occupied as usual in the side yard. Today Myron and Lydia sat together, studying the pages of a picture book wherein were depicted many sorts of wild animals, both terrestrial and off-world.

"Good morning all!" called Olivano. "What are you doing with yourselves today?"

"We are exploring the universe, from top to bottom," said Wayness. "We look at pictures, and talk. Lydia sometimes reads from the books and Myron draws pretty pictures when he is in the mood."

"Myron can do anything," said Lydia.

"I don't doubt it an instant," said Olivano. "You are also very clever."

"Lydia reads quite well," said Wayness. She pointed to a picture. "What animal is that, Lydia?"

"It is a lion."

"How do you know?"

Lydia gave Wayness a puzzled look. "The letters read 'LION.' "

Wayness took the book, turned the page, covered the picture and asked: "What animal is on this page?"

"I don't know. The word reads 'TIGER,' but we won't know really until we see the picture."

"Quite right!" said Wayness. "There might have been a mistake. But not this time! The picture shows a tiger and the letters spell 'TIGER.' "

Olivano asked: "What of Myron? Does he read too?"

"Of course he reads—probably better than you do. Myron, be a good boy and read something."

Myron cocked his head dubiously to the side, but said nothing.

"In that case, show me an animal that you like."

It seemed that Myron had ignored the question, then

suddenly he turned a few pages and displayed the picture of a stag, with mountains in the background.

"That is a handsome beast indeed," said Olivano. Wayness put her arm around Myron's thin shoulders and hugged him. "You are very clever, Myron."

Myron pulled in the corners of his mouth by way of response.

Lydia looked at the picture. "That is a 'STAG.' "

"Quite right! What else can you read?"

"Anything I like."

"Really?"

Lydia opened a book and read:

'Rodney the Bad Boy.'

"Very good," said Wayness. "Now read the story." Lydia bent her head over the book and read:

'Once there was a boy named Rodney who had learned a bad habit: he scribbled in picture books. One day he drew some foolish black lines across the face of a fine sabretooth tiger. This was a serious mistake, since a fairy owned the book. She said: "That was a naughty trick, Rodney, and now you shall have the teeth of the poor tiger whom you made so ugly."

'Instantly two long heavy teeth grew from Rodney's mouth, so long that when he lowered his head the points rested on his chest. Rodney's father and mother were very annoyed, but the dentist said that the teeth were healthy and there were no cavities, and that probably they need not worry about braces. The main thing was for Rodney to brush the teeth well, and to wipe them with a napkin while he was eating.'

Lydia put the book down. "That is enough for now."

"And very interesting too," said Wayness. "Rodney will probably not make the same mistake again."

Lydia nodded and returned to the pages of the picture book.

Olivano spoke to Wayness. "I am astonished. What have you done?"

"Nothing. It is already there. I gave it a chance to happen, and meanwhile I hugged them and kissed them, which they seem to like."

"Yes, of course," said Olivano. "Who wouldn't?"

"They might have known how to read before. Myron, have you been reading for a long time and keeping it secret?"

Myron had been drawing on a sheet of paper. He looked up at Wayness from the corner of his eyes, then returned to his drawing.

"If you don't care to talk, you can write something on this piece of nice green paper." Wayness put the paper in front of him.

Again Myron squinted up from the side of his face. When he saw that Wayness was smiling at him, he took up his pencil and wrote: "We have never read before. It is easier than chess. But there are many words I do not know."

"We will repair that lack, perhaps even today. Now show Dr. Olivano how well you can draw."

Without enthusiasm Myron began to draw, using his pencils. Then he took up his color flow-pens and brushed here and there. On the paper appeared a great stag with spreading antlers. He stood looking from a landscape similar to the depiction in the book, but quite different in detail. If anything, the drawing was more precise and the colors more striking than those in the book.

"That is absolutely enchanting," said Olivano. "Myron, I salute you."

"I can draw too," said Lydia.

"Of course you can," said Wayness. "You are also a wonderful little creature."

Wayness, glancing toward the house, saw Irena watching from the window. "We are being observed," she told Olivano.

"So I noticed. We must bring these matters to her attention."

Lydia's shoulders sagged. "I don't want any medicine."

Olivano asked: "What medicine?"

Lydia looked off toward the loom of the mountains. "Sometimes when the wind blows I want to run, and then they give us medicine, so that everything is dark and we are tired."

Olivano said: "I will see that they give you no more medicine. But you must not run when the wind blows."

"Clouds ride on the wind, and birds fly sidewise. Weeds roll and tumble and bump down the pampas."

"Lydia thinks she must join the clouds and birds and weeds," said Wayness.

Lydia found the idea amusing. "No! Marin; you are foolish!"

"Then why do you run?"

Lydia's words came slowly. "First there is the wind, and I know things are starting. Then I begin to hear far voices. They are calling to me. They say—" Lydia made her voice low and husky "—'Weerooo! Weerooo! Are you there? Weerooo!' They are calling to me, from in back of the mountains, and I start to feel strange, and then I run out into the dark."

Wayness asked: "Do you know who is calling?"

"It might be the old men with the yellow eyes," said Lydia dubiously.

"Does Myron hear the voices?"

"Myron becomes angry."

"Running through the night is a bad habit, and you must change," said Olivano. "When the night is dark and the wind blows strong and cold, you will surely get lost and fall down among the rocks and the thorns and die. Then there will be no more Lydia, and the people who love you will be sad."

"I will be sad too," said Lydia.

"That is exactly correct. So, you will stop running?"

Lydia became anxious. "They will still call me!"

Wayness said: "I do not go running every time someone calls to me."

"That is proper conduct," said Olivano. "You must act the same way."

Lydia nodded slowly, as if agreeing to take the matter under consideration.

Olivano turned to Wayness: "It's time for our conference with Irena. Today we have some serious matters to discuss."

"In regard to the hair?"

Olivano nodded. "I may be forced to make some harsh decisions before too long. They never come easy."

Wayness became apprehensive. "What sort of decisions?"

"I'm not sure yet. I'm waiting for some test reports." He led the way to the front door, where Irena silently admitted them into the house.

Dr. Olivano put on his best professional manner. "I'm happy to confirm that the virus is no longer a threat; there have been no new cases."

Irena acknowledged the news with a curt nod. "I am quite busy today, and if that is all—"

"Not quite. In fact there are several matters which we must discuss. Shall we sit?"

Irena wordlessly turned away and went into the sitting room. Olivano and Wayness followed, and seated themselves gingerly on the couch. Irena remained standing.

Olivano spoke, choosing his words carefully. "In regard to the children, I can only call their progress phenomenal. It is hard to assign credit, but clearly the children like Marin, and respond to her, and she has been able to break down their isolation."

Irena said crisply: "That, of course, may be beneficial, but I have been warned that they are of a manic disposition and should not be over-stimulated."

"That is incorrect," said Olivano coldly. "Lydia and Myron are highly intelligent individuals desperately anxious to become normal. I understood none of this until Marin provided some insights. Then the problems started to show themselves."

Irena darted a glittering black glance toward Wayness. "There were no problems whatever. They lived quietly and happily until Marin appeared on the scene. Since then, their conduct has become erratic, even peculiar."

"That is true," said Olivano. "They are commencing to demonstrate extraordinary abilities, far beyond what is considered 'normal.' In a few years these abilities will become less dramatic, or even disappear, which is the usual sequence of events. But for now, the improvement in their personalities is so notable that we must do our best to maintain the momentum; don't you agree?"

"Yes, of course, but with certain reservations."

Olivano dismissed Irena's 'reservations' with a gesture. "Last week I took away some hair samples. They have provided information which, frankly, I find almost incredible. Let me ask you this: have you been dosing the children with medicines or tonics of any kind?"

Irena's eyes narrowed. She delayed several seconds before responding. "Not recently." She attempted a light tone. "Where did you get that idea? Surely not from the hair?"

Olivano nodded somberly. "The hair of both children show striations recurring at weekly intervals. The striations yield no identifiable compounds, which indicates that the medicine is a complex organic substance, or mixture of substances, too dilute to leave a signature other than the fact that they were administered. So now, I will ask you again as to what medicine you have been giving the children?"

Irena attempted an airy tone. "Only their regular tonic, which, in my opinion, has kept them as well as they are today."

"Why did you not tell me about this so-called 'tonic'?"

Irena shrugged. "It is nothing of consequence. The doctor who prescribed it explained that it strengthened the nerves, and was also good for the digestion."

"May I see this tonic?"

"It's all gone," said Irena. "I used the last some time ago and discarded the bottle."

"And you have no more?"

Irena hesitated a single instant. "No."

Olivano nodded. "These are my instructions. Do not administer any medicines or tonics whatever. Is this understood?"

"Of course; still, the children are sometimes difficult. When the wind blows at night, Lydia becomes unmanageable and wants to run out across the pampas. During these times, a sedative becomes necessary."

Olivano nodded. "I can understand that you may have a problem. I will prescribe a safe sedative, but you must not use it except under extreme circumstances."

"As you like."

"I will reiterate, to make sure there is no misunderstanding. I do not want you dosing the children except with my prior approval. You would be doing them harm and I would surely know and I would have no choice but to take them to an environment where they were protected."

Irena stood, face sagging in dejection and defeat. She started to speak, then held her tongue.

Olivano rose to his feet. "I'll have a word or two with the children, then I will be going." He nodded to Irena and departed. Irena turned toward Wayness. She spoke in a harsh low voice: "I cannot fathom you! Why have you done these things to me?"

Wayness could think of nothing to say, and Irena's distress stirred her own latent guilt at being in the house under false pretenses. At last, lamely, she said: "I have intended nothing to harm you."

"My life is no longer my own!" Irena's mouth began to work, and her words came in wild harsh mutters. "Only one year more. One accursed year! Then it might have been over! I would flee—I would flee now, only there is nothing for me: no solace, no refuge! I am miserable, even before I die, and then who knows? Who knows? It is for this reason that I am afraid!"

"Madame Irena, please calm yourself! I'm sure things are not as bad as you fear!"

"Ha! You know nothing, except to smarm and snivel and now I do not know what to do."

"Why are you worried? Is it about Professor Solomon?"

Irena's face instantly froze. "I have said nothing, do you hear? Nothing!"

"Of course. Still, if you care to talk, I will listen."

But Irena had turned on her heel and in three long steps had lunged from the room.

Wayness gloomily went out into the yard, where she

took herself in hand. She could not afford to be soft; if deceit and dissimulation were the worst compromises she must make, she could count herself lucky. And after all, Myron and Lydia were to be considered. Irena had mentioned a year: what was to happen in a year? Wayness felt certain that it would not have been to the advantage of the two children.

Dr. Olivano had departed. Madame Clara presently called the children in for their lunch. Wayness sat on the edge of the sandbox and ate the sandwich she had brought from the hotel.

Toward the middle of the afternoon Wayness diffidently asked permission to take the children for a walk. Irena gave a graceless assent and Wayness took her two charges to a confectionery on the square, where Lydia and Myron gravely consumed hot cocoa and fruit tarts mounded high with whipped cream. Wayness wondered what would happen to them when she went away. Dr. Olivano would look to their physical well-being, and as for their emotions— Wayness heaved a sigh. She must harden her heart to such considerations. As for her own affairs, they were not going at all well. She was not a whit closer to Moncurio's whereabouts now than on the day of her arrival. There had been no opportunity to search the house—though what she might expect to find she had no idea. She was supported only by hope, because she could think of no alternatives to what she was doing. She studied Myron and Lydia, who, so she noticed, were studying her in turn. Wayness saw that they had enjoyed their treats to the last crumb. Next she took them to the town bookshop, where she bought a terrestrial atlas, a big picture book of natural history, a dictionary, and an astronomical atlas.

The three returned to Casa Lucasta. Irena took note of the purchases but made no comment; Wayness would have been surprised had she done so.

The next morning, when Wayness arrived, she found Myron and Lydia already hard at work, building a kite to their own design, using splints of split cane and dark blue film, secured by strips of cohering tape. It was an intricate construction five feet long, comprising an extravagant array of wings, vanes, foils, spoilers, and flared conduits. Wayness found the kite fascinating to look at, but doubted whether it would fly.

The kite was not finished until middle afternoon, when the wind started to blow erratically, in gusts followed by periods of dead calm. Myron and Lydia nevertheless prepared to fly the kite. Wayness, after indecision, decided not to interfere, though she was sure that the kite would meet disaster.

The two, carrying the kite, crossed Calle Maduro and picked their way out upon the waste of stone and bush which spread away to the south. Wayness followed behind.

Lydia held the string while Myron carried the kite downwind, the film chattering and the various vanes and foils fluttering. Myron turned; the wind caught the kite and, contrary to Wayness' pessimistic expectations, swept it up—higher, higher, higher, as Lydia paid out the string. She turned a quick smile over her shoulder toward Wayness. Myron watched the ascent with neither surprise nor enthusiasm, but with a gravity which was almost stern. High soared the kite, ruling the wind, each of Myron's peculiar vanes and surfaces performing faultlessly. Wayness watched, marvelling.

The wind waxed and waned, the kite acknowledging the changes with small adjustments, sometimes swooping or dipping somewhat, but otherwise paying no heed to the vagaries of nature. Myron's kite ruled the skies!

A gust of wind, stronger than any before, struck down from the mountains. The kite string broke and fell slowly to the ground. The kite, liberated, swung majestically away downwind on a mission of its own, and its ultimate descent could not be discerned.

Myron and Lydia stood motionless, looking after the kite for some time, mouths drooping but showing no other emotion. Wayness thought that the flight had been successful. She thought that Lydia and Myron also were satisfied. Myron turned, gave Wayness one of his most unfathomable stares. Wayness said nothing. Lydia dutifully began to roll up the string. As soon as the job was done, all returned to the house, Myron and Lydia pensive rather than crestfallen.

For a time the three sat on the couch, looking through the new books. Wayness was startled to find that Myron was reading the dictionary, scanning page after page, though without any evidence of enjoyment or interest. "That is natural enough," Wayness told herself. "It is not an exciting book."

Irena returned from work, even more tired and distraught than usual. She went directly to her room, without a word to anyone. Shortly afterward Wayness took her leave and returned to the hotel.

During the evening Olivano telephoned. He asked: "And how went your day?"

"Well enough. Lydia and Myron built a beautiful kite, and it flew beautifully too. But the string broke and for all I know, the kite is still flying somewhere off across the pampas. When I left the house, Lydia was inspecting the picture of a stegosaurus and Myron was studying a chart of the Gaean Reach. He had already read the dictionary. Clara was surly and Irena ignored me."

"Just another day at Casa Lucasta," said Olivano. "As for me, I received the complete analysis of Irena's blood today, and it is as I have long suspected: she has been taking some sort of drug which the analyst is unable to name, except to suggest that it is off-world in origin."

"I've wondered about this too," said Wayness. "In the morning, when she leaves for work, she is quite neat and in command of herself; in the afternoon she can hardly wait to get home and comes running in like a scarecrow."

Olivano went on in his most toneless voice: "Everything taken with everything, it has become clear to me that Irena is not a suitable custodian for Lydia and Myron. I intend to take them to a better environment as soon as possible."

Wayness slowly adjusted herself to the news, which was bleak. "How soon will that be?"

"The legal processes will take two or three days, depending upon whether old Bernard's leg is hurting him or not. After that, there is no reason for further delay, but it always occurs. It would be better for everyone concerned if you were not on hand at this time."

"So when must I go?"

"Sooner rather than later, I fear."

"Two days? Three days?"

"Three days at most, or so I would estimate. I will be glad to have the matter settled, since I am starting to suffer from nervous anxieties. The situation at Casa Lucasta does not seem stable."

X.

Wayness slumped back into the chair and stared numbly off across the room. Time passed; emotion gradually drained from her mind, leaving only a lump of resentment, directed toward everything and everyone, including Dr. Olivano and his indomitable rectitude.

Wayness finally managed a sour shaky laugh. Dr. Olivano's responsibilities must be for the children, and her sense of betrayal was irrational. Dr. Olivano, after all, was not a member of the Naturalist Society.

Wayness rose to her feet and went to the window. Her circumstances were bleak; she was no closer to Moncurio than when she had first arrived in Pombareales—perhaps even farther away, since now she had antagonized Irena Portils, the single strand of connection to Moncurio.

Three days, at most, remained to her, and she could think of no constructive course of action other than searching the house. To date, there had been no opportunity; either Madame Clara or Irena was always on hand. Even had she been able to search, Wayness suspected that the effort would have yielded nothing, except for enormous embarrassment if she were caught.

She brooded down across the square, which was almost deserted. Tonight the wind blew strong, fluttering foliage and moaning on its way past the hotel. It was to be hoped that Lydia would not hear voices calling: "Weerooo! Come to us, come!" and decide to run.

Wayness felt too restless for bed. She donned her gray

cloak, and leaving the hotel walked quickly along the silent streets to Calle Maduro. Overhead the stars glittered hard and brilliant in a black sky; low in the west hung the Southern Cross.

Tonight the town was quiet: few folk were abroad. The cantinas were almost empty, though the red and yellow lights with which they festooned their fronts shone bravely through the dark. From the Cantina de Las Hermosas came the sound of a voice raised in song—perhaps issuing from the throat of Leon Casinde the pork butcher, thought Wayness.

The winds whipped down Calle Maduro, sighing through the shrubs and weeds of the pampas. Wayness stopped to listen, and thought to hear a low mournful tone drifting down from the upper air, though she could distinguish no voices. She continued up Calle Maduro. The small houses were pale in the starlight. Casa Lucasta was dark. Everyone had gone to bed, to sleep, or perhaps to lie awake thinking.

Wayness stood in the shadows of the empty house. There was nothing to be seen, nothing to be heard but the wind.

For ten minutes she waited, the wind flapping her cloak, not at all sure why she was here in the first place, though she would not have been surprised to see a small thin shape emerge from Casa Lucasta and run out across the pampas.

Nothing of the sort occurred. The house remained dark. At last Wayness turned away and slowly returned down Calle Maduro, and back to the Hotel Monopole.

In the morning Wayness awoke with the mood of the night before still with her. The day outside her windows was overcast, and the wind had ceased to blow, so that the sky seemed to exert a curious oppressive weight.

As Wayness consumed her breakfast, her mood changed, and she began to scold herself. "I am Wayness Tamm of Riverview House! I am said to be a very talented person, also intelligent. Therefore, I must start to demonstrate these qualities, or feel foolish when I look into the mirror. So far I have been too diffident; I have been waiting for information to float past on a silver tray! This is poor strategy! I must do something more dramatic! Such as — what?" Wayness considered. "If I could only convince Irena that I meant Moncurio no harm, perhaps she might help me — especially if I offered her money." Wayness considered further. "I don't dare bring up the subject — that's the sad truth; indeed, I'm afraid of Irena."

Nevertheless, Wayness set out for Casa Lucasta in a mood of determination. She arrived just as Irena was leaving for work. "Good morning," said Wayness politely. "It almost looks like rain, doesn't it?"

"Good morning," said Irena. She glanced around the sky as if she had never noticed it before. "Rain is not usual here." She gave Wayness a vague smile and went off down Calle Maduro.

Wayness looked after her, shaking her head in perplexity. Irena was a strange one, and no mistake!

Wayness went to the door and touched the chime button. She waited. After an interval nicely calculated to express a maximum of contempt and resentment, the door was opened by Clara, who at once turned and went back to the kitchen, darting a single admonitory glance back over her shoulder. The message is clear, thought Wayness. "I am not one of Clara's favorites either."

The children were at their breakfast in the dining room. Wayness greeted them, then took a seat at the end of the table and watched as they finished their porridge. Myron, as usual, was stern and lost in thought, Lydia seemed a trifle peaked.

"Last night the wind blew hard," said Wayness. "Did you hear it?"

"I heard it," said Lydia, and added virtuously: "but I did not run."

"Very wise! Did you hear voices?"

Lydia squirmed in the chair. "Myron says that the voices are not really there."

"Myron is right, as he always seems to be."

Lydia returned to her porridge. Wayness took occasion to survey the room. Where could she reasonably hope to find information pertaining to Adrian Moncurio, supposing that it existed? Much would depend upon Irena's attitude toward such information. If she deemed it of no great value, it might be almost anywhere—even in the drawers of the sideboard yonder, where Irena kept miscellaneous household papers.

Clara went out to the utility porch. Wayness jumped up, ran to the sideboard, opened drawers looked here and there, hoping that the name 'Moncurio,' or 'Professor Solomon' might catch her eye.

Nothing.

Lydia and Myron watched with neither surprise nor concern. Clara returned to the kitchen; Wayness resumed her seat. Lydia asked: "Why did you do that?"

Wayness said in a half-whisper: "I was looking for something. I will tell you later, when Clara cannot hear."

Lydia nodded, finding the remark eminently reasonable. She lowered her own voice: "You should ask Myron. He can find anything, because he can detect where things are."

A quiver of excitement played along Wayness' skin. She looked toward Myron; could it possibly be? the idea strained credibility. She asked in a tentative voice: "Myron—can you find things?"

Myron's nose twitched, as if in deprecation of the purported skill. Lydia said: "Myron knows everything. Or almost everything. I think it is time he was starting to talk, so that you could hear what he has to say."

Myron paid no heed and pushed away what remained of his porridge.

Lydia studied him soberly, then told Wayness: "I think he will talk when there is something he wants to say."

"Or when he is helping us find something," said Wayness.

Movements from the kitchen suggested that Clara's attention had been attracted by the conversation.

"Well, then," said Wayness heavily. "What shall we do today? The weather is dreary but it's not too cold, and we can go out into the yard." Where, thought Wayness grimly, they could talk without fear of Clara listening.

However, rain had started to fall, so that the three

remained in the sitting room, looking at the terrestrial atlas.

Wayness explained the Mercator projection. "So on this flat paper you have the entire surface of Old Earth. These blue areas are oceans and these others are continents. Do either of you know where we are now?"

Lydia shook her head. "No one has ever told us,"

Myron, after a single glance, put his finger on Patagonia.

"Correct!" said Wayness. She turned pages in the atlas. "All these countries are different, and every place has its own special flavor. It is great fun traveling here and there, going from one old city to another, or exploring beautiful wild places, and even on Old Earth the wild places still exist."

Lydia looked dubiously down at the maps. "What you say must be true, but these maps are confusing, and they give me a funny feeling. I'm not sure whether I like it or not."

Wayness laughed. "I know that feeling very well. It is called 'wanderlust.' When I was your age, someone gave me a book of poems from the early times. One of these poems affected me strongly, and haunted me for days, so that I avoided the book. Do you want to hear the poem? It is quite short and it goes like this:

> " 'On we rode, the others and I,
> Over the mountains blue and by
> The Silver River, the Sounding Sea,
> And the robber woods of Tartary.' "

"That is pretty," said Lydia. She looked at Myron, who had cocked his head to the side. "Myron thinks it is very nice. He likes the way the words sound together. Do you know any others?"

"Let me think. I don't have a good memory for poems, but here is one called 'The Lake of the Dismal Swamp.' It is sad and eerie.

> " 'They made the grave too cold and damp
> For a soul so brave and true.
> So she's gone to the Lake of the Dismal Swamp

Where all night long by a firefly lamp
She paddles her birch canoe.' "

After a moment Lydia said: "That poem is also very nice."

Lydia looked toward Myron, then turned to Wayness with a marvelling expression on her face. "Myron has decided to write to you!"

Sitting up straight Myron took pencil and paper. Using neat quick strokes he printed a message. "The poem is beautiful, and the words are beautiful. Say it again."

Wayness smilingly shook her head. "It would not sound so well the second time."

Myron gave her so mournful a look that Wayness relented. "Very well. I'll do it just this once." She repeated the poem.

Myron listened attentively, then wrote: "I like that poem. The words fit together well. I shall write a poem when I have time."

"I hope you will show it to me," said Wayness. "Or even read it aloud."

Myron pursed his lips, not yet ready to go so far.

Lydia asked: "Do you know any other poems?"

Wayness reflected. "There is a poem I learned when I was very young and a fine poem it is, too. I think that you will like it." She looked from face to face; both were alert and expectant. "It goes like this:

" *'Pussycat Mew jumped over a coal*
And in her best petticoat burnt a great hole.
Poor Pussy's weeping, she'll have no more milk
Until her best petticoat's mended with silk.' "

Lydia was pleased with the poem. "Though, of course, it is very sad."

"Possibly," said Wayness. "But I suspect that the pussycat went quickly to work and mended her skirt, so that she was once again served her milk. That is what I would have done, at any rate."

"And I, as well. Do you know any more poems?"

"Not at the moment. Perhaps you should try to write a poem, and Myron also."

Lydia nodded thoughtfully. "I will write a poem about the wind."

"That is a good idea. Myron, what about you?"

Myron wrote: "I must decide what to write about. The poem will sound like the 'Lake of the Dismal Swamp,' because that seems a good way to write poems."

"Both of your ideas sound interesting," said Wayness. She turned her head to listen. Clara had once again gone out to the utility porch. Wayness looked around the sitting room. There was no desk or cabinet in which Irena would have kept private papers.

Lydia asked again: "What are you looking for?"

"A paper with the address of a man named 'Adrian Moncurio.' Either that, or a paper with the address of 'Professor Solomon' who is the same man."

Clara came back into the kitchen. She looked through the doorway, making a swift appraisal of what might be occurring. She turned away. Neither Myron nor Lydia had anything to say.

Myron snatched up his pencil and wrote. "There is not a paper like that in the house."

Wayness leaned back and stared toward the ceiling.

The day passed. Outside the rain fell steadily: large heavy drops which did little more than bring out the scent of damp concrete and damp soil. Irena came home and Wayness took her leave. In a dispirited mood she walked through the rain to the hotel.

On the following day the overcast exerted a dank pressure upon the landscape. Wayness arrived at Casa Lucasta to find that Irena had not gone to work. She gave no explanation, but evidently did not feel well and, after a muttered colloquy with Clara, went up to her room. Half an hour later Clara draped a black shawl over her head, donned her overcoat, took up her shopping bag and trudged from the house.

A light rain was now falling, constraining Wayness and the two children to the sitting room.

Clara was gone. Wayness listened, but there was no

sound from upstairs. She spoke in a low voice: "I will tell you something about myself. I have kept it secret from everyone. Since I want your help, I will tell you this secret.

"I was born on a world which is very wild. No one lives there except many different kinds of animals and a few people who guard the world. But there are other people who want to kill most of the animals, and build big cities and destroy the beauty of this world."

Myron wrote: "They are fools."

"I think so too," said Wayness. "In fact, some of them are wicked people, and have even tried to kill me."

Lydia looked at Wayness large-eyed. "Who could do such a terrible thing!"

"I don't know. But I am trying my best to stop them, to save my beautiful world. There is a man who can help me. I think you know him. His name—" Wayness stopped speaking. She raised her head and listened. What had she heard? Whatever the sound had been, it was not repeated. She lowered her voice still further. "His name is Adrian Moncurio." She spoke in a low voice, almost breathless with urgency. Again she tilted her head to listen. Then: "Moncurio called himself Professor Solomon; perhaps you know him under this name. He came to Pombareales and got into trouble. He said he had found a treasure of gold doubloons in a secret cave. He was not telling the truth. The cave was fictitious, and the gold doubloons were mostly lead. He sold as many as he could, then when his trick was discovered, he fled from Earth, and now I must find him. Do either of you know where he is?"

The two had listened in an uneasy silence. Lydia said: "Myron knows, of course. Myron knows everything."

Wayness looked at Myron and started to speak, but was interrupted. Into the room came Irena, her hair in disorder, her skin the color of old mustard. She cried hoarsely: "What are you talking about? I can hear this sly murmuring and it is something I cannot tolerate! What is it then!"

Wayness stuttered and groped for words. Myron spoke in a clear easy voice: "I have composed a poem. Do you want to hear it?"

Irena stared, her jaw dropping to draw the lines of her haggard face even deeper. "You are talking!"

"I will speak my poem."

Irena started to speak in a peculiar strangled voice. Lydia called out sharply: "Listen to Myron! He has decided to speak!"

"This is the poem. It is called 'The World of the Nineteen Moons.' "

Irena cried out: "Enough of this nonsense!" She stared at Wayness. "Who are you? What do you want here? You are no social worker! You must leave this house at once; all you have done is damage!"

Wayness said furiously: "The damage was not done by me! Are you not happy that Myron is speaking, that he is mentally sound? Truly, you are a terrible woman!"

"This is the poem," said Myron. "I have just composed it now." He pitched his voice low:

> " 'He swindled them all with the lead doubloons
> He had found in fictitious caves.
> Now he's gone to the World of the Nineteen Moons
> Where, out on the desert of Standing Stones,
> He plunders the sacred graves.' "

Lydia said: "That is a lovely poem, Myron."

Irena started to blurt something, then stopped short, and spoke carefully: "Yes, yes, we must see about this. It is wonderful that Myron is improving. Just one minute, and then I wish to hear you speak some more." Irena turned and went into the kitchen.

Wayness jumped to her feet. "Quick," she muttered. "We must go very quickly. Follow me." She started for the entry hall and the front door.

Irena burst into the sitting room, brandishing a heavy kitchen knife. "Now there will be an end to it!" She lunged at Wayness; the knife drove down. Wayness jerked away and the knife slashed her shoulder. She reeled over backward and Irena was on her, knife on high.

Lydia screamed: "No, no!" She seized Irena's arm, and the knife shook loose, fell to the floor.

Wayness ran to the door. "Come!" she cried. "Lydia! Myron! Come!"

Irena recovered the knife and advanced upon her. Wayness cried: "Run out the back way! Quick, quick, quick!" She stood in the doorway. "Irena, you must—"

Irena gave a great scream and leapt forward; Wayness stumbled out upon the terrace. Over Irena's shoulder she glimpsed the face of Clara, home from her shopping, face contorted in a wolfish grin. The door slammed. From within came scream after scream. Wayness turned and ran down the street to the nearest inhabited house. She burst through the door and while an astonished old woman looked on, ran to the telephone and called the police, and also informed the dispatcher that an ambulance might be needed.

XI.

The time was late afternoon. The overcast had broken and the sun illuminated the central plaza of Pombareales with a wan and cheerless light. The wind blew swirls of dust and bits of litter across the stone flags.

Wayness lay on the bed of her room in the Hotel Monopole. Her wound had been treated and she had been told that aside from a hair-line scar, she would suffer no permanent consequences from the attack.

She had been sedated and only now had started to rouse herself from a semi-stupor. Presently she sat up and looked at the clock. The telephone chime sounded. Doctor Olivano's face appeared on the screen. He inspected her. "Are you well enough to receive a visitor?"

"Certainly."

"I'll order up a pot of tea."

"That would be nice."

A few minutes later the two sat at the table in the corner of the room. Olivano said: "Irena is dead. She stabbed herself in the throat. First she tried to kill Myron and Lydia. It was Clara who saved them. She held Irena away with a broom, until the police arrived. She is a doughty old bird. Irena then rushed into the dining room, lay herself down on the table, and did some bloody work."

In a faint voice Wayness asked: "What of the children?"

"They were both cut and slashed, but not seriously. They are in good condition. They want to see you."

Wayness looked out the window. "I don't know if that is a good idea or not."

"How so?"

"I have become very fond of them both. If I had a home, I would take them there and keep them. But I have no home at the moment. What will become of them? If it were anything bad, I would take them anyway and leave them with my uncle for a time."

Olivano showed her a crooked smile. "They will be well taken care of. In fact, I too have become fond of them, against every precept of my profession."

"I see."

Olivano leaned back in his chair. "I had a talk with Clara. She is stoic and matter-of-fact, and declares that she knew that tragedy was on the way. She rambled here and there, and it took an hour to learn what I am about to tell you—in something less than an hour, or so I hope.

"To begin with, Irena was very beautiful when she was young, but unpredictable and restless; also she loved money and resented being born into a poor family. She became a dancer and joined a troupe of harlequins who traveled off-world. At one far place or another—Clara is vague in connection with places—she met Moncurio, and took up with him. In due course they returned to Pombareales, and Professor Solomon sold his fake doubloons, until the swindle was discovered and they fled for their lives.

"Years passed, and Irena returned to Pombareales with a pair of apparently feeble-minded children. Irena gave out the story that she had been deserted and had known nothing of the swindle, and so was allowed to live more or less in peace. Irena confided to Clara that the children were not her own but must be raised by a rigid routine until they approached adolescence, when certain mental powers would be at the maximum. At this time, according to Irena, the children would assist in the search for buried or hidden jewels. Moncurio and Irena both believed that they would become very wealthy. From time to time Moncurio sent them small sums of money, and kept Irena supplied with the proper 'medicines' for the children and herself."

"Drugs or no drugs, she was an extremely wicked woman."

"Undeniably so. Well then, that is that. It is a pity that you failed to secure the information you needed, but you are a resourceful person and no doubt will somehow make do."

"Yes; probably so," said Wayness coldly. She still had not forgiven Dr. Olivano his delinquencies.

"The children are resting now. You are of course at liberty to see them if you care to do so." He rose to his feet. "But I could tell them that you came to see them, and then were called away on very important business."

Wayness nodded bleakly. "It is probably best that way."

CHAPTER VIII

I.

At Fair Winds Agnes had gone off on holiday to Tidnor Strands. She would be gone two weeks; during this interval her niece Tassy, a bouncy energetic girl of eighteen, would take care of Pirie Tamm and see to his comfort.

Pirie Tamm agreed to the arrangement without enthusiasm. Tassy was comely, plump, with a round cheerful face, dimples, blonde curls, innocent blue eyes and boundless self-confidence. Before leaving, Agnes had assured Pirie Tamm that while Tassy was lively and exuberant, she was conscientious to a fault, and would do her best to please him.

And so it was. Tassy instantly diagnosed in Pirie Tamm the tragic case of a lonely old gentleman, brooding away the final hours of his life. She decided that she must bring at least a modicum of color and adventure to Pirie Tamm's daily routine. While he consumed his breakfast, Tassy stood to the side, ready with fresh marmalade, anxious to proffer hot toast, gently insisting that he eat his nice prunes, which he detested, and recommending neither salt nor pepper for reasons which had been made clear to her in a magazine article, but which now she could not quite recollect. She reported upon the weather and the scandals affecting her favorite celebrities, and described the plot of a cinematic presentation she had recently enjoyed. She mentioned the latest dance craze, 'Nervous Knee-caps,' which was performed to a loud shrill music of coughs, squeals and grunts. It was a fascinating exercise, said Tassy, involving hands, knees and pelvis; perhaps Sir Pirie would like to learn the step? Pirie Tamm said that while the prospect was intriguing, his doctor would surely object, and also, where in thunder was the salt and pepper? A man could not eat eggs without salt and pepper!

"Oh yes you can, and you must," said Tassy. "It is much healthier for you. That is the new wave of medical thinking!"

Pirie Tamm rolled his eyes to the ceiling and wondered if Agnes were enjoying herself at Tidnor Strands?

Late one afternoon, as Pirie Tamm sipped his sherry, Tassy notified him that he was wanted on the telephone. He scowled and muttered a curse. "This is not a civilized hour to be making phone calls and disturbing people at their sherry! Who is it?"

"He gave no name and I forgot to ask. He's a rather handsome young man, though I should say a bit too severe and grim. However, he seems basically decent, and I decided to let him speak with you."

Pirie Tamm stared at her with sagging jaw. At last he said: "Your powers of divination are remarkable."

Tassy nodded complacently. "It has always been one of my great gifts."

Pirie Tamm rose to his feet. "I had better speak to the fellow."

The face looking from the screen was, as Tassy had declared, personable and somber. Various subtle signs suggested to Pirie Tamm that here was an off-worlder. "I am Pirie Tamm. I don't think I know you."

"Wayness may have mentioned me. I am Glawen Clattuc."

"Indeed, indeed!" exclaimed Pirie Tamm. "Where are you?"

"At the Shillawy spaceport. Is Wayness still with you at Fair Winds?"

"Not at the moment, I'm sorry to say. She set off for Bangalore, and I have not heard from her since. You are coming to Fair Winds, I hope?"

"Only if it is convenient for you to have me."

"Of course!" Pirie Tamm gave directions. "I'll expect you in about two hours."

Glawen arrived at Fair Winds and was made welcome by Pirie Tamm. The two took dinner in the wood-paneled dining room. Pirie Tamm told Glawen what he knew of Wayness' adventures. "Her last call came from Trieste. She told me very little, because she feared that my telephone messages were being intercepted. I was skeptical but nevertheless I called in a team of experts. They found three spy cells, and a telephone tap as well. We are convinced that the mechanisms were installed by Julian Bohost. You are acquainted with him?"

"All too well."

"As of now, the house is protected and we may talk freely—though, to be candid, I still feel a constraint."

"You don't know what, if anything, Wayness has learned?"

"Unfortunately, no. Simonetta preceded us to Gohoon Galleries, and removed the records of sale. Wayness therefore was forced to work from a different perspective. She used the analogy of a ladder, with the Charter and the Grant on a middle rung. Simonetta, knowing who bought the material, was able to search up the ladder. At our end, we found items of Naturalist material, and traced it back down the ladder toward the original buyer."

"It was wasted effort," said Glawen. "I know the first buyer. His name was Floyd Swaner, and he lived at Idola on the Big Prairie. Simonetta learned his identity—evidently as you have mentioned, at Gohoon Auctions—and ever since she has concentrated on Floyd Swaner. She still seems to believe that Charter and Grant are somewhere on the Swaner premises, since she has burgled his property and tried to marry his grandson."

Pirie Tamm gave a disconsolate grunt. "Where does Julian come into the picture? Is he in league with Simonetta?"

"I suspect that each is trying to use the other, and each keeps dismal plans for all eventualities at the back of his or her mind. I'm afraid that bitter times lie ahead."

"And what are your plans?"

"I'll be leaving directly for Idola, and if the Charter and Grant are not at hand, then I'll start climbing the ladder toward that middle rung."

II.

Glawen flew across the ocean to Old Tran, now known as Division City, at the heart of the continent. A local service flew him two hundred miles west to Largo, on the Sippewissa River. He arrived at twilight and took lodging at an old inn on the banks of the river. He telephoned Pirie Tamm, but learned nothing new; Wayness had not called.

In the morning Glawen rented a flitter and flew north across the Big Prairie, to arrive an hour later at Idola: a small town which, like many other small towns of Earth, had survived in its present identity for thousands of years*. Glawen landed the flitter and took directions to the Chilke homestead. He was told: "Fly north till you come to Fosco Creek, about five miles. Pretty soon Fosco Creek makes a grand loop: swinging first to the east then up and around to the west. Look down; you'll see a barn with a green roof and a house beside some big old oak trees. That's the Chilke place."

Glawen took the flitter back into the air and flew

---

*Excerpt from 'Reflections upon the Morphology of Settled Places'– LIFE, Volume 11, by Unspiek, Baron Bodissey:

"Towns behave in many respects like living organisms, which across time evolve and adapt so exactly to the landscape, the weather, and the requirements of the inhabitants that there is very little thrust for change. Parallel to these considerations the forces of tradition exert a like effect upon the character of the town; and indeed, the older the town, the more rigid its tendencies toward immutability."

through the bright morning, over broad fields yellow with ripening grain, and so came to Fosco Creek. He followed the line of willows and alders, and presently came upon the loop. Below he saw the oft-burgled barn and the house where Eustace Chilke had spent his childhood.

Glawen landed the flitter in the yard, and was greeted by a pair of nondescript dogs and three tow-headed children, who were playing in the dirt with toy trucks and fragments of oddly-shaped green stones.

Glawen jumped to the ground. The oldest child said respectfully: "Good morning, sir."

"Good morning," said Glawen. "Is your name Chilke?"

"I am Clarence Earl Chilke."

"Fancy that!" said Glawen. "I know your Uncle Eustace."

"Really? Where is he now?"

"Far away, across the stars, at a place called Araminta Station. Well, I had better make myself known to the house. Who is home?"

"Nobody but Grandma now. Our mother and father have gone to Largo."

Glawen went to the front door of the house, where a woman of late middle age awaited him. She was strong and stocky, with a round good-humored face in which Glawen could see unmistakable signs of Eustace Chilke himself. "My name is Glawen Clattuc," he said. "I have a letter from Eustace which introduces me."

Ma Chilke read the letter aloud:

" 'Dear Ma:

This will introduce my good friend Glawen Clattuc, who is a fine fellow, unlike most of my friends. We are still looking for some of Grandpa's stuff, which has never been found. He'll ask you some questions, or so I expect, and maybe he'll want to look in the barn. Let him do anything he likes. I don't know when I'll be home again, but I'll tell you for sure that I am often homesick, especially when I am threatened by Simonetta Clattuc. If you see her, punch her in the nose, and

tell her it was from me. Then run because she is
a powerful woman. I'll be home one of these days.
Don't let the dogs sleep on my bed. My best love
to you and every one else except Andrew, for
reasons he knows best.

Your dutiful son,
Eustace' "

Ma Chilke blinked and wiped her eye on her sleeve. "I
don't know why I get sentimental. The rascal hasn't showed
his face around here for a long time. 'Dutiful son' — there's
a good joke."

"Eustace is a wayward type, no denying that," said
Glawen. "Still, at Araminta Station he is considered an
important man."

"In that case, he had better stay on and count his
blessings, since he's been run out of most places in disgrace. Of course, I'm just talking foolish. Eustace is at
heart a good boy, if a mite restless. I guess he has told you
about his Grandpa Swaner."

"So he has."

"That was my father, and he was a rare bird! But sit
yourself down, to be sure! Let me pour you some coffee.
Can you eat?"

"Not just now, thank you." Glawen seated himself at
the kitchen table. Ma Chilke poured coffee and set out a
platter of cookies, then pulled up a chair of her own.
"Daddy was a wonder, what with his purple owls and
stuffed animals and all the funny old bangles. We've never
quite known what to make of him, nor Eustace either, if
the truth be told. It seems, somehow, that all his nonsense skipped a generation and landed in poor Eustace. I
don't know whether I'm sorry or not; there was always so
much windy talk of far places and distant worlds and
great treasures in wonderful gems. Eustace loved it and
couldn't get enough of it. Grandpa was a little cruel sometimes. He promised Eustace a fine space yacht for his
twelfth birthday, and poor Eustace was so excited he
could talk of nothing else. I warned him not to brag about
his space yacht around the school yard, since no one

would believe him; and they'd tell him he had a screw loose as well. I don't think Eustace cared much one way or the other. His grandpa had given him a big atlas of the Gaean Reach and Eustace studied it for hours on end, deciding where to fly his new space yacht, and how he was going to land on lonely desolate worlds where no one had ever set foot before and put up a sign reading 'Eustace Chilke, been here and gone.'

"Grandpa Swaner never bought Eustace the space yacht but he did take him on a voyage somewhere, and that was enough in itself to put the wander-fever into the poor boy, and we've seen precious little of him all these many years." Ma Chilke sighed and slapped her hand down on the table. "So now you've come to rummage through Grandpa Swaner's things like all the rest. I should charge admission!"

Glawen asked: "Have many others come here to look?"

"Yes indeed, and I ask them all: 'What is it that you are looking for? If I knew I might give you a hint.' Although what I was saying to myself was, 'if I knew, I'd go get it for myself.' "

"No one ever told you?"

"No one. And I suppose that you won't tell me either."

"I'll tell you if you won't tell anyone else."

"I agree to that."

"It's the Cadwal Charter, which was lost. Whoever finds it controls the world Cadwal. There are good people looking for the Charter and bad people. Eustace and I are with the good people. I'm making it very simple, of course."

"So that's why I've had so much trouble with the barn. It's been burgled at least three times. About ten years ago a big heavy-set woman showed up. She was dressed to kill and she wore a big important-looking hat, so I took her for a celebrity, or a grandee of some kind. She said her name was Madame Zigonie, and that she wanted to buy the stuffed moose. I said that it was not my moose, but that the owner would no doubt let it go for a thousand sols.

"She gave a snort and said that she, too, had lots of things she'd let go for a thousand sols.

"I asked her to make an offer, but she wanted to study

the moose first. I told her it was an ordinary moose, with horns and a long ugly face, and that I didn't have time to take her out to the barn just then. She became huffy and we had words, and she stalked away. A week later the barn was burgled and when we went to look the moose had been vandalized, with all its cotton guts strung out; I sewed the creature back up."

"What did they take?"

"Nothing so far as I could see. They had turned over boxes of papers. Truth to tell, I found it hard to believe that a woman like Madame Zigonie would work so hard to burgle a barn. I put it down to sheer spite."

"I don't think spite was involved," said Glawen. "She was looking for the Charter. Floyd Swaner bought it at auction and disposed of it no one knows where or how. Which brings me to the question: who did he deal with?"

Ma Chilke gave her head a jerk of disdain. "I marvel now when I think of them! Touts, agents, collectors, nature-fakers and a few ordinary mental cases. I could spot one a mile away. They all walk as if their feet hurt, and before they go near something they want, they give you a glance to see if you are watching. Toward the end Grandpa dealt mainly with a man called Melvish Keebles. His address? I have no idea. Another gentleman came asking just a few days ago and I told him the same thing."

"Who was this other gentleman?"

Ma Chilke frowned toward the ceiling. "Bolst? Bolster? I took no great notice. He was a talker fast and free, with a voice like oil. Boster? Something like that."

"Julian Bohost?"

"That is the name. Is he a friend of yours?"

"No. What did you tell him?"

"About Keebles? I told him what I knew, which is nothing, except that Keebles seemed to be an agent for a dealer in Division City."

"Did he look in the barn?"

"I made him pay two sols for the privilege, then went out with him, which put his nose out of joint. He poked around here and there, and looked into Grandpa Swaner's account books, from forty years ago, but he soon lost interest and only glanced at the moose. He asked if there were any other papers or documents, that he might pay a good price if he found something to interest him. For instance, were there any papers Grandpa Swaner had hidden away? And he said in a lordly way: 'Why not bring these papers out, my good woman, and perhaps there will be another two sols in it for you.'

"I told him there were no such papers, that whenever Grandpa Swaner came into some books or documents, he traded them away at once, to Melvish Keebles. He wanted Keebles' address, of course. I told him that I had not even thought of Keebles for years, and what kind of a woman did he take me for, that I should know the private address of all these shady characters? He looked foolish and said he had not meant it that way. I told him in the future I would appreciate it if he kept a civil tongue in his head, and this seemed to puzzle him even more, and he apologized. So I told him I knew nothing whatever of Melvish Keebles, save that he was something of a rascal. Mr. Bohost thanked me and went away, and I began thinking of the old days and I remembered 'Shoup.' "

"Who is 'Shoup'?"

"I can't say for sure, but I expect that he was another of Grandpa's cronies, or perhaps some kind of a dealer over in Division City, because when Grandpa and Keebles talked together, it was always 'Shoup this' and 'Shoup-that.' " Ma Chilke sniffed and blinked. "I don't like to think back; it always makes me blue. When Grandpa was alive, there was always something going on. That purple vase is one of his things, and those green ornaments as well; in fact they came to him from Keebles, and Grandpa prized them highly, so that when the children got into the boxes and started playing games with them, I took them up and fixed them along the mantle, as you see. There are more in the barn, and more vases and such things, and of course the moose."

Glawen returned to Division City, and lodged himself at one of the airport hotels. During the evening he studied the city directory. Almost at once he found the notice:

SHOUP AND COMPANY
Art supplies of All Kinds
Import and Export
We also deal in curios and exotic artifacts.
Off-world services a specialty
5000 Whipsnade Park, Bolton

In the morning Glawen rode by public transit to Bolton, a semi-industrial suburb at the northern verge of the city, where he found 5000 Whipsnade Park without difficulty. The premises, a square squat structure of concrete foam five stories high, was occupied exclusively by Shoup and Company.

Glawen entered the structure and found himself in a large showroom encompassing the entire first floor. Shelves, tables, bins and racks displayed art supplies of every description, to be sold both at retail and wholesale, for delivery anywhere in the Gaean Reach. To the left was a cashier's office and a shipping counter.

Glawen approached a sales clerk, who wore what seemed to be the Shoup uniform. A patch under the breast pocket of his gray tunic read:

D. Mulsh
At your service

D. Mulsh, a stocky young man with a cherubic pink face, fair hair and an air of complacent good humor, was busy at a display of articles whose function Glawen could not guess. The objects resembled small handguns and were of decidedly menacing appearance, with a hand grip, a trigger, a metal snout and a reaction chamber. Glawen asked: "What sort of weapons are those? I thought Shoup sold art supplies."

Mulsh smiled politely. "It is a fair question: why do we sell guns along with our art supplies? Some folk think they are used to kill amateur artists. Others suspect that artists use them to extort money from the public when all else fails."

"Which is the correct theory?"

"Neither. The guns allow anyone to execute beautiful panes of colored glass. The process is simple. Notice! I insert this green cartridge into the reaction chamber, and arrange a target of clear glass. When I pull the trigger I project a molten squirt which fuses permanently to the clear pane. The user can select cartridges of as many colors as he likes, to produce panes of the most intricate design glowing in absolutely rapturous colors. May I fit you out with a kit?"

"The idea is appealing," said Glawen. "But at the moment I am looking for something else."

"If it can be had, we have it. That is the motto of Shoup and Company. Just a moment while I ship off this kit." Mulsh took a box to the counter. He told the clerk: "Label this off to Iovanes Faray at Anacutra, and ship." He turned to Glawen: "Now then, sir! What can I sell you? A gross or two of the glass-melt kits? A dozen artist's models? A ten-ton block of Canova marble? Thirty-five ounces of moth dust? A bust of Leon Beiderbecke? All are on special for the day."

"At this particular moment I want something far less complicated."

"Such as what?"

"A trifle of information. One of your customers is Melvish Keebles. I must ship him a parcel and I have lost his address. I'd like you to look it up for me, and here is a sol for your trouble."

Mulsh looked askance at Glawen and waved away the proffered money.

"Most odd! Just yesterday another man approached me with the same request. All I could tell him was that I knew nothing of this 'Keebles,' and that he must apply upstairs at 'Accounts' or 'Billing.' With the best will in the world, that is all I can tell you."

Glawen frowned. "This man who came in yesterday: what was he like?"

"Oh—nothing extraordinary. He was a bit taller than you, about your age, I would say. Nice-looking chap, and well-spoken. Fancied himself a bit, if you ask me."

Glawen nodded. "Where did you say to go?"

" 'Accounts' on the fifth floor, or you can ask Miss Shoup herself. She is the boss."

"Surely she is not the founder of the business?"

"Indeed not! Six Shoups preceded her down the years, though she may well terminate the line, if current indications can be trusted." Mulsh looked over his shoulder. "I'll give you a tip. If you talk to Miss Shoup, don't smile at her or call her 'Flavia' or try to be familiar; she'll snap your head off."

"I will heed your advice," said Glawen. "By the way, the man who came in yesterday: did he get Keebles' address?"

"I don't know. I was off duty when he left."

Glawen rode the lift to the fifth floor, which like the first was a single large chamber. No attempt had been made to disguise the stark structural fabric of the building. The concrete ceiling beams were white-washed; a seamless sheath of resilient sponge covered the floor. The wall to the right was flanked by a counter, overhung by signs: 'Billing,' 'Accounts,' 'Employment' and others. Elsewhere a dozen desks were scattered here and there, seemingly at random. Everywhere men and women clad in the neat Shoup uniform worked earnestly and for the most part in silence. When conversation became necessary, hushed voices and brevity of expression were employed, so that the room seemed uncannily quiet.

Glawen squared his shoulders, put on his most businesslike manner, marched briskly across the room to stand by the counter under the sign 'Accounts.' Almost at once he was approached by a young woman named T. Mirmar, according to the label on her tunic. She spoke in a half-whisper: "Yes, sir?"

Glawen brought out a card and wrote on it: 'Melvish Keebles.' He put the card in front of T. Mirmar. Modulating his own voice he said: "I have some books to be shipped to this gentleman. Would you be kind enough to note down his exact mailing address?"

T. Mirmar looked at him and shook her head. "What is it about this 'Keebles' person? You're the second to ask since yesterday."

"Did you give the gentleman yesterday the address?"

"No. I sent him to Miss Shoup, who would want to deal with such a request. I don't know what she did, but for information you had best apply to Miss Shoup as well."

Glawen sighed. "I was hoping to simplify my inquiries. Would ten sols get me the address?"

"From me? What an idea! No, thank you."

Glawen sighed again. "Well then: where is Miss Shoup?"

"Yonder." T. Mirmar indicated a desk at the far end of the room, occupied by a tall gangling woman somewhat past her first youth.

Glawen studied Miss Shoup for a moment. "She is not quite what I expected," he told T. Mirmar. "Am I mistaken, or is she angry about something?"

T. Mirmar glanced across the room. She said in a flat voice: "It would not be proper for me to comment, sir."

Glawen continued his covert inspection of Miss Shoup. She was not at all well-favored, and Glawen could easily understand why the sixth generation of the Shoup family might be the end of the line. She wore the short-sleeved Shoup tunic, though it emphasized her narrow chest and thin white arms. The white dome of her forehead was topped by a few dismal ringlets of mouse-gray hair. Below were round gray eyes, a small thin nose, a small pallid mouth and a button of a chin. She sat bolt upright and her expression seemed stern, passionless, aloof. If she were not angry, thought Glawen, neither was she overflowing with zest and vivacity.

There was no help for it. Miss Shoup must be approached, and as expeditiously as possible. He turned back to T. Mirmar. "Should I just walk over to her desk?"

"Of course! How else could you get there?"

"I was concerned about formality."

"There is none at Shoup and Company; just good manners."

"I see. I will do the best I can." He walked across the room. Miss Shoup did not raise her eyes until he halted in front of her desk. "Miss Flavia Shoup?"

"Yes?"

"My name is Glawen Clattuc. May I sit down?" He

looked about for a chair; the nearest was at a desk forty feet away.

Miss Shoup appraised him for a moment, eyes as round and impersonal as those of a codfish. "Usually, when visitors find no chairs by my desk, they take the hint."

Glawen managed to contrive a strained smile. It was an odd remark, he thought: not at all in accord with Shoup and Company's reputation for politeness. Perhaps Miss Shoup intended only a witticism. "The hint is taken! I will be as brief as possible. Still, if you prefer that I stand, I shall do so."

Miss Shoup showed a thin smile. "As you like."

Glawen fetched the chair, emplaced it beside the desk. He seated himself after performing a small punctilious bow which he thought might mollify Miss Shoup but she spoke more crisply than ever: "I do not enjoy mockery, no matter how subliminal the level at which it is expressed."

"I am of this same opinion," said Glawen. "Unfortunately, it is pervasive and I ignore it as if it did not exist."

Miss Shoup raised her near-colorless eyebrows a hundredth of an inch, but made no comment. Glawen recalled Mulsh's warning against any attempts at familiarity with Miss Shoup. The warning, he thought, was redundant. The silence grew strained. Glawen said politely: "I am an offworlder, as perhaps you have already divined."

"Of course." The words were spoken without emphasis, but carried an overtone of distaste.

"I am a Naturalist from Araminta Station on Cadwal, which is a Conservancy, as you may know."

Miss Shoup said to him incuriously: "You are a long way from home."

"Yes. I am trying to recover some documents which were stolen from the Naturalist Society."

"You have come to the wrong place. We keep no such articles in stock."

"I thought not," said Glawen. "However, one of your customers may be able to help me. His name is Melvish Keebles—but I do not have his current address, which is why I have come to you."

Miss Shoup's mouth twitched in a thin smile. "We

cannot issue such information without explicit instructions from the customer."

"That is ordinary business practice," said Glawen. "I had hoped that in these special circumstances you might be flexible. I assure you, incidentally, that I mean Melvish Keebles no harm; I only want to ask regarding the disposition of some documents which are of importance to the Conservancy"

Miss Shoup leaned back in her chair. "I am totally flexible. I am Shoup and Company incarnate. My policy is company policy. I can change it ten times a day if I choose. I make a virtue of caprice. As for Keebles, whether or not you intended his disadvantage, you would say the same things; hence, your words carry no weight."

"Yes; I fear that is true," Glawen admitted. "You have put the matter logically."

"I know something of Keebles. He is a scapegrace. Many folk indeed would like to find him, including five ex-wives, none of whom he troubled to divorce or notify of the others. The entire membership of the Shoto Society would be pleased to lay hands on him. Of all my customers, Keebles would protest the loudest if I gave out his address."

Glawen began to wonder whether Miss Shoup might not, very quietly, be enjoying his frustration. He said somberly: "If facts would influence you—"

Miss Shoup leaned forward and clasped her hands in front of her. "I care nothing for facts."

Glawen pretended an ingenuous interest, while despising himself for the dissimulation: "If so, by what means are you influenced?"

"There are no certain methods. You might appeal to my altruism. I would laugh at you. Flattery? Try all you like; I will listen with interest. Omens and portents? I fear nothing. Threats? One word and I would order my clerks to beat you well. They would do so, and paint you in a variety of indelible colors. A bribe? I already have more money than I could spend in a thousand years. What else is there?"

"Ordinary human decency."

"But I am extra-ordinary, or hadn't you noticed? It is not by my choice that I am human. As for 'decency,' the word was defined without my participation; I am not bound by it."

Glawen reflected a moment. "I've been told that yesterday someone else asked you for Keebles' address. Did you give him the information?"

Miss Shoup became very still. Her fingers stiffened. Her neck muscles suddenly corded, and she spoke. "Yes. So I did."

Glawen stared at her. "What name did he use?"

Miss Shoup clenched her fingers into a small bony fist. "It was a false name. I checked his hotel. They knew nothing of him. He made a fool of me. It will never happen again."

"You don't know where to find him?"

"No." Miss Shoup's voice was calm and cold. "He sat where you are sitting and told me he was from off-world, that his father wanted to establish an artists' supply house, and had sent him to Earth to study Shoup and Company's operations. He said that he had expected a dreary time of it, until he had met me; and now he saw that he had been wrong. He said that intelligence was the most fascinating trait a woman could have, and that we must have dinner together. I said, certainly, that would be delightful, and since he did not know the city, he should come to my house. This seemed to suit him very well. As he was leaving he said that his father wanted a certain Melvish Keebles to be his agent but did not know how to find him, and had I any suggestions. I said that by chance Keebles was one of my customers and that I could solve his problem on the spot, and I did so. He thanked me and went off. I went home and arranged a quiet dinner, with fine wine and good food. We would dine overlooking the lake, with candles on the table. I dressed in a black velvet gown I had never worn before and I made some special changes, then sat down to wait. I waited a long time, and in the end I lit the candles, started the music, drank the wine and dined alone."

"That was an unpleasant experience."

"Only at first. Halfway through the second bottle of wine I was able to be amused. Today I am back in my own world, though I have developed a loathing for handsome young men which extends to you. I see you clearly. As a class you are a crass and brutal pack of animals, stinking of rut, proud in the majesty of your genital organs. Some people have an insane aversion to spiders, others to snakes; I detest young men."

Glawen rose to his feet. "Miss Shoup, I have a hundred things to say to you, but you would like none of them, so I will bid you good day."

Miss Shoup made no response.

Glawen departed the chamber. He rode the lift down to the showroom on the ground floor, and went to the table with the display of glass-melt guns. He was approached almost at once by D. Mulsh, who asked: "How went your interview?"

"Well enough," said Glawen. "Miss Shoup is a remarkable woman."

"So she is. I see that you are still interested in the glass-melt guns. Can I sell you a kit today?"

"Yes," said Glawen. "They seem to be very useful items."

"You will enjoy it," said Mulsh heartily. "It is amazingly versatile."

"This particular kit I will present to a friend, and I'll have you ship it to him from here."

"No problem whatever, though I must charge you shipping costs."

"Quite all right."

Mulsh took the parcel to the shipping counter. "You may give the girl particulars." He took Glawen's money and went off to the Cashier. Glawen told the girl: "Label the parcel to Melvish Keebles. The address is in your files."

The girl punched buttons; the label machine ejected a label, which the girl affixed to the parcel. Glawen said: "On second thought I will carry the parcel with me."

"Just as you like, sir."

Glawen left the premises of Shoup and Company. Once out on the sidewalk he examined the label. It read:

Melvish Keebles
Argonaut Art Supplies
Crippet Alley, Tanjaree, Nion
Pharisse VI ARGO NAVIS 14-AR-366

Glawen returned to his hotel at the Division City airport. From his room he called Fair Winds, but there still had been no word from Wayness.

"I can't imagine where she has taken herself!" Pirie Tamm fretted. "No news may be good news, but it also can be very bad news."

"I agree," said Glawen. "What's worse, I can't take the time to go look for her; circumstances simply don't allow it. I'm going off-world at once."

"As for me, there is nothing I can do but wait," gloomed Pirie Tamm.

"Somebody has to stay at home," said Glawen. "When Wayness calls, tell her that I've gone off-world, up another rung of the ladder, and that I will be back as soon as possible."

III.

At Tammeola Spaceport near Division City, the ticket agency's integrator sorted through routes, schedules, layovers and connections and computed for Glawen the most expeditious passage to the world Nion. The readout was valid only for a single hour's time-slot, after which circumstances might or might not change. There were also provisos in regard to transit between junction points. If the scheduled service were late, altered or canceled, then the carefully computed passage must be modified. In short, the element of luck still controlled circumstances. Glawen's adversary had a day's head start — which might mean much or nothing, and Glawen refused to speculate in regard to pooobilities.

Glawen boarded the *Madelle Azenour* which would convey him to the junction at Star Home on Aspidiske IV, at the head of the Argo Navis Sector. At Star Home he would travel by local feeder packet to Mersey on Anthony Pringle's World, where another local packet would take him outward, through the Jingles, into the most remote parts of the Reach and finally down to the city Tanjaree on Nion, by the yellow-white sun Pharisse.

Aboard the *Madelle Azenour* time went by smoothly and pleasantly, with nothing to do but eat, sleep, watch the stars slide past, and enjoy such recreational facilities as were available. Glawen studied his fellow passengers with care, since quite possibly his adversary might be aboard the same ship. In the end he decided that the young man who had deceived Miss Shoup so heartlessly had chosen either another route or another schedule.

In HANDBOOK TO THE INHABITED WORLDS Glawen learned that Nion had first been explored in the remote past, during the first great surge of men across space. The human tide had slackened and then receded, notably from the far side of the Jingles, leaving Nion in near-isolation for thousands of years.

Nion, according to the HANDBOOK, was a medium-large planet (diameter: 13,000 miles; surface gravity: 1.03 Earth normal; sidereal day: 37.26 hours), attended by a numerous retinue of satellites. While the climate was generally mild, the topography was diverse and the habitable areas separated by deserts, steep-sided plateaus, tracts of weird wonderful forests and 'water-fields.' These latter were suspensions of pollen blown from forests and 'flower-fields' into areas originally lakes and seas, where the sedimented pollen became the substance known as 'pold.'

The fauna, principally insects, is of no great consequence.

The HANDBOOK declared: "In order to understand the intricacies of life on Nion, one must understand pold. There are hundreds of types of pold, but basically they are either 'dry,' derived from loess-like beds of pollen and spores transported by the wind, drifted and ultimately compacted; or the 'wet,' from deposits laid down in the ancient lakes and seas. The sub-varieties of pold derive from age, curing and blending, the action of morphotic agents, and thousands of secret processes. Pold is ubiquitous. The soil consists of pold. Beer is brewed from pold. Natural raw pold is often nutritious, but not always; some deposits are poisonous, narcotic, hallucinogenic, or vile-tasting. The Gangrils of the Lankster Cleeks are experts; they have built a complex society upon their manipulation of pold. Other peoples are not such connoisseurs, and eat pold like bread, or pudding, or as a substitute for meat. The flavor of pold depends, obviously, upon many factors. Often it is bland, or somewhat nutty, or even sour, like new cheese.

"By reason of pold, everywhere available, hunger is

unknown. Still, for a variety of reasons, the population remains sparse.

"Visitors to Nion will find it hard to avoid the consumption of pold, whether dining at a fine restaurant or one less esteemed—for the simple reason that pold is plentiful and easy to prepare, and the tourist will complain in vain.

"A warning may properly be inserted here. Due possibly to the plenitude of pold, the work ethic is little in evidence, and the tourist must be prepared for casual service at even the best hotels. 'The easy way is the best way': this is the basic premise of Tanjaree society. Be prepared, and control your temper! The folk of Tanjaree are actually agreeable, if a trifle vain and self-conscious. Social status is all important, but it is based upon subtleties and conditions which are quite incomprehensible to the visitor. To make a crude generalization, status derives from avoiding work and, with an ineffably cavalier flourish, inducing someone else to undertake the task. Hence, at an outdoor restaurant on the Mall, the patron will try to give his order to one of the three waiters on duty, all of whom will ostentatiously turn away, until the patron cries out for attention and perhaps starts to make a scene. To participate in an undignified altercation is to lose tremendous face. The nearest waiter reluctantly condescends to take the order, but service will be slow, and the order will eventually be served by a kitchen flunky while the waiter stands with hands clasped behind him, absorbing status at the expense of the exasperated patron, the other waiters and the debased kitchen flunky.

"A second warning, even more urgent, may be in order: Tanjaree is the single cosmopolitan center of Nion. Other settlements are controlled by local conventions which the tourist will find strange, sometimes unpleasant and not infrequently dangerous, should the tourist foolishly attempt to enforce his own theories upon the local population. On Nion human life—especially that of the offworlder—is not considered sacrosanct. The tourist is warned not to go off on solitary expeditions into the outback without local advice and assistance. Many hundreds of tourists have suffered some very peculiar fates by ignoring this warning.

"As a consequence of the environment, the early inhabitants had evolved without interaction or mutual coherence. In the process societies of considerable disparity were formed. The first inhabitants of Tanjaree had included a clique of biologists dedicated to the creation of a super-race through genetic manipulation.

"The descendants of these so-called 'Over-men' survived in the Great Tangting Forest, where they had become freaks and monsters with savage intelligence and horrifying habits."

The HANDBOOK continued: "At the present time, these beasts have become the focus of touristic interest, and are no longer in danger of extermination. A tube of clear glass conducts a road twenty miles long through the Tangting forest, along which charabancs convey parties of tourists in safety, while the monstrous 'Over-men' scream and slaver and lunge at the glass and perform obscene antics, for the titillation of the tourists.

"Elsewhere, the various folk of Nion continued to follow their ancient conventions, oblivious to the strange off-world people who came to marvel at them and to buy, purloin, seize or otherwise gain possession of their handiworks and sacred tokens. Certain of the peoples had become surly and even hostile toward strangers and remain so to the present day. Some are actively dangerous, notably the rock-workers of Eladre, who have carved their delicate and intricate city from the substance of a mountain. The Shadow-men become murderers during certain lunar phases. The Gangrils not only subsist upon pold, but transform it into mysterious new substances, with unpredictable psychic effects. For many centuries the Gangrils had maintained a subservient caste assembled from kidnapped off-worlders, tourists, and the like, which functioned to test the drugs derived from their 'pold.' This particular habit, among others, has gained them an unsavory reputation. Despite their seemingly benign manners, they are regarded with suspicion, and tourists are warned never to approach the Gangril settlements alone; there have been too many reports of naive off-worlders accepting what they thought to be hospitality from the blandly smiling Gangrils, only to discover that they had ingested an experimental drug, and that they were being closely scrutinized for clues as to the drug's effect.

"There are other folk, also considered quaint, who lack all menace: most notably the clans of vagabond jesters who roam the world in gaudily decorated caravans, performing eccentric dances, farces and burlesques, feats of musical virtuosity, comic ballads, operettas, and whatever else enters their minds."

The HANDBOOK offered a summation, to the effect that Nion was a world of unique touristic interest, though it lacked much in the way of creature comforts and the tourist must be prepared to make concessions, especially in connection with pold. Tanjaree, the entry port and tourist headquarters, was a small city of no great distinction, regulated by standard Gaean laws and conventions; elsewhere the folk were so strange and their conduct so incomprehensible that they might have been members of indigenous or alien races. Such was the information provided by the HANDBOOK.

In due course the *Madelle Azenour* landed at Star Home on Aspidiske IV. This was his first and most important junction point and immediately his schedule, so meticulously crafted at Tammeola, failed him, by reason of a rerouted carrier; but two days later he secured passage aboard a cargo ship to Mersey on Anthony Pringle's World at the edge of the Jingles. Here his connections were favorable, and he boarded the *Argo Pilot*, which took him through the Jingles, a region of bright and dim stars, gas balls, dark scoriated hulks, sullen spheroids of neutron metal, orphan planets and orphan moons, to the back of the sector and down to Tanjaree on Nion.

The Spaceport occupied a strip along the edge of a low plateau, with the city Tanjaree at its base surrounding a small lake.

Glawen underwent entry formalities, which included dosages of universal prophylactic, fungicide, anti-virals and buffers to absorb the first shock of the toxic local proteins. He was also subjected to an unusually careful search of his travel-bag and his person, which resulted in the seizure of his handgun. "Weapons of this sort are not allowed on Nion," he was informed. "There are too many situations which become volatile in the twinkling of an eye, and the knives and kukris of Nion are bad enough."

"All the more reason to allow me my gun for self-defense."

The complaint went unheeded. Glawen was tendered a receipt. "You may reclaim the weapon upon your departure."

Leaving the terminal building, Glawen stepped out into the glare of light from the sun Pharisse. The sky, a cloudless expanse of purple-blue, seemed tremendously wide, by reason of the far horizons. He went to the railing which guarded the brink of the plateau and looked down over Tanjaree. It was a city of modest size, separated by a circular lake. To the west was the old town, or native quarter: a random scatter of low white domes and slender spires, almost dwarfed beneath a dozen or so prodigious dendrons growing among the structures. They stood, so Glawen estimated, over two hundred feet tall, on massive black boles which separated into a sprawl of heavy branches, bending at the tips to the weight of blue fruiting globes, about ten feet in diameter.

The new town, to the east of the lake, showed a street layout only marginally more rational than the unabashed chaos of the old town. An avenue skirted the lake. Where it passed in front of the large tourist hotels and other tourist services, it broadened and was known as 'The Mall.' Narrow streets and alleys slanted away in all directions through the rather shabby districts away from the waterfront. The structures, large and small alike, were fabrications of lumpy plaster, apparently wadded into place by hand, with all dimensions and measurements being estimated by eye. There were no sharp corners, neither right angles nor verticality save in those instances which occurred by accident. The effect was one of organic growth and—initially, at least—not unpleasant. Most of the structures were two stories high, though the tourist hotels fronting on the lake were often of three or even four stories.

Glawen turned away from the view. A small structure nearby displayed a sign: TOURIST INFORMATION. Glawen went to the structure and entered. The premises were furnished with a long table, chairs, a rack of brochures. Behind the table sat a pair of young women, dressed in sleeveless white frocks and sandals. They were appealing creatures, thought Glawen, strikingly similar, with delicate features in pale faces, chestnut curls and slight small-breasted bodies. Both wore ribbons in their hair: pink on the girl sitting to the left, blue on the one to the right. They took note of Glawen with similar expressions of polite inquiry. The girl with the blue ribbon asked: "How best can we serve you, sir?"

"First of all," said Glawen, "I need a hotel. Can you make me a recommendation and—if possible—book me a room?"

"Of course! That is our function!" The girls exchanged smiles, as if at a private joke. Pink Ribbon said: "There are twenty hotels in Tanjaree. Six are rated 'First Class'; five are 'Second Class.' The others are somewhat less convenient. There are also shelters where lodging is provided the penurious."

Blue Ribbon said: "Before we can accommodate you to your precise taste, we must learn your preferences. Which category do you prefer?"

"Naturally, I prefer the best," said Glawen. "The question becomes, can I afford it?"

Blue Ribbon handed him a sheet of paper. "Here are the hotels and their rates."

Glawen glanced down the list. "I see nothing to alarm me. Which is the best?"

Pink and Blue exchanged smiles. "That is a hard question to answer," said Blue. "Departing tourists have much more definite opinions upon which is the worst."

"Hm," said Glawen. "Perhaps I should ask: which hotel provokes the fewest angry complaints?"

Pink and Blue considered a moment, then took counsel with each other. "The Cansaspara, perhaps?" suggested Pink. "The Cansaspara would be my guess," said Blue. "Unfortunately three ships have arrived during the last three days, and none have departed. The Cansaspara is booked solid."

"A pity," sighed Pink. "I like the Cansaspara Arcade."

"It is nice," agreed Blue.

Glawen looked from one girl to the other. Both were charming, he thought, though a bit languid and indirect in the conduct of their duties. He said: "I have some business I must transact as soon as possible, so book me anywhere you can."

"The Superbo and the Haz Warrior are about equal in their amenities," said Pink. "Do you have a preference?"

"Not really. The Superbo would seem a bit more relaxed than the Haz Warrior."

"You are a thoughtful man," said Blue. "Evidently you know something of the Haz; am I correct?"

"I'm afraid not. But for the moment—"

"The Haz are almost extinct. A few remain, under the Croo Cleeks, but they no longer sail their desert-boats. In the old days they captured tourists and forced them to fight duels."

Blue gave a shudder. "It is all in the past: the midnight camps, the music, the wild dances, the weird Haz honor!"

"Very picturesque," said Glawen. "But it must have discouraged tourism."

Pink and Blue both laughed. "Not at all! The tourist need not fight. The warrior would mock him, and pull his nose, and offer to fight blindfold, or with his hands tied. If the tourist still demurred, he would be called a dog, a thief and a tourist. The women would spit on his feet and cut the bottom out of his trousers—but he would be allowed to return to Tanjaree alive, with much material for reminiscence."

"Interesting," said Glawen. "But now, between the Superbo and the Haz Warrior—"

"There is little difference," said Blue. "At the Haz Warrior, they play Haz music and pretend to despise the tourist, but they offer no violence."

Glawen said: "I think I prefer the Superbo. Be so kind as to—"

"Both the Superbo and the Haz Warrior are fully booked," said Pink. "We will place you at the Novial."

"Anywhere, since I am in a bit of a hurry."

"An instant only!" said Blue. "We are famous for the quickness of our fast speed!"

"The Novial it is then, though their pold is far from classic."

"It's good enough for me," said Glawen. "I am not yet a connoisseur. You may book me into the Novial."

"Just so," said Blue. "If you need good pold, go to one of the kiosks. The Gangril formulations are best."

Pink thrust out her tongue. On the tip rested a small black pastille. She said: "At this very moment I am sucking on a wafer of tikki-tikki, which is a Gangril formulation. The flavor is sharp but subtle, and the formulation soothes me."

Blue stated: "Tikki-tikki often eases the aggravations of my work."

Glawen said decisively: "I must leave, before I become an aggravation."

"You are no aggravation!" declared Pink. "We like talking to you, and we have nothing better to do."

Blue said: "Here is a map of Tanjaree." She made marks. "This is where we live. If you are bored, you may come to call, and taste our truest pold."

Pink suggested: "Or we could walk beside the lake and count the moons, and recite the proper poems."

Blue said: "Or we could visit the serai and watch the mad harlequins as they dance and play their concertinas."

"I am bewildered by so many choices," said Glawen. "However, I must first see to my business, which is most urgent."

"If you like, I will give you a wafer of nging," said Pink. "The effect is to minimize the importance of serious business. It allows one to live without tension or care."

Glawen smilingly shook his head. "Thank you again." He looked at the map. "The Novial is where?"

Blue made a mark. "First, we must book you your lodging, or all might come to naught."

"I will do so at once," said Pink. "I had forgotten the gentleman's requirements."

Glawen waited while Pink spoke into the telephone, then nodded to Glawen. "Your lodging is secure, but you must report to the Novial at once or it might be let to someone else. As you see, things go briskly here at Tanjaree."

"You have made that clear," said Glawen. "Please mark Crippet Alley on the map, and also the Argonaut Art Supply Company."

Blue made careful indications, which Pink verified and approved. Glawen again expressed his thanks and departed.

IV.

A long rickety escalator lowered him to the lakeside avenue. He looked up toward the sun Pharisse. To judge by the altitude, the time was perhaps an hour into the afternoon. The reckoning, however, might be misleading, since Nion's sidereal day was something over thirty-seven hours long.

Glawen set off along the avenue and a few minutes later arrived at the Novial Hotel. He entered the lobby: a nondescript chamber neither spacious nor elegant. He approached the reception counter where sat a dapper young clerk, engaged in an animated telephone conversation. He was two or three years older than Glawen, with plump shoulders, full jowls, sleek black hair, limpid brown eyes under fine expressive black eyebrows. He wore dark green pantaloons, a yellow blouse decorated with two panels of intricate designs in black and red. On his head, he wore a jaunty black toque—evidently the last cry in fashion. After a single swift glance toward Glawen from the corner of his eye, he turned away from the counter and continued to talk into the telephone. On the screen Glawen glimpsed the face of another young dandy, wearing a similar toque, also rakishly aslant.

A moment passed. Glawen waited, his patience slowly eroding. The clerk spoke on, with an occasional chuckle. Glawen became restive. He began to tap his fingers on the counter. Time was passing; every minute might be important! The clerk creased his eyebrows in annoyance, then looked over his shoulder and brought the conversation to an end. He swung about and asked: "Well, sir? What are your needs?"

Glawen composed his voice. "Lodging, naturally."

"Unfortunately, sir, the hotel is complete. You must go elsewhere."

"What! The tourist office only just made my reservation!"

"Really?" The clerk shook his head. "Why am I not told of these things? They must have called elsewhere. Have you tried the Bon Felice?"

"Of course not. I was booked into the Novial; I came to the Novial. Does that sound at all unreasonable to you?"

"I am not the unreasonable one," said the clerk. "That word best describes the person who, when notified that no accommodation exists, continues to wheedle and argue. It is this conduct I define as unreasonable."

"Just so," said Glawen. "When the Tourist Information Office telephones down a booking, what is the procedure?"

"It is simple enough. The official on duty, which is to say, myself, carefully inscribes the name upon this board, and there is no scope for mistake."

Glawen pointed to the board. "What is the name in that blue square to the side?"

The clerk rose wearily to his feet. "This square? It reads: 'Glawen Clattuc.' So then?"

"I am Glawen Clattuc."

For a few seconds the clerk stood silent. Then he said: "You are lucky. That is our 'Grand Suite.' In the future you should take pains to explain your arrangements more carefully; we cannot function in the absence of facts."

"Yes, of course," said Glawen. "You are a marvel of efficiency. Now show me to the 'Grand Suite.' "

The clerk flashed Glawen a glare of astounded outrage. "My rank is high! I am office manager and deputy executive vice-president! I do not lead lodgers here and there about the hotel!"

"Who does so, in that case?"

"At the moment, no one. The porter has not yet arrived, and I have no idea as to how the housekeepers have arranged their schedules. You may either wait here until the proper employee reports for duty, or you may walk down yonder corridor to the end, and pass through the last door on the left. The lock code is ta-ta ta."

Glawen went to the specified door, tapped ta-ta ta upon the lock panel. The door slid ajar; Glawen stepped through the opening. He found himself in a room of no great size, with a table to the right and a bed along the left wall. The bathroom occupied an alcove. Glawen stood looking about the room in wonder. Had there been some sort of mistake? Could this truly be the 'Grand Suite'?

For the moment it must serve; other concerns pressed upon him. Journey's end was at hand, and Destiny was waiting somewhere along Crippet Alley. He tossed his travel bag upon the bed and left the room.

In the lobby the clerk watched his approach sidelong; then, raising his fine black eyebrows, ostentatiously turned away, so that when Glawen came to make the customary complaints, he could look about with an air of indifference which, by infuriating off-world patrons, served to enhance his self-esteem.

Glawen paid him no heed. Looking neither right nor left he crossed the lobby and departed the hotel. The clerk looked after him glumly, his self-esteem deflated to its original condition.

Out on the avenue, Glawen paused to take stock of his surroundings. Pharisse had moved no great distance across the sky; eight hours, perhaps, of daylight remained before what would be a long slow dusk. Low in the sky floated a number of pale wraiths: some of Nion's numerous satellites, in phases, crescent to half-full. At the moment the air was still, and the lake reflected the low white domes and minarets of Old Tanjaree on the opposite shore.

Glawen set off on his fateful mission, trying to insulate his mind against both foreboding and hope—a task complicated by uneasy speculations regarding the man who had beguiled Miss Shoup: where was he now?

Glawen came to Crippet Alley and turned aside, passing instantly from the enclave of the off-worlders into an environment where the local population pursued its own quiet purposes. They seemed a sedate gentle folk, living a

languid pace perhaps influenced by the long thirty-seven
hour day of Tanjaree. Like Pink and Blue, they were of no
great stature, with chestnut hair, delicate features and gray
eyes. The alley itself was irregular and crooked, sometimes
narrow and overhung by the upper stories of houses along
the way, at times expanding into a small irregular plaza,
perhaps with a thick-trunked dendron at the center.

It gradually came upon Glawen that there was something strange about Crippet Alley: it was unnaturally quiet.
There were no loud voices or music or clangor; only the
slide of soft footsteps and a muted whisper from the stalls
and shops.

Glawen arrived at the Argonaut Art Supply Company:
a two-story structure, somewhat more imposing than others along the alley. A pair of windows to either side of the
door displayed on the left a number of small mechanical
toys; to the right, a sampling of the art supplies offered for
sale within the shop: modeling tools; waxes, plasters and
clays; equipment for the decoration of fabric, along with
dyes and mordants; pigments, stains and solvents; kits of
graduated andromorphs. The merchandise had a settled
look, as if it had not been shifted for a long time.

Glawen entered the shop: a dim cluttered chamber with
the high ceiling and walls stained dark brown. The room
was very silent; Glawen saw that he was alone save for a
middle-aged woman with short blonde-gray hair who sat
behind a counter reading a journal. Her complexion was
fair; she wore a neat blue smock.

Glawen approached the counter; the woman looked up
from her journal with an amiable, if incurious, expression.
"Yes, sir?"

Glawen found that his mouth was dry. The moment
had come and he was nervous. He found his voice: "Is Mr.
Keebles at hand?"

The woman looked off across the room, frowning as if
pondering the question. She decided upon a reply. "Mr.
Keebles? He is not here."

Glawen's heart sank. The woman added: "Not at the
moment." Glawen released his pent breath.

Having responded to the question, the woman returned

to her journal. Glawen spoke patiently: "When will he be back?"

The woman looked up again. "Before long, or so I should think."

"In minutes? Hours? Days? Months?"

The woman showed a dutiful smile. "Really now! What a funny thing to say! Mr. Keebles has only just gone off to the bathroom!"

"Then we are thinking in terms of minutes," said Glawen. "Am I right?"

"Certainly not days, nor months," said the woman primly. "Not even hours."

"In that case, I will wait."

The woman nodded and went back to her reading. Glawen turned and gave the room a more detailed inspection. At the back was a flight of rickety stairs and, to the side, a shipping counter, where his eye was caught by a glint of green. Approaching the counter, he saw a tray containing half a dozen green jade clasps, three inches in diameter, much like those he had noticed in Ma Chilke's sitting room, though these were chipped and cracked, or otherwise damaged. Odd! thought Glawen. He looked toward the woman and spoke: "What are these jade pieces?"

The woman tilted her head to look. She reflected a moment. "Ah, yes! The jade buckles! They are 'tanglets,' from the Plain of Standing Stones, around the other side of the world."

"Are they valuable?"

"Oh yes! But it is dangerous to collect them, unless one is an expert."

"Is Mr. Keebles such an expert?"

The woman gave her head a smiling shake. "Not Mr. Keebles! He gets them from a friend but they are becoming scarce, which is a pity since they bring good prices." She turned her head. "Here is Mr. Keebles."

Down the stairs came a small man with a ruff of white hair. His chest and shoulders were lumpy; his head hunched forward on a short neck. Round pale blue eyes studied Glawen warily. "Well, sir, and what is it you are needing?"

"You are Melvish Keebles?"

The pale blue eyes appraised Glawen without friendliness. "If you are a salesman or an agent, you are wasting your time—and, more importantly, mine."

"I am neither salesman nor agent. My name is Glawen Clattuc. I would like a few words with you."

"In what connection?"

"I can't explain until I ask you a question or two."

Keebles curled his thin lips. "I take this to mean that you want something but are not disposed to pay for it."

Glawen smiled and shook his head. "I think that our transaction will bring you at least some small profit."

Keebles gave a shuddering groan. "When will I get clients who think in something other than trifles?" He waved his hand toward Glawen. "Come; I will listen to you, for a few moments at least." He turned away and led Glawen along a passage, into a room of irregular dimensions, as dim and fusty as the shop itself. A row of windows in openings canted and askew, no two alike, overlooked a dreary yard. "This is my office," said Keebles. "We can talk here."

Glawen looked around the room. The furnishings were scant: a desk, four gaunt tall-backed chairs of bent cane, a red and black rug, a rank of cabinets, a side-table stacked with oddments. A shelf supported a dozen ceramic statues, each about sixteen inches high, representing monsters of the Tangting Forest. Glawen found them arresting, by reason both of superb workmanship and the impact of the subject matter, since they were the most hideous and disgusting objects of his experience.

Keebles seated himself at his desk. "Pretty things, are they not?"

Glawen turned away. "How can you bear to look at them?"

"I have no choice," said Keebles. "I can't sell them."

"The tourists will take them off your hands," said Glawen. "They will buy anything, the more horrifying the better."

Keebles snorted. "A hundred thousand sols for the twelve?"

"That seems a high price."

"Not so. One of the Tangting monsters is a freak. He models his fellows in clay for recreation. I will take them to Earth and describe them as fascinating works which pose a hundred psychological puzzles and sell them to a museum." He jerked his thumb toward a chair. "Sit down and explain your business. Please be brief, since I have an appointment by and by."

Glawen seated himself. His father Scharde had once remarked that candor should not be avoided merely because it represented truth. In the case at hand, Keebles would believe nothing, so that truth served the same purpose as mendacity. Not the entire truth, of course. That would be a diet too rich for Keebles.

"I have just come out from Earth, to negotiate some business for a client. It's nothing to do with you, I hasten to say, except that while I was looking down a list of general business agents, I noticed your name. There can't be too many Melvish Keebles in the profession, and to make a long story short, I decided to call on you."

Keebles listened with no great interest. "Go on."

"You are the Melvish Keebles who at one time worked with Floyd Swaner?"

Keebles nodded. "Those were good days, and I doubt if I will see their like again." He leaned back in his chair. "Where did you learn of our connection?"

"From Swaner's daughter. She still lives out on the Big Prairie."

Keebles turned his eyes up toward the ceiling and seemed to reflect upon times past. "I remember her, though her name escapes me."

"She is Mrs. Chilke. I'm not sure that I have ever heard her first name."

" 'Chilke,' so it was. And what took you out to the Big Prairie?"

"Simple enough. Like you, I am an agent of sorts, and one of my clients is the Naturalist Society. More accurately, I work in their interests as a labor of love; there certainly is very little profit involved. Are you a member?"

"Of the Naturalist Society?" Keebles shook his head. "I thought the Naturalists were defunct."

"Not quite. But you support Society goals?"

Keebles showed a thin smile. "Everyone is against sin. So who disagrees with the Naturalists?"

"No one—until he sees a chance for profit."

Keebles laughed soundlessly, in soft little pants. "That is the rock which tears the bottom out of the boat."

"In any case, the Society is trying to revive itself. Quite some time ago—and I think you know of this—a secretary named Nisfit sold off all the Society archives and kept the money. The Society is trying to recover as many of the missing documents as possible, and wherever I go, I keep my eyes open. Hence, when I learned that you were located here, I thought I would make some inquiries."

Keebles said indifferently, "All this is long ago and far away."

"According to Mrs. Chilke, Floyd Swaner sold a parcel of these documents to you. Are they still in your possession?"

"After all these years?" Keebles again gave his soft panting laugh. "Not very likely."

Glawen felt a pang of discouragement; he had been hoping against hope that Keebles might still possess the Grant and the Charter. "You have none of them whatever?"

"Not a one. Books and documents are not my line of work."

"What happened to the documents?"

"They left my hands long ago."

"Do you know where they are now?"

Keebles shook his head. "I know to whom I sold them. What happened next I can't even guess."

"Is it possible the buyer still has them in his possession?"

"Anything is possible."

"Well then: to whom did you sell them?"

Keebles, leaning back, put his feet on the desk. "We are now moving into the quiet area, where words are golden. This is where we take off our shoes and go on tiptoe."

"I've played such games before," said Glawen. "Someone has always stolen my shoes."

Keebles ignored the remark. "I am not wealthy, and

information is my stock in trade. If you want it you must pay for it."

"Words are cheap," said Glawen. "Is your information worth anything? In short, what do you know?"

"I know to whom I traded the Naturalist documents, and I know where to find him now. That's the information you want, isn't it? So what is it worth to you? Quite a bit, I should imagine."

Glawen shook his head. "You are not being realistic. The Naturalists can't afford a large outlay, and I can't pay out money on speculation. The man might have disposed of the material long ago."

"Life is unpredictable, Mr. Clattuc. To gain something you must risk something."

"A sensible man considers the odds. In this case, they are not good. Your friend might have sold the material long ago to someone he can't remember; or, if he still owns it, he might refuse to let it go, for any number of reasons. In short, your information might earn me a small commission. More likely it will bring me nothing more than a wild goose chase."

"Bah," muttered Keebles. "You worry too much." He removed his feet from the desk and sat up in the chair. "Let's get down to brass tacks. What will you pay for the information?"

"What information?" demanded Glawen. "I can't offer anything until I know what I'm getting. Telephone your friend and ask if he still owns everything you sold him, or whether he sold off any segment of the material, and if so, what. I will pay you five sols to make the call, and wait for the answer."

Keebles gave a roar of indignation. "The time I waste haggling with you is worth twice as much!"

"Perhaps so, if you could find someone willing to pay." Glawen laid five sols on the desk. "Make the call, get the facts, and we'll go on from there. Do you want me to wait in the outer office?"

"I can't call now," grumbled Keebles. "It's the wrong time of day." He glanced at the wall clock. "Also, I have another appointment. Come back this evening, at sunset or a bit later. It still may not be a convenient hour to call, but nothing is convenient on this cursed world, and I still can't fathom the thirty-seven hour days."

V.

Glawen walked back along Crippet Alley, pondering his interview with Melvish Keebles. Everything considered, the affair had gone about as well as could have been hoped, even though Keebles had left him in a state of nerve-wracking suspense.

Nonetheless, he had made progress, of a sort. Keebles had agreed to telephone the other party to the transaction, tacitly acknowledging the presence of this person upon Nion. Glawen wondered whether the admission had been an indiscretion which Keebles had regretted. If so, it indicated a carelessness which surely was not characteristic of Keebles; if not, the significance could only be that Keebles considered the business trivial, with little prospect of profit for himself—and this seemed the most likely explanation. As for the other party to the transaction, it could hardly be anyone other than Keebles' long-time associate, now collecting tanglets out on the Plain of Standing Stones—a dangerous business, according to the woman who seemed to serve as Keebles' clerk, though perhaps she might be another of the wives he married so casually.

Crippet Alley expanded into a square, than narrowed again. More folk were abroad than before: for the most part the slight delicate-featured natives of Tanjaree, with here and there a man or a woman from one of the outer districts, of markedly different physiognomy and costume, in Tanjaree that they might visit the markets. No one paid Glawen the slightest heed; he might have been invisible for all the attention he aroused.

The long afternoon lay ahead. Glawen returned to the Novial Hotel. In the lobby the clerk leaned forward upon the counter. "The dining room is now prepared for the mid-afternoon service. Shall I announce that you will shortly be on hand to take your pold?"

Glawen stopped short. Mid-afternoon service? How many meals were consumed during the course of a thirty-seven hour day? Breakfast, lunch, dinner, mid-morning and mid-afternoon services, at the very least. What happened during the long hungry nineteen-hour nights*? Glawen temporarily put the question from his mind. At the moment, he was hungry. "I doubt if I am ready for pold," he told the clerk. "Is standard cuisine available?"

"Naturally! A certain class of tourist will take nothing else, which is a pity, since pold gratifies, sustains and lubricates. It is wholesome and cannot be defeated. Still, you may eat as you like."

"In that case I will take the risk."

In the restaurant Glawen was handed the 'Tourist's Menu,' from which he made a selection. As an unsolicited side-dish, he was served a slab of pale cream-yellow pold which, when he tasted it, yielded a bland nutty flavor. He found no incentive to linger in the dining room and as soon as possible went out upon the avenue. The time was still early afternoon. Pharisse seemed welded to a spot on the sky. To east and west the pale daylight moons eased unobtrusively along their tracks. Across the lake the domes and spires of Old Town shimmered in reflection on the surface of the water.

Glawen went to sit on a bench. The Plain of Standing Stones, according to Keebles' clerk, was halfway around the world. Noon at Tanjaree was midnight on the Plain of

---

*Note: Among certain of Nion's societies, including that centered upon Tanjaree, nocturnal meals, their content and degree of elaboration, were based upon phases and states of the moons. A person who ate the wrong sort of pold while, let us say, the moon Zosmei was on high would have committed a vulgar and laughable solecism, so that forever after he would be known as a bumpkin.

Standing Stones, and dusk, correspondingly, would be early morning, so that it became clear why Keebles felt impelled to delay his telephone call.

Glawen brought out the packet of informational folders he had received at the Tourist Information Office, from which he took a map of Nion in Mercator projection, printed in a variety of colors. Vertical lines created thirty-seven segments, corresponding to the thirty-seven hours and fifteen minutes of the sidereal day. The origin—0 o'clock, or midnight—passed through Tanjaree.

Nion's surface area was roughly four times that of Earth: a disparity magnified by the absence of oceans and large seas. Colors indicated physiographic detail: gray for dry sea bottom, olive green for water fields, blue for open water, pink for the vast steppes. Clots of population surrounded the three principal cities: Tanjaree; Sirmegosto, six thousand miles south and east; Tyl Toc four thousand miles due west. Additionally, there were several dozen isolated towns scattered across the planet, including many tourist destinations: Hooktown, near the Tangting Forest; Moonway on the Plain of Standing Stones; Whipple's Camp, under the Scintic Crag; also a spatter of even smaller villages. Black lines connecting the populated areas were identified as 'nomad routes.'

Glawen found the Plain of Standing Stones in the segment marked '18,' halfway around the world. Here was the town Moonway, the William Schulz Buttes to the north and the Gerhart Pastels to the south.

Glawen studied the map for a few moments, then folded it and replaced it in his pocket. He rose from the bench and walked along the avenue to a bookseller's shop near the Cansaspara Hotel. He bought a tourist's guide, entitled:

NION: WHERE TO GO, WHAT TO DO! Also, where not to go and what not to do, if you value your life and sanity. (Yes: sanity! See section on Gangril pold).

Nearby was an outdoor café. Glawen found a table somewhat to the side and seated himself. The other patrons were for the most part off-worlders: tourists chattering and remarking upon the contradictions of Tanjaree, in their estimation a place forlorn and shabby, but truly exotic and of course incomprehensible. Some recounted their experiences with pold; others excitedly spoke of their excursion to the Tangting Forest and its mind-numbing habitants. In the sky Pharisse seemed to hang steady and still among its retinue of moons.

Glawen started to read in the tourist guide, but was interrupted by the arrival of a waiter wearing a maroon uniform with a flowing black cravat. "Your order, sir?"

Glawen looked up from his book. "What is available?"

"We offer a full range of potations, sir. They are listed here, on the menu." He indicated a card and started to turn away.

"Wait!" cried Glawen. "What is a 'Tympanese Tonic'?"

"It is a local beverage, sir, with mildly stimulating effects."

"It is derived from pold?"

"Yes, sir."

"What is 'Meteor Fuel'?"

"It is another mild stimulant, sir, and is sometimes taken before foot races."

"Also, derived from—"

"A different sort of pold, sir."

"The lady yonder: what is she drinking?"

"That is our 'Corpse Reviver.' It is a secret recipe of the Gangrils and is popular among tourists with modernistic views."

"I see. What about these 'Teas imported from Earth'? Are they also pold?"

"Not to my knowledge, sir."

"You may bring me a pot of green tea, if you please."

Glawen returned to the guidebook and found a section entitled: 'The Plain of Standing Stones.' He read:

> One cannot think of the Standing Stones without reference to the Shadowmen, who to this day lurk in the neighborhood. They are aptly named, if only because they are little more than

shadows of their remarkable progenitors, each of whom strove incessantly for honor and devoted his life to the performance of mighty deeds. The Shadowmen of today are somber, taciturn, intensely superstitious, and so introverted as to be impenetrable. Etiquette guides each phase of his life, so that he seems overwhelmed by its minutiae, and his conduct is predictable. The casual visitor to Moonway, who chances to come upon one of the Shadowmen during the course of his excursion, will see a person stolid as a rock, and quite imperturbable. But let the visitor make no mistake: this aloof gentleman will cut his throat without a qualm if he finds the tourist tampering with his sacred objects. Still, do not be deterred from a visit to the Standing Stones; they are remarkable, and you will be safe so long as you conform to the regulations.

The Shadowmen of today must be viewed in the perspective of their history. It is a melancholy record: the textbook case of isolated Gaean settlers who, over the centuries, have developed a unique society with intricate conventions. These conventions become ever more elaborate and generate ever greater intricacy until eventually they control, dominate and finally strangle the society, which thereupon becomes moribund. The process always bewilders the casual observer who contrasts the Golden Age of the society with its contemporary squalor. Most often the process is associated with a powerful religion and an insensate priesthood; in the case of the Shadowmen, the compulsive force was the glory to be won by excellence at the great game.

Two thousand years ago the society reached its zenith. The population was divided into four septs: North, East, South and West. Four or five thousand stones had been erected by champions to mark their graves. Which came first: the Games or the Stones is a matter of conjecture and is in any case irrelevant. The Games began as demonstrations of agility and speed, in which young men raced a dangerous course across the tops of the stones. Presently the races began to include contact—shoving, tripping, wrestling—as valid ploys in the winning of races. Next, came the Iron Races, which were not so much races across the tops of the stones as complicated strategies involving leaps, runs, swordplay. Skill in the use of weapons became as important as agility. The Games had always engendered passions; the four septs now found themselves involved in blood feuds and vendettas, which consumed much of their energies.

But not all. The rules of combat were complicated. Upon arriving at the age of fourteen the young man allowed his hair to grow long and carved a hair-buckle for himself from a nodule of fine jade. These buckles—'tanglets,' as they were known—became more than ornaments; they were repositories of the owner's mana, and represented his manhood; they were his dearest possession. As soon as he had carved his first tanglet and had submitted it for the approval of the elders, the young man was ready for the games.

First, he must await a proper concatenation of the moons: this was all-important. The moons, their phases, cycles and positions controlled the lives of the Shadowmen. When the moons finally came to a favorable conjunction, the young man climbed upon the stones. If he were of a cautious disposition, he made his first trials against other first-tanglet youths. Usually, at worst, he would be thrown down or jump without mortal damage, though he was required to give up his tanglet to the victor, at an important ceremony and with a maximum of ceremonial pomp, at which the victor was exalted and the loser shamed. The loser, seething with bitter humiliation, must carve a new and menacing tanglet for himself.

In due course, he might become quick and skillful, and start winning tanglets, all of which he wore on the rope of hair which dangled down the back of his head. If he were conquered, or cast down, or killed, he surrendered all his tanglets and his hair rope. If, however, he were a victor and a champion, at the age of twenty he was entitled to associate with ten fellows. Together they cut ten stones from the quartzite cliffs a hundred miles to the south. These stones would then be transported across the plain, inscribed and erected. The youth by this ritual became a man, and sooner or later would be buried at the foot of his stone, along with his tanglets.

Such were the Games: first, foot races across the stones; in the end passionate challenges, killings and revenges which at last exhausted the virility of the Shadowmen and reduced their numbers to a paltry few hundred.

The Shadowmen of today wear no tanglets; however, they carve imitations which they sell to tourists, and which they insist have been dug from a secret grave known only to themselves; be warned! These articles are fraudulent! An authentic tanglet is extremely valuable which fact has tempted predatory entrepreneurs from elsewhere. Usually—one might say, always—these persons are found dead among the stones with their throats cut.

At the western verge of the Standing Stones is the settlement Moonway, so-named by reason of the superstitions which still control the lives of the Shadowmen. Moonway is not so much a city as it is a combination of trading post, tourist center and village. The three hotels—the Moonway, the Jade Tanglet, the Banshee Moon—are about equivalent. The Moonway is said to exercise greater caution against sand-fleas than the others; all may be negligent. Bring insecticide and spray your bed before retiring. Otherwise you may be roundly bitten.

NOTE: The Shadowmen are apparently mild and patient. This is only partly true, as you will

learn if you molest, touch, ridicule or sometimes
so much as notice a bald woman. Your throat will
be cut at once; the woman has dedicated her hair
to a moon-sequence for a purpose important to
her. Never smile at a Shadowman; he will return
your smile, and with a quick motion of his arm
you will find yourself smiling from two mouths,
though not with double the amusement. Further,
no one will protect you or punish the Shadowman, since you will have been amply warned
against improprieties, as you just have been.

A good thing to keep in mind, reflected Glawen. He
relaxed in his chair and sat watching those who passed by
along the avenue: off-worlders from the nearby hotels;
slender chestnut-haired denizens of Tanjaree; Gangrils,
sleepy-eyed, also slight of physique and with hair often of
a coppery-russet, rather than chestnut, the men wearing
loose knee-length black breeches and colored shirts, the
women in white breeches of exaggerated amplitude, black
blouses and odd little green hats.

Glawen suddenly realized he had not been served his
tea. The waiter who had taken his order stood nearby,
looking idly off across the lake. Glawen wondered whether
it was worth the effort to make an angry representation,
from which, so he realized, the waiter would turn with an
air of ineffable scorn and fatigue. And Glawen would seem,
in the end, a red-faced expostulating boor. He considered
the options open to him, and the easiest was to decide that
he had not wanted tea in the first place. He adopted this
course of action with a sigh of resignation, only to find that
at the very same moment his tea had been served by a
kitchen boy. "Wait," said Glawen. He lifted the lid of the pot
and sniffed at the contents. Tea or pold? It smelled like tea,
of one variety or another. "Very well," Glawen told the boy.
"This seems to be tea."

"So it does," said the boy.

Glawen looked at him sharply, but decided that the
remark had been made innocently. "Very well," said Glawen
austerely. "You may go." In the end, so he told himself, it

was impossible to defeat the kitchen; they served as they saw fit and the customer must consume whatever he found on his plate, regardless of his own suspicions or better judgment.

His attention was taken by the coming of a ramshackle vehicle along the avenue: a great box, painted in garish designs, forty feet long and fourteen feet high. It rode on six tall wheels, all affixed independently to the chassis, so that they tilted, wobbled and canted as the vehicle lurched along the avenue. It was guided by a fat round-faced man with a bushy black mustache and a wide-brimmed black hat, who sat on a bench on top of the vehicle from where he manipulated the controls. Behind him a low fence enclosed the top surface; within this area a half dozen urchins of indeterminate sex, wearing ragged gowns which sometimes exposed their bottoms, sometimes not. Other folk leaned through the windows, waving and saluting the onlookers. The fat man with the black mustache heaved at his controls; the vehicle careened to a halt; a side panel dropped aside and folded open to become a stage twelve feet wide running the length of the vehicle. Out upon the stage came a small man with a droll face, nose splayed, eyes drooping and melancholy, mouth sagging into dewlaps: the face of an unhappy pug dog. He wore a blue garment bedizened by a hundred tags and tassels, with a low narrow-brimmed hat. He came forward to the front of the stage, seated himself into empty air, but just in time a hand reached from within and thrust a stool under the descending fundament. He grimaced and leered at the folk watching from the café, reached an arm into the air, apparently without purpose, but another arm from within placed a stringed instrument into his grasp. The clown struck a set of chords, plucked a fragment of a tune in an upper register, then sang a plaintive ballad which told the tribulations of a vagabond's life. As he played a coda, a pair of fat women rushed out on the stage, to jig and jump and tumble while the clown played a quick-step. He was joined at the other side of the stage by a younger man with a concertina; the women redoubled their exertions, their great breasts bouncing, arms flailing. They kicked so high that they seemed to fall over backwards but instead turned amazing back somersaults which showed flashes of fat haunch and rocked the stage when they alighted. Finally they seized the sad-faced clown and hurled him out over the onlookers who screamed and ducked, but he had been attached by a wire to a long pole which took him, never missing a beat on his instrument, orbiting out and around in a great swing and safely back to the stage.

The fat ladies were replaced by three girls in full black skirts and golden-brown blouses who were joined by a burly youth masked and costumed as a demon of demented lust. He chased the girls about the stage in a frenzy of acrobatic exercises during which he attempted to disrobe the girls, and bear them to the ground. As the cavortings came to a climax, with two of the girls bare-breasted and the demon tugging at the skirt of the third, Glawen felt the most minuscule stir. He looked quickly around and reached to seize the wrist of a girl eight or nine years old. Her hand was already in his pocket; her face was only a foot away from his own. He stared into her slate-gray eyes, and squeezed at her wrist. She released what she had fixed upon. Glawen saw that she was preparing to spit into his face. He released his grip and she walked away without haste, turning a single scornful glance over her shoulder.

On the stage a juggler was busy with a dozen rings. He was followed by an aged woman who blew on a heavy bass horn and played a plectrum with her bare feet, chording with one set of toes, striking with the other. She was presently joined by a rachity clown as old as herself who played two bagpipes and a nose-flute simultaneously to produce a music of three parts. The finale consisted of ten adults forming an orchestra while six small children danced jigs and circlets and rounds and finally ran out among the audience holding trays for offerings. The girl who approached Glawen was the same who had tried to pick his pocket. Without comment he dropped some coins into the tray; without comment she moved on. A moment later the vehicle rumbled away to play before another café at the far side of the Cansaspara Hotel.

Glawen looked up toward Pharisse, which had edged somewhat down the sky. He returned to the guidebook and read about the vagabond entertainers who roamed Nion in their lumbering vehicles. There were, so it was estimated, perhaps two hundred such vehicles, each with its own traditions and special repertory.

"They are almost like wild creatures, so strong are their nomadic instincts!" declared the guidebook. "Nothing could persuade them to limit their freedom. Their status is low; other folk consider them mad and treat them with tolerant contempt, quite ignoring the fact that some of the performances display efforts of great creativity, not to mention a high degree of technical virtuosity.

"For all the zest and vivacity of their performances, the vagabond life is far from a romantic idyll. After a long journey they arrive at a destination in jubilant mood. Before long they become restless and fretful and once more strike out across the wilderness to a new destination. They are not a frivolous people but, rather, as if obeying the universal tradition, would seem to be ordinarily melancholy. As children they learn to perform as soon as they can walk. Their adult lives are marred by petty jealousies and the pressure to excel; their old age is anything but tranquil. As soon as the old man or woman fails at his performance, or plays sour notes at his music, he loses the respect of his fellows and is given only grudging and perfunctory recognition. Now, when he or she performs, the audiences will still marvel at their amazing energy and abnormal agility as they drive themselves to amazing new levels of performance, until finally they totter and fall, or play an embarrassing luxuriance of sour notes. Then it is over and they become apathetic. During the next journey the vehicle stops briefly in the middle of the night, with the moons spilling across the dark sky. The oldster is thrust from the vehicle and given a bottle of wine. The vehicle departs, and the old buffoon is left alone. He will sit upon the ground; perhaps he will watch the moons slide past for a time, or perhaps he will sing the song he has prepared just for this occasion; then he drinks the bottle of wine and stretches out to sleep a sleep from which he will never awake, for the wine is drugged with a soft Gangril poison."

Glawen pushed the book aside; he had learned as much as—or more than—he cared to know. He leaned back in the chair, glanced up at Pharisse and wondered whether he should order an item of pastry from the cart now being wheeled among the tables. To the other side of the café a young man, tall and of good physique, rose from the table at which he had been sitting, his back half-turned toward Glawen who watched him depart with no more than idle attention. By the time Glawen's interest was aroused the young man was walking away. Glawen still managed to see that he wore dark green trousers cut to a close fit, a cobalt blue cape, and a small loose-crowned brimless hat.

The figure disappeared up the avenue, his gait easy, confident, almost a swagger. Glawen tried to recall what he had glimpsed, and thought to recapture the image of a well-shaped head with a neat cap of thick dark hair; a clear skin and classically regular features. Despite the lack of distortion or deviation, Glawen was half-convinced that he had seen the man before.

Glawen settled back into his chair. He consulted his watch; there was time for a nap before his rendezvous with Keebles. He rose, departed the café, and returned to the Novial Hotel.

A different clerk was on duty: an older man with sparse gingery hair and a prim beard. Glawen asked that he be called without fail at twenty-seven o'clock since he had an important engagement. The clerk gave a curt nod, made a note, then resumed his study of a fashion journal. Glawen went to his room, removed his outer garments, threw himself down upon the bed and soon fell asleep.

Time passed. Glawen's slumber was disturbed by a tingle of pain at the side of his hip. He turned on the light, and found that he had been stung by a black insect. Outside the window the sky was dim with dusk. The time was twenty-eight o'clock. He jumped up, destroyed such insects as were conveniently to hand, splashed water into his face, dressed and left the room. As he strode through the lobby the clerk jumped to his feet and leaned forward over the counter. He called out in an aggrieved voice: "Mr. Clattuc! I was about to call you, but it seems that you have taken matters into your own hands."

"Not quite," said Glawen. "I was awakened by an insect. The room is infested. I will be out for a few hours; please make sure that the room is fumigated in my absence."

The clerk resumed his seat. "The janitor evidently forgot to use insecticide when he cleaned your room. I will make sure that your complaint is received in the proper quarters."

"That is not enough. You must deal with these insects now."

The clerk said stiffly: "Unfortunately, the janitor has gone off duty. I can only assure you that the matter will be resolved to your complete satisfaction tomorrow."

Glawen spoke in a careful voice: "When I return from my business, I shall look about the room. If I find any insects, I shall capture them and bring them here, and you will not enjoy what use I make of them."

"That is intemperate language, Mr. Clattuc."

"I was not awakened by a temperate insect. Heed my warning!"

Glawen left the hotel. Pharisse had dropped from the sky and twilight had come to Tanjaree, working a wonderful transformation. Across the lake Old Town, illuminated by the glow of soft white lights, seemed only half-real: a city of fairy-tale palaces. A dozen moons drifted across the sky, showing subtle variations of color: creamy-gray through white and silver-white, the palest of pinks and equally soft violet, each moon reflecting its image in the lake. Nion, according to the guidebook, was often known as 'The World of the Nineteen Moons.' Each of the moons was named and every inhabitant of the planet knew these names as well as he knew his own.

Glawen turned into Crippet Alley, and was surprised to find that, by virtue of its illumination, the street now seemed charming and gay. Apparently every householder had been required to hang out a light globe to his own taste, resulting in a welter of colored globes set as if in celebration of a festival. Glawen knew that aesthetic impulse had been far from anyone's mind; the lights were as they were because it was easier than a more uniform arrangement.

Many folk were still abroad, though not the previous crowds. Some were natives; others were tourists, strolling at their leisure, pausing to look into the shop windows, or patronizing the little café. Glawen, an hour late for his appointment with Keebles, pressed along the street as rapidly as possible. He stopped short. A man wearing a blue cape had passed him by; Glawen glimpsed a pale preoccupied face, features set in a mask. Glawen turned and looked back, but the dark blue cloak was lost in the welter of lights and moving shapes. Glawen continued along Crippet Alley and presently arrived at the Argonaut Art Import and Export Company. There were lights on within the shop; as before, the door was unlocked, even though the posted closing hour was twenty-seven o'clock and the clerk was no longer on duty behind the counter.

Glawen entered, closed the door behind him. He stood a moment looking around the cluttered interior. Everything was as he had left it earlier in the day. He heard nothing and there was no sign of Keebles.

Glawen went to the passage leading back to Keebles' office. He halted, listened: no sound. He called out: "Mr. Keebles! I'm here—Glawen Clattuc!"

The silence seemed more profound than ever.

Glawen grimaced. He looked behind him, up the stairs, then ventured forward along the passage. Once again he called: "Mr. Keebles?"

As before: no response. Glawen peered into the back office. A corpse lay on the floor. It was Keebles. His arms and ankles had been bound; blood oozed from his mouth. His eyes were open and bulged enormously in horror. His trousers had been cut open and it was clear that Keebles had been tortured.

Glawen bent and touched Keebles' neck with his knuckles. Still warm. Keebles had been dead only a short time. If the clerk had not forgotten to call Glawen, Keebles might still be alive.

Glawen stared unhappily down at the corpse, and the

mouth which now would never reveal the information he had come so far to learn.

Why had Keebles been killed? There were no overt signs of pillage. The desk drawers were closed, as was the cabinet. In a nook at the far end of the room, a door opened on a makeshift porch and the yard beyond. The door was bolted from the inside; the murderer had not used it in his operation.

Glawen returned his attention to the desk. He searched in vain for a notebook or an address file or something similar which might identify Keebles' associate. Careful to leave no fingerprints, Glawen searched the desk drawers. He came upon nothing of interest. He looked into the cabinet, where he discovered a small safe, the doors of which swung open. The contents, again, were of no immediate interest.

Glawen stood thinking. Keebles had intended to make a telephone call. On the desk was the telephone screen and the keyboard. Using a pencil Glawen punched the 'Options' button, and then the code for 'Listing of recent calls.'

The most recent call had been made to the Moonway Hotel, at Moonway. The others were local calls, made earlier in the day, and impossible to identify.

From the front of the premises came a soft sound: a rattling at the door which evidently had locked itself after Glawen had closed it.

Glawen peered cautiously down the passage. Against the lights of the street he saw a pair of constables who were trying to open the door in silence.

For a second Glawen stood transfixed. Then, on long swift strides he ran to the back door. He slid back the bolt, opened the door and stepped out upon the porch. He closed the door and stood listening, then he went to stand in the shadow of a shed. A moment later a pair of constables rushed around the structure, gave the yard a perfunctory scrutiny, then entered Keebles' office by the back door.

In an instant Glawen was over the back fence. By the light of a dozen moons he picked his way through rubbish and rubble, and pits filled with puddles of foul-smelling water.

The waste area gave upon a small back alley, with

392   JACK VANCE

small lumpy structures to either side. Thirty yards ahead
a tavern spilled colored light into the street. From within
came the mutter of guttural voices, a strange whining
music, and occasionally the high-pitched whinny of
drunken female laughter. Glawen walked briskly past, and
in due course, after several false turnings, came out on
the lakeside avenue.

As he walked he pondered. The coming of the constables so hard upon his own arrival did not seem to be
coincidence. They had been notified—by someone who
knew that Keebles was dead. Glawen worked out a
sequence of events which he found reasonable, if a number
of assumptions were accepted. Assume that the young man
in the blue cape were the same handsome young man who
betrayed Miss Flavia Shoup; assume that he had arrived at
Tanjaree almost at the same time as Glawen. Assume that
he had taken note of Glawen and perhaps recognized him.
Assume that he had approached Keebles and had received
the same response given to Glawen. With these assumptions in place, then the sequence of events became clear.
Arriving at the Argonaut Art Import and Export Company,
the man had compelled Keebles to yield his information,
then had killed him if only to deny Glawen the same
information. Upon leaving the office, the murderer had
observed Glawen in Crippet Alley and had thereupon notified the constables of the horrid crime and the murderer's
presence upon the scene.

Even if the sequence were faulty in part, Glawen was
impelled to travel to Moonway at best speed.

Glawen returned to the Novial Hotel. The clerk gave
him a distant nod, but clearly was not in a cordial mood.
Repairing to his room, Glawen found that someone had
strung up a mesh hammock, to be used should the insects
become troublesome.

Glawen changed his clothes and returned to the lobby.
The clerk had judiciously absented himself until his guest
had settled down for the night. Glawen went to the public
telephone. The Halcyon Travel Agency in the Cansaspara
Hotel was still open, so he discovered, and would remain so
until thirty-two o'clock.

CHAPTER IX

I.

The Halcyon Travel Bureau occupied a glass-enclosed office to the side of the Hotel Cansaspara lobby. A placard read:

> HALCYON TRAVEL BUREAU
> *Travel services of every description.*
> TOURS, EXCURSIONS, EXPEDITIONS
>
> Visit the far-flung backlands in comfort and safety. See the real Nion! Study the habits of mysterious peoples and observe their orgiastic rites! Dine under the hurtling moons at the Feast of a Thousand Polds, or enjoy a sumptuous service of your own familiar cuisine!
> ONCE IN A LIFETIME CHANCE!
> TRANSPORT GUIDES INFORMATION

Glawen entered the office. At the desk sat a tall dark-haired woman, handsome, trim of figure and clearly of off-world origin. A plaque on her desk read:

> T. DYTZEN
> Agent on duty.

She spoke: "Sir? Can I be of help?"

"I hope so," said Glawen. He seated himself in the chair

beside the desk. "What is the best connection to Moonway? I want to get there in a hurry—now if not sooner."

T. Dytzen smiled. "Have you been long on Nion?"

"I arrived just today."

T. Dytzen nodded. "Before the week is out, you will stop using words like 'hurry' and 'soon' and 'immediately.' Well, let us see what can be done." T. Dytzen worked her information screen. "There are a number of carriers, but none are large-scale or well organized. Semi-Express is the only line keeping to a schedule, but you have just missed the evening flight; it left at twenty-nine twenty. It puts down at Port Frank Medich, and arrives at Moonway about twelve o'clock; that is to say, local dusk at Moonway. I mention this just to give you an idea of flight-time."

"I see. What else is available?"

T. Dytzen consulted the screen. "At thirty-two forty the regular Blue Arrow service leaves Tanjaree, but it makes six local stops and arrives at Moonway tomorrow at twenty-six o'clock."

"What else do you have?"

T. Dytzen proposed several other services which sooner or later put into Moonway. "These are for the most part air-vans, not too fast, with a passenger capacity of thirty or forty. They are cheap to operate and make a tolerable profit for the owners, but essentially there is not enough traffic to support fast service to these outlying camps and villages. So you use what is available and call it 'adventure.' The tourists complain very little."

"Can I hire a flitter? One way or another, I must get out to Moonway and fast."

T. Dytzen gave her head a dubious shake. "I don't quite know what to tell you. There is little choice between Murk's Deluxe and Sky-waft. I cannot recommend either. Murk's vehicles—I have heard them called 'contraptions'—are not dependable and those at Sky-waft are no better; in fact they may be worse. Neither will rent a vehicle without a pilot, to make sure the tourist does not decide to fly over Tangting Forest. Still, if you like, I will call Murk's, to find what they have on hand."

"Please do."

T. Dytzen touched telephone buttons, which presently induced a surly response. "What do you want, then? I was sound asleep."

"Strange," said T. Dytzen. "Your advertisement says: 'Expert service, night and day; we never sleep!' "

"That only happens when we have vehicles to rent."

"And now you have none?"

"I have two, but they are in service."

"The advertisement states that Murk's Deluxe maintains a fleet of a dozen vehicles of several types."

"That is an old advertisement. Call some other day, if you will." The telephone screen went blank.

T. Dytzen told Glawen: "I expected nothing more. Still, for the sake of perseverance, I will call Sky-waft." She touched telephone buttons. There was no response whatever.

"Sky-waft appears to have closed for the day," said T. Dytzen. "Tomorrow I will ask why its advertisement reads: 'DEPENDABLE! VIGILANT! ALWAYS ON THE JOB!' " She ruminated. "Perhaps your best recourse is the Provincial Mail Service at eleven o'clock during the forenoon. It makes a number of stops, as many as seven or eight, and arrives at Moonway about noon local time—which is to say close on thirty-seven or thirty-eight o'clock."

"Are there no other aircraft? What about private vehicles? Or freight services? There must be someone making deliveries around the outback."

"So there are," said T. Dytzen. She looked in a directory. "Most of the offices will be closed at this time."

"There might be a schedule of departures at the port."

T. Dytzen gave a noncommittal nod and tapped the callbuttons. She spoke, was transferred to another office, spoke again, waited and spoke to a third individual. After a brief conversation, she turned from the telephone to Glawen. "You are in luck. All-world Cargoes is making deliveries in the Moonway sector. The carrier departs Bay 14 at the spaceport in about half an hour. I spoke with the pilot; he says he will take you out for twenty sols. Is that satisfactory? It's about what you would pay on the Semi-Express."

"I'm agreeable to the price, but when does he arrive?"

T. Dytzen spoke a few words into the telephone, then turned back to Glawen. "Arrival is an hour or so later than Semi-Express time."

"Sign me aboard."

T. Dytzen spoke a few more words, then turned away from the telephone. "Go directly out upon Bay 14 and stand by the front of the carrier. Don't be conspicuous or tell anyone what you are doing. The pilot will approach you. My fee, incidentally, is five sols."

II.

Glawen returned to the Novial Hotel, where he found the clerk once again at his post. He checked out, to the clerk's indignation. "Have all our meticulous efforts gone for naught?"

"I don't have time to explain," said Glawen. "But two facts are certain. Pharisse will rise in the morning and you will never see me again."

Glawen went at best speed to the spaceport. At the canteen he bought packets of biscuits, cheese, salted fish, pickles, and four flasks of imported beer, then went out upon the freight dock. He found Bay 14, where a cargo carrier of medium size had been loaded and made ready for departure. He went to stand in the shadows near the control cupola.

Five minutes later a tall thin man wearing a short-sleeved work suit came along the dock, walking with a loose and easy stride which Glawen thought might indicate a correspondingly easy temperament. He looked to be about Glawen's age, with cropped flax-yellow hair, guileless blue eyes, features of no particular distinction. He halted in front of Glawen. "I am Rak Wrinch, and I drive this vehicle. Do you have something for me?"

"Just some money."

"That will do nicely."

Glawen paid over twenty sols.

Wrinch looked up and down the dock. "Jump up into the cab, and keep out of sight."

Five minutes later the carrier lifted from the spaceport and slanted up through the night toward its cruising altitude. Overhead drifted the moons of Nion, lambent globes of many soft shades and sizes, sometimes eclipsing, sometimes seeming to race, sometimes rollicking like happy children. Glawen thought that it might be easy to attach mystical meaning to their interplay.

Wrinch verified what Glawen had already assumed: that he was an off-worlder from Kyper City on Sylvanus. He looked sidelong at Glawen. "You've never been there?"

"Never," said Glawen. "Sylvanus is one of the many worlds I know nothing about, except that it is somewhere in Virgo."

"True. It's not so bad a place, as worlds go. Every year the Bang-bird Festival draws in tourists from everywhere. You must have heard of the Bang-bird races."

"I'm afraid not."

"These creatures are called 'birds' only out of politeness. Mix up a dragon, an ostrich and a devil, and you have a bang-bird. They stand twelve feet high, walk on two legs, with long necks and tall heads; they are vicious unless treated carefully when young, and are not stupid. Still, they are useless for anything but saddle-animals, and every year they run the Grand Champion Races at Kyper City. The riders are a special caste and religious, since they are almost always killed by the birds in the end. But the rider who wins the Grand Race becomes a great celebrity, with much money, and never rides again."

"The races must be quite a sight."

"Indeed. There are always two or three riders thrown, and then there is turmoil while the birds stop to kill the riders, whom they hate, so the tourists always go away in awe. Where is your home?"

"Araminta Station on Cadwal, at the back of Perseus."

"I never heard of Cadwal either." He refused Glawen's offer of food. "I ate before departure."

"What time will we arrive at Moonway?"

"You are in a hurry?"

"I would like to arrive before the Semi-Express, if possible."

"Out of the question, I must put down at Port Klank to discharge three pumps for the water system. After Port Klank, by rights I should make for Yellow Blossom, then Moonway, but I suppose I could call at Moonway first and then cut north to Yellow Blossom. That would save an hour or two."

"And time of arrival?"

"About fourteen o'clock. How is that?"

"It will have to do."

Wrinch looked curiously at Glawen. "Have you been there before?"

"No."

"It is a fascinating place. The Standing Stones are sometimes called monuments to ancient heroes, but they are more; they represent the ancient heroes themselves: personalities which have never died. During certain lunar patterns they come out and play the old games again. Tourists who are caught out among the Stones at these times are killed at once, though ordinarily the Shadowmen are a quiet lot, without much to say. The moons control their emotions. If the tourists fail to follow the rules which are posted for them, their throats are cut."

Glawen found his eyes growing heavy; he had missed much sleep. At the back of the cab were a pair of settees; Glawen stretched out on one and, after checking the auto-pilot, Wrinch laid his long frame down on the other. The two slept, and the carrier flew alone through the night.

Glawen was awakened by a jar and a thud; he raised himself to find daylight outside and Pharisse several hours high. The carrier had landed upon the spongy surface of a small plateau. To the west, north and south spread a wide landscape of other such plateaus, rising above the inter-vening sea bottom. To the east, and near the carrier, a dozen concrete buildings stood in a line, facing what appeared to be experimental plots of off-world vegetation.

Wrinch had already jumped down from the cupola, to see to the delivery of his freight. With three other men he went to the rear of the carrier; the doors were opened, several items of cargo were unloaded with the help of a small lift-truck; then the doors were slammed shut and, after a moment of conversation, Wrinch climbed back into the cupola. He made marks on his manifest, adjusted the auto-pilot, and once again the carrier took to the air.

"That was Port Klank," said Wrinch. "Some agronomists from Earth, either visionaries or madmen, are trying to grow terrestrial flora on a soil which is essentially pure pold. They claim the chemistry is right; that no toxic metals are present, only the macro-molecules typical of metamorphosed pold. So they use bacteria to break down these molecules, along with the viruses of Nion and experimental soil conditioners. They claim that in ten years each of these plateaus will look like a forested island instead of what you see today."

"What about water?"

"There's plenty of sub-surface water. I just delivered three high-pressure pumps. There is also a vast reservoir of water in the pold itself. Some of the scientists talk about rain and rivers and the seas coming back, but that is far in the future—I hope. Planetary engineers make me nervous."

The day went by. Pharisse moved westward, its own motion augmented by the eastward movement of the carrier. At ten o'clock Pharisse sank behind the horizon. The long dusk faded through golden apricot and plum, and finally all color disappeared, leaving the night to the moons. At first there were three. Wrinch named them off: "Lilimel, Garuun, Seis. I know them all. The Shadowmen are the real experts. They stand and point, and suddenly something happens—another moon appears, or one moon passes under another and they all groan or hiss or fall down on their knees. One day I made a delivery and something happened among the moons and they started to attack a fat old tourist who had done nothing except come out of the hotel and stand on the porch. He ran inside and hid in the lounge. The Shadowmen told the manager that he would be cut into eight pieces if he ever showed himself again, so he left at once. It appears that while on a guided walk among the Standing Stones the old tourist went behind one of the stones to urinate. No one had known until the moons identified the culprit."

The night advanced. Three more moons entered the sky: Zosmei, Maltasar, Yanaz, according to Wrinch.

Glawen gave them scant attention. "Relax," said Wrinch. "We are making good time. I can't get any more out of this old cow. Anyway, we're almost there."

Glawen looked down toward the land below. "Is that the Plain of Standing Stones?"

"Not yet." Wrinch pointed to the east. "Here comes Sigil. The Shadowmen believe that if Sigil eclipses Ninka, on that instant the universe will come to an end. This isn't a bad bet, since Sigil orbits well out past Ninka."

Time passed. Glawen sat forward on the edge of the seat. Wrinch finally said: "We are now over the Plain of Standing Stones. See those lights off to the left? That's the camp of the Western Tribe. In a minute you should see the lights of Moonway. There are three hotels. The Moonway is the best. Do you have reservations?"

"No."

"The Moonway naturally tends to fill up first. Still it's worth a try. Now you can see the lights."

"What about you? Will you be stopping over?"

"My schedule won't allow it. I'll cut up to Yellow Blossom, then continue around."

"Maybe I'll see you back in Tanjaree."

"I hope so. You know where to find me."

The carrier slanted down toward Moonway. Wrinch pointed out Moonway Hotel. "It's the big place at the center. The colored lights are on entertainers' wagons; there are always three or four troupes parked at Moonway. They cavort and do mad tricks and amuse the hotel guests, so they are tolerated."

The carrier landed. As soon as Wrinch opened the cupola door, Glawen took his travel bag and jumped to the ground. "Thank you, and goodbye."

"Goodbye and good luck."

III.

Glawen half-walked half-ran toward the Moonway Hotel: a massive structure of concrete and glass, more or less regular after the architectural canons of Nion which rejected flat surfaces and hard edges, and accepted verticality only because, in its absence, the building would fall down. To right and left extended two-story residential wings, with a garden terrace surmounting the main structure, where patrons of the hotel dined under festoons of dim green and blue fairy-lights. Not far from the hotel entrance three of the nomad wagons had been stationed, each as gaudy and garish as any Glawen had seen in Tanjaree. To the side vagabonds sat at their ease, drinking pold beer from tall misshapen crocks, while iron pots hanging on tripods bubbled over fires. At the sight of Glawen, a number of urchins ran out to join him. Mistaking Glawen's accelerated pace as a desire for exercise, they called out: "We'll race you, sir, for some money! See? All of us carry money! We will run you a fine race!"

"No thanks," said Glawen. "No race today."

"We run backwards! How can you lose? Are you a fast runner, sir?"

"I'm very slow. You must race with your fathers, or grandmothers."

"Ha, ha! No chance; if we won, they would beat us!"

"Too bad," panted Glawen.

"We will race with each other. Give us money for a prize!" "We will carry your burden!" The largest tried to snatch away Glawen's travel bag. Glawen held the bag high. "I need no help. Go play elsewhere."

The urchins ignored his instructions. They surrounded him, running backwards just in front, plucking at his sleeves, hooting and jeering. "Coward! Do you fear to race?" "He runs like a fat old lady." "He has long thin toes; that's why he wears funny shoes." "Oh, he's a strange one!"

From one of the tables a large bewhiskered man jumped to his feet and came forward. "Leave off, you vermin! Can't you see the gentleman is not amused!" He addressed Glawen. "Sorry for the annoyance, sir! Children have no manners nowadays! Still, they are easily pleased; if you toss them a few coins they would never call you 'skink' or 'tight-gut' again!"

"I don't mind at all," said Glawen. "Excuse me; I am in a hurry." He continued toward the hotel. The vagabond shrugged, kicked the children out of his way and returned to his beer.

Entering the Moonway, Glawen found himself in a spacious lobby with a high ceiling. A sleek young clerk, apparently an off-worlder, presided over the registration desk. He took note of Glawen's scuffed travel bag with raised eyebrows and a fastidious droop to his mouth. His voice, however, was impeccably correct: "I am sorry, sir, but unless you have a reservation, I cannot offer you accommodation. We are booked solid. I suggest that you try either the Magic Jade, or the Maudley—though I believe that they are also full."

"I'll see about accommodation later," said Glawen. "My first need is for information." He placed a sol on the counter. The clerk pretended not to notice. "Perhaps you can help me."

"I will do my best, sir."

"Do you keep records of incoming telephone calls—specifically, a call from Tanjaree which would have arrived early this morning?"

"We keep no such records, sir; they would serve no purpose."

Glawen grimaced. "Were you on duty at about twenty-eight o'clock this morning?"

"No, sir. I came on duty at ten o'clock this afternoon."

"Who was on duty then?"

"That would be Mr. Stensel, sir."

"I would like a few words with him, and at once. The matter is rather urgent."

The clerk went to his telephone, spoke a few soft words, listened and turned back to Glawen. "Mr. Stensel is just finishing his supper. If you will go to the couch yonder, to the side of the clock, Mr. Stensel will join you almost immediately."

"Thank you." Glawen went to the designated couch and seated himself.

The lobby was a cheerful airy place, despite the ponderous construction of the walls. Rugs, striped black, white, red, blue and green, covered the floor; the ceiling, thirty feet above, had been decorated with motifs of the Shadowmen: patterns of barbaric extravagance and passion, somehow kept under restraint. A panel suspended over the registration desk displayed colored disks representing the moons currently in the sky. They appeared low to the left of the panel, rose to the height of their arc and curved down to disappear off to the right.

Three minutes passed. A plump little man, balding and brisk, dressed only slightly less formally than the clerk on duty, approached. "I am Mr. Stensel. I understand that you have a question or two?"

"So I do. Sit down, if you please."

Mr. Stensel seated himself on the couch. "Now then: how may I help you, sir?"

"You were on duty this morning at twenty-eight o'clock?"

"That is correct, sir; it is my regular shift."

"Do you remember a telephone call from Tanjaree at about this time?"

"Hm." Mr. Stensel appeared to cogitate. "This is the kind of detail that quickly becomes lost."

Glawen gave him two sols, and Mr. Stensel smiled. "Strange how money lubricates the memory. Yes; I remember the call; indeed, I recognized the caller, since he telephones often. It was Mr. Melvish Keebles."

"Right. To whom did he speak?"

"To one of our long-term guests, Mr. Adrian Moncurio the archaeologist. You may have heard of him, since he is quite well known."

"You did not overhear the conversation?"

"No, sir. That is not proper conduct, under any circumstances. Another gentleman asked me the same questions only a trifle more than an hour ago, and I told him the same."

Glawen's heart sank. "Did this other gentleman give his name?"

"No, sir."

"What did he look like?"

"He was nicely dressed, of good appearance, and exceedingly pleasant, so I thought."

Glawen brought out another two sols. "You have been most helpful. Where can I find Mr. Moncurio?"

"He occupies Suite A, which opens onto the front verandah. Leave the lobby, turn to the right. Suite A is at the end. You may or may not find Mr. Moncurio on the premises, since he keeps odd hours, and sometimes goes out to explore among the Stones when the moons are favorable. He is highly skilled in such matters, and can judge the moons to a nicety. Otherwise, he would long ago have been killed."

"Are the moons right now?"

Mr. Stensel looked toward the panel. "As to that, I can't say, since I have never studied the subject."

"Thank you." Glawen left the lobby, turned to the right and ran to the end of the verandah, where he found Suite A. Glimmers of light seeped past the window-blinds. Glawen took heart; it appeared that someone was at home. He pressed the bell button.

A minute passed, while Glawen's tension mounted. From within came the sound of slow movement. The door slid aside; in the opening stood a dark-haired full-figured woman of no great stature. Despite the incursions of middle age, she still commanded elements of youthful charm. Her thick hair was cut short and square around her head in a style prompted either by high fashion or by stark practicality. She examined Glawen with bright black eyes. "Yes, sir?"

"Is Mr. Moncurio in?" Glawen was annoyed to hear the anxious catch in his voice.

The woman shook her head and Glawen's heart sank once again. "He's out in the field, doing his archaeology." She stepped to the doorway, looked right and left along the verandah, then turned back to Glawen. "I can't understand his popularity. Suddenly, everyone must see Professor Moncurio, and no one will wait."

"Where can I find him? It is very important!"

"He is out in the Stones somewhere. The moons for a change are good. I suspect he's off down Row Fourteen. Are you another archaeologist?"

"No. Is there anyone who could help me find him?"

The woman gave a sad laugh. "Not I, for sure, with my poor legs. But he won't go far, since he must be back before Shan goes down, which is less than two hours." The woman pointed toward a pale blue moon. "When Shan sets, the Shadowmen will come in a rush, looking for throats to cut."

"Where is Row Fourteen?"

"Simple! Go down Column Five, which is the aisle yonder, count fourteen rows. Then turn to the left and go three or four columns, and Adrian should be nearby. If not, don't go looking for him! The Stones are confusing in the moonlight; you might easily lose your way. The pold is already black with spilled blood."

"Thanks; I'll be careful." Glawen started away. The woman called after him: "Watch for the others; remind them of the time!"

Glawen approached the Standing Stones. They loomed above him, twenty feet or so tall, massive in the moonlight. He entered Column Five; to either side the ranks receded and finally disappeared into the blur of mingled moonlight and darkness.

Glawen went at a half-run down Column Five, counting rows. At Row Eight he stopped to listen. The only sound was the flux of blood in his own ears. He continued: a shadow moving among the other shadows. At Row Twelve he stopped again, straining to hear sounds which might guide him.

Had his senses deceived him? Had he heard a voice? If so, it had been soft and diffident, as if wanting to make itself known, yet fearful of being overheard. Odd!

Glawen turned aside into Row Twelve and ran on long stealthy steps past three ranks of stones, to Column Eight. He stopped again to listen. Silence! An ominous sign. If a friend had come out to join Moncurio, there would be conversation, or so it would seem. He set off along the column. Almost at once the call came again, as low-pitched and wary as before. The stones muffled sound; Glawen could not fix on the direction of the voice, or its distance; still it did not seem far.

Glawen went along the row to Column Nine, and turned to the right. Two more rows would bring him to Fourteen. He must not lose himself among the stones! Step by step he went forward. There were presences near, baleful and alert. Something came running through the dark to pounce on his back; he swung around. Nothing was there. His nerves had fooled him. He stood staring in all directions, listening for another call, or noise: anything he could fix upon.

It came: from near at hand a sudden laugh, an unpleasant roar, mocking and triumphant. Then came a babble of voices, a thud of sinister import; after a few breathless instants—a cry of awful fury.

Glawen put aside caution and ran toward the sounds. After a few feet, he halted to orient himself. He heard hurrying footsteps; looking along the column he saw a human shape. It approached at a peculiar lurching gait. Suddenly, with a sobbing gasp of frustration, it stopped short, bent low, made a hurried adjustment; then, free of its former restraint, ran forward and collided full into Glawen. Nine of the nineteen moons illuminated a stricken face. Glawen cried in amazement: "Wayness!"

She stared up, first in shock, then in incredulous joy. "Glawen! I can't believe that it's you!" She turned, looked over her shoulder. "Baro is back there: he's a murderer! He dropped Moncurio into a tomb and left him for the Shadowmen. He caught me and said I was more interesting alive than dead and started to undress me. I hit him with a spade and he fell down. I tried to run away but I could not run fast with my trousers down around my ankles." She darted another glance over her shoulder. "We had best go to the hotel for help! Baro is a devil!"

From between the stones a shape darker than the shadows moved forward into the light of the moons. Glawen recognized the man he had glimpsed in Crippet Alley and at the Cansaspara café.

Wayness gave a soft cry of distress. "It's too late."

The man came slowly forward. He halted ten feet away. Some trick of posture or perhaps his supercilious grin stirred recollections in Glawen's mind and he knew the man's identity. "It's Benjamie the spy! Benjamie the traitor!"

Benjamie laughed. "Of course! And you are the noble and pure Glawen Clattuc! I sent your father to Shattorak! I suppose you are annoyed with me."

"Very much so."

Benjamie came a step closer. Glawen wondered what he was carrying behind his back. "So here we are," said Benjamie, "you and I, and now we shall see who is the better man: nice good Glawen or bad Benn Barr! And pretty Wayness will rejoice with whomever is alive at the end!"

Glawen somberly considered Benjamie, who stood an inch taller than himself and was heavier by twenty pounds. Benjamie was quick and light footed; his confidence was superb.

Glawen told Wayness: "Run back to the hotel. As soon as you're well away, I'll get clear of this fellow and join you."

"But Glawen! What if—" She could not bring herself to finish.

"If you hurry, there should be time to help Moncurio before Shan goes down. As for Benjamie, I will do what needs to be done."

Benjamie gave a contemptuous laugh. "Stay here!" he told Wayness. "If you run I'll catch you." He strode forward. Glawen saw that he was carrying a short-handled spade. "This won't take long." He feinted, then swung the spade so that it should slash Glawen's neck. Glawen jumped aside and pressed his back against a tall Standing Stone. Benjamie jabbed with the spade; Glawen again jerked aside; the spade rang against the stone. Glawen seized the handle; the two wrestled for possession: twisting one way, then the other. Glawen saw that Benjamie was preparing a surprise. He first wrenched and hauled with the shovel in order to set Glawen up in an exposed stance. Glawen obliged, prompting the surprise: a sudden kick to the groin. Glawen twisted his hips and slipped the kick. Grasping the foot he instantly thrust hard, to send Benjamie hopping backward. Glawen wrested away the spade, struck it down hard on Benjamie's shoulder, and Benjamie hissed in pain. He charged like a bull, grappled Glawen, bore him back so that Glawen's head cracked against the Standing Stone. Glawen felt sick and dazed. Benjamie drove his fist into Glawen's cheek; Glawen struck Benjamie's belly; it was like hitting a board.

For a few moments there was confusion: a tangle of grunting bodies, flailing arms, contorted faces. Pain and fear were forgotten; each thought only of the other's destruction. Benjamie attempted another kick; Glawen caught the leg, pulled, twisted; there was a snap and Benjamie fell over backward, his ankle broken. He raised himself slowly on his hands and toes, then lunged, and caught Glawen off-balance. Benjamie worked himself behind Glawen, thrust his forearm against Glawen's throat. Grinning in jubilation Benjamie constricted his muscles so that Glawen's eyes bulged and his chest pumped in vain for air.

Glawen reached back his right hand, caught Benjamie's hair and pulled back with all of his waning strength. Benjamie made fretful noises and tried to shake the hand loose. For an instant he allowed his arm muscles to slacken. Glawen drew his head far back and askew. With his left hand Glawen jabbed at Benjamie's throat, at the site of a sensitive nerve. Benjamie's grip relaxed. Glawen broke loose; gasping, he turned and with all his strength drove his knuckles into Benjamie's larynx. He felt the crushing of cartilaginous structures; croaking and wheezing, Benjamie fell over backwards, to sit slumped against a Standing Stone, to stare at Glawen with dull bewildered eyes.

Glawen, still panting, picked up the spade. He spoke to Benjamie: "Think of Shattorak."

Benjamie slumped back against the stone. Glawen saw that he was only half-conscious.

Wayness came forward. She watched Benjamie in fascinated horror. "Is he dead?"

"Not at the moment; he's probably in a state of shock."

"Will he survive?"

"I don't think so. If I did, I'd break his head with the spade. Perhaps I should do it anyway."

Wayness clutched his arm. "No, Glawen, don't!" Then she said: "No, I don't mean that. He can't be allowed to live."

"He's dying. In any case he can't walk, and the Shadowmen will be here before long. Where is Moncurio?"

"Back here." Wayness led the way to an excavation, covered over with a slab of stone. "He is below the stone. It's very heavy."

Prying with the spade and exerting all his strength, Glawen managed to slide the stone back a few inches. He called down: "Moncurio?"

"I'm down here! Get me out! I thought you were Shadowmen."

"Not yet."

With Wayness assisting, Glawen thrust back the stone, inch by inch, until Moncurio was able to wriggle through the gap. "Ah, air! Space! Freedom! What a wonderful feeling! I thought that I was done for!" Moncurio paused to brush dirt from his clothes. In the moonlight Glawen saw a tall robust man of late maturity, only a trifle soft in the midriff. His thick silver-gray hair matched his brisk mustache. A wide brow, a nose long and straight, a well-shaped chin lent dignity to his face; his eyes, however, under drooping eyelids were large, dark and moist: the eyes of a spaniel.

Moncurio finished dusting off his clothes. He spoke with emotion: "A true miracle! I had given up hope! My life was flashing before my eyes! You two came at the most fortuitous moment!"

"It wasn't all that fortuitous," said Glawen.

Moncurio looked at him uncomprehendingly.

Wayness said: "I came out looking for you. I saw Benjamie drop you into the hole; then he attacked me. Glawen rescued both of us. Benjamie is now lying yonder; he may be dead."

"And a good thing too!" declared Moncurio with feeling. "He wanted information; I told him everything I knew and for gratitude he pushed me into the hole. I consider him a very discourteous fellow."

"No doubt as to that."

Moncurio looked around the sky. "Shan slants low!" He consulted his watch. "Twenty-four minutes remain. Now then!" he said with sudden energy. "Help me cover the tomb! Otherwise the Shadowmen will become nasty-minded and poison the water."

The three set to work. Moncurio at last was satisfied. "That will have to do, since Shan is almost down and Res is under Padan. The Shadowmen know what has been going on and they are delirious with rage. It is seven minutes to the hotel. Nine minutes remain before Shan is gone."

The three returned at a smart pace along the rows and columns. Presently they broke out into the open.

"We can't stop here," declared Moncurio. "In five minutes Shan will be gone, but some reckless juvenile might decide to try for instant honor and cut our throats here and now, and make his peace with the moons later."

"This is a precarious place to live," observed Glawen.

"In many respects, yes," said Moncurio. "But the true archaeologist ignores hardship. He must make sacrifices for his science!"

The three continued back toward the hotel. Moncurio spoke on. "It is not all romance and glory, I assure you! No profession is less forgiving! One mistake, and the reputation of a lifetime is demolished! Meanwhile, the financial rewards are minimal."

"A good tomb robber seems to do quite well," mused Wayness.

"In that regard, I have no opinion," said Moncurio with dignity.

The three reached the safe grounds surrounding the

hotel complex. Far to the west pale blue Shan sank below the edge of the old sea-bottom.

Ten seconds passed. From the Stones came a wild cry, of vindictive glee.

"They have found Benjamie, or Ben Barr—whatever his name," said Moncurio. "If he was not yet dead, he is dead now." Moncurio turned away and went to the door of Suite A. He halted and turned. "Once again, I thank you both for your help. Perhaps we will meet tomorrow, and take a cup of tea on the verandah. So now: goodnight!"

"Just a moment," said Wayness. "We also must ask you a few questions."

Moncurio said stiffly: "I am extremely tired; could not your questions wait?"

"And suppose you died during the night?"

Moncurio gave a bleak laugh. "Your questions would be the least of my worries."

"We won't take too much of your time," said Wayness. "You can rest while we talk to you."

"I suppose I can spare you five minutes or so," grumbled Moncurio. He opened the door; the three entered his sitting room. From the bedchamber came a woman's voice. "Adrian? Is that you?"

"Yes, my dear! Two friends are here on a matter of business; you need not come out."

The voice, now somewhat querulous, said: "I could serve tea, I suppose."

"Thank you, dear, but they will only be here a minute."

"As you like."

Moncurio turned back to Glawen and Wayness. "You undoubtedly are aware that I am Adrian Moncurio, archaeologist and social historian. I fear that I did not catch your names."

"I am Glawen Clattuc."

"I am Wayness Tamm. I think you know my uncle, Pirie Tamm. He lives at Fair Winds, near Shillawy."

Moncurio was for a moment taken aback: here was a new dimension to the case. He gave Wayness a quick sidelong glance, as if to divine her motives. "Yes, of course! I know Pirie Tamm well. But what are your questions?"

Glawen asked: "Did you speak with Melvish Keebles yesterday?"

Moncurio frowned. "Why do you ask?"

"He might have mentioned Benjamie, or Ben Barr, as you knew him."

Moncurio grimaced. "Keebles called and left a message, but I was busy out in the field. When I returned his call, I had no answer." Moncurio dropped into a chair. "Perhaps you will tell me what this is all about."

"Certainly. Some time ago Keebles sold you a collection of Naturalist Society documents. He said that you still might have them in your possession."

Moncurio raised his fine gray eyebrows. "Keebles is wrong. I traded the parcel to Xantief in Trieste."

"You looked through the parcel before you traded it?"

"Naturally! I am a careful man!"

"And you kept nothing?"

"Not so much as a torn photograph."

"What of Keebles? Did he keep anything?"

Moncurio shook his head. "This stuff was not in Keebles' line. He took it in trade from a certain Floyd Swaner, now dead. In exchange, Keebles gave Swaner a set of tanglets." He took a green jade medallion from a shelf, and fondled it lovingly. "This is a tanglet, which the ancient Shadowmen used to certify the glory of their champions. Nowadays tanglets are much in vogue among the collectors." He replaced the tanglet on the shelf. "Unfortunately, they are ever harder to find."

Glawen asked: "And the Naturalist documents—you know nothing about them—for instance, where they are now?"

"Nothing, beyond what I have told you."

After a moment Wayness heaved a sigh. "I came down the ladder, rung by rung: Gohoon Galleries to Funusti Museum to Mirky Porod to Trieste, to Casa Lucasta, and finally to Moonway."

"I came up the ladder, from Idola on the Big Prairie to Division City to Tanjaree to Moonway."

"Moonway is the middle rung, where we should find what we are looking for—but Moonway is as empty as the rest."

Moncurio asked: "What are you seeking? Could it be the Cadwal Charter and Grant?"

Wayness nodded sadly. "They have become very important, even critical, if Cadwal is to remain a Conservancy."

Glawen asked: "Did you know they were missing?"

"When I first saw the Naturalist documents, I noticed that the Charter and the Grant were missing. Keebles never saw them, of this I am certain. All of which means that he did not receive them from Floyd Swaner."

"This surely was Smonny Clattuc's opinion," said Glawen. "She burgled the Chilke barn any number of times and eviscerated the stuffed moose, but never came up with anything."

"So what could have happened to the Charter and Grant?" asked Moncurio.

"That is the mystery we are trying to solve," said Wayness.

"Grandpa Swaner left everything to his grandson Eustace," said Glawen. "Smonny tried to get hold of Chilke's property in every way she could think of, including marriage, which of course Chilke avoided. Life was too short, he said. Now it seems that no one—Chilke, Smonny, Wayness, you, I, no one—knows what has happened to the Charter and the Grant."

"An interesting problem," said Moncurio. "I can offer no clues." He pulled at his mustache, then glanced over his shoulder toward the bedchamber. The door was slightly ajar. Moncurio quietly crossed the room, eased the door shut and returned to his previous place. "We must not disturb Carlotta with our talk. Ha hm. It seems that you have gone to great pains in your search." He looked toward Wayness. "Did I hear you mention 'Casa Lucasta'?"

"You did."

Moncurio phrased a question with care. "Interesting! We are speaking of 'Casa Lucasta' in—I forget the name of the town."

"Pombareales."

"Yes, of course. And how go things in that odd little corner of Old Earth?"

Wayness considered. "The folk of Patagonia have long

memories. They are still on the look-out for an archaeologist named 'Professor Solomon.' "

"Bah!" Moncurio gave an uncomfortable laugh. "You are referring to a promotional scheme which went sour. The idea was to advertise a new tourist complex, but at the last minute the principals backed off, and I was left in an exposed position. It's the old, old story, from which I emerged a cynic, I can assure you!"

Wayness gave an incredulous laugh. "A tourist resort on the pampas, with wind blowing weeds back and forth?"

Moncurio nodded with dignity. "I advised against the scheme, but when everything collapsed I was left alone to face the hysteria. They accused me, if you can believe it, of larceny, swindling, fraud, chicanery and much else. I was lucky to escape."

"That is how it seems to everyone," said Wayness.

Moncurio ignored the remark. "You visited Casa Lucasta?"

"Often."

"And how is Irena?"

"Irena is dead."

Moncurio's face sagged in dismay. "What happened to her?"

"She killed herself, after trying to kill the two children."

Moncurio winced. "And the children: what of them?"

"They are safe. Madame Clara said that you and Irena kept them dosed with drugs."

"That is a malicious distortion! I did the children a great service in taking them from the Gangrils. On Nion life means nothing."

"Still—why drug them on Old Earth? That is no great favor!"

"It was for the benefit of us all! I can easily explain, though you may not easily understand. Listen then! I learned something of the Gangril drugs—not much; just a smattering. They are able to reinforce certain functions of the brain and suppress others. Clairvoyance is an ability they can enhance.

"Now then! I am an archaeologist of not inconsiderable reputation!" Moncurio put on an expression of stern and inflexible dedication. "My first responsibility is to science; I am unswerving in this regard! Still, from time to time I am able to discover hidden treasures which allow me to finance my researches."

"Uncle Pirie describes you as a 'tomb robber,'" said Wayness.

"That is a bit uncharitable," said Moncurio. "Still, I am a practical man, and I make no bones of it. The heroes of the ancient Shadowmen were buried with their tanglets. A set of such tanglets is worth a fortune. But only one tomb in sixty yields more than three or four and only one in a hundred is a hero's tomb. To dig into a single tomb is both tiresome and dangerous; I have evaded death by inches many times. If a clairvoyant person could indicate which of the tombs contained a set of hero's tanglets, in a year we could leave Moonway forever and live in prosperity the rest of our lives. And there you have the explanation for Irena, the drugs and the two children. Irena loved money above all else; I knew that she would be fanatically faithful."

The door leading into the bedchamber burst open and Carlotta stormed out into the sitting room. "I have heard enough! Do you think me deaf, dumb and blind? I am neither a Gangril, nor a robber, nor am I 'fanatically faithful'! I am disgusted with what I have heard! You would be treated to the rough edge of my tongue if we were alone!"

"Carlotta, my dear! Let us be temperate!"

"I am being temperate. I will call you a scoundrel, a festering sore and a human jackal. That is temperance and it must suffice. I will send for my belongings tomorrow." Carlotta marched through the front door and out into the night. The door thudded shut.

Moncurio paced back and forth, head lowered, arms clasped behind his back. "I am dogged by adversity; it must be my destiny! After travail and endless patience, not to mention expense, my plans lie in shards!" He glanced sharply at Wayness. "Who informed you of my address? Was it Clara? I have never trusted that woman!"

"Myron told me."

"Myron?" Moncurio's jaw dropped. "How did he know?"

Wayness shrugged. "Clairvoyance, perhaps."

Moncurio resumed his pacing. Glawen and Wayness rose to their feet, bade Moncurio goodbye, and followed Carlotta out into the night.

Standing by the railing at the edge of the verandah they looked toward the ghostly ranks of the Standing Stones.

"I am still frightened," said Wayness. "I was sure that I would be killed."

"It was a near thing. I should never have let you go off by yourself." Glawen put his arms around her; they embraced.

Wayness spoke at last. "So—what now?"

"At the moment I can't think of anything sensible. My head seems to be whirling. I would like to find us a civilized dinner with a bottle of wine. I have had nothing to eat for days on end except some bread and cheese and a bite of pold. At the moment I don't even have a room."

"No problem there," said Wayness. "I have a very nice room."

CHAPTER X

I.

From Tanjaree on Pharisse and through the Jingles to Mersey, thence to Star Home on Aspidiske VI; then back toward the center of the Reach: so went the voyage, without excitement or notable event. There was little to do but watch the stars slide by and to speculate in regard to the question: where was the Charter, and the Grant-in-Perpetuity?

Glawen and Wayness spent hours in conjecture and cogitation, but in the end they returned to what seemed a set of basic facts. Charter and Grant had definitely been taken and sold by Frons Nisfit, along with other Naturalist documents. This was proved by Smonny's conduct at Gohoon Galleries. She had discovered a notation confirming the sale of Charter and Grant to Floyd Swaner, which had prompted her to excise the page and to concentrate her attention upon the Chilke ranch and Eustace Chilke himself.

Such was Basic Fact A. Basic Fact B was that Charter and Grant had not left Floyd Swaner's possession. There was no reason to doubt both Keebles and Moncurio that Floyd Swaner had not included the items among the Naturalist Society materials he had traded to them for tanglets. Basic Fact C was that Floyd Swaner had bequeathed all his belongings to Eustace Chilke, his grandson. However, on several occasions Chilke had declared that he knew nothing of such documents; and that the most notable items of his inheritance consisted of several stuffed animals and a collection of purple vases.

"The conclusion is plain," said Wayness. "Charter and Grant, despite all of Smonny's attempts to locate them, are still somewhere among Floyd Swaner's effects—that is to say, the objects he bequeathed to Eustace Chilke."

The two sat in the after saloon, watching the stars shift across the dark sky. Glawen said: "It seems then that we must trespass once more upon the patience of Ma Chilke. She must be very bored with this business by now."

"She won't be bored if we explain that the tanglets are valuable."

"That may soothe her. The documents are probably in some perfectly obvious place, where no one has troubled to look."

"It's a good theory, except that at the Chilke ranch there don't seem to be any such obvious places, except those which are used all the time."

"Perhaps they are among Chilke's boyhood keep-sakes—old letters, high school yearbooks and the like—we might find an inconspicuous envelope labeled 'Memoranda' or something of the sort. In fact—" Glawen stopped short.

" 'In fact'? What does that mean?"

"It means that I thought of somewhere to look. I don't mean the stuffed moose."

II.

Glawen and Wayness emerged from the Tammeola spaceport into the light of early morning. Immediately boarding the slideway, they rode north to Division City and thence by local air service to Largo on the Sippewissa River. As before, Glawen rented a flitter: they flew north and west into the heart of the Big Prairie, over Idola and beyond to where Fosco Creek, lined by cottonwoods and weeping willows, made its great loop and there, below, was the Chilke farmstead.

On this occasion Ma Chilke was alone, without even the children on hand. Glawen and Wayness alighted from the flitter and approached the house. Ma Chilke came to the door and stood waiting with hands on hips. She greeted Glawen with formal cordiality, and gave Wayness a sharp inspection, which Wayness bore with as much aplomb as possible. Ma Chilke turned back to Glawen and spoke, rather tartly: "Instead of keeping to business and going out after Mel Keebles, it looks like you went out and got this young lady instead."

Glawen grinned. "I could explain my reasons, if you were interested."

"Don't bother," retorted Ma Chilke. "I can guess your reasons, and depending upon what you were looking for, they make sense. Are you planning to introduce us?"

"Mrs. Chilke, this is Miss Wayness Tamm."

"Pleased to meet you." Ma Chilke backed into the house. "Come in. So long as I hold the door open, the flies will take advantage."

Ma Chilke took her guests through the kitchen and into the parlor. Glawen sat on the couch, with Wayness beside him. Ma Chilke surveyed them without affability. "So what is it this time? Did you find Mel Keebles?"

"Yes. It took some doing. He was out on a far world a long ways from home."

Ma Chilke shook her head in disapproval. "I just can't understand it; surely there is nothing out there as good as what we have at home. Most often things are worse! I have heard of places where a black slime covers you every time you lay down to sleep. Is that nice?"

"No," said Wayness. "Definitely not!"

Ma Chilke went on. "I don't want to look out my window and find a snake sixty feet long looking back at me. I take no pleasure in that sort of thing."

"There is no explaining why people go out among the stars," said Glawen. "It might be curiosity, or the love of adventure, or the prospect of great wealth; and sometimes people simply want to live by their own rules. Sometimes they are misanthropes, or sometimes they have made Old Earth too hot for themselves."

"Like Adrian Moncurio," suggested Wayness.

Ma Chilke frowned. "Adrian who?"

"Moncurio. You've probably heard the name before, since he was a friend of both Grandpa Swaner and Melvish Keebles."

"I remember the name," said Ma Chilke. "I haven't heard it for years. He had something to do with the purple vases and the green jade buckles."

"This is one reason we are here," said Glawen. "These purple vases are burial urns and they are valuable to collectors."

Wayness said: "The same applies to the jade buckles. They are called tanglets. Before we go, I will put you in touch with someone who will help you sell them at a good price."

"That's kind of you," said Ma Chilke. "The things really belong to Eustace, but I don't suppose he'd mind if I sold a few of them. I can use the money, certainly."

"To start with, you should put them in a safe place, and don't let the children play with them."

"Good advice!" Ma Chilke had become noticeably more amiable. "Perhaps you would like a cup of tea? Or a glass of cold lemonade?"

"Lemonade would be wonderful," said Wayness. "Can I help?"

"No thanks, I'll only be a minute or two."

Glawen asked: "May we look at the ATLAS OF FAR WORLDS your father gave to Eustace?"

Ma Chilke pointed. "There it is yonder: the big red book at the bottom of the stack." She took herself into the kitchen.

Glawen withdrew the book and brought it back to the couch. "First: to Cadwal." He looked at the index, then turned pages. The planet maps were for the most part Mercator projections, covering the whole of a double page. On the back of the maps was printed pertinent information: a historical synopsis, physical data, statistical tables; odd, unique or noteworthy facts. To many of these informational pages someone, perhaps the young Eustace, perhaps his grandfather, had clipped or otherwise attached additional material.

Glawen opened the book to the 'Cadwal' map. On the back of the left-hand page a large buff envelope had been taped. Glawen looked up. Ma Chilke was still in the kitchen. He detached the envelope, opened the flap, looked within. He gave Wayness an inscrutable glance, tucked the envelope into the inside pocket of his jacket.

Wayness asked in a whisper: "Is it?"

Glawen answered in a husky voice: "It is."

Ma Chilke entered from the kitchen, carrying three tall glasses of lemonade on a tray. She extended the tray to Glawen and Wayness and, glancing down at the Atlas, asked: "What world is that?"

"Cadwal," said Glawen. "It's far away." He indicated a small red square on the eastern shore of the continent Deucas. "This is Araminta Station, which is our home, and where Eustace is living now. He has become an important person."

"Fancy that!" marveled Ma Chilke. "When he was growing up, nobody called him 'Eustace'; they called him

'Useless'! For a fact, he was a moody child and when everyone else went north, Eustace went south. But he had a saving grace: he could always make me laugh! Even though I often wanted to whack him. But Grandpa always took up his cause, and the two were great friends. Strange how things turn out! Eustace being an important man, after so many years!"

After a moment's pleasant reflection Ma Chilke again looked to the map. "Where are the towns and roads and cities?"

"You won't find any on Cadwal," said Wayness. "The first explorers considered it a world too beautiful and too full of natural wonder to be spoiled by human settlement, so they made Cadwal a Conservancy. Folk may come to visit and enjoy the natural conditions, but no one is allowed to alter the environment, or dig for volcanic jewels or bother the native beasts, no matter how savage or repulsive they are."

"Keep your savage beasts and welcome to them!" declared Ma Chilke. "I have troubles enough with gophers."

Wayness rose to her feet. "I will be sure to call Alvina, my friend in Trieste. She is a dealer in tanglets and will certainly get in touch with you. I think that she is honest; still it can't do any harm to mention my name."

"That is very kind of you."

"We are happy to be helpful."

"Did you ever meet up with that other gentleman?"

"Julian Bohost?" asked Glawen. "No. He sent out one of his friends, who was even worse."

Glawen and Wayness took their leave. The flitter raised from the ground; the Chilke farmstead receded into the afternoon haze.

Glawen brought out the buff envelope and gave it to Wayness. "You verify. I'm afraid to look."

Wayness opened the envelope and withdrew three documents. "This is the Charter," she said. "The original Charter!"

"Good news, so far."

"This is the Grant-in-Perpetuity. It appears to be authentic." She glanced down the page. "It is simple enough—a deed to property described as the planet

Cadwal, with its astrographical coordinates. Title is vested in the Naturalist Society, contingent upon the payment of timely fees. Transfer of title can be effected quite easily, or so it seems; but neither Frons Nisfit nor anyone else has transferred title.":

"Very good news, again!"

"True—with qualifications, which we will discuss. The third document is a letter addressed to Eustace Chilke and signed by Floyd Swaner. It reads:

" 'Dear Eustace:

" 'To my intense surprise I came upon these papers mixed among a random lot I picked up at auction for practically nothing. The documents, however, are of incalculable value—in fact, they convey title to the planet Cadwal.

" 'The nominal owner is the Naturalist Society, and if it were an active responsible entity I would instantly return the papers to what must be considered their rightful owners. However, I have made inquiries and I discover that this would be a most unwise course of action. The Society is moribund; its membership is senile and its officers, with one or two exceptions, are dilettantes. In short, the Naturalist Society is dying if not dead, but not yet aware of the fact.

" 'The Cadwal Conservancy is an institution of which I approve. However, as I write, death is approaching me no less definitely than it is overtaking the Naturalist Society. Therefore, I am appointing you the custodian of these documents, until they can be transferred into the secure keeping of a new and revitalized Naturalist Society, or its successor—always toward the goal of ensuring the integrity and permanency of the Cadwal Conservancy.

" 'My only specific instructions are these: do not allow well-meaning but impractical theoreticians to exert any control over you; make sure that your associates are competent, experienced

and tolerant folk, without ideological axes to
grind.

" 'If you feel that the task I have imposed
upon you is beyond your capability, carefully
select some mature person whose dedication to
the ideals of conservancy is beyond question, and
turn the task over to him, or her.

" 'Essentially, you must fly this one by the
seat of your pants—as I know you will do in any
case, no matter how solemn my instructions and
how earnest my warnings.

" 'I take this means for transferring the documents to you for several reasons, one being that
when I die and you are not at hand, any property
I bequeath to you will cheerfully be expropriated
by your brothers and cousins, aunts, uncles,
mother and father. Or it will be stored in the barn
along with the stuffed animals. I have written you
letters at several of your addresses instructing
you to look in a place whereof you know for
something of value; one of these letters should
reach you and, so I believe, will lead you to these
documents. Goodbye, or so I fear, Eustace. I am
not afraid of death; I just don't think I will like it
very much.

Floyd Swaner' "

Wayness looked at Glawen. "That is the lot."

"Grandpa Swaner's ideas are much like our own, which
means that we are spared the need for ignoring them."

"Which makes things easier for everyone," said Wayness, "including Chilke, since we can quite justifiably take
his cooperation for granted, and assume that he would
instantly transfer the documents to us."

"Chilke will be happy that his duties have been discharged so easily. Still, it would be nice to name something
after him: a swamp, a bird, a mountain, or even the new
labor camp at Cape Journal: the 'Eustace B. Chilke Memorial Penitentiary.' "

"Chilke might like it better without the 'Memorial.' "

"Probably so."

At Largo the two took lodging at the Old River Inn overlooking the wide Sippewissa River. Wayness immediately telephoned Pirie Tamm at Fair Winds.

"Wayness!" cried Pirie Tamm. "This is a surprise indeed! Where are you?"

"On the way back from Bangalore. My studies have gone well; I have learned seven new vibrations."

Pirie Tamm said cautiously: "I'm sure it will all be very helpful."

"The Pandit is pleased with my progress. He feels that my feet are pointed in the right direction, at the very least."

"Knowing the Pandit, I consider that high praise," said Pirie Tamm dryly. "You are on your way to Fair Winds?"

"Yes, with a friend. I thought I should forewarn you. Will it be convenient?"

"Of course. Who is the friend?"

"It's a long story and it will keep until we see you. What has been happening at Fair Winds?"

Pirie Tamm was silent a moment, and seemed to calculate his response. He spoke in a careful voice: "My health is good, and my hip is definitely on the mend. The rhododendrons are putting on a spectacular show; Challis is green with envy, since she considers hers supreme in the field. I have seen nothing of Julian Bohost, which is just as well. The man is a pest and insufferable as well. What else has been going on? Let me see. For some strange reason the Society is enjoying quite an upsurge of interest; during the last month I have enrolled over twenty new members."

Wayness studied Pirie Tamm's face. She spoke enthusiastically. "That is really good news, Uncle Pirie! We can only hope that the trend continues!"

"Just so," said Pirie Tamm. "It is all quite extraordinary and I must consult the by-laws to assure myself on one or two small points. When will you be arriving at Fair Winds?"

"Just a moment, Uncle Pirie. Let me consult my friend. We may have some business to transact along the way." Wayness moved off the screen. Pirie Tamm heard muffled voices. He waited. Wayness returned. "Uncle Pirie, we have decided to stop over for a day or two at Shillawy, and we urgently want you to join us there."

"That is no problem," said Pirie Tamm. "I shall enjoy the excursion. Where shall we meet, and when?"

"We travel tomorrow, so it will be the morning after. We will stop at your favorite hotel; I forget the name at the moment, but no matter; it will come to me in a moment. Until the morning of the day after tomorrow, then!"

"Until then! I am anxious to hear your news!"

III.

Glawen and Wayness arrived at Shillawy during the small hours of the night. They went directly to the Sheldon Hotel and slept until nine o'clock, when they received a call from Pirie Tamm. "Perhaps this is early, perhaps not, since I do not know what you have in mind. In any case, I prefer to err on the side of promptitude."

"Quite right, Uncle Pirie!" said Wayness. "We have much to talk about and many things to do. But for now you might like to know that we have been successful in our quest. We have everything we set out to look for."

"That is very good news! But who is the 'we'?"

"Glawen Clattuc is with me."

"Aha! So that is how the wind blows! Well, I am not at all surprised. In any case, I will be happy to see him again."

"Meet us in the lobby; we'll be down in five minutes."

The three breakfasted and spoke together at length. Glawen and Wayness reported upon their adventures; Pirie Tamm spoke of his own fears and speculations.

"It is clear that Julian is up to mischief," said Wayness. "We still can't relax."

"Especially since Julian is working with Smonny."

Wayness' mouth drooped. "But that's not certain — or is it?"

"Either Namour or Smonny sent Benjamie to Araminta Station. Here on Earth Julian was directed to the Shoup Art Supply by Ma Chilke, but Benjamie was the one who romanced Miss Shoup and then went out to Nion. That indicates a connection between Julian and Smonny. It's probably only temporary, since Smonny and the LPF are ultimately pulling in different directions. But for now I imagine that each wants to make use of the other."

Wayness jumped up. "Why are we delaying here? Let's get this thing over as quickly as possible, before someone tries to interfere."

"You are making me nervous." Glawen rose to his feet. "The sooner we accomplish our business the better."

"Very well," said Pirie Tamm. "Today we witness the end of an era."

IV.

Pirie Tamm, Wayness and Glawen returned to Fair Winds, arriving late in the afternoon.

"It is too late to arrange a full-scale banquet," said Pirie Tamm. "The occasion, of course, demands nothing less, but we shall content ourselves with a festive dinner."

"Just as well," said Wayness. "I could not work up the proper jubilation. Also, Glawen would not be permitted to sit at the table, since he has nothing to wear except the clothes he is standing in."

Pirie Tamm summoned Agnes. "This is Glawen Clattuc," he said. "Do we have any decent clothes in the spare wardrobe to fit him?"

"I'm sure we do, sir. If the gentleman will come with me, we'll have a look."

"Also, tell Cook to expect three for dinner. Perhaps she will roast some plump ducklings with plum sauce, or a nice joint of beef. Nothing elaborate, you understand."

"Very good, sir. I will give her the message."

Glawen and Wayness bathed and dressed in fresh garments. They descended to find Pirie Tamm waiting for them in the drawing room. "It is a bit brisk out on the verandah, and sunset is a good half-hour past. Therefore, we will take our sherry indoors this evening. Wayness, as I recall, you are partial to the Fino."

"It's all good, Uncle Pirie."

"That is my opinion as well. Glawen, do you like sherry, or would you prefer something else?"

"Sherry will do nicely, thank you."

The three seated themselves. Pirie Tamm held aloft his glass. "It seems fitting that we should take this occasion to salute the noble Naturalist Society, which functioned such long centuries with grace and dignity, and commanded the genius of so many extraordinary men!" Pirie Tamm paused to reflect. "It is perhaps a rather lugubrious toast, but I offer it nevertheless, in the same reverent spirit which the ancient druithines sang their paeans of catharsis."

"Let us know when we can drink," said Wayness.

"Now!" said Pirie Tamm. "To the Naturalist Society!"

Glawen proposed a second toast. "To the intrepid and incomparable Wayness!"

"It may not be in the best taste, but I'll drink anyway," said Wayness. "To myself!"

Pirie Tamm refilled the glasses. Wayness proposed a toast: "To Glawen and Uncle Pirie, both of whom I love dearly, and also to Xantief, Grandpa Swaner, Myron and Lydia, the Countess and her dogs, and many others!"

"Let me specifically include Miss Shoup and Melvish Keebles," said Glawen. "For no particular reason."

Pirie Tamm once again raised his glass: "We have celebrated the past, its grandeurs and gallantries, but there are new challenges to face, new deeds to do, new mysteries to solve, and, yes, new enemies to conquer! The future confronts us with—"

Wayness protested. "Please, Uncle Pirie! I'm still limp from the past! So far as I am concerned, the future can wait until we have used up some of this very agreeable, very relaxing present."

Pirie Tamm became contrite. "Of course! So it shall be! I fear that I was carried away by the flow of my own rhetoric. We shall attend to the future when it becomes convenient."

Agnes entered the room. "Dinner is served."

In the morning the three made a leisurely breakfast. Glawen asked Pirie Tamm: "Are you certain that we are not an inconvenience? If so—"

"Do not so much as think of it. When you go I will be alone again. You must stay as long as you can."

"There is work for us to do," said Wayness. "It's urgent

that we draft a temporary Charter and by-laws to protect
the new Conservancy until the work can be done properly."

"It is a sound idea," said Pirie Tamm. "At this moment,
I can see how the Conservancy could be snatched away
from you, and without any great difficulty—although it
would be necessary to mitigate or even cancel your testimony by killing you."

"If Benjamie were alive, I'd feel more vulnerable," said
Wayness. "He killed with no qualms whatever. I don't think
Julian has killed anyone yet."

"The prospect of working here is pleasant," said
Glawen. "Still, I am concerned about Cadwal and what
might be going on. I'm sure that it can't be good."

The telephone rang. Pirie Tamm went to the screen.
"Yes?"

"Julian Bohost here," said a voice.

"Well, Julian, what do you want?"

"I would like to call at Fair Winds, to discuss a matter
of some importance. What time would be convenient for
you?"

"One time is as good as another."

"I will be there in half an hour, with my associates."

Half an hour later Julian Bohost arrived at Fair Winds
with an entourage of two men and two women. Julian wore
a suit of pale blue and white stripes, a white shirt with a
teal blue cravat and a white broad-brimmed hat. The other
four persons were about Julian's age or a few years older,
and were without notable distinction.

Pirie Tamm ushered the group into the drawing room.
Wayness and Glawen were seated on the couch. Julian
pretended surprise but his efforts were unconvincing. He
introduced his companions: "Mr. and Mrs. Spangard, Mr.
Fath, Miss Trefethyn. Over here is Mr. Pirie Tamm; then
Wayness Tamm and Glawen Clattuc, from Cadwal."

Pirie Tamm asked: "Can I offer you coffee? Or tea?"

"No thank you," said Julian. "We are here not on a
social occasion, but on serious business."

"I hope to our mutual profit."

"As to that, I can't say. Mr. and Mrs. Spangard are
accountants; Mr. Fath and Miss Trefethyn are attorneys-at-

law. All four, I might add, are new members in good standing of the Naturalist Society, as I am myself."

Pirie Tamm performed a perfunctory bow. "I congratulate all of you. Be seated then, or stand, as you like. I think there are chairs enough to go around."

"Thank you." Julian selected a chair, settled himself into a casual attitude and surveyed the group. He spoke in a slightly nasal voice: "By way of preamble let me state that we have studied the Naturalist Society by-laws in great detail."

"Excellent," said Pirie Tamm heartily. "That is a good example for us all."

"No doubt," said Julian. "In any case, I believe that recently you have enrolled a number of new members into the Society."

"Quite so. Twenty-two during the last month, so I believe. It is both surprising and a good portent for the future."

"The total membership now numbers how many?"

"Counting associate members and non-voting members?"

"Just voting members."

Pirie Tamm gave his head a melancholy shake. "Not too many more, I am sorry to say. There is Wayness, myself, and two others. We have had three deaths in the last six months. Twenty-two plus you plus this four adds up to twenty-seven."

Julian nodded. "That is my count. I have here the proxies for the members not present at the moment. Except for the two elderly members you have mentioned, the entire membership is represented in this room. Do you care to examine the proxies?"

Pirie Tamm smilingly waved away the proffered envelope. "I am sure that they are correct."

"They are eminently correct," said Julian. "We have, therefore, assembled a quorum."

"So it would seem. What do you wish to do? Raise the dues? I would argue against this step, at least for the present."

"The dues are adequate. Please be good enough to

declare this an official meeting of the Naturalist Society, as stipulated in the by-laws."

"Very well. As Secretary and ranking officer, I declare this an official meeting. Now you must wait for a moment or two until I find the minutes of the last meeting, which, as is customary, I will read to you. Let me think. What did I do with the official record?"

Julian rose to his feet. "Mr. Chairman, I move that the reading of the minutes be eschewed on this occasion."

"I second," said Mr. Spangard.

Pirie Tamm glanced around the room. "All in favor? All opposed? The 'ayes' have it; the minutes will not be read, which is something of a relief, I must say. Is there old business to be transacted?"

The room was silent.

"No? Is there new business?"

"Yes," said Julian.

"Chair recognizes Mr. Bohost."

"I wish to indicate Paragraph Twelve of the by-laws wherein it is stated that the secretary may be removed from office at any time, by a two-thirds vote of the membership."

"Thank you, Mr. Bohost. That is an interesting point. Your remarks have been noted. The chair recognizes Mr. Fath."

"I move that Mr. Pirie Tamm be removed from his office as secretary and replaced with Julian Bohost."

"Any second to the motion?"

"I second," said Miss Trefethyn.

"All in favor raise their hands."

Julian and his four friends raised their hands. Julian said: "The proxies vote aye. There are eighteen votes here."

"The motion is carried. Mr. Bohost, you are now the new Secretary of the Naturalist Society. You may take charge of the meeting forthwith. I congratulate you and I wish you a long and happy tenure. As for myself, I am old and tired; I am delighted to witness this influx of new energy into the grand old Society."

"Thank you," said Julian. He darted a suspicious glance toward Glawen and Wayness. Why were their faces so mild and bland?

Pirie Tamm said: "The Society files are in my study. Please remove them at your earliest convenience. Assets are approximately nil. I usually make up the short-fall from my own pocket. Mr. and Mrs. Spangard will no doubt study the accounts in detail, once you have installed them in your own offices."

Julian cleared his throat. "Now then! A final small piece of business. The Society's principal asset is the deed to Cadwal planet. As we know, it has been missing for a very long time."

"True. We have not publicized this fact for obvious reasons."

"You will be happy to learn that the loss may be remedied. Mr. Fath and Miss Trefethyn tell me that the Society may petition the Gaean Court of Planetary Affairs to declare the old grant lost, irretrievable and invalid, and to issue a replacement. This is standard practice, so I am told, and can be accomplished without difficulty. I mention this principally for the benefit of Miss Tamm and Mr. Clattuc, inasmuch as they have long taken an adversarial position to the Life, Peace and Freedom Party which now will conduct a thorough reconstruction of the so-called Conservancy."

Glawen shook his head slowly. "Wrong again, Julian. If the Peefers want to loot a planet, they must look elsewhere."

"Don't call us 'Peefers'!" snapped Julian. "You have no more legal standing. As soon as the new grant is executed—"

"But it won't be executed."

"Oh? Why not?"

"Because we have found the original."

Julian stared, his lower lip trembling. Mr. Fath muttered into his ear. Julian said sharply: "In that case, the grant is part of the assets of the Naturalist Society. Where is it?"

Glawen reached to the shelf at his back, sorted through papers, selected one and tossed it to Julian. "There you are."

Julian, Mr. Fath and Miss Trefethyn bent their heads over the document. Mr. Fath suddenly jabbed at the document with his finger. "So that is your game!"

Julian asked in bewilderment: "What did they do?"

"They sold Cadwal for one sol 'receipt of which is hereby acknowledged.' It is signed 'Pirie Tamm' and dated yesterday."

"You will find the sum of one sol duly entered into the Naturalist Society account," said Pirie Tamm.

"That is fraud!" cried Julian. He snatched the document. " 'Sold to that association known as the CADWAL CONSERVANCY for the sum of one sol.' " Julian turned to Mr. Fath. "Can they do that?"

"In short simple words: yes. It has been done. This grant, if you notice, is now stamped, VOID BY REASON OF SUPERSESSION."

Julian turned to Glawen. "Where is the new grant?"

"Here is a copy. It has been recorded. The original is in the safe deposit."

"You are still Secretary of the Naturalist Society," said Wayness. "It is a fine new career for you!"

"I resign," cried Julian in brassy tones. He swung around to his friends. "There is nothing more here for us; we are in a den of conservationists; they sting like wasps and bite like serpents. Let us go." He clapped the hat on his head and stalked from the room, followed by his four friends.

Wayness asked Pirie Tamm: "Who is Secretary of the Naturalist Society now?"

"Not I," said Pirie Tamm. "I fear that there is no more Naturalist Society. It is over and past."

THE BEST IN
SCIENCE FICTION

☐ 54310-6	A FOR ANYTHING	$3.95
☐ 54311-4	*Damon Knight*	Canada $4.95
☐ 55625-9	BRIGHTNESS FALLS FROM THE AIR	$3.50
☐ 55626-7	*James Tiptree, Jr.*	Canada $3.95
☐ 53815-3	CASTING FORTUNE	$3.95
☐ 53816-1	*John M. Ford*	Canada $4.95
☐ 50554-9	THE ENCHANTMENTS OF FLESH & SPIRIT	$3.95
☐ 50555-7	*Storm Constantine*	Canada $4.95
☐ 55413-2	HERITAGE OF FLIGHT	$3.95
☐ 55414-0	*Susan Shwartz*	Canada $4.95
☐ 54293-2	LOOK INTO THE SUN	$3.95
☐ 54294-0	*James Patrick Kelly*	Canada $4.95
☐ 54925-2	MIDAS WORLD	$2.95
☐ 54926-0	*Frederik Pohl*	Canada $3.50
☐ 53157-4	THE SECRET ASCENSION	$4.50
☐ 53158-2	*Michael Bishop*	Canada $5.50
☐ 55627-5	THE STARRY RIFT	$4.50
☐ 55628-3	*James Tiptree, Jr.*	Canada $5.50
☐ 50623-5	TERRAPLANE	$3.95
☐	*Jack Womack*	Canada $4.95
☐ 50369-4	WHEEL OF THE WINDS	$3.95
☐ 50370-8	*M.J. Engh*	Canada $4.95

Buy them at your local bookstore or use this handy coupon:
Clip and mail this page with your order.

Publishers Book and Audio Mailing Service
P.O. Box 120159, Staten Island, NY 10312-0004

Please send me the book(s) I have checked above. I am enclosing $ _____
(Please add $1.25 for the first book, and $.25 for each additional book to cover postage and handling.
Send check or money order only—no CODs.)

Name _____
Address _____
City _____ State/Zip _____
Please allow six weeks for delivery. Prices subject to change without notice.

MORE SCIENCE FICTION
BESTSELLERS FROM TOR

☐	53676-2 ARSLAN	$3.95
☐	53677-0 *M.J. Engh*	Canada $4.95
☐	54333-5 CV	$2.95
☐	54334-3 *Damon Knight*	Canada $3.50
☐	54622-9 THE FALLING WOMAN	$3.95
☐	54623-7 *Pat Murphy*	Canada $4.95
☐	53327-5 THE INFINITY LINK	$4.95
☐	53328-3 *Jeffrey A. Carver*	Canada $5.95
☐	50984-6 KILLER	$3.95
☐	*David Drake & Karl Edward Wagner*	Canada $4.95
☐	50024-5 LAND'S END	$4.95
☐	50026-1 *Frederik Pohl & Jack Williamson*	Canada $5.95
☐	54564-8 NIGHTFLYERS	$3.50
☐	54565-6 *George R.R. Martin*	Canada $4.50
☐	55716-6 PHANTOMS ON THE WIND	$3.50
☐	55717-4 *Robert E. Vardeman*	Canada $4.50
☐	55259-8 SUBTERRANEAN GALLERY	$3.95
☐	55258-X *Richard Paul Russo*	Canada $4.95
☐	54425-0 THE WANDERER	$2.95
☐	54426-9 *Fritz Leiber*	Canada $3.25
☐	55711-5 WORLD'S END	$2.95
☐	55712-3 *Joan D. Vinge*	Canada $3.50

Buy them at your local bookstore or use this handy coupon:
Clip and mail this page with your order.

Publishers Book and Audio Mailing Service
P.O. Box 120159, Staten Island, NY 10312-0004

Please send me the book(s) I have checked above. I am enclosing $ _____
(Please add $1.25 for the first book, and $.25 for each additional book to cover postage and handling.
Send check or money order only—no CODs.)

Name _____
Address _____
City _____ State/Zip _____
Please allow six weeks for delivery. Prices subject to change without notice.

BESTSELLERS
FROM TOR

☐ ☐	50570-0	ALL ABOUT WOMEN *Andrew M. Greeley*	$4.95 Canada $5.95
☐ ☐	58341-8 58342-6	ANGEL FIRE *Andrew M. Greeley*	$4.95 Canada $5.95
☐ ☐	52725-9 52726-7	BLACK WIND *F. Paul Wilson*	$4.95 Canada $5.95
☐ ☐	51392-4	LONG RIDE HOME *W. Michael Gear*	$4.95 Canada $5.95
☐ ☐	50350-3	OKTOBER *Stephen Gallagher*	$4.95 Canada $5.95
☐ ☐	50857-2	THE RANSOM OF BLACK STEALTH One *Dean Ing*	$5.95 Canada $6.95
☐ ☐	50088-1	SAND IN THE WIND *Kathleen O'Neal Gear*	$4.50 Canada $5.50
☐ ☐	51878-0	SANDMAN *Linda Crockett*	$4.95 Canada $5.95
☐ ☐	50214-0 50215-9	THE SCHOLARS OF NIGHT *John M. Ford*	$4.95 Canada $5.95
☐ ☐	51826-8	TENDER PREY *Julia Grice*	$4.95 Canada $5.95
☐ ☐	52188-4	TIME AND CHANCE *Alan Brennert*	$4.95 Canada $5.95

TOR SCIENCE FICTION
DOUBLES

☐	50010-5	THE BLIND GEOMETER	Robinson	$3.50
☐	50114-4	THE NEW ATLANTIS	LeGuin	Canada $4.50
☐	55952-5	BORN WITH THE DEAD	Silverberg	$2.95
☐	55953-3	THE SALIVA TREE	Aldiss	Canada $3.95
☐	55964-9	THE COLOR OF NEANDERTHAL EYES	Tiptree	$3.50
☐	50204-3	AND STRANGE AT ECBATAN THE TREES	Bishop	Canada $4.50
☐	50362-7	DIVIDE AND RULE	de Camp	$3.50
☐	50363-5	THE SWORD OF RHIANNON	Brackett	Canada $4.50
☐	50275-2	ELEGY FOR ANGELS AND DOGS	Williams	$3.50
☐		THE GRAVEYARD HEART	Zelazny	Canada $4.50
☐	55963-0	ENEMY MINE	Longyear	$2.95
☐	54302-5	ANOTHER ORPHAN	Kessel	Canada $3.95
☐	50854-8	EYE FOR EYE	Card	$3.95
☐		THE TUNESMITH	Biggle	Canada $4.95
☐	50813-0	FUGUE STATE	Ford	$3.50
☐		THE DEATH OF DOCTOR ISLAND	Wolfe	Canada $4.50
☐	55971-1	HARDFOUGHT	Bear	$3.50
☐	55951-7	CASCADE POINT	Zahn	Canada $4.50
☐	55879-0	HE WHO SHAPES	Zelazny	$2.95
☐	50266-3	THE INFINITY BOX	Wilhelm	Canada $3.95
☐	50983-8	HOME IS THE HANGMAN	Zelazny	$3.50
☐		WE, IN SOME STRANGE POWER'S EMPLOY,		Canada $4.50
		MOVE ON A RIGOROUS LINE	Delany	

Buy them at your local bookstore or use this handy coupon:
Clip and mail this page with your order.

Publishers Book and Audio Mailing Service
P.O. Box 120159, Staten Island, NY 10312-0004

Please send me the book(s) I have checked above. I am enclosing $ _____
(Please add $1.25 for the first book, and $.25 for each additional book to cover postage and handling.
Send check or money order only—no CODs.)

Name _____

Address _____

City _____ State/Zip _____

Please allow six weeks for delivery. Prices subject to change without notice.